SELECT EDITIONS
LARGE TYPE

SELECT EDITIONS
LARGE TYPE

**This Large Print Book carries the
Seal of Approval of N.A.V.H.**

Reader's
Digest

CONTENTS

FRANCESCA'S KITCHEN

PETER PEZZELLI

IT TAKES a grandmother to show
how a little wisdom, a lot of
patience, and a good batch of
home cooking can solve almost
any problem.

Chapter One

THERE was no point in taking chances, so the first thing Francesca Campanile did after boarding the plane and finding her seat by the aisle was to open her pocketbook and take out her rosary beads. Rolling one of the dark, smooth beads between her thumb and forefinger, she whispered a quick Hail Mary and made the sign of the cross, while ahead of her, at the front of the cabin, a smiling stewardess was just beginning to give her cheerful recitation about what everyone should do in case the cabin lost pressure in flight or the plane plummeted into the ocean or crash-landed after take off. The knowledge that there were little air masks that popped out of the ceiling and flotation devices under her seat did little to reassure Francesca that she hadn't been completely out of her mind just stepping on board. In truth, as whenever she flew, which wasn't often, it almost seemed as if the stewardess was telling them all these things just to make passengers like Francesca feel even more scared out of their minds—if that was possible.

Francesca sat there, pondering her rosary beads, until the jet engines began to whine and the plane lurched forward, giving her a start. As the plane pulled away from the terminal, Francesca reached into her pocketbook again, pulled out a set of photographs, and clutched them to her heart, looking anxiously about at the people all around her. The plane was packed.

Francesca dreaded flying. The flight from Tampa would take close to three hours, and she intended to spend every second of that time in prayerful meditation, until the plane safely touched down in Providence. The young man sitting next to her, who had been leafing through a magazine, glanced her way and noticed the rosary beads and the photographs.

"A little nervous about flying?" he said with a kind smile.

Francesca shrugged. "I'm an old lady, so who cares if I die? But if you ask me, this thing is nothing but a big sardine can with wings. It's a crazy way to get from one place to another."

"Well, I guess you have a point," the man said, laughing. "But it's still the *fastest* way to get from one place to another."

"Ayyy, there's more to life than speed," answered Francesca.

"Not when you're in a hurry," he kidded. "Besides, they say flying is the safest way to travel—you know, statistically anyway. So you shouldn't worry."

"I'm a grandmother. All I do is worry."

"You sound just like *my* grandmother."

"We're all the same."

The young man laughed again before nodding at the photographs in Francesca's hand. "Your family?" he asked.

"My grandchildren," said Francesca, smiling for the first time since she had come on board. "See," she said, passing one of the photographs to him, "those are my two grandsons, Will and Charlie. They live out in Oregon with my daughter Alice and her husband, Bill. They moved west a few years ago after Bill took a job with some big company out there." She paused for a moment and then let out a sigh. "Seems silly to pick up your wife and children and move so far away just for a job."

The engines gave a brief roar as the pilot maneuvered the plane along the runway into its position behind the other planes waiting to take off. The sound gave Francesca another start.

"And who's in the other pictures?" asked the young man.

"My daughter Roseanne's three kids," she replied, passing him another photo. "Rosie lives here in Florida with her husband, Frank. That's Dana and Sara, the two girls. Dana's a teenager now, and Sara's not far behind. And that's little Frankie; he's the youngest. They all came to the airport today to put me on the plane. I hated to go. Breaks my heart to say good-bye."

"I'm sure they must come home sometimes to visit you," offered the young man. "That must make you feel good."

"Oh, sure," said Francesca, heaving another sigh. "I fly out to see all of them once or twice a year, and sometimes they fly home to Rhode Island to see me, but it's not the same as having people close to you all the time. You never feel like you're a part of each other's lives, the way you're supposed to feel about your family."

Francesca paused and let her thoughts drift back to the two weeks she had just passed at the home of her daughter and son-in-law.

Roseanne was her oldest, and Francesca missed her terribly when they were apart. They were much alike, she and her elder daughter, both headstrong and independent. Consequently, they quibbled over just about everything. The way Rosie had decided to wear her hair these days—so short, instead of beautiful and long, the way it used to be— what was that all about? And the scandalously skimpy bikinis she let the girls wear to the beach. The television shows she let Frankie watch and those crazy video games she let him play. And the way Rosie made her marinara sauce or fried up the eggplant, which wasn't at all the way she had been taught by her mother. From the moment she had awakened every day to the moment she had gone to bed, it seemed as if Francesca had spent her entire visit bickering with her daughter.

It had been wonderful.

Francesca understood, of course, that her daughter and son-in-law had discovered their own way of doing things. They were a family, and their life together had acquired a unique rhythm, which was beautiful and perfect in its own way. Besides, Francesca knew how to make it up to them. When things got too frazzled, she would offer to stay at home with the kids so Rosie and Frank could have a night out together just by themselves. She pitched in by helping Roseanne keep the house clean. Most of all, she cooked.

Francesca loved to cook, and she loved to watch people eat what she had cooked. It was one of her greatest pleasures in life. She had a special touch in the kitchen. She didn't need to go shopping to prepare a meal. Given five minutes to poke around in the cupboards and the refrigerator, Francesca could roust up enough ingredients to make something that would set mouths to watering.

And so, when it came time for Francesca to go home, when they all drove out to see her off at the airport, there were hugs and kisses and tears galore. There were promises to call as soon as she made it home and promises to visit again soon. Little Frankie had been draped over his father's shoulder. He had waved his little hand and called, "Bye-bye, Nonna," to her, the sound of his voice so sweet that it had brought the tears anew to her eyes.

Now, as she sat there with the photos, knowing that she must be boring this poor young man to tears of his own, she felt a wave of sadness wash over her. "Anyway," she finally said, "that's about the best I can do right now—see my family whenever I can. That's why I get on these stupid airplanes and fly all over the country even though they scare me to death. I carry my pictures and these rosary beads so if the worst happens, at least I won't be alone."

With that, she let the young man go back to reading his magazine. She was grateful for the conversation, for it had made her feel a little better. Just the same, as the engines roared and the plane began its takeoff, Francesca took hold of her rosary beads and the pictures of her grandchildren and began to pray.

There was no point in taking chances.

No ONE was there to greet Francesca when the plane arrived at the airport in Warwick, a few miles outside of Providence. Usually, Joey could be counted on to pick her up. Thirty-two and unmarried, Joey was the youngest of Francesca's three children and the only one to stay close to home. This time, however, Joey himself was away on vacation. He and his rugby friends had decided to take a trip to Australia to see, his sisters and mother could only surmise, if banging into one another's heads felt any different in that part of the world than it did in New England. Joey would be gone for the better part of a month, so Francesca was on her own.

Not that she minded. When the plane landed, Francesca made her way out with the rest of the herd. She collected her one small suitcase and then headed to the exit. She was unperturbed by the blast of cold air that swept across the parking lot to welcome her when she stepped outside. It affected her little that the bright Florida sunshine was replaced by the pale, gray shroud of a January sky hanging gloomily over the city as she rode home in the taxi. And she didn't mind trudging through the crusty snow that blanketed the walkway to her front steps; the cab driver, after all, was kind enough to carry her suitcase for her. These were all things for which Francesca had prepared herself. How could she have done otherwise? She was a New Englander, born and bred.

There was, however, one thing for which Francesca was never quite ready, something that always took her by surprise whenever she came home. The silence.

Alone in the hallway, unwinding the scarf from around her neck, Francesca felt the heavy stillness of the house pressing in around her. She tugged off her overcoat, hung it in the closet, then reached down to collect the pile of bills the mailman had deposited through the slot in the front door. Everything was still addressed to Mr. and Mrs. Leonard Campanile. Leo had been gone for over eight years, but Francesca had never changed the name on her mailing address to reflect the fact that she was a widow. Somehow, seeing their names together kept a glimmer of hope burning inside that her husband was still in the parlor watching television or sitting at the kitchen table reading the paper. She half-expected to find him there waiting for her every time she walked through the front door; that half of her felt it keenly when, inevitably, she did not.

Francesca went to the kitchen, set the mail on the table, and turned to look out the window over the sink. If the interior of her home seemed gloomy to her, the exterior was positively bleak. It was late afternoon, and the barren trees and shrubs swayed back and forth in the cold wind, while the sun slowly fell off to the west. A thin cover of hard, frozen snow lay across the backyard.

Francesca gave a little sigh, turned away from the window, and went to the refrigerator. She did not feel hungry, or if she did, she didn't care. She closed the refrigerator door and walked out of the kitchen to the front hall. Her daughter would be waiting by the telephone back in Florida, anxious to hear that her mother had made it home safely. Francesca would call her from the bedroom and then lie down to rest. She turned toward the staircase.

"Leo," she called as she started up the stairs, "I'm home."

"TONY, you call these tomatoes?"

Tony, the grocer, who was putting cucumbers on the shelf, looked at Francesca and gave a shrug. "That's what it said on the carton, Mrs. Campanile," he replied with a good-natured smile.

"The cardboard boxes these came in probably have more flavor," she suggested ruefully. "I should find another market."

"Ayyy, what do you expect?" laughed Tony. "Nobody has good tomatoes this time of year."

"That's what you always say. The supermarket down the road probably has some nice tomatoes that actually taste like tomatoes. These things don't even *look* like tomatoes."

Tony chuckled, for this was a scene that had been played out many times in his little corner market just down the street from Francesca's house. Both of them knew full well that despite the lower prices and the greater selection in the huge supermarkets, Francesca preferred the comfort and convenience of her own neighborhood market. Nobody had a better meat selection than Tony's Market, and the produce, despite her occasional gripes in the winter, was the best around. But there was more than the meat and the produce that kept her coming back.

Here, everyone knew her. When she walked in, she was always greeted with a "Hello, Mrs. Campanile!" or a "What will you have today, Mrs. Campanile?" It was nice to come to a place where you always found the same faces and everybody knew you.

The dearth of decent tomatoes, however,

was a source of true consternation to Francesca. Not that she blamed Tony. She understood that, no matter where she shopped, the bland, flavorless varieties shipped in from somewhere overseas were all that she would find in the middle of the winter. But how she longed for those beautiful native tomatoes of last summer!

Leo, of course, had kept a tomato garden for years, and there was no end to the uses to which she would put her husband's beautiful tomatoes. Marinara sauces, pizza, salads, sandwiches. Her favorite, though, was a simple tomato salad. Francesca would start by cutting up the tomatoes and tossing them into a bowl with a healthy dose of olive oil. Next, she would add a clove or two worth of diced garlic, some chopped basil and oregano picked fresh from her own little garden, then salt and pepper. Finally, she would toss it all together once or twice, and she was done. The memory brought a wistful smile to her face. Francesca let out a long sigh.

"Cooking for the family tonight?" asked Tony, bringing her back from her reveries.

"I wish, Tony," she answered. "No, it's only me. I was just in the mood for some nice tomatoes, that's all. Something to make me forget about this cold weather."

"I know what you mean," Tony confessed. "Tell you the truth, I won't eat those things myself. Just be patient. It'll be summer before you know it, and we'll have some nice tomatoes."

Francesca continued to collect the few things she needed from the market. In truth, she could have managed with what she already had at home. But it had been two days since she had returned from Florida, and this was the first time she had stepped outside. The previous day had been spent unpacking, washing her clothes, and getting her closet back in order. Then there were bills to be paid, appointments to be confirmed to have her hair done and to get a checkup from the doctor. Francesca liked to have everything in order, so she started each day by making a list of things she needed to do. It kept her busy and made the days pass more quickly.

Francesca took her time shopping. She had no place in particular to go and nothing else to do. Most of her old friends from the neighborhood were gone, some having moved to warmer climes, some to retirement centers, and some directly to the next life. She pushed her cart up to the checkout counter, where Tony's wife, Donna, waited by the cash register.

"Find everything you need, Mrs. Campanile?" she asked. "I see you have your milk and bread. That's good. They say we might get some snow later today."

"Oh, yes," Francesca replied as she put her groceries up on the counter. "I've got everything I need, not that I'm one of those nervous Nellies who thinks the sky is falling every time she sees a few snowflakes, but it never hurts to be prepared."

"We might get six or seven inches," Donna said as she scanned the groceries. "Sounds like it will be a good night to stay home."

Francesca nodded. What else would I do? she thought.

A FEW fragile flakes were already drifting down when Francesca left the market and started home. It was late morning, nearing lunchtime, and the cars zipped up and down the road as she walked along the sidewalk.

Clutching the handles of the cloth bag in which she carried her groceries, Francesca made her way along the sidewalk, keeping a watchful eye on the pavement lest she slip on a patch of ice. She soon rounded the corner off the main road and walked up the street to her house. The street climbed a steep hill, but her legs were more than equal to the task. When she made it to the house and through the front door, she hurried to put away her groceries.

The little red light on the telephone answering machine was flashing when she came into the kitchen. She gave the button a tap and listened to the messages while she sorted the groceries. The first was from Alice: "Hi, Mom. It's me. I talked to Rosie yesterday. She said you guys had a good time together at her house. Will and Charlie were wondering when you're going to visit us. They miss your lasagna. Give me a call. Love you."

A beep, then the next message, this one from Roseanne: "Hi, Mom, it's me. You home? I talked to Alice yesterday. Told her about your trip. Heard you guys might get a bunch of snow up there today, so I hope you get home soon before it starts. Call me."

A succession of beeps without messages followed, then: "Hello. This is the West End

Public Library. Some books you reserved have come in. We'll hold them for a week. Thank you."

Francesca put the groceries away and picked up the telephone to call Alice in Oregon. She called Rosie a little while later. When she was finished talking to Rosie, Francesca hung up the phone, erased the messages on the answering machine, and paused to look out the back window. The kitchen was her favorite room in the house, not so much because of her love of cooking, but because of the beautiful view it afforded of the city. When the leaves were off the trees, you could look out across the backyard and see all the way downtown to the dome of the State House and beyond. Turning over in her mind the third message on the answering machine, she stared thoughtfully at the drab shroud of gray clouds. The snowflakes were now coming down with greater urgency. Deep within, part of Francesca was urging her to just stay inside and curl up on the couch and take a nap. Another part of her, though, longed to be out of the house once more. She fretted about it for only a minute before deciding to pull her overcoat and hat back on.

"This is New England," she told herself while she fished the car keys out of her pocketbook. "It's supposed to snow in the winter."

THE librarian was gazing out the window at the thickening snowfall when Francesca walked in.

"Hello, Rebecca," said Francesca.

"Hi, Mrs. Campanile," she said, taking nervous note of the snowflakes on Francesca's shoulders. "We're closing at two today," she advised her. Then, worriedly, she said, "It looks like it's really starting to come down out there. Are the roads getting bad?"

"No, honey," Francesca answered with a smile. "If an old lady like me can drive through this weather, so can you. You're too young to worry about a few flakes of snow."

. "Ugh," the young woman sighed. "I hate driving in the snow."

Francesca set a sturdy cloth bag atop the desk, one of many she kept at home in the closet by the front door, ready for every occasion; this one she used to tote her books to and from the library. "I understand you have some new books for me," she said.

Rebecca found the items reserved for

Francesca and placed them on the desktop next to her computer. She opened the cover of the first book and passed a handheld scanner over the bar code on the inside of the front cover. "Hmm, what are you studying this time?" she said, looking over the book's cover with curiosity. *"Perspectives on Vietnamese Culture,"* she read. "Sounds interesting. Plus a Fodor's guide to traveling in Vietnam," she noted as she scanned the next book and then the language tapes. "Looks like someone is getting ready to take a trip to Southeast Asia."

"Just in my mind," chuckled Francesca. "Flying to Florida was far enough for me. I just like to study new things now and then, especially during the winter."

Francesca collected her things and was just starting to go when someone called from the back of the library. "Frannie, is that you?" came a familiar voice.

Francesca looked about and saw Peg, one of her library friends, beckoning to her from the computer room in the back. The library offered seniors free classes in Word and Excel, but Francesca rarely set foot in that room. Though curious about the machines, she had yet to put her fingers on a keyboard. She nodded a thank-you to Rebecca and strolled over to talk to her friend, who had slipped back into the room.

Francesca saw that Natalie and Connie, another two of her friends, were seated at the other computer terminals. They both waved hello. The three old women, all of them bundled up in bulky sweaters, had their eyes glued to their computer screens.

"You should give this a try," suggested Natalie. "It's a cinch."

"What for?" replied Francesca. "I'd rather read a book."

"Don't know what you're missing," said Connie. "It's fun, and e-mail's a great way to keep in touch with people."

"That's what they invented stamps and envelopes for," said Francesca. "There's nothing like getting a handwritten letter."

"*Letter?*" Peg laughed along with the other two women. "Nobody writes letters anymore."

"Yes, I know," said Francesca grumpily. "That's another thing I miss these days." She gave a sigh. "Well, at least I know how to use the telephone whenever I want to hear someone's voice."

Peg gave Francesca a thoughtful look.

"What's with the puss on your face today, Frannie?" she asked. "Everything okay?"

"Oh, yeah," said Francesca, giving a shrug. "Just feeling a little blue, that's all."

"What about? You just got back from Florida, right? Everything okay down there with your family?"

"Yes," Francesca replied. "They're all fine. It's just that . . ." She paused and looked away.

"What?" said Peg.

By now, Natalie and Connie had turned away from their monitors and were listening to what Francesca had to say. Francesca looked back at them, unable to suppress the glum expression on her face.

"I don't know," she answered. "It's just that I keep thinking about my daughters and my grandchildren. They're all so far away. You'd think that after all these years, I'd be used to it by now, but it just seems to feel worse every day. Lately, I just feel useless."

"Don't we all," sighed Connie.

"Don't worry, Frannie," said Peg. "It's just the winter getting you down, that's all. It's cold and dark outside, and we're all cooped up inside. It happens to me sometimes, too, especially in January."

"Me too," Natalie added.

"Nighttime's the worst for me," said Connie. "Sometimes all I do is sit in my kitchen and think about my children."

"It's so strange, isn't it?" said Francesca. "I can remember a time when I couldn't wait for mine to all finally grow up and move out of the house and just stop driving me crazy. Now, a day doesn't go by without my wishing that I could have them all back upstairs at night, sleeping in their beds. I'd pay anything to have them small like that again for just one more day, to see them wake up and come downstairs for breakfast in the morning."

"Who wouldn't?" said Peg. "But life goes on. You can't waste your time wishing you could turn back the clock. Besides, you still have your son close to home."

"Ayyy, that one," scoffed Francesca. "He might as well be living on the far side of the moon. The only time I see him is when he's hungry or he wants me to do his laundry. The kid needs a wife."

"Yeah, but then what would there be for you to do?" asked Natalie.

"You know, you're not being very helpful," replied Francesca ruefully.

At that, the four women all laughed.

Feeling a little better, Francesca looked across the library to the front desk, where Rebecca was pulling on her overcoat. "Well, I guess I better get going. Looks like Chicken Little's getting ready to throw us all out any second." Francesca turned to go.

"Hey, Frannie," said Peg, "try not to worry, okay? Before you know it, it will be spring, and things will look a lot brighter."

LATER that evening, Francesca stood at her kitchen counter, beating some eggs in a bowl. She stirred in a little milk and some bits of cheese before pouring it all over a batch of ground beef and onions she had sizzling in a frying pan atop the stove. While everything simmered, she threw together a salad of lettuce and cucumbers, with a little oil and vinegar; then she turned her attention back to the eggs, moving them around with a spatula to keep them from sticking to the pan. When they were cooked, she pushed them onto a plate, added a splash of Tabasco sauce, and poured herself a little glass of red wine. Francesca put everything onto a dinner tray and carried it into the den.

She set the tray on a TV table and sat down on the sofa, listening to the intensifying storm. The wind had started to howl and to toss great handfuls of icy snow, which sprittered against the windowpanes like grains of sand. The sound of it made Francesca shiver, and she pulled a throw over her legs. Her thoughts drifted to Florida and Oregon and Australia. She looked up and let her eyes scan the photographs of her children and grandchildren covering virtually every square inch of the den's walls.

Francesca reached over and popped the first of the language tapes into the cassette player on the table by the sofa. As the tape started to play, she lifted her wineglass to her family. *"Salute,"* she told them. "Sleep tight tonight, my sweets."

Then she took a sip of wine and began to eat her supper.

BY LATE morning, the clouds had drifted away, leaving behind clear skies as far as the eye could see. The January sun was not strong enough to melt away any of the snow. It was still quite cold outside. Francesca stood and gazed out the front window. From outside, she could hear the scraping of snow shovels and the roaring of a power snow-blower somewhere nearby. Turning away from the window, she began to walk about the house, looking for something constructive to do to pass the time. She knew she shouldn't even think about going outdoors again. Just the same, Francesca had been born with what her own mother had called *una testa dura:* an exceedingly hard head. Such being the case, she was finding it very difficult to resist the temptation to take a stroll around the block, just to see how the rest of the neighborhood had made out after the storm. It occurred to her that the bill pay-ments neatly stacked on the kitchen table provided a convenient excuse; it was time to put them in the mail.

What harm would there be in a quick jaunt down the street to the nearest mailbox?

Francesca pondered the answer to that question a short while later while picking herself up out of a snowbank on the side of the main road. The walk down her hill had proven to be more treacherous than she had imagined. The road had been plowed, but the snow had been pushed up onto the sidewalks, forcing her to walk along the road's edge. When she rounded the corner at the bottom of the hill onto the main street, she had found that the cars and trucks were already whizzing along, often within inches of her elbow. Determined to reach the mailbox a few hundred yards or so down the road, Francesca had been looking back over her shoulder for approaching cars when she had suddenly lost her footing and toppled sideways into the snow. She had landed in a snowbank with a less-than-graceful flop and let out a string of Italian epithets she had learned from her mother. She then stood and trudged on, the snow caked on her hat and up and down her entire backside so that, to motorists overtaking her, she appeared to be a very grumpy walking snowman.

The humor of the sight was not lost on a group of teenaged boys milling about on the front steps of a tenement house as Francesca trod by on her way to the mailbox. Fuming as she was, Francesca took little note of them. She dropped the bills into the mailbox and turned to go back the way she had come.

Chapter Two

"BLESS me, Father, for I have sinned."

It was Saturday afternoon, and Francesca was making her confession, as she often did before evening mass. Something about acknowledging her sins had a way of lifting her spirits and getting her through the week to come. A lift was what she needed, for she was in decidedly ill humor and had been all day.

She was experiencing considerable soreness in her hip and shoulder, the result of her encounter with the snowbank earlier in the week. A few doses of pain reliever would have done wonders for her. Francesca, however, disdained taking medicine of any kind; she preferred to just grit her teeth and bear it. Two nights of poor sleep, though, had left her tired and irritable. She would have to give in later on and take something before bed. A few aspirin and a good night's rest after confession and mass were sure to chase away the pain and brighten her mood by morning. Till then, though, she was as amiable as a lioness with a thorn in her paw.

"It's been six weeks since I last confessed," she continued.

"Ah, Francesca, where have you been?" Father Buontempo said pleasantly from behind the curtain inside his cubicle. "It's been so long I was beginning to wonder what had become of you."

"Hey," Francesca snapped, "you're supposed to at least pretend not to know who I am when I'm giving you my confession. What kind of priest are you?"

"Sorry," he replied. This wasn't the first time he'd had an exchange of this sort with his parishioner. Still, he couldn't help himself from adding, "But how could I not know it's you? You're one of my best customers." Then he sighed. "Sometimes you're my only customer. Do you know what it's like sitting in here by yourself all afternoon?"

"Never mind about that," Francesca grunted. "I've got problems of my own."

"All right," he relented. "What have you been up to now?"

"I took the Lord's name in vain," Francesca answered, getting straight to it. "I didn't mean to do it, but it just slipped out, more than once, after I fell down in the snow."

"Were you hurt?" asked Father Buontempo, truly concerned.

"Mostly my pride," admitted Francesca. "I
guess having too much of that is something
else I should confess."

"Is that all?"

"No," said Francesca after a moment's
pause. "Something else has been on my
mind."

"What is it?"

Francesca took a deep breath. "It's hard to
explain," she replied, "but lately, God has
been getting on my nerves. Is that a sin?"

"Hmm, that's a new one," replied the
priest. "I guess it depends. Why don't you tell
me what you mean when you say God is getting on your nerves?"

Francesca hesitated for a time, trying to
put into words exactly the way she felt. It had
been building for some time now, and she
wanted desperately to get it off her chest. "I
just don't know what He wants from me,
that's all," she lamented. "I feel useless these
days, and I can't get rid of the idea that it's all
His fault. What is my life supposed to be all
about now that He has taken my husband
and my children have grown up and moved

away? What am I without my family? I know I'm old, but does that mean everything's over for me?"

"Those are hard questions," answered Father Buontempo, "questions we all ask ourselves at different points in our lives. God's will isn't always clear, so there's certainly nothing sinful about seeking to understand it. Accepting His will once we understand it can be the hard part." He paused to assess whether his words were helping her. Then he continued, telling her, "But you ought to remember that even though your children might be far away, they love you and think about you every day, just like you love and think about them. You're always together in your thoughts and prayers."

"It's not enough," said Francesca. "I need more from my family. *They* need more from me, even if they don't know it."

"Perhaps. But maybe it would help to consider that your children and grandchildren are not your only family. You're also part of God's greater family. Everyone you meet is a son or daughter or sister or brother, everywhere you go. In a special way, each of them needs you, and you need them."

"Maybe," muttered Francesca, not completely convinced.

"Be patient," the priest told her. "When God is ready, He'll make whatever it is that He wants you to do next clear to you."

"No chance He could give me a hint in the meantime?"

"Sorry, I don't think He works that way. You'll just have to wait."

"And what do I do while I'm waiting?"

"For starters, you can say three Our Fathers," he told her. Then he absolved Francesca of her sins, real and imagined, and sent her on her way.

After mass, Francesca stopped by the market to pick up some vegetables and a few pieces of meat to put in a soup she was planning to make. She liked soups, especially in the winter. As she looked over the selection of meats, Francesca's eye fell upon the weekly special: a nice pork tenderloin roast that would be perfect for Sunday dinner. In her mind, she could already see the meal on the table, the beautiful roast at the center, beside it some roasted potatoes and a platter of sautéed rabe and a fresh-baked loaf of bread.

The vision quickly faded, though, as the realization that there would be no one to share such a meal with her invaded her thoughts. Just the same, Francesca picked up the roast and put it in her basket.

"That's a nice price for that roast, isn't it?" said a smiling Tony when Francesca brought everything to the cash register.

"Too good to pass up," Francesca agreed.

"Cooking for the family tomorrow?" he asked.

"Nope," replied Francesca, shaking her head. "Just me."

"That's a lot of meat for just one person," Tony joked.

"Oh, no," explained Francesca. "This is going in the freezer for someday and somebody; who knows when or who?"

"And what about you in the meantime?"

"Me?" she said with a shrug. "I guess tonight I'll just make myself some soup . . . and then I'll wait."

"BLOOD pressure is fine," said the doctor. He removed the cuff from Francesca's arm. Then he took the stethoscope and listened to her heart for a few moments, before placing the cold metal disk on her back. "Big breath, please," he asked.

Francesca took a deep breath.

"Now out," said the doctor.

Francesca had come in for her yearly checkup. She didn't care much for going to the doctor, but it kept her son and daughters from nagging her about taking care of her health. Francesca had been in such gloomy spirits earlier that morning that she had almost canceled the appointment. She looked at the doctor, who was now leaning back against the counter facing the examination table. He was a young man, late thirties. If she had to go to the doctor, Francesca ordinarily would have preferred to be examined by someone closer to her own age. Doctor Johnson, however, to whom she had gone for years, had retired the previous spring, leaving this new doctor, Doctor Olsen, to take over the practice.

"Let's see," the doctor continued as he scanned his notes, "your heart sounds good, weight's just where it should be, and all your blood work looks fine."

"So I guess that means I'm going to live?"

she asked, not particularly cheered by his findings.

"If I had to put it into medical terms, I'd say that you're healthy as a horse."

"Then how come I feel so rotten all over?"

"Well, I'd say it's because of that fall you told me about. You'd be surprised by how long it takes to fully recover from a jolt like that." The doctor then tapped his pen against his clipboard and eyed her thoughtfully. "You know, I don't think there's anything wrong with you other than what I've told you, but this time of year can get you down as well. We call it *seasonal affective disorder*—SAD."

"Sad. That sounds about right," said Francesca, chuckling for the first time since she came to the office. "What causes it?"

"Lack of sunlight this time of year," he explained. "As the days get shorter, so do our tempers, if you know what I mean."

"What do you do for it?"

"Try to get out in the sun a few minutes each day. Getting more sleep will help as well. You're a healthy person, so you should also try to find something to keep your mind active to pass the time."

"I'm tired of just passing the time," Francesca told him with a sigh. "I want to fill it and live it." She sat there sulking for a time. "Maybe I should get myself a job," she suggested.

"There's no reason why you can't still work if you want to."

"Really?" she said. She had made the suggestion as a joke.

"I mean, just part-time," said the doctor. "I wouldn't want to see you working more than a few hours every week. Not that you couldn't, but unless you need the money, why would you?"

Francesca turned the idea of getting back in the job market over in her mind. For a moment, it seemed like an intriguing possibility. But then another thought brought her down. "It's been years since I worked outside the house," she told him. "Last time was before I had children. Who would hire me now, and to do what?"

"I don't know," admitted the doctor. "But it's never too late to learn something new, something you might enjoy. You'll just have to keep your eyes open and wait to see what comes up."

"Wait," she muttered. "Seems like all I do these days is wait."

The doctor helped her put on her coat and held open the door. "See you next year, Mrs. Campanile," he said pleasantly.

"If God wants," Francesca replied, giving him a nod. Then she picked up her pocketbook and headed out to the front desk to schedule next year's appointment.

THE newspaper lay in a plastic bag at the bottom of the front walk when Francesca looked out the window early the next morning. She let out a grunt of consternation. Once upon a time, the paperboy would have made certain that he tossed her newspaper up onto the front step so that it would stay dry, and she wouldn't need to traipse through the snow or rain to retrieve it. Nowadays, though, one person in a car did the job of ten paperboys. This arrangement, she presumed, is what some people referred to as progress. Francesca did not think of it that way. Whoever it was that drove by every morning never stopped but simply flung the papers out the window, letting them land wherever.

At lunchtime, the newspaper still rested on

the same spot. Lately, the headlines had been proclaiming nothing but gloom, something that Francesca felt she already had in ample supply; there was no need to hurry out to get more. Besides, it was a bitter-cold day, and she had been disinclined to brave the elements that morning. Instead, she had spent the early part of the day upstairs, rummaging through the bedroom closets. It always amazed Francesca to discover how much clutter her children had left behind. No matter how many times she straightened out the attic or closets, she inevitably found something that she had previously overlooked. On this particular morning, she held up a little blue cardigan sweater that Joey had last worn for Christmas when he was four years old. She recalled how he had looked so adorable that everyone had just wanted to pick him up and hug him for all they were worth.

Francesca breathed in the scent of the wool and squeezed the little sweater to her heart. Tears ran from her eyes, until she carefully placed the sweater back on its hanger. Then, drying her cheeks with the back of her hand, she closed the closet door and returned downstairs.

Later, Francesca finally went out for the newspaper while the last of the soup from the previous weekend was heating up on the stove. She looked over the newspaper while she sat at the kitchen table, eating her soup. She gave the front page a cursory examination before going to the obituaries. Relieved to find that none of her acquaintances had chosen to leave this world, she set the paper down for a moment and gave a sigh. As she stared blankly across the room, her gaze fell on the clock above the stove, and suddenly she became acutely aware of the passage of time. It was then that Francesca realized what had been troubling her. She was sick of the feeling that she was just sitting on the sidelines, watching life go by. She longed to get back in the game—for however long God would allow her to play.

Francesca looked down at the newspaper. Not sure of exactly what she was looking for, she turned to the help-wanted section. Her gloom turned to dismay as she scanned the ads and found nothing for which she was even remotely qualified.

Francesca then put the paper down again. She had just about made up her mind to forget the whole thing when her eye spied a small help-wanted ad near the bottom of the page. She leaned closer and read it carefully. Somewhere inside the back of her mind the light of a new idea flickered to life. She sat there for a time, wondering what she should do. It would help to talk to someone. She *needed* to talk to someone, but who? Rosie and Alice were sure to have a conniption if they found out what she was contemplating, and Joey was off to the other side of the world. She stayed there, turning the matter over in her mind, until at last she came to a decision and stood. A few minutes later, bundled up in her coat and hat, Francesca grabbed her book bag and opened the front door. "I've waited long enough," she muttered. Then she stepped outside, locked the door behind her, and went to the car.

"YOU want to do *what?*" Peg gaped at Francesca with wide-eyed incredulity. Francesca had found her in the library computer room. Natalie was there as well, gazing at Francesca with much the same look. Connie, she suspected, would have made the same face had she not been off in some other part of the library.

"Frannie," Peg continued, "I can understand you want to keep busy, but do you really want to be a nanny for someone else's brats?"

"It's not really a nanny the ad said she's looking for," Francesca tried to explain. "It's more like 'a responsible person' is what it said, to look after a couple of children at their home for one or two hours after school every day. What's so bad about that?"

"That's how it starts," warned Natalie. "Trust me, you don't know what parents are like these days. First they tell you they'll be home at five, next they ask if you would stay a little later because they're busy at work, and before you know it, they're out till all hours, gallivanting around while you're stuck there watching *their* kids. Believe me, I've seen it happen."

Peg nodded her head in agreement. "She's right, Frannie. These people will take advantage of you. It happened to my daughter. She agreed to watch one of her neighbor's kids one day after school. The next day, the mother asked my daughter to do it again. All of a sudden, the mother's calling from work practically every day, asking her to watch the little girl for her. It went on like that until one night when the parents didn't pick her up until almost ten o'clock. That's when my daughter finally put a stop to it."

"How sad for that little girl," said Francesca. Her two friends were not telling her anything she didn't already know. In a land of plenty, there were so many children who went without the simple things that counted most in life.

"Forget about it," Natalie advised. "Why would you want to do it in the first place?"

"I don't know," Francesca admitted. "It's almost like asking me why I breathe. I don't understand how or why it happens, but I know if I stop doing it, it's all over for me. That's kind of the way I feel about this whole thing. It's just a way to keep me breathing."

"If I were you, I'd stop and take a deep breath and think about this some more before I went ahead," said Peg.

Just then, Connie appeared at the door. Peg and Natalie filled her in on Francesca's plan. "What are you, crazy?" she exclaimed.

"They've already asked me that," replied Francesca.

"But who are these people?" asked Connie. "What do you know about them?"

"Nothing," replied Francesca with a shrug. "The ad just said, 'Working mother seeks responsible person,' to watch her kids after school. That's all I know."

"All the more reason you shouldn't do it," said Natalie. "You never know what kind of creeps you might end up involved with."

"Oh, don't worry, girls," Francesca told them. "I know how to take care of myself. Besides, who's to say that I'll even get the job? And there's nothing that says I have to take it even if they offer it to me. I just want to give myself the chance."

"Well, it's your life," said Peg, turning back to her computer. "But if you asked me, I'd say you're looking for trouble."

"Maybe, but what else is life for?" she replied.

Later, Francesca left the others to their computers and stopped by the front desk to check out some books on babysitting. She tucked them into her book bag and headed to the exit.

Chapter Three

"MOM?"

The voice came to Loretta Simmons from someplace far away, like an echo in a canyon.

"Mom."

It came around again, this time closer and more insistent.

"Come on, Mom. We're gonna be late!"

Facedown in the pillow, clenching the bedsheets beneath her, Loretta Simmons opened her eyes. Wearily, she lifted her head off the pillow, pushed aside the hair hanging over her eyes, and looked into the face of her son, standing at the edge of the bed. She glanced at the clock. Seven twenty-five. Great, she had forgotten to set the alarm again. There was no way the kids would make the bus; she would have to drive them to school again. Dropping her head back onto the pillow, she let out a sorrowful groan and squeezed her eyes shut once more.

Up to that point, Loretta had been lost in a very pleasant dream, the last remnants of which were now quickly receding from her memory. It was the type of dream she seemed to have with growing regularity lately. Whenever she had it, there was always something oddly familiar about it. She recalled standing on a balcony overlooking a shimmering, moonlit bay. A warm breeze caressed her face, while down below, calypso music rose above the sighing of the gentle surf. She wasn't alone, of course. Standing there with her on that beautiful balcony was a man. There was something very familiar about him as well, even though she never could quite make out his face.

"Tell me you'll stay," she recalls saying to him in the dream.

"Of course," he told her, reaching out for her hand.

"Tell me you love me."

"With all my heart."

It was all something right out of a romance novel, but just the same, it all came out so heartfelt, so dramatically real to her. It swept her away—the secret passion, the longing in her heart. But then, just at the moment when the man finally took her in his arms, the voice had come and chased the whole magical scene away.

"Get up, Mom," insisted her son, nudging

her in the arm. "We're going to be late for school!"

"Go get dressed, Will," Loretta grunted. "I'll be up in a minute."

"I'm already dressed," he replied. "When are you going to make breakfast? I'm hungry."

"You're nine years old," she complained. "Can't you make your own breakfast? Pour yourself a glass of juice. Make some toast."

"We have no juice, and the toaster is broke, remember?" her son impishly reminded her.

Loretta let out another groan. "Is your sister up?"

"In the bathroom, brushing her hair, where else?"

"Okay." His mother yawned, dragging herself from beneath the covers. "Go. I'm up."

Loretta stood and shuffled out into the hallway. As she passed the bathroom, she rapped her knuckles against the door.

"Don't be all day in there, Miss America," she warned her daughter. "Get a move on." Then she trudged downstairs to make herself a cup of instant coffee.

Will was sitting on the living room couch,

playing a video game on the television. Beside him, on the end table, rested a paper plate holding several saltine crackers and an open jar of peanut butter.

"Turn that thing off," Loretta cried, "and get ready for school." She followed that up by screaming upstairs, "Penelope Simmons, get yourself down here. *Now!*"

Penny descended the stairs a few minutes later. She was a pretty girl with blue eyes and dark, straight hair like her mother's. However, her choice of attire that morning—a flimsy blouse and a skirt much too short for a sixth grader—elicited sharp criticism from her mother. The daily dress review before school had become something of an ordeal ever since she had turned eleven.

"Absolutely not!" cried Loretta. "Where did you get that outfit?"

"My friend Jenna let me borrow it. We're the same size."

"I don't care. Besides, it's the middle of winter. At least put a sweater on. You look ridiculous."

"Tell me about it," chimed in Will, always willing to add fuel to the fire.

"Shut up, game boy," sneered his sister. "Try minding your own business."

"Whatever."

As it usually did on a school day morning, the decibel level continued to increase as the time to depart for school drew nearer. By the time Loretta managed to get herself dressed, collect her own things for work, and bustle with them out the door, she was in full throat, leading the chorus of bickering. She glanced back inside just once and gave a dismayed sigh at the untidy state of things in the living room and kitchen. There was nothing to be done about it now, so she slammed the door shut and hurried them all off to the car. With barely a look in the rearview mirror, she backed the car out of the driveway and tore off down the road.

"Now remember," she told her two children a short while later when she pulled the car up to the school's front door, "you'll have someone new staying with you today until I come home. Please try to be nice to her. Be polite. Especially you, Penny."

Loretta watched until the two of them were safe inside before tearing off again down the road. With any luck, she would be only fifteen or twenty minutes late for work.

HAD it not been for the Snickers bar in her desk drawer, Loretta would have eaten nothing at all at lunchtime. Her head was banging and her stomach growling, but she had no time to eat anything more substantial. She was behind in her work and needed her lunch break just to catch up.

Loretta worked in downtown Providence as a legal assistant in the law offices of Pace, Sotheby, and Grant. Much of her day was spent typing up and reviewing contracts, articles of incorporation, and other legal documents. It was a fast-paced office that demanded speed and attention to detail. Arnold Grant, for whom Loretta did most of her work, might forgive her for arriving a few minutes late every now and then, but he would never tolerate any diminution in the quality of her work. Dexter Sotheby was cut from the same cloth. Loretta didn't dare disappoint either of them.

Bill Pace, the founding partner of the firm, was her favorite of the three. A sweet, avuncular old gentleman, he had reduced his role over the years to simply overseeing the operation and occasionally schmoozing with clients. A widower for some years, he had no children or grandchildren to occupy his days, so the office was something of a second home. Pace passed the bulk of the workweek in his office perusing the *Wall Street Journal,* when he wasn't working on his putting game. On this day, as occasionally happened, a stray golf ball came rolling out of his office door and across the lobby floor, evidence that the firm's senior partner had once again misread the cut of his office carpet. The ball caromed off the leg of a chair and rolled along until it came to rest next to Loretta's desk.

Loretta leaned out from her cubicle and looked down the hall to his office. "Too much club!" she called out playfully.

With shirtsleeves rolled up and one suspender slipping off his shoulder, Pace emerged from his office, examining the club head of a new putter. The old man stopped at Loretta's desk, rubbed his chin, and regarded the ball for a moment.

"Looks like an unplayable lie," he grumbled before discreetly stooping down to pick it up.

With that, he sauntered off, the putter riding atop his shoulder. He returned a short time later, bringing with him a cup of coffee, which he placed on her desk. "That's for not reporting me to the rules committee," he said, giving her a wink.

"Why thank you," said Loretta, delighted to have something to perk her up and perhaps relieve her headache. "But *I'm* the one who should get coffee for *you*."

"Bah," he replied with a wave of his hand. "That's about all they'll let me do around here these days."

Noting that his tie was askew, a not-uncommon state of affairs with him, Loretta crooked her finger for him to come closer. He leaned over the edge of the desk while she fixed it for him.

"How are your children?" he asked. "Growing up fast, I bet."

Loretta smiled. "Some days I think they're not growing up fast enough, if you know what I mean."

"What you need is a good man in your life, to help you appreciate it all," said Pace. He patted his midsection and gave a little cough. "I'd, uh, offer myself, but I'm afraid these old bones are just about fully depreciated."

"Oh, I wouldn't say that," she replied, "but *you* could use a good woman to look after you."

"Have anyone in mind?" he said.

"Sorry." She shrugged. "I'd offer myself, but while a good man would be nice, what I could really use is a wife."

"Hmm, can't help you in that department," chuckled her boss. "But I'll keep you posted." He patted his tie and gave her a nod. "Thanks for keeping me presentable." With that, he tossed the putter over his shoulder once more and strolled back to his office.

"Thanks for the coffee," she called after him.

Loretta sighed and turned her attention back to her computer.

Later that afternoon, she finally allowed herself a break and took a walk to the ladies' room. On the way back to her desk, she stopped to chat with Shirley, one of the other legal assistants. Like Loretta, Shirley was single and in her early thirties.

"So, how goes the rat race?" Shirley asked when Loretta settled into the chair next to her desk.

"The rats seem to keep getting farther ahead," said Loretta wearily. She closed her eyes for a moment and massaged her forehead. "And I have such a headache today."

Shirley looked at her with concern. "Is it bad?"

"I just need something to eat."

"I'll say," said Shirley. "You're so skinny, it makes me sick. All I do is look at food, and I get fat. How do you stay so thin?"

Loretta shrugged. "I guess I just don't look at food that often."

Though she had said it in jest, it was really quite true. Loretta seldom had time for more than coffee and toast for breakfast. Lunch consisted of a sandwich and another cup of coffee, purchased in the deli downstairs. She rarely ate anything between meals. By the time Loretta staggered home from work, the best she could manage for herself and the kids was takeout from a restaurant or frozen dinners out of the fridge. Loretta would have liked to do better, at least at supper time, but she simply didn't have the energy.

"So, how are your kids doing?" asked Shirley. "Find them a new babysitter yet?"

"She starts today," answered Loretta. "I was beginning to think that I'd never find someone."

"Who is she?" said her friend. "Where did you find her?"

"I put an ad in the newspaper," explained Loretta. "It ran for a week. Do you believe that only two people responded?"

"Who did you hire?"

"A grad student who goes to school at the Rhode Island School of Design. Her name's Brenda. She seems dependable enough."

"Who was the other one?" Shirley pried.

"The other one was nice, too, I guess," answered Loretta. "But she was this old Italian woman, and I wasn't sure she could handle the kids. Plus, I don't know, there was something about her, something that made me feel . . ."

"What?" said Shirley.

"She made me feel guilty," Loretta finally confessed.

"How on earth did she do that?" laughed her friend.

"Well, when I asked her if she had any experience, she started to tell me about her own children and her grandkids, and a little about the rest of her family. It sounds like she's very close to them all."

"What's wrong with that?"

"Oh, nothing," said Loretta. "It just made me wonder about a lot of things, that's all. As you know, my family life has never exactly been an episode out of *The Brady Bunch*. And then, of course, there was the look on her face when she asked about Will and Penny's father, and I told her that David was long gone and that the two of us had never married. She didn't say anything, but I could tell she didn't approve. I think she's an old Catholic, just like my mother."

"Old Catholics tend to be like that," opined Shirley.

"I suppose," said Loretta. "But I just don't need that whole guilt scene right now. In any case, I decided to hire the girl."

"I'm sure she'll work out fine," Shirley told her.

"Me too," said Loretta, brightening.

And with that, she stood and walked back to her desk. When she settled into her chair, she noticed the red light on her telephone blinking, telling her that someone had left a message.

THERE WERE MOMENTS when Loretta was reminded that the framework of her life was constructed with all the stability of a house of cards. Touch it, remove one single card, and everything would come toppling down into a heap.

It was a state of affairs of which she had grown acutely aware over the years since David had gone, leaving her to raise two children by herself. Loretta lived in dread of the multitude of common everyday occurrences that could wreak havoc on her life. What if the car broke down? What if the heat stopped working? Who would she call to fix it, and how much would it cost? Money—or more accurately, the lack of it—always weighed heavily on her mind. What if she should get so far behind in her bills that the telephone company or the cable television company or the electric company disconnected her service? Or what if any of a million possible other things went wrong? Like on this particular day, what if she called home and discovered the babysitter she had just hired had not yet shown up to look after the kids when they got home from school?

"What do you *mean* there's no one there but you and Will?" said Loretta in a panicked whisper when she returned Penny's call. "Brenda should have been there a half hour ago."

"Well, Brenda's not here, Mom," replied Penny. "I had to get the key from behind the mailbox to open the door."

Loretta put her hand to her forehead and squeezed her eyes closed. She took a deep breath to calm herself while trying to decide what to do. She opened her eyes in time to see the door to Arnold Grant's office open. Her stomach tightened. Grant emerged from his office and began to walk her way. Though she felt more like crying, Loretta turned the telephone receiver to her shoulder and forced herself to give him a smile, despite noting the file folder in his hand. She knew what was coming next.

"Loretta, would you be able to take a look at this for me and write it up right away? I need it in an hour for a meeting."

"Of course. I'll get right to it, Mister Grant," said Loretta, wincing inside, hoping he couldn't hear the muffled voice of her daughter coming from the telephone receiver. When her boss left, she put the receiver back to her ear.

"Mom? Mom? Are you still there?"

"Yes, Penny, I'm here."

"Mom, don't worry about it," her daughter insisted. "Brenda just walked in. Do you want to talk to her?"

"I most certainly do," said Loretta. "But I can't right now. Go do your homework. I'll talk to Brenda when I get home."

Brenda had a plausible excuse for her tardiness when Loretta finally returned home and spoke with her that evening—something about an important meeting with her academic advisor. Loretta was too tired to attend to the details. Brenda apologized profusely and assured her that she would not be late again.

Loretta gave Brenda a second chance.

The next afternoon when Loretta called to check that Brenda had arrived on time, all she got was a busy signal. At least she felt certain everyone was safely home. Just the same, she fretted all afternoon at the persistent busy signal that greeted her every time she called. It wasn't until she got home that night and let Brenda go on her way that Will informed her that Brenda had spent the entire afternoon talking on the telephone.

Loretta's blood pressure inched up another notch.

The following morning, Loretta left a note by the telephone, asking Brenda to please leave the line free. To her relief, the line rang when she called home that afternoon. Brenda answered it right away and let her know that Will and Penny were home. Everything was fine. That night, however, her son and daughter had little to say as they sat in front of the television eating pizza. They ignored her when she asked them how their day had gone. She suspected something was wrong, but she could pry nothing out of them.

A nagging worry persisted through the next morning, until she finally decided to do something about it. Loretta worked through lunch and asked to leave early. When the time came, she pulled on her coat, grabbed her purse, and hurried out to her car.

Loretta was alarmed to see a second car in addition to Brenda's parked out front when she arrived home. It was nearing four o'clock, and the sun was falling away fast. The lights in the upstairs bedrooms were lit. Will and

Penny, she guessed, were in their rooms. As she strode up the front steps, she leaned over to look in through the front window.

Then she understood. There on the living room couch lay Brenda with a young man. Thankfully, the two had not fully disrobed, but they were obviously giving each other a very extensive anatomy lesson. When she threw open the front door and walked in on them, Loretta stared at the young man with icy malice, until he hastily collected his belongings and escaped out the door. Then she turned her glare to a red-faced Brenda.

"I can explain, Mrs. Simmons," Brenda said anxiously as she tried to straighten herself up.

"I'm sure you can," replied Loretta. "But don't bother."

Later, after she had sent the young woman packing, Loretta sat on the bottom of the stairs and stared forlornly at the floor. She let out a sigh, rested her elbows atop her knees, and propped her chin up on her hand. Will and Penny came down and sat side by side on the stair above her. They had been hiding out upstairs until Brenda had gone. "We didn't want to have to tell you, Mom," said Penny. "We know how hard you tried to find somebody."

"I know," said Loretta. "I'm sorry about all this."

"We don't need anybody," said Will, trying to cheer her up. "We're old enough to stay by ourselves."

"He's right, Mom," his sister agreed. "We can do it."

Loretta reached back for their hands and pulled them down closer to her. She gave each of them a kiss on the head.

"Thanks, guys," she told them. "But I'm never going to leave you all alone. Never." She took a deep breath and stood.

"What are you going to do?" asked Will.

"The same thing I always do. Go to plan B."

"What's plan B?" he said.

"I'll tell you when I know for sure," Loretta answered. She walked into the kitchen and sifted through the papers on the counter until she found the one she was looking for. She picked up the telephone and dialed the number she had scribbled on the paper. It rang only twice before the person answered.

"Hello, Mrs. Campanile," she said. "Sorry to bother you. This is Loretta Simmons. . . ."

Chapter Four

FRANCESCA sat at the kitchen table after she hung up the telephone. The call from Loretta Simmons had taken her by surprise. It was a Thursday evening, and over a week had passed without any word from the young woman since their interview.

As the days went by and it became obvious that the woman must have chosen someone else to look after her children, Francesca had decided that perhaps it was all for the best. Peg and the others were right; she probably wasn't ready for this sort of thing. Just that night, while she had sat at the table eating a bowl of minestrone, Francesca had decided to forget all about it, to put the whole matter out of her mind—and then the telephone had rung.

To say that she had been caught off guard would have been a great understatement. More startling, though, was when the Simmons woman had asked Francesca if she would be able to start Friday, the very next day! Francesca had been so astonished, she couldn't say no. Of course she could come tomorrow, Francesca had told her. As she mulled the whole thing over, an odd feeling of dread mixed with anticipation filled her. She stood to take her empty bowl to the sink. "What did I just get myself into, Leo?" she said aloud as she washed the bowl and deposited it into the dish drainer. "Am I crazy, or what?"

FRANCESCA found the key to the house tucked behind the mailbox, just where Loretta had said she would leave it. She hesitated, standing in the cold outside the front door. There was, she fully realized, no one home, but just the same, she wanted to make a good impression entering the house for the first time. Francesca always believed that every home has a personality all its own, its own soul almost, something that radiates its own energy. As she inserted the key and turned it, Francesca sensed an air of shyness and uncertainty in this home, something that gave the impression that this was a place not quite sure of itself. That being the case, she entered slowly and respectfully, giving it time to grow accustomed to her presence.

Francesca stepped inside and closed the door. She stood there for a time, surveying the interior of the home while she removed her coat and hat. Little had changed since her initial visit to the house, when she had first interviewed for the position. It was not dirty by any means, but the place had the look of organized disarray, which one would expect in a house presided over by a working mother raising two children on her own.

Francesca removed her boots and slipped on her house shoes before stepping into the living room, where she cast a trained eye upon the surroundings. Though almost the end of January, holiday decorations still adorned the windows and an artificial Christmas tree stood in the corner. The pillows on the couch were tossed helter-skelter, and several days' worth of what looked to be unread newspapers were strewn across the coffee table. On the end table by the couch, she spied a small pile of crumbs, evidence that someone recently had been munching on a snack while watching the television.

The kitchen was a disaster. When she walked in, Francesca found the counters littered with school papers, mail, and a variety of other clutter. The sink was piled with dirty dishes, cups, and utensils.

Francesca made her way out of the kitchen and back to the front and looked up the staircase. The first few steps presented a narrow passage, as there were shoes, hairbrushes, books, and other items piled there. Though curious to go upstairs, Francesca decided against the idea. She had already seen enough to understand what this mother was up against. Francesca went back to the living room and sat down on the couch to wait for the children.

A short time later, she jumped up when she heard the sound of children's voices outside the front door. When the two youngsters stepped inside, Francesca stood like a lady-in-waiting, her hands curled into each other in a gesture of respectful anticipation.

The boy and girl eyed her warily as they stood in the front hall, peeling off their coats and hats.

For her part, Francesca's heart melted the moment she beheld the two children. They were adorable! The girl, she could see, was just on the cusp of adolescence. With her long, dark hair and slender features, she was destined to be a beautiful young lady someday, but for now, she was still very much a child.

The boy was smaller than his big sister, his hair equally dark but full of delightful curls, which rolled and tumbled over his forehead. His big, inquisitive eyes peered at her through wire-rimmed eyeglasses, and he looked like a professor of entomology who had just come across a rather interesting-looking bug.

"Hello, children," she said in a hesitant voice. "My name is Mrs. Campanile, your new babysitter."

The girl gave her a haughty stare. "*My* name is Penny," she replied with a tone of youthful defiance, "and I'm not a baby, so I do not need a babysitter."

"*Penny*," the boy whispered, "remember what Mom said."

"Oh, that's quite all right," Francesca assured the boy. "My mistake. It's just that the two of you are so much more grown up than I had anticipated." This remark seemed to put his sister more at ease. "I suppose your sister is right," Francesca went on. "We'll have to come up with something else to call me besides your babysitter." This she said while moving toward the coffee table, to block their view of the manual on babysitting sticking out of the bag of books she had brought along to keep her occupied while she waited alone. To her relief, neither seemed to notice.

"And what is your name, young man?" Francesca asked the boy, even though she already knew.

"I'm Will," he said.

"Well, how nice," she told him. "I have a grandson named Will who's just your age. It's a pleasure to meet you both."

"Yeah, I guess," said Penny, walking past her to the kitchen. Will followed close behind, giving Francesca a quick glance over his shoulder as he passed.

"If there's anything you need . . ." Francesca called after them, but neither of them replied. Not wanting to interfere in their after-school routines, Francesca simply watched them go. She stayed in the living room, listening to them exchange whispers as they rummaged through the refrigerator. She smiled, for it was a scene she knew well. Many things had changed since she raised her own family, but one thing had remained constant: Children always come home hungry from school.

A few minutes later, Will and Penny reemerged from the kitchen. To Francesca's dismay, Penny carried a bag of potato chips and Will a bowl of ice cream. There was nothing wrong in having an afternoon snack, but she wanted with all her heart to tell them to have something more wholesome. She understood, however, that it was not her place to do so. The two children paraded by her again and, without a word, marched upstairs to their rooms. Not sure of what to do next, Francesca returned to the couch and pulled out the book on babysitting.

"SORRY I'm a little late," said Loretta when she bustled through the front door, clutching a grocery bag in one arm and a cloth bag containing her work shoes and purse under the other. She dropped the cloth bag onto the floor, kicked the door shut behind her, and hurried toward the kitchen.

The clock on the mantel read five forty-five. Loretta was fifteen minutes late, but Francesca didn't mind. In truth, she had become engrossed in her books and the time had gone by quickly.

"The market was *such* a zoo!" the younger woman lamented as she hurried past Francesca with the grocery bag.

"Eh, Friday night. What did you expect?" said Francesca, strolling over to the kitchen door. She peeked in, curious to get a look at what Loretta had brought home. "Planning to cook for the family tonight?" she asked.

"Oh, no," said Loretta with a laugh. "Who has time to cook? Besides, I can just about boil water."

"It's not so hard to learn," said Francesca.

"Maybe someday, when I have the time. But for now, they have some really nice pre-pared food at the markets. It's so convenient. You bring it home, toss it in the microwave, and dinner's served. No mess. No fuss. No pots and pans to clean up. Can't beat that."

"I suppose," said Francesca as she watched the young mother take plastic containers out of the bag and put them on the table. "What did you get?"

"Meat loaf," said Loretta, opening one of the containers. "Plus some mashed potatoes and vegetables. It's really good."

"That's nice," said Francesca. "Well, I'm sure you and the children will enjoy it," she added before turning back to the living room to collect her things. By the time Loretta came out of the kitchen, Francesca had already pulled on her boots and overcoat.

"I hope they weren't any trouble for you," said Loretta, rummaging through her pocketbook while the older woman tugged a hat over her ears.

"Oh, no," said Francesca, giving her a smile. "They were perfect. We had a nice chat when they came home, and then they went straight upstairs to . . . well, I guess to do their homework." She started for the door.

"Oh, don't go yet," said Loretta, still searching through her pocketbook. "I haven't paid you for today," she said. "Where *is* that checkbook?"

"Please, don't worry about it," Francesca told her. "Today was a chance to introduce ourselves. This one's on me."

"Oh, no, that's not right," protested Loretta. "It's the end of the week, and you deserve to be paid for your time today."

"Believe me, it's really not necessary. Make it up to me next Friday," said Francesca, giving her a pat on the hand. "Now, go have supper with your children. That's more important."

With that, Francesca bid her good night and went to the door. After she had traversed the front walk and settled into her car, Francesca hummed a tune to herself as she buckled up and put the key in the ignition. When she turned it, the engine coughed like a smoker in the morning before rumbling to life. She gave in to a little yawn, for it had been a long day. Putting the car in gear, she pulled away from the house, unaware that three pairs of curious eyes were watching her from the windows.

LORETTA watched until the old woman had driven off. When the car was out of sight, she turned from the window and started back to the kitchen. She regarded the cluttered table and the sink full of dishes. She had hoped Mrs. Campanile would stay in the living room and spare her the humiliation of seeing the disaster all around while she put out the food for supper. Instead, the old nosebag had waltzed right in. As if that weren't insult enough, there was the not-so-subtle dig about learning how to cook! That's all she needed right now—to have a guilt trip laid on her by her babysitter.

Loretta poked her head out the kitchen door to call the kids for supper, but by then, they were already pushing and elbowing their way down the staircase.

"Hey!" cried Loretta. "How many times have I told the two of you, no roughhousing on the stairs?"

"She started it," complained Will.

"Just go wash your hands for dinner," Loretta told them.

"Oh, Mom, *where* did you find her?" exclaimed Penny a short time later when the three had gathered at the table to serve themselves. "She must be like—I don't know—a hundred and *fifty*."

The young girl served herself a helping of mashed potatoes and carried her plate to the living room to watch TV while she ate.

"Really, Mom," Will chimed in just before stuffing a forkful of meat loaf into his mouth. "Where did you find that Mrs. Compa-bompa-whatever-her-name-is anyway? At a nursing home?" With that, he took his plate and sauntered off to join his sister.

"That's enough from the two of you," his mother called after him. "She seems like a very nice woman. And her name is Mrs. Campanile. You can call her Mrs. C if that's too hard for you."

Not wanting to dwell further on the subject, Loretta changed the conversation. "So, I hope no one has any big assignments due on Monday," she told them. "If either of you do, get working on it now, because I'm not going to want to hear about it on Sunday night at ten o'clock."

"I have a team project I'm working on with Jenna," announced Penny. "So I'll need to use the computer tonight."

"But I was going to go online to check out the Yu-Gi-Oh! website!" cried Will.

"My schoolwork is more important than your stupid gamecard thing," replied his sister.

"It's not fair, Mom," he protested. "All she's gonna do is instant message her friends."

"Enough!" pleaded Loretta. "Let your sister work for a little while; then you do whatever you want on it later. The two of you are old enough to sort this out between yourselves. If you can't do that and this constant commotion continues, I'll just get rid of the computer, and that will be that."

"Whatever," said Penny.

"So, what's the deal, Mom?" asked Will. "Is she coming back on Monday?"

"Mrs. Campanile? I certainly hope so."

"How come?"

"Because at the moment, I don't have a plan C," she told him.

EARLY Saturday afternoon, Francesca stopped by the library to drop off the books on babysitting she had taken out. Peg and the others were there when she walked in, each of them browsing through the videos for something to watch on television that night.

Francesca gave them a full report, shrugging. "At least I didn't have to do any cooking or cleaning—not that I wasn't tempted. And I was so *bombalit'* yesterday morning, trying to get myself organized, that I didn't even think to make something for the kids to eat after school. You should have seen the junk they ate!"

"Let them eat what they want," said Peg with a dismissive wave. "You're better off. You do it once, and they'll expect it all the time. Besides, you never know if one of them might have a food allergy."

"Food allergy?"

"That's right," agreed Natalie. "Didn't all those babysitting books tell you anything? Lots of kids these days are allergic to peanuts and God knows what else. You've got to be careful."

"So, give us the dirt," said Peg. "Was the house a mess?"

"Oh, not so bad," Francesca told them. "Things were a little lived-in, if you know what I mean. I thought about straightening up a little before the mother got home—"

"Don't you dare!" huffed Peg.

"Don't worry. I didn't lift a finger," Francesca assured them.

Connie leaned closer and gave her a nudge. "So, what about the kids?" she said with a twinkle in her eye. "What were they like?"

"Oh, you should have seen them!" cried Francesca, holding her hands over her heart.

"Really cute?" sighed Natalie.

"You would pinch their cheeks for an hour if you saw them."

"Hey, cute is what cute does," warned Peg. "It's the cute ones that are always the most trouble."

"Well, you might have a point there," said Francesca. "I didn't exactly hit it off with the two of them. I don't think they're bad kids— I didn't get that impression at all—but they need something."

"What?" her three friends asked in unison.

"I don't know yet," said Francesca, "but I'll figure it out."

Later that afternoon, Francesca went to church. She arrived early and prayed the rosary. Francesca loved the quiet, contemplative minutes in the church before mass.

On this particular evening, however, the rosary and the mass did not prove to be the elixir to her spirits they normally were. From the opening prayers through Communion, Francesca struggled to pay attention, her mind dwelling on her first day with the Simmons children. She was feeling a little guilty about not telling her own children what she was up to, even though she was of the firm opinion that it was her business and none of theirs. She felt an additional twinge at not having been completely forthright with her friends at the library. They were right, of course, that there were people who would take advantage of someone caring for their children. Somehow, though, Loretta Simmons did not strike her as being one of them. She understood that, until she knew the young mother and her children better, she would have to tread lightly.

Feeling a bit glum, Francesca gave only a brief hello to Father Buontempo when she walked out of church after mass. The winter night had fallen like a dark cloak over the city, and she shivered as she picked her way across the parking lot to her car. When she installed herself behind the steering wheel and turned the key, the engine did not turn over right away, adding a layer of apprehension to her ruminations. On the third try, it roared to life, and Francesca put it in gear before it had a chance to stall.

When she pulled up to the house, Francesca was surprised to see a car parked out front. She pulled into the driveway and hurried up the front walk to the door. When she stepped inside, she threw off her coat and hat and went straight to the kitchen. There she found a young man sitting at the table, perusing the newspaper. The young man said nothing but merely looked up, gave her a smile, and went back to reading the paper. Peeved at such a complacent greeting, Francesca tried to force herself to frown at the young man, but it was no use, for inside, her heart was soaring. How could it not?

Joey was home.

FRANCESCA FILLED a pot with water and put it on the stove. She threw in a pinch of salt, turned the heat up, and covered the pot. While she waited for the water to boil, she peeled and diced two cloves of garlic. She slid the garlic into a frying pan already coated with olive oil, then added a pat of butter and a sprinkling of crushed red pepper before setting the heat on low to let the garlic simmer.

Joey was still at the table, looking over the sports section. He had barely spoken two words since his mother had walked in. This reticence was not due to indifference on his part. Joey, Francesca well understood, had simply inherited his father's preternatural state of perpetual calmness. Francesca had rarely known her son to raise his voice in anger or to fly off the handle the way his mother and sisters were prone to do.

"All I have is linguine and some lettuce and cucumber for a salad," she told him. "If I'd known you were coming, I would have stopped at the market."

Joey shrugged and jutted out his chin slightly, as if to say that whatever she made would be more than sufficient.

Francesca took the lid off the pot. The

water had come to a rolling boil, and she was greeted by a great puff of steam. She ripped open the package of linguine and dumped the long, brittle strands into the hissing water.

"Go get some cheese out of the fridge," she said over her shoulder as she stirred the linguine with a big fork. "Get the Romano. I like that better than the Parmesan."

"You're the boss," said Joey. He pushed away from the table, stood, and walked to the refrigerator with a slight limp, evidence of a recent rugby injury.

"I wish you would give up playing that crazy game of yours," she told him. "You're getting too old, you know. One of these days, you're going to really hurt yourself. Then you'll be sorry."

Joey poked his head into the refrigerator to find the cheese. Then he limped back to his chair and set the cheese on the table.

When the linguine was finished cooking, Francesca poured it all into a strainer in the sink. She gave the strainer a shake before depositing the steaming strands into the frying pan with the garlic and olive oil.

Joey eagerly folded the newspaper and put it aside when he saw his mother carrying the frying pan to the table. She set it in the center of the table on top of an oven pad and nodded for him to help himself while she finished preparing the salad. Joey filled one bowl for himself and another for his mother before digging in. Francesca was happy to note that, by the time she sat down to eat, he was already working on a second helping.

"I missed this." He sighed contentedly as he twirled the linguine onto his fork.

Narrowing her gaze, Francesca reached out and pushed some of Joey's curly hair away from his forehead to reveal an ugly-looking lump. "Look what you do to the beautiful face your father and I gave you. How did you manage to get *that?*"

"I caught somebody's boot when I went down to get the ball during the match against—"

"Stop. Don't tell me anymore. I'm sorry I asked."

Joey shrugged and turned his attention back to his bowl of linguine. Francesca studied him for a few moments.

"So," she asked him, "did you find it?"

Joey looked up at her with a questioning look. "Find what?"

"You know, what you've been looking for," she answered. "Did you find it down there on the other side of the globe?"

"What makes you think that I'm looking for something?"

"Everybody's looking for something. It's what life is all about. Searching for the right things to make you feel whole, especially when you've lost something. But you know, you can run around the world all you want, but what you're looking for is right here," she said, poking his chest above his heart. "That's what will tell you what to look for and when you've found it—if you just pay attention instead of running away." She paused. "It's been almost four years, you know. It's time to start listening again."

Joey gave another one of his shrugs, telling her there was no use in pursuing the subject. Instead, he glanced over to the bowl on the counter. Francesca shook her head, gave him a gentle slap across the top of his head, and went to get the salad.

"It's good to have you home," she told him.

"It's nice to be home," he said. "So, what have *you* been up to? Find what *you've* been looking for?"

"Wouldn't *you* like to know," answered his mother with a grin as she set the salad on the table. "Now shut up and eat."

Joey stayed for a while after dinner, telling Francesca about his trip to Australia, until the jet lag hit him and his eyes began to droop. Francesca knew there was little use in trying to convince him to just stay and sleep in his old bed that night, so before it got too late, she shooed her yawning son out the door. She didn't want him falling asleep at the wheel on the way back to his apartment. Before Joey left, she instructed him to return the next day for Sunday dinner—and to bring his laundry. She stood at the door and watched him drive off. It made her sad to see him go, but at least now she had an excuse to thaw out that nice pork roast she'd been keeping in the freezer.

Chapter Five

"MY, AREN'T we looking bright-eyed and bushy-tailed," said Shirley as she passed Loretta on Monday morning. "Coffee should be ready any minute," she added cheerfully.

The weekends never seemed to provide Loretta with the extra rest that her body

craved. The one just past had been no different. Instead of sleeping in on Saturday morning, Loretta had dragged herself out of bed
and set about straightening up the house before the kids awoke. She was determined to
get things in better order before Mrs.
Campanile returned on Monday afternoon.
Why she should be concerned with the old
woman's opinion of her housekeeping, Loretta
could not quite say. Nonetheless, the thought
of it was enough to prod her into action.

Operations commenced in the living room,
where at long last she boxed the Christmas
ornaments, dismantled the tree, and carted it
all back to the basement. Loretta then broke
out the vacuum cleaner. It wasn't long,
though, before the howling of the machine
shook the children from their slumber. Will
and Penny soon descended the stairs and
started their Saturday morning ritual of lying
around watching cartoons and eating in front
of the television, oblivious to the crumbs
dropping on the floor where Loretta had just
vacuumed. Their cups and plates later found
their way right back into the sink, which she
had only just emptied. The whole cycle began
anew as the weekend progressed, and come

Monday morning, as she stood at the doorway trying to herd Will and Penny out to the
car, Loretta realized with dismay that the
downstairs was in much the same state that it
had been in on Friday night.

Once settled behind her desk, Loretta let
out a yawn while she waited for her computer
screen to come aglow. Shirley soon appeared
with the promised cup of coffee.

"So, how's the RISD girl working out as a
babysitter?" asked Shirley, sitting back on the
edge of Loretta's desk.

Loretta rolled her eyes. "Didn't I tell you? I
had to get rid of her." She recounted the un-
settling circumstances that led to the grad student's dismissal.

"What a little tramp," huffed Shirley. "So,
who's going to watch the kids now?"

"Guess."

"Not the old Italian lady you told me
about," laughed Shirley. "You said you didn't
like her because she made you feel guilty."

"She does," answered Loretta. "But it
wasn't like I had a lot of options. At least
when I called her, she showed up."

Shirley was about to pry out more details
about the babysitter situation when Mr. Pace

walked through the door. It was early for the senior partner to arrive at the office; most mornings, he didn't saunter in until after ten o'clock.

"Good morning, Mister Pace," they said in unison.

"Good morning, ladies," the old gentleman said amiably as he stood by the closet, pulling off his overcoat. "Please, don't look so surprised to see me. I do have to work sometimes, you know." He took out a hanger, stuck it inside the coat, and stuffed the whole thing haphazardly into the closet. "That coffee looks wonderful," he added hopefully.

"I'll get you a cup," said Shirley, and off she went.

Pace strolled over to Loretta.

"Busy day planned?" she asked.

"New client coming in today. New England Trucking. It's a family business. The Hadleys. Known them for years, so the powers that be pulled me out of the mothballs to make it look good." He sat back against the desk in just the same spot Shirley had vacated and straightened his tie. "Funny," he went on, "but I can remember back when the Hadleys first started the business. They used to be just a little mom-and-pop operation back in those days. Now, of course, the son's taken over, and they're buying up other small companies all over the region. Anyway, we're helping them close on two deals just this week alone."

Loretta grasped the meaning of this last remark. Multiple closings meant multiple hours, usually extra hours, to prepare the required piles of legal documents. She'd be going home late at least one night that week. "Sounds like we're all going to be busy," she said, trying her best to hide the faint air of dread in her voice.

"I'm afraid so," sighed Pace as he ambled off to his office.

Loretta eyed the calendar. The week ahead looked even longer to her than it had just a few moments earlier. Occasionally being obligated to work late hours came with the territory, and Loretta was not one to complain. She accepted it as part of the job. Her only concern was that her new babysitter might not feel the same.

FRANCESCA went to the window and peered out to the street. It was nearing four o'clock on Wednesday afternoon, and the winter sun was already dipping toward the tops of the leafless trees. The old woman folded her arms and tapped her foot. Standing there, fretting about Will and Penny until she saw them come into sight, had, in just three days, become something of a daily routine for her. The school bus, according to their mother, dropped them off at the corner up the street at three forty-five each afternoon. Given a few minutes to traverse the sidewalk home, the children should have arrived at the doorstep by ten minutes to four.

She turned away from the window and regarded the interior of the house. The kitchen was still a catastrophe, but it had not escaped her notice when she arrived on Monday afternoon that the Simmons woman had at least managed to put away the Christmas decorations. It was all Francesca could do to keep herself from helping. Whenever she was seized by the notion, however, Peg's stern admonition to not get too involved echoed in her ears.

At the sound of voices out on the doorstep, Francesca whirled around to see the door swing open and Will and Penny come bustling into the front hall, where they unceremoniously dropped their backpacks. "Hello, children," Francesca greeted them as they peeled off their coats and hats. Their cheeks were bright red from the cold, giving their faces irresistible glows.

"Hello," they mumbled after tossing their hats and coats onto a nearby chair. Without another word, as had been the case every other day, the two children went straight to the kitchen. This was always a painful moment for their new afternoon governess, who looked on helplessly as they marched back out with their treats in hand. That Will and Penny should have craved something sweet after school was perfectly understandable to Francesca. What grieved her was that they ate nothing but junk.

Penny headed directly upstairs. "I have to get on the computer, so don't bother me," she warned her brother.

"I don't care what you do," Will replied. He gave Francesca a cautious look. "I'd like to watch some TV. Is that all right?"

"Of course," said Francesca, delighted that one of the children had finally said something to her other than hello or good-bye.

Will slouched over to the couch and plopped down. Francesca watched him turn the television on and scroll through the channels until he found one of those crazy animated adventure shows Rosie and Alice let her grandsons watch. The young boy breathed an audible sigh of relief and tore the plastic wrap off his snack cake. Francesca recognized that sigh, that unmistakable signal children gave after six hours of school-day stress when they finally could unplug their minds in the safe refuge of their own home.

"Tough day at school today?" said Francesca, hazarding an attempt at a conversation.

His eyes glued to the television, Will gave a shrug in reply. For a moment, Francesca expected him to say something, but instead he took a bite of the cake. She took a seat on the chair adjacent to the couch and reached into her book bag for a magazine.

"I got a fifty on my math quiz," Will suddenly confessed in a dejected voice, his gaze never straying from the television. "And Tubs Bennett hit me in the head with a snowball at recess."

"Which felt worse?" asked Francesca. She was pleased that her query elicited the hint of a smile from the boy.

"Good question," he replied.

"Who is this Tubs Bennett?" asked Francesca, pressing ahead.

"He's a big goof in the sixth grade," lamented Will. "He likes to push around little kids, especially me, because he says my glasses make me look like Harry Potter."

"What grade is Harry in?" Francesca asked, feigning ignorance.

"He doesn't go to *our* school!" exclaimed Will, his face brightening at the ludicrous question. "You *know*, he's the wizard, from the stories! Haven't you ever heard of Harry Potter?"

"Hmm, a wizard," mused Francesca, hoping to string the boy along. "Perhaps we could get him to turn Tubs Bennett into a toad."

"Ha!" laughed Will. "That would be great. Maybe while he's at it, he could change the grade on my math quiz too!"

"I'm afraid you'll have to accomplish that trick on your own," suggested Francesca.

The boy turned his attention back to the television.

Francesca was pleased to have finally initiated some repartee, however slight, with one of the children. She was just about to congratulate herself when the telephone rang.

"I'll get it!" shrieked Penny from upstairs. To her disappointment, it was her mother, calling to speak with Francesca.

"Hello, Mrs. Campanile," Loretta began when Francesca picked up the telephone. "I hope the children are behaving for you today."

"Of course," said Francesca.

"That's good," she said. "I was wondering if you might stay a little later today. I'm going to be busy here for a few more hours."

"Yes," Francesca assured her, "of course it's all right. Don't worry. I'll stay with them until you come home."

"Thank you so much," said Loretta. "That's a big relief."

"But just one thing—what about dinner for the children?"

"Actually," Loretta said meekly, "do you think it would be a problem . . . I mean, if it wouldn't be too much trouble, would you mind making dinner for them?"

Francesca could scarcely contain her glee. "Of course," she replied, her thoughts already racing through the possibilities, for surely there was something in the cupboards or fridge that she could whip up for the two youngsters. "I'd be happy to do it."

"Great," said Loretta. "We have plenty of frozen dinners."

Francesca was not certain that she had heard correctly.

"Frozen dinners?"

"Yes, they should be right there when you open the freezer."

Francesca went to the refrigerator and, with phone in hand, opened the freezer door. She extracted one of the frost-covered boxes. "You want me to cook these?" she asked.

"All you have to do is pop them into the microwave," Loretta assured her. "Do you know how to work the microwave?"

"Yes," Francesca replied, trying to maintain her composure.

"I'm sure you'll be hungry, too, so just help yourself to whatever you like," Loretta added brightly. "I think there might be a fettuccine Alfredo in there."

Francesca swallowed hard. The young woman could not imagine the pain this suggestion inflicted on her. "Thank you," she said after pausing for a moment, "but I'll wait to have dinner at home."

Francesca stared forlornly at the refrigerator door after she hung up the phone. She cast a miserable eye about at the seldom-used oven, the cluttered counters, and the sink full of dirty dishes. Her heart grieving, Francesca called for Will and Penny to come to the freezer to pick out their suppers.

If preparing the frozen meals had not been painful enough, watching the children eat them, sitting as they were on the living room couch instead of at the table, was pure torture. It seemed to Francesca that she was being punished for some crime, or perhaps it was some penance she was being forced to per-form, to cure her of her pride and stubborn-ness. Whichever the case, she turned away from the two children and looked upward.

"Forgive them, God," she sighed under her breath. "They know not what they do."

Later, Francesca was sitting in the living room, doing a crossword puzzle, when a weary-looking Loretta finally walked through the door. "Thank you for staying," said Loretta, smiling gratefully. "I hope dinner wasn't too much trouble."

"No trouble at all," Francesca answered. "Do you think you will be working late again tomorrow?"

Loretta let out a sigh. "I'm afraid there's

that possibility. I understand if it's a problem for you to stay again."

"Oh, no"—Francesca smiled—"it won't be a problem. But would you mind if I ask you a question?"

"Go right ahead," said Loretta.

"I was wondering," Francesca began, ignoring the voices of her library friends screaming in her ears, "do your children have any food allergies?"

WHEN Will and Penny came home from school the next day, they were immediately distracted by a delightful and unexpected smell. They looked in the kitchen just as Francesca was removing a tray of freshly baked chocolate chip cookies from the oven. She had made the cookies from scratch, mixing the ingredients at home, and brought everything with her, tray and all, so that all she needed to do was toss it into the oven.

"Hello, children," Francesca said, setting the tray atop the stove.

"Wow, those smell good, Mrs. C," said Will, taking a step into the kitchen.

"Who did you make those for?" Penny inquired, her chilly demeanor starting to melt.

"My son," Francesca told them. "He loves chocolate chip cookies."

"Oh," said Penny, trying to hide her disappointment.

"But you know something?" Francesca said. "I think you both could have one, if you like."

"Are you sure?" asked Penny, her face brightening.

"But first," interjected Francesca, "that table needs to be cleared off, and these counters need to be straightened up. Do you think you two could do that for your mother while I let these cool?"

Despite the old woman's smile, there was a certain sternness in her eye as she proposed this bargain, which seemed not to cause the boy any great concern. His sister, however, considered more carefully. "Is there anything *else* we have to do?" Penny asked.

"Yes," said Francesca, confirming the young girl's suspicions. "You have to wash your hands after. *Then* you can have a cookie."

"That's good enough for me," enthused Will. "Let's get going!"

It didn't take long for the two to clear the

table. The counters were a bit trickier, but the children organized everything as best they could. When they finished, true to her word, Francesca let them both try one of the cookies, but not before pouring each of them a glass of milk and making them sit at the table.

"Sit, and eat those right there," Francesca told them. "I don't want you getting crumbs all over your mother's carpets. And make sure you drink all that milk." She took a seat at the table and watched them, delighted at the looks of pleasure on their faces as they munched away. Before they had a chance to ask, Francesca suggested they could each take another. The words had scarcely left her lips before two more cookies were swiped from the plate.

"So, what do you think?" she asked when they had both swallowed their last bites. "Were there enough chocolate chips? My son likes lots in his cookies."

Before they could answer the question, the telephone rang.

Francesca picked up the receiver. "Hello," she said. "Yes, everything is going just fine. They've been angels. They had a snack, and now they're just about to go do their homework." Francesca gave the two children a look. Reluctantly, Penny and Will trudged into the living room to find a spot where they would still be close enough to eavesdrop. "You think you might be late again this evening?" said Francesca, a smile breaking out across her face. "Don't worry, Mrs. Simmons. Yes, of course I can take care of dinner. . . ."

"Where are you going?" said Will when Francesca emerged from the kitchen a few minutes later and put on her coat.

"Just out to the car for a minute. I'll be right back."

Francesca returned shortly, carrying two grocery bags.

"What's that you got?" Will called after her.

"Frozen dinners," Francesca breezily replied. "Go do your homework. I'll call you when it's time to eat."

Once in the kitchen, Francesca put the bags on the counter and pulled out two half-gallon plastic containers. The tubs, two of the many old ice-cream containers she saved to store leftovers in, held tomato sauce and meatballs from her freezer at home.

She peeked in the other bag to make sure it still held the box of spaghetti and the little container of grated cheese she had also brought along just in case she had been called upon to cook dinner. That little bit about frozen dinners had only been a white lie, Francesca reflected as she pried off the tops of the sauce and meatball containers. Most of this dinner was frozen at the moment—but it wouldn't be for long.

There were a thousand other meals Francesca might have conjured up for dinner that evening, but to her recollection, no child she had ever encountered disliked spaghetti and meatballs. Just the same, she held her breath when she called the children back to the kitchen and set the pot of steaming, sauce-drenched noodles and meatballs on the table.

Any misgivings Francesca might have had about the meal she had prepared were instantly dispelled when she saw the hungry looks on the children's faces when they came to the table. "Get some clean bowls," she said, giving Penny a nod. To Will she said, "And you get some forks and spoons."

The two did as they were told and watched eagerly as Francesca filled their dishes. To her chagrin, however, the two took their dinners and waltzed away toward the living room.

"Ayyy!" Francesca exclaimed, stopping them dead in their tracks. "Where are you two going?"

"To watch TV while we eat," said Will.

"In my house," Francesca replied coolly, "when I cook a meal, people sit down at the table and eat it together."

"Well, this is not your house," said Penny. She was summoning up as much defiance as she could but was finding it difficult, given the fact that she was dying to get a taste of the spaghetti.

Francesca cowed the girl with a withering look. "This might not be my house, but that's my food I just cooked, so you do what I say if you want to eat it."

"But you didn't say anything last night," countered Will.

"I didn't cook that meal," Francesca replied. "I just thawed it out. This one's all mine—so back to the table, you two."

The two siblings looked at each other for a moment and reluctantly trudged back to the table. Francesca filled a plate for herself, and the three sat down together to eat.

"Now, isn't this nice?" said Francesca. She waited for an answer, but the two children already had their mouths full. "Sit up straight when you eat," she said. "And then both of you can tell me all about your day at school."

"AM I a bad mother?"

It was lunchtime, and Loretta was sitting at a table in the deli on the first floor of the office building where she worked.

"Bad?" said Shirley, sitting opposite her. "Of course not. What on earth makes you ask such a question?"

"My babysitter—my nanny—whatever you want to call her," muttered Loretta. She dropped her tuna sandwich onto her plate, dabbed the corners of her mouth with a paper napkin, then started to tear the napkin bit by bit into little pieces.

"Oh, boy. What's happened now?" said Shirley. "Don't tell me you caught *her* making out on the couch with some guy."

"Oh, shut up," huffed Loretta. "How could you even think such a thing?"

Loretta tried to sulk in silence, but Shirley's curiosity had been piqued. "Come on," she prodded, "tell Auntie Shirley all about it. What did your nanny do that's got you looking so blue?"

Loretta let out a long, weary sigh. "Okay, you want to know what happened? Last night, she cooked the kids spaghetti and meatballs without even asking me."

"Uh-huh." Shirley nodded thoughtfully. "And how was it?"

"What?"

"The spaghetti and meatballs."

"Delicious," griped Loretta. "So were the cookies."

"She made cookies?"

"Homemade chocolate chip."

"I see," said Shirley. "Was that all?"

"No," answered Loretta. "Before I came home, she made the kids straighten up after dinner so that the whole kitchen was the neatest it's ever been when I got home."

"What a witch," said Shirley, deadpan. "I can understand why you're so upset."

"It's not funny," cried Loretta. "I know it sounds stupid, but I felt embarrassed, almost . . . I don't know . . . humiliated."

"Oh, come on," said Shirley with a dismissive wave. "Why would you feel that way? It was only a plate of pasta."

"I told you, she's an old Catholic. They have this way about them. Without even trying, they make you feel guilty. Trust me, I know. Remember, my mother is an old Catholic."

"And what does she have to say on the subject?"

Loretta rolled her eyes and shook her head. "Never mind," she sighed. "Don't even go there. That's another story."

"Loretta," said Shirley with a kind grin, "hasn't it occurred to you that maybe all this lady wants to do is help? If you asked me, I'd say she's just what you need right now."

Loretta slouched back in her chair and pouted. In her heart, she knew Shirley was probably right. Thinking back to the previous evening, even she wasn't quite certain just what it was that had caused her so much grief when she had come home to find a nice plate of leftover spaghetti waiting for her at the place her children had set for her at the table. Mrs. Campanile had covered it in foil to keep it warm, as she did with the leftover cookies. Walking through the door, cold and weary, Loretta could not have denied that there was something wonderful about that delicious smell of food that greeted her. Later, though, after Mrs. Campanile had gone on her way, and she sat down to eat her supper, Loretta had wanted to break down in tears when Will said to her, "Isn't that spaghetti and meatballs delicious, Mom? I wish you could cook like that."

"I don't know," Loretta admitted gloomily. "Maybe you're right. I know my life is a mess, but it's *my* mess. I feel like I should be able to sort everything out by myself. I just need a break. A chance to catch my breath. Then I could get things in order. Instead, I just bounce from one thing to another, and I feel like—"

"Like you're doing everything wrong?"

Loretta narrowed her eyes in an icy glare. "You know," she grumbled, "you're not being very helpful."

"Sorry," said Shirley. "Just joking. But I wish you would listen to yourself. You just got finished saying you need a break. Maybe this Mrs. What's-Her-Name is it. Why not let her try to help?"

Loretta was about to try to explain why when she caught sight of someone stepping out of the elevators. She leaned forward to get a better view. Her spirits suddenly began to rise.

At seeing her changed demeanor, Shirley

turned around to see Ned Hadley, the scion of New England Trucking, stepping into the lobby. As Hadley hurried toward the revolving doors, he glanced toward the two women, nodded a greeting, and gave them a wink.

"Boy, he is *so* stuck-up," said Shirley, her voice dripping with disdain.

"Yeah, I guess you're right," said Loretta, nodding in agreement, even though she was inclined to a slightly more favorable opinion.

Now, at hearing Loretta's less-than-convincing tone of voice, it was Shirley's turn to let out a grumble. "Don't even think about it," she warned her friend.

Loretta smiled and gave a dismissive wave. "Who, me?" she said, acting as though she had no idea of her friend's meaning. She knew full well, though, that young Mr. Hadley had shown an interest in her during the past few days. Whenever Loretta came into the room or passed him in the corridor, he gave her a smile and made some pleasant, casual remark. "How's my girl today?" he might say with disarming charm as he passed her desk. Or, at seeing her approach, he'd say, "Here's some sunshine coming my way!"

Loretta was too experienced to be taken in by his artful banter. As an attractive woman in business, she endured it almost every day. As a single, stressed-out mother, however, she was still too young not to be flattered by the attention. Besides, the thought of having a knight in shining armor show up to take care of her was a pleasant daydream.

"Get those little notions right out of your head, young lady," said Shirley, bringing her back. "That man has the word *cad* stamped all over his face. The guy just got divorced. Trust me, I've seen his kind in action. He's just out looking for an easy score."

"Gee, thanks," said Loretta. "I didn't know I was so easy."

"You know what I mean," Shirley replied with a huff. "Just be careful, is all I'm saying, and make sure you give him the brush-off if he comes on to you."

Loretta settled back in her chair and smiled. "My word of honor," she said with fingers crossed.

"Good girl. So, anyway, what are your plans for your terrible nanny now that she has offended you with her cooking?"

"Oh, I don't know," confessed Loretta,

"but it's Friday, and tonight at least, *I'm* taking care of dinner—somehow."

Shirley chuckled. "KFC, here you come," she said.

Later that afternoon, after the firm had finished the closings for New England Trucking and the blizzard of papers had subsided, Loretta was free to go home. She hurried to the closet to get her coat and hat. On the way out, she walked by the glass walls of the conference room, now empty save for Ned Hadley, who was on his cell phone. At seeing Loretta, he flashed a winning smile and beckoned her to come in.

Despite Shirley's admonitions at lunch, Loretta returned his smile and stepped into the conference room. She was curious, and as far as she knew, curiosity killed only cats.

"TOMORROW night?"

"Just for a few hours," said Loretta. "Maybe seven to ten?"

They were standing in the front hall by the door, where Francesca was getting ready to leave. Will and Penny were off in the kitchen, tearing open the boxes of Chinese food their mother had just brought home. Francesca was happy to be going home on time. Joey had called that morning to tell her he might stop by in the evening to pick up some laundry she was doing for him.

"I know it's kind of last minute," Loretta went on. "I totally understand if you have other plans."

Other than five-thirty mass, Francesca had no plans for Saturday night and would have been delighted to say yes, but her thoughts turned to her son. Occasionally, he came unannounced for dinner on Saturdays before going out for the night. Given that she had yet to breathe a word to her son and daughters about what she had been up to these days, alarm bells were certain to go off from Providence to Oregon if he came home to find her gone.

"I don't want to say no," she told Loretta, "but I can't say yes just yet. Could I let you know tonight, or tomorrow morning?"

"Of course," said Loretta. "Call me as late as you want tonight or any time tomorrow."

Francesca patted Loretta on the hand, then went on her way.

Later, when Joey arrived at the house, Francesca was in the basement, pulling the last load of clothes she had just washed for him out of the dryer. At hearing the front door open, she called for him to come down to give her a hand. Joey descended the stairs and paused on the bottom step. "I don't know, the service isn't as good here as it once was," he joked in that gentle way of his, the one that reminded Francesca of her husband.

"Oh, really," she said with a harrumph. "And how is that?"

"I never used to have to carry laundry," her son explained. "Somehow, it just ended up in my bedroom, like magic."

"Hey, you want that kind of service again, you'll have to get yourself a wife," observed his mother.

Joey let out a harrumph of his own and picked up a clothes basket.

Back upstairs, Francesca instructed him to dump the clothes onto the kitchen table and set the basket on the floor. She took a seat and began to fold the clothes, while Joey stood at the sink, staring out the back window.

"You hungry?" she asked. "I have some leftover 'scarole and beans in the refrigerator."

"Nah, thanks," said Joey. "I'll get something later on."

"Will I be seeing you this weekend?"

"Well, not tomorrow night," he said.

"No, why not?"

"I'm going out."

"A date?" said Francesca with interest. "Anyone I know?"

"No, she's nobody," Joey replied. "Just someone I met."

Francesca let out a huff. "That's what you always say. 'She's nobody.' It's about time you stopped wasting your time with nobodies and found yourself a *somebody,* somebody you can settle down with—or at least bring home to meet your mother."

Joey turned from the window and leaned back, his arms folded against his chest. "You know I tried all of that once already, Ma," he said. "Didn't work out for me. And it was just as well. I like things better this way."

"What's better about going through your life without someone who really loves you and wants to take care of you?" said Francesca. "That's no way to live."

"Well, it works for now," said Joey. He brought the subject to a close by turning back toward the window, and in so doing he noticed the message light blinking on the telephone. "You have some messages. You wanna hear them?"

"No, leave them," said Francesca. "I'll listen to them later," she added quickly.

"Whatever," he answered. Then, giving her a quizzical look, "You know, I tried to call you this afternoon, and yesterday too. You've been out a lot lately. Anything up?"

"What, are you writing a book?" snipped Francesca.

"Nope," said Joey, ever placid. "Just asking."

"Well, don't ask me about my business, and I won't ask you about yours," she told him.

"But you ask me about my business all the time," Joey said.

"That's because I'm your mother, and it's my right!"

"You're the boss."

Francesca waited until later on, after she had seen Joey off at the door, before checking the answering machine. As she had suspected, there were messages from Alice and Rosie. She had to call Florida and Oregon. But now that she was certain Joey would be occupied on Saturday night, she was eager to let the Simmons woman know that she would be available to babysit.

Chapter Six

WHEN Francesca arrived the following evening a little before seven, Will answered the door and let her in before fleeing to the relative quiet of the living room couch, where he safely lost himself in a video game. The situation upstairs, where the Simmons woman was hurrying to get ready, was not so tranquil. At issue seemed to be the location of a pair of earrings that *someone* must have misplaced when she was snooping in her mother's jewelry box, even though she had been told a thousand times not to. For her part, Penny was denying the accusations with shrill professions of innocence.

It was, a chuckling Francesca decided, just a typical mother-daughter melee. She had endured enough of them through the years with her own daughters to recognize the signs.

"Staying out of the line of fire?" she said to Will on her way to the kitchen with a big paper bag.

The boy rolled his eyes. "It's like this every time when she's getting dressed to go out," he sighed.

"Does your mother go out a lot?" asked Francesca.

"Hardly ever," answered Will. "But it's always a disaster." Then, nodding to the bag, "Whatcha got?"

"A few things for later on," she replied. "Come and see."

Will paused the video game he was playing and jumped off the couch to follow her into the kitchen. He stood by Francesca's side as she reached into the bag. The old woman smiled. "I thought these might come in handy in case anyone wanted to play a game," she said, pulling a deck of cards out of the bag.

"What else?" he asked.

"And I brought this in case we watch a movie or something good on TV," she continued, producing a bag of popping corn.

The prospect of hot, buttered popcorn seemed to spark some interest, but only a little. "Anything else?" Will asked.

"Just this," said Francesca, reaching deep to get hold of a glass-covered cake dish. She lifted it out, set it on the table, and lifted the cover to reveal the chocolate cake she had baked that afternoon.

"Now you're talking," he said happily.

Penny suddenly made an appearance at the kitchen door. "What's all that?" she said with a look of eager curiosity.

"Just a couple of treats for later," Francesca told her, "if you're both good. Maybe we'll make some hot chocolate too."

They heard the front doorbell ring, and Will and Penny exchanged nervous glances. The two children fell in behind Francesca as she marched off to the front door.

"Hi—Ned Hadley," said the young man straightaway when Francesca opened the door. She looked past him to the driveway, where a sleek black sedan was idling.

"Francesca Campanile," she replied, unimpressed. "Come in."

Before Hadley had finished stepping into the front hall, Francesca had already scrutinized him from head to toe. She noticed everything: the cut of his clothes, his shoes, the way he carried himself. He was handsome enough, with his sandy brown hair and regular features, and he obviously had more than a few dollars in his pocket, but there was something vaguely annoying about his smile and the easy manner with which he nodded and winked at Will and Penny, who were keeping their distance a few steps back.

"Hi, kids," he said with a smarmy grin. "Where's Mom?"

"I'm ready," came Loretta's voice from the top of the stairs. She was standing there putting on an earring.

A few moments later, Loretta descended the stairs. Wearing a very feminine but conservative black dress, she looked quite lovely. She wasted no time putting on her coat and then gave each of the kids a kiss. "Promise you'll be good," she said.

"I'm glad you found your earrings," Penny whispered to her.

"Me too," her mother whispered back.

"Will you be home late?" asked Will.

"Not very," his mother assured him, "but when I get home, you should already be asleep. Okay?" With that, she let them go.

"You two go and have a good time," said Francesca. "Just drive carefully. It's dark and icy out there."

"Don't worry," said a grinning Hadley. "She'll be in very good hands." He nodded to the door. "Shall we, Loretta?"

The moment their mother and Hadley

stepped outside, Penny and Will hastened to the window. Francesca came up behind the two children and looked out the window. "Nice car," opined Will once the car was out of sight, "but I think that guy is weird."

"Me too." His sister nodded.

Me three, thought Francesca. Then, aloud, "Well, now, anybody in the mood for popcorn?"

FRANCESCA took a card from Penny and passed one of her own to Will, who in turn passed one to his sister. Francesca let out a grunt of displeasure. She was on the lookout for a queen, but it was proving elusive. On the count of three, they passed cards again. This time, Francesca's eyes lit up when the hoped-for queen finally appeared in her hand. Without pause, she thrust her hand out into the middle of the table to grab one of the two spoons resting there.

Too late!

With screams of delight filling the air, two smaller hands shot out first and snatched the spoons away. Will threw his cards on the table to reveal four jacks. Penny showed four kings.

Gloating in their victory, the two burst out in laughter and waved the spoons at her. "We won," said Will. "Now pay up!"

"Hmm, I don't know about that," answered Francesca. "I think maybe I was just hustled by a couple of cardsharps. I should probably just take that cake and head on home." This suggestion elicited a howl of playful protest. The bowl of popcorn was empty, and the two youngsters were eager for their next treat.

"Okay, okay," laughed Francesca, getting up from the table. She was very pleased with herself, for the night was turning out better than expected. She had feared the children would retreat to their usual sanctuaries of the upstairs computer and the television. Instead, they had followed her into the kitchen. To her surprise, it was Will who suggested they play a game of cards. Spoons just happened to be an old favorite of Francesca's.

When the hot chocolate was ready, Francesca filled three cups. She cut three slices of cake, transferred them to plates, and set them down in front of the children.

Will took a big bite of cake and washed it down with a gulp of hot chocolate. Penny cast a look at the stove. "Mrs. C, will you ever cook supper again for us?" she asked.

"We'll see," Francesca replied. "If your mother has to come home again late some night after work, she might ask me."

"Mom's been coming home late a lot lately," said Will.

Penny took a bite of her cake. "That's just the way her job is sometimes," she said.

"Your mother works very hard," Francesca told them. "She does it for you two, to keep a roof over your heads and food on the table. And sometimes she comes home very tired. That's why you should do all you can to help out, picking up after yourselves and keeping things in order."

"Did you ever have to work late when you had kids?" asked Will, his eyes peering at her through his wire-rimmed glasses. Francesca chuckled to herself, for she realized that Tubs Bennett was right; sometimes Will did look like Harry Potter.

"Well, I didn't have a job outside the house," she replied. "My husband had his own business fixing cars, and sometimes I would help him by taking care of the books and paying the bills. But my most important job was taking care of my house and my family." She paused and gave them a warm smile. "That was another day and age. Life was different then."

"Like how?" asked Penny.

"For one thing, families stayed a lot closer in those days," explained Francesca. "When I was little, my grandparents lived upstairs. We had relatives all around the area. I couldn't walk anywhere in the neighborhood without seeing someone whose family came from the same *paese* as my grandparents."

"The same what?" asked Penny.

"*Paese.* The same town or village back in Italy. Didn't you ever hear the word *paesan?* That's where it comes from."

"I thought it meant someone who likes pizza," said Will.

"Well, I suppose that might be partly correct." Francesca chuckled. "But the long and the short of it was that there were always people watching out for me. I think that's what the problem is today. People are always moving around, never setting down roots, and never really getting to know their neighbors."

"You sound just like Grandma Jane," observed Will.

"I didn't know you had a grandma," said Francesca.

"She lives in New York," he said. "We don't see her much."

"That's too bad. I'm sure she must miss you both a lot."

Penny fidgeted. "She and Mom don't get along," she said.

"I see," said Francesca, nodding. "But you know, you shouldn't worry if your mother and grandmother don't always seem to get along. Mothers and daughters have been arguing with one another ever since . . . well, ever since there have been mothers and daughters. It doesn't mean that they don't love each other."

Francesca took the deck of cards in hand. "How about you finish your cake, and we'll play another few hands before it's time for bed. I want you both asleep before your mother gets home."

DESPITE ample experience to the contrary, Loretta always hoped for the best. So whenever she met a man who offered the slightest prospect of bringing a measure of warmth and love to her life, she pushed the hard lessons of experience from her mind and let hope have its day. Loretta told herself that Ned Hadley had many appealing qualities—a reasonably handsome face; bright, playful eyes; a pleasant enough personality; and a certain charm about him. He also had a membership at a private country club, to which he took Loretta that night for dinner.

As she settled in at the table, Loretta looked about at her surroundings. She had to admit that it was a nice place to have dinner on a first date. Just the same, as she took her menu in hand, Loretta could not escape the feeling that all of Hadley's assets were offset by one annoying liability: his cell phone.

From the moment they left the house, it seemed that hardly two minutes passed without them being interrupted by the ringing of his telephone. He invariably picked up and began chatting away, as if Loretta were not even there. He was doing so just at that moment at the club, while the waiter did his best to explain the specials. The young man soon gave up the effort and promised he would return shortly to take their orders.

"Sorry," said Hadley after finally hanging up. "Just business. You know how it is. It never ends."

More than one of his conversations had ended with a hushed "I'll call you later," leaving Loretta to wonder what kind of business he was talking. Despite the misgivings, she still held out hope that the evening would turn out better than it started.

"You know, Ned," she suggested playfully, "it might be easier for us to talk if maybe you just . . . I don't know, turned that thing off?"

As he tucked the phone into his jacket pocket, Hadley chuckled and gave her an odd sort of half smile, as if to say that he wasn't sure of just exactly what she meant. He picked up his menu and began to study the entrées. "So, sunshine girl," he said easily, "what looks good tonight—besides you, of course?"

Loretta flashed a perfunctory smile in reply even though she did not feel the least bit flattered. She was, in fact, beginning to feel that she would rather go home. Had she not been famished at that particular moment, she might have suggested it. Instead, she returned her gaze to her menu and kept it there until she saw the waiter returning to take their orders.

"Has everyone made up their minds?" he asked pleasantly.

Loretta closed her menu and gave a barely audible sigh.

"Well, I don't know about you," she said to Hadley, a thinly masked hint of disappointment in her voice, "but I think I've just about made up mine."

After dinner, as Hadley drove her home, Loretta sat quietly listening to the hum of the tires against the road. Her companion was once again engaged in conversation, but not with her. As annoying as the constant interruptions had been, they had in some ways been a blessing. Hadley seemed incapable of discussing anything other than the glories of golf and the trials and tribulations of his family's trucking business.

When they arrived at the house, Hadley abruptly ended his conversation, snapped the telephone shut, and tossed it aside. "I'm sorry," he said in a heavy voice. "I'm afraid I haven't been very good company this evening. Here I am with a beautiful woman, and all I've done is talk to other people on that silly phone. I don't know why I get like that. It's just everything, I guess. I've had a lot going on, you see. The business. My divorce . . ."

Hadley proceeded to explain that, despite

his outward bravura, he was on the inside the most wretched man on the planet. Since the breakup of his marriage, he told her, he had known only sadness and loneliness. He went on for a time, until finally his voice trailed away, a forlorn expression coming over his face.

Loretta didn't know what to say. For the first time all evening, Hadley was behaving like something other than a self-assured boor. He was acting vulnerable and human. Perhaps she had judged him too quickly. This new person might be one worth getting to know better. As they sat there in awkward silence, the car's engine idling, she let a moment pass before turning to him. "Would you like to come in and maybe talk for a while?"

"Okay," he said, a smile curling the corners of his mouth as he turned the engine off. "I'd love to come in."

Francesca greeted them at the door when the two walked up the front steps. Loretta laughed to herself, for she had noticed the older woman standing at the living room window, keeping watch like a nervous mother waiting up for a teenaged daughter.

"I hope the children weren't any trouble, Mrs. Campanile," said Loretta when she and Hadley came inside.

"No trouble at all," she assured her. "They both went right upstairs to bed like little angels." She began to put on her coat. "Did you have a nice time tonight?"

"Very nice," said Hadley before Loretta could reply.

"Oh, good," said Francesca, giving him a suspicious glance. "Well, good night, Mrs. Simmons. I'll see you on Monday."

Loretta stood at the door and watched while Francesca got into her car.

"Alone at last," said Hadley as he ambled into the living room. He took off his coat and tossed it across the arm of the sofa.

"Why don't you sit and relax," suggested Loretta. "I'll get us something to drink. Some wine or maybe coffee, if you like."

"Please, don't go to the trouble," said Hadley, settling onto the sofa. He looked up at her and patted the seat cushion beside him in a gesture of invitation. "Why don't you just come and join me?"

No sooner had she seated herself at a discreet distance from him than, without warning, Hadley reached out and took her in his arms, professing an uncontrollable passion for her. He pulled her close and pressed his mouth to hers. Stunned by this clumsy amorous assault, Loretta did her best to fend off his advances.

"What are you doing?" she hissed, trying to squirm out of his embrace. In that moment, it all became clear that his confession in the car had been nothing but a ploy aimed at winning him an invitation to come inside. Loretta was furious at herself for not having seen through the ruse.

"Come on, Loretta," Hadley implored, holding her tighter. "The kids are asleep upstairs. They'll never know."

"Never know *what?*" answered Loretta.

"You know," said Hadley. "We're both grown-ups here. You know how much you—"

"Mom?"

The small voice coming from the stairs froze Hadley. By the time Will came into view and peeked over the railing into the living room, Hadley had retreated to the opposite end of the sofa.

"What is it, Will?" said Loretta. She hurried over to him, mortified at the prospect that her son might have overheard the goings-on in the living room.

"It's Penny," Will explained. "She's sick. I think she's gonna throw up."

Loretta turned to Hadley, who was doing his best to avoid eye contact. "I'm sorry, Mister Hadley," she told him in a tone that conveyed not the slightest bit of warmth, "but I think you'll have to leave now."

Hadley cleared his throat. "Yes, of course," he said, getting to his feet. "I understand completely." With that, he took his coat in hand and made haste for the door. "Could I call you again sometime?" he asked with astonishing boldness.

"How about if I call you?" snipped Loretta, holding the door open for him.

Hadley stepped outside, then suddenly stuck his head back in through the door. "But do you know my number?" he asked.

"Doesn't everybody?" said Loretta. Then she unceremoniously pushed his head out and slammed the door shut. Feeling like every drop of energy had been wrung out of her, she turned to Will and slumped back against the wall.

"Is he gone?" said Penny, coming to the

top of the staircase. She looked down at her mother with worried eyes.

"I guess you're not getting ready to throw up," Loretta observed.

"I'm feeling a little better," her daughter said sheepishly.

"Sorry, Mom," said Will. "We couldn't think of anything else to do to make him go away."

"Thanks, guys," said Loretta, putting her arm around her son to lead him back to bed. "Sorry for all the fuss."

"He's not coming back, is he, Mom?" Penny asked.

"Nope," said Loretta. "That's one thing I can promise you."

"GOOD weekend?" said Shirley. The inevitable cup of coffee in hand, she was sitting back against the edge of Loretta's desk.

"Let's just say it was forgettable," she replied with a weary sigh, "and leave it at that."

"Oh, come on," prodded Shirley. "You can do better than that. Tell me how Saturday night went with *You-Know-Who*."

Loretta gaped at her friend. "How did you know about that?"

"Oh, I have my ways," said a smug Shirley. "So, go on. Tell me what happened!"

"Nothing happened," said Loretta with firmness, "absolutely nothing." Then, rolling her eyes, she added, "Thank God."

"Ooh," cooed Shirley. "Sounds intriguing. I did warn you, of course, but you wouldn't listen. So, come on. Let's have it."

"Some other time," Loretta told her. "Maybe someday when you start writing for the tabloids."

"Oh, you're no fun." Shirley pouted. She then leaned closer and looked with concern into Loretta's face. "Hey, kid, you look a little peaked today. Are you feeling all right?"

"Just really tired," said Loretta with a shrug.

Shirley reached out and put the back of her hand against Loretta's forehead. "You feel a little warm," she said. "I think you might be coming down with something."

"Thanks, Mom," Loretta said, smiling.

Later that morning, Mr. Pace ambled by Loretta's desk. On his shoulder rode a new putter he was intending to put to the test.

"Good morning, Loretta," he greeted her pleasantly.

"Good morning, Mister Pace," she said.

Pace lingered for a moment. Looking vaguely ill at ease, he fidgeted with the putter and cleared his throat. "I heard through the grapevine that you and Ned Hadley had dinner Saturday night," he began. "I have one or two friends at that club, you see."

Loretta cringed; she wanted to crawl under her desk. Was there anyone who didn't know about her pathetic attempt at a social life?

"I, um, hope all went well," he said delicately.

"It depends on how you'd define the word *well*," answered Loretta. She looked up and gave him a dejected shrug.

Pace let out a grunt of consternation. "I've known the Hadleys for years," he said. "Wonderful, good-hearted people, but the son is a bit of a . . . well, he has something of a reputation."

"Don't worry," Loretta told him with a rueful smile, "I managed to keep *my* reputation intact—just barely."

"Good girl," said Pace, seeming much relieved. "I should have said something to you when I first saw him taking an interest, but I thought it best to not interfere. Nobody likes it when the old man goes around butting his nose into other people's business."

"Well, from now on, feel free to butt your nose into my business any time you want," Loretta assured him. She started to stand, intending to fix Pace's tie, which was once again dreadfully askew, but suddenly feeling light-headed and weak, she plopped right back down in her chair.

"Are you not feeling well?" said Pace.

"I don't know," said Loretta anxiously. "All of a sudden, I'm cold all over, and it feels like my head weighs a thousand pounds."

"Did you get a flu shot this year?" he asked her.

"The kids got them, but I didn't bother," said Loretta, starting to shiver. It felt like she was sitting in the middle of a walk-in freezer.

Pace clicked his tongue and shook his head. "You should have bothered," he told her. With that, he took her gently by the arm and helped her stand. "Come on. I think we'd better get you home."

Despite Mr. Pace's fretful pleas to let him or someone else take her home, Loretta insisted on driving herself. By the time she made it home, Loretta had neither the energy nor the inclination to do anything other than drag herself upstairs and drop into bed. She tugged the blankets over herself, intent on burrowing in and staying there to keep warm, but then she let out a groan, realizing there was something she needed to do first. Rolling onto her side, she reached for the telephone, brought it onto the bed, and dialed a number.

"Hello, Mrs. Campanile. It's Loretta Simmons," she said with a dry cough when Francesca's answering machine picked up. "I'm home sick with the flu today, so there's no need for you to come. In fact, it would be much smarter if you didn't. I don't want to spread this around. I'll call you tomorrow." Then she hung up the phone, dropped her head back onto the pillow, and promptly fell asleep.

Chapter Seven

WHEN she opened her eyes many hours later, Loretta realized that she had lost all conception of time since she had put herself to bed that morning. She tried to sit up, but her head was throbbing.

Penny was at the side of her bed. Looking

down with worried eyes, she reached out and touched her mother's face.

"Hi, Mom," she said, stroking her hair. "I was waiting for you to wake up. Are you okay?"

It was all Loretta could do to keep her eyes open. "I will be," she moaned. "It's just the flu." She looked around the room. "Where's your brother?"

"Downstairs, doing his homework."

"His *homework?*" scoffed Loretta. "Is he feeling sick too?"

"Doesn't look like it." Penny shrugged.

"Do me a favor, sweetie. Get me the Tylenol and a cup of water."

"There's already some right here," answered Penny.

Loretta lifted her head and looked at the bedside table. A bottle of Extra Strength Tylenol stood there along with a small teapot and cup. "Now, how on earth did that get there?" she said.

"Probably Mrs. C," offered Penny.

"No," said Loretta. "I left a message for her not to come today."

"Guess she didn't get it, because she came."

While Penny poured the tea, Loretta sat

up, opened the bottle of pain reliever, and shook out two tablets. The tea was cold, but it served to wash the pills down. Loretta had a vague recollection of someone tucking the blankets around her earlier that afternoon. In her fevered state, Loretta had imagined it to be her mother. Now she realized it must have been Mrs. Campanile.

"Are you guys hungry?" Loretta asked feebly.

"No," Penny answered. "Mrs. C cooked us supper."

"What did she make?"

"It was this kind of weird pie thing she made in the frying pan," said her daughter, "a frittatt, or something like that, with potatoes and eggs—and onions, I think."

"Okay, honey," said Loretta. Then, with a yawn, "I'm going to rest. Set the alarm for me so I can get up and help you guys get ready for school tomorrow."

"Oh, don't worry," Penny assured her. "Mrs. C already made us get our clothes all ready for tomorrow morning."

"HELLO, Mrs. Simmons?" Francesca called.

No reply. Standing at the front door, a bag of groceries clutched in her arm, Francesca pushed the door open and peeked inside. It was late in the morning, and to all appearances, no one was home, a circumstance she found quite puzzling. Just the previous day, the poor Simmons woman had been bedridden; it astounded Francesca to think that she might have gone to work. Then she heard a stirring from upstairs. She leaned in through the door and heard it again; then all was quiet once more.

Francesca tucked the house key back behind the mailbox and stepped inside. As she stood in the front hall, removing her coat and hat, she noted that the children's backpacks were nowhere in sight, a sure sign that the two had made it out to school that morning. Stepping near the staircase, Francesca gave a glance up, recalling the previous day, when she had ventured upstairs for the first time to check on the Simmons woman. The children's bedrooms, she had discovered, were in remarkable disorder, littered with games, toys, shoes, and clothes. Restoring some semblance of order in the children's rooms was a project she longed to tackle. But for the moment she had other plans, and in any event, she did not wish to disturb their mother's rest. And so Francesca moved to the kitchen, set the groceries on the counter, and went to work.

Sometimes when she was alone at home, Francesca talked to herself as she went about her business. In truth, she wouldn't talk so much to herself as she would to her husband, Leo, who, despite having passed on to the next life, remained for her every bit as good a listener as he had been in this life.

It was nearing noon, and she had been talking a blue streak, when she heard the sound of footsteps descending the staircase. By this time, Francesca had already straightened up the counters and washed the children's breakfast dishes. A simple broth mixed with pastina and sliced carrots simmered on the stove. Wiping her hands on her apron, she turned just as Loretta trudged into the kitchen and deposited herself at the table. The young woman was a pitiable sight, her face dreadfully drawn and wan.

"Oh, it *is* you, Mrs. Campanile," she said feebly. "I thought I heard your voice. Were you on the phone?"

"Oh, you poor thing," said Francesca. "I must have been talking to myself again. I'm so sorry for waking you."

"It's okay," Loretta told her. "I needed to get up for a while."

"How are you feeling?" said Francesca. "Think you could manage a little something to eat? I made some soup."

"It's worth a try," said Loretta, "but Mrs. Campanile—"

"Francesca," the older woman interrupted her as she ladled out the broth and pastina into a bowl.

"Oh, okay. Francesca," Loretta continued. "It's very kind of you, coming to the house so early today and staying late with the children last night, but I really don't think I can afford—"

"You want cheese on that?" asked Francesca before Loretta could finish whatever she meant to say.

"Um, no thank you," said Loretta. "I don't want you to go to any more trouble."

"What trouble?" said Francesca, turning back to the table with the steaming bowl of soup. "There you go, Mrs. Simmons—"

"Loretta," the younger woman interrupted

her. She looked up at Francesca with tired eyes and mustered a weak smile.

"Okay, Loretta it is," said Francesca, returning her smile. "Now just eat this while I finish what I'm doing here."

"What exactly are you doing?" inquired Loretta.

Francesca began to dice up some garlic. "I'm making some tomato sauce," she explained.

"How do you make the sauce?" said Loretta, sounding sincerely curious. "I mean, if you don't mind my asking."

"Oh, it's the easiest thing in the world," laughed Francesca. "Just watch while you eat your soup."

When she was finished slicing the garlic, Francesca slid it into a pot with some olive oil and turned up the heat. In a few moments, the garlic's strong but pleasing aroma was wafting through the air, giving the kitchen the warm smell of a trattoria.

"Now what?" asked Loretta.

"Now a little bit of meat," she replied, opening a small package of ground beef. She crumbled the meat in her hand and let it drop bit by bit into the pot.

"All you have to do is brown it a little," Francesca said. She stirred it all around with a spoon, then went back to the cutting board, sliced up a piece of pepperoni, and pushed that into the pot as well. "I like to add that for flavor," she explained.

Francesca then opened two cans of kitchen-ready tomatoes and poured them into the pot before adding a sprinkling of basil and oregano. She gave it all a good stir, covered the pot, and turned the heat down low. "And that's that," she said, wiping her hands on her apron. "Now we just let it cook on its own for a while. All that's left to do is boil some pasta when it's time for dinner."

"You make it look easy," Loretta said wearily.

"Anyone can do it," Francesca told her. "You just have to have a little patience."

"Maybe," said Loretta, sounding less than convinced.

"So, how was your date on Saturday with your gentleman friend?" Francesca asked. "Will you be seeing him again?"

"Not if I can help it," groaned Loretta. "He was a creep."

"Hmm, I thought as much when I met him, but I didn't want to say so. Nobody likes it when an old lady interferes."

"You know, you're the second person to tell me something like that. Do me a favor. In the future, feel free to interfere."

"I'll try to remember," Francesca told her with a kind smile.

Loretta slouched back in her chair. A sad, weary expression came over her face. "Are there any good men left out there for someone like me?" she lamented.

"Oh, they're out there . . . somewhere," Francesca assured her. "You're a young, attractive woman. The right man will show up at your door someday."

"Yeah, but then how do you get him to stay?" said Loretta.

"I don't know," Francesca replied, "but in my day, the first thing you did when you met a man you wanted to keep was give him something good to eat. You know, a lot has changed in the world since I was young, but that old saying about the way to a man's heart is as true now as it was then. Sounds silly, but it works."

"It would be nice to have a man cook for *me*," Loretta opined, her face brightening a little.

"Well, that's a nice fantasy," chuckled Francesca, "but I wouldn't hold my breath waiting for it."

"I guess you're right," sighed Loretta. "So that leaves it up to me. Maybe you could show me the ropes someday."

"Any time. But for now, you should get right back in bed."

"Yes," said Loretta. "Thank you so much for the soup." Her voice quavered slightly. She stood.

"Come on," said Francesca, taking her by the arm. "You need to get your rest. We'll talk later."

THE doorbell rang.

Francesca looked at the clock and frowned. It was a few minutes past one. Who could be coming to the house at that hour? She went to the front door, opened it a crack, and beheld a dapper, older gentleman waiting out on the front step. The collar of his long gray coat was turned up against the chill wind. It was a sunny day, but it had suddenly turned quite blustery. He held a cardboard box from which protruded a white bag holding a loaf of bread. The tops of some plastic containers were also visible.

"May I help you?" she said, fixing him with a skeptical gaze.

"Good afternoon, ma'am," he said affably. "I've come to deliver this to Loretta Simmons. I hope this is the right house."

"Who are you?" said Francesca.

"My name is Bill Pace. Loretta works for me at the firm."

"And *I* work for Loretta right here," countered Francesca, narrowing her gaze at him. "You talk just like a lawyer."

"Well, I guess that's because I *am* a lawyer." He paused and gave her a smile. "So I take it that I have come to the right place."

"Oh, yes." Francesca nodded. "But we have the flu here, you know. You probably shouldn't come in—*Dio mio*, hold on!"

A great gust of wind had just slammed into the house and blew a cloud of snow off the tops of the bushes. Francesca opened the door wide. "Come inside before you get yourself blown away."

"Thank you," he said, stepping quickly inside.

As he came in, Francesca regarded him more closely. He was, she suspected, about the same age as herself. He had a pleasant face with bright blue eyes, like her own. Time had left its mark on his features, but the creases in his forehead and the crow's feet by his eyes were, to Francesca, simply signs of a well-lived life.

"So, Mister . . . what was it again?"

"Pace," he answered. "And I'm sorry, your name is . . . ?"

"Francesca Campanile."

"My, that's a beautiful name," he said.

"Thank you. I've always liked it," replied Francesca, inwardly flattered by the remark. "I'm the nanny," she told him.

"How nice," he said. "Tell me, how is Loretta feeling?"

"Not so great," said Francesca. "She's upstairs sleeping right now. Do you want me to wake her and tell her you're here?"

"No," replied Pace. "I can only stay a

minute." He gave the air a sniff. "Hmm, it smells like something good is cooking."

"Oh," she said, "just a little tomato sauce for dinner."

Pace nodded. "Ah, I recognized that smell as soon as I walked in the door," he said in a wistful voice.

Francesca studied his face before giving in to a smile. She nodded at the box. "Why don't you bring that into the kitchen, and maybe I'll let you have a little taste."

"Now that's an offer I couldn't refuse," said Pace, his eyes lighting up. He followed Francesca into the kitchen.

"Sit there," she said, gesturing to a chair. She then took the box from him, set it on the table, and began to take out its contents. "A nice loaf of bread," she said, giving the bag a sniff. "What else?"

"That's chicken-and-escarole soup in the plastic containers," said Pace as he removed his coat and sat down. "And there are some veal cutlets and vegetables in the others. I bought it all at Angelo's on the Hill on the way over."

"I haven't been to that restaurant in years,"

said Francesca. "My husband and I used to take our kids there."

"One of my favorite places," said Pace.

Francesca began to transfer the containers to the refrigerator. The loaf of bread she set on the counter next to the stove. "You're a nice boss, to bring all this food," she said.

"Well," said Pace with a shrug, "I just thought some soup would make Loretta feel better, and the meat and vegetables would save her the trouble of cooking supper for the kids. I hadn't realized that she was already in such good hands."

"Oh, don't worry," Francesca assured him. "None of that food will go to waste. Speaking of which . . ." Francesca took a knife and lopped off a chunk of the bread. This she again cut in half to open it up and set it on the plate. Then she removed the lid from the pot and dipped the ladle into the bubbling sauce. She drew forth a healthy sampling, poured it across the bread, and set the steaming treat in front of Pace, pushing a paper napkin his way.

Wasting no time, Pace pulled the bread apart and lifted a piece to his mouth. A look of pure pleasure came over his face. "Ooh," he sighed happily. "This brings back memories."

Francesca watched him with interest, noting the easy, practiced manner in which he tore the bread and used it like a sponge to mop up the remaining sauce from the plate.

"Mmm, I love the pepperoni," he said.

"I only cut up a couple of small pieces," chuckled Francesca. She eyed him more closely. "You know, for a Yankee, you have an educated taste in Italian food."

Pace looked up at her and smiled. "Oh, I'm not so much of a Yankee as you might think," he told her. "My mother was a pretty fair cook in her day, you know; my wife too."

Francesca detected a hint of sadness in his voice. She stole a glance at the wedding ring on his finger.

"Does your wife like to cook?" she asked.

"She did," he answered. "She passed away several years ago."

"Oh, I'm sorry to hear that," said Francesca. "Children?"

"No, we never had any. We had lots of nieces and nephews to spoil, but they're all grown up now. I still have a brother, but he moved out to Phoenix a few years ago, and my sister and her husband are down in Florida." He paused and shook his head. "People move around so much these days."

"Eh, it sounds like my family," said Francesca, throwing her hands up. "Everybody's living all over creation. What can you do?"

"Not much," said Pace, absentmindedly fidgeting with his wedding ring. He gave a sad smile. "Funny," he said, "but after all these years, I still wear this. I don't know why."

"Ayyy, probably for the same reason I still wear mine since my husband died," said Francesca. "It just won't come off."

"I know what you mean," said Pace with a sympathetic sigh. "It's like a part of you, isn't it?"

"No, you don't understand," said Francesca, tugging at her own ring. "What I mean is, it just won't come off. I can't get the stupid thing over my knuckle anymore."

Pace burst out laughing. Francesca could not help joining him.

A moment later, Pace dabbed his mouth with the napkin and pushed himself away from the table. "Well, on that note, I suppose

I should be getting back to work," he announced, getting to his feet and putting on his long gray coat.

As the two walked to the front hall, the wind outside rattled the windows in the living room.

"Well, thank you, Mrs.—"

"Francesca," she said before he could finish.

"Well, thank you, Francesca," he corrected himself. "That was as nice a lunch break as I've had in quite a while."

"Don't mention it," Francesca replied with a hint of a smile.

"Perhaps we'll see each other again sometime."

"I'll talk to my boss," said Francesca. She nodded good-bye and watched him step out the door and descend the front steps. When Pace drove away, Francesca gazed off into the distance for a time before looking down at the ring on her finger. She gave a little laugh and looked up toward the heavens.

"Don't worry, Leo. The ring's still on good and tight."

THREE forty-five that same afternoon found Francesca keeping watch at her usual post at the living room window. By this time, the wind outside was howling for all it was worth. Penny and Will finally came into sight. Leaning into the teeth of the wild wind, they trod gamely up the street. When they made it to the front walk, Francesca unlocked the door and hurried back to the kitchen.

"Oh, boy," cried Penny when she and her brother clamored in through the door. "It is *so* windy!" As usual, the two dropped their backpacks on the spot and began to peel off their coats and hats.

"*Shush!*" called Francesca. "Keep it quiet. Your mother is sleeping. Now take off your boots and come into the kitchen."

The two rushed in. Francesca couldn't help smiling when she saw their rosy red cheeks and wide, expectant eyes. "Have some soup," she said. "You both must be frozen like ice cubes."

Francesca filled two mugs, set them on the table, and gave each of the children a spoon.

"It's good," said Penny after taking a taste. "Did you make it?"

"Nope." Francesca shook her head. "That came from a restaurant, but I'll make you soup of my own someday." She sat down at the table with them. "Tell me about your day at school."

"Numskull lost his math book," said Penny.

"I didn't lose it," protested the boy. "I just can't find it."

"What's the difference?" his sister chimed in.

"This is a serious matter," warned Francesca. "Last I remember, you weren't doing so well in math, Will. Am I right?"

"Yeah," he sighed.

"You've looked everywhere?"

He gave a discouraged nod in reply.

"Okay," said Francesca. "Well, first you should go up to your bedroom and straighten up and see if maybe you didn't lose your book somewhere in that mess. If it's not there, or someplace else in the house, then you'll just have to say a prayer to Saint Anthony."

"To who?" the two asked in unison.

"Saint Anthony," said Francesca, surprised at the curious looks on their faces. "Don't you know who Saint Anthony is?"

"Never heard of him." Penny shrugged.

"Saint Anthony's a good saint," Francesca explained. "He's the one to pray to when you lose something. Works for me every time. The thing you have to remember is that if he helps you find something, like your book, then you have to pay him back by putting some money in the poor box the next time you go to mass."

"Mass?" said Will. "You mean like going to church?"

"Yes, of course," she answered.

"But we don't go to church," said Penny.

This admission came as no surprise to Francesca. She knew their parents had never married, so it stood to reason they probably were not churchgoers. "I see," Francesca said thoughtfully after a moment's contemplation. Then, forcing a smile, "Well, I still think it's a good idea for you to pray to him anyway. It can't hurt, right?"

THE next day, Francesca was sitting at Loretta's kitchen table, matching up socks from a basket of clothes she had just washed and dried, when Loretta came downstairs. It was midafternoon, well after lunchtime.

"Don't say it," Francesca told her before she could open her mouth. "I saw the clothes starting to pile up, so I just decided to do a quick load to pass the time before the children came home."

"But Mrs. . . . I mean, Francesca," began Loretta. "It's really too much to ask—"

"You didn't ask," Francesca cut in. "I just did it, because it needed to be done."

Loretta took a seat at the table.

"You're looking a little better," observed Francesca.

Loretta nodded. "I'm still a little woozy, but my fever's down. I should be getting back to work."

"Trust me, you're not doing anyone a favor by hurrying back to the office before you're better. Take an extra day. I'm sure your boss Mister Pace would tell you the same thing."

Loretta gave her a curious look. "How did you know his name was Mister Pace?" she asked.

"He came here yesterday while you were sleeping," Francesca explained, to Loretta's obvious surprise. "He brought some nice soup and bread, and some meat and vegetables too. I gave the kids the food for dinner."

"Funny how oblivious you are to everything when you're asleep," said Loretta.

"That's what sleep is for," replied Francesca. "It's so important, but everybody tries to ignore it. It's like my daughters, who are always complaining that they feel so tired and blue. Try going to bed an hour earlier, I tell them. They'd feel ten years younger in a week. But young people don't want to listen."

Loretta smiled. "I remember you told me you have two daughters. Do they live in Rhode Island too?"

"Florida and Oregon," Francesca replied ruefully.

"I see," said Loretta. "Do you miss them, being so far away?"

"Only every minute of the day," said Francesca. "That's how we old mothers are, you know."

"I'm not sure if all of you are that way," said Loretta, "at least not in my case."

"No? Tell me, where does your mother live?"

"Upstate New York," Loretta answered.

Francesca eyed Loretta for a moment. She had been around long enough to know when someone was holding inside a story that needed telling. "What do you say to my putting some water in the kettle," she offered, "and maybe you and I can have a cup of tea? And you can try one of the pizzelle I made this morning."

"I would love some tea," admitted Loretta. "But tell me, what in the world are pizzelle?"

"You'll see." Francesca laughed. "You'll see."

The two women went into the living room. Loretta insisted on carrying in the tray with the pot of tea. She set it atop the coffee table, while Francesca brought in the plate of pizzelle. They sat on the couch, and Loretta filled their cups with tea.

"This is a pizzella," said Francesca, handing Loretta one of the round, waferlike cookies. "You see, it's sort of like a little pizza. You make them like waffles, except these are thinner."

Loretta noted its golden brown color and delicate snowflake design. "It smells wonderful."

As they nibbled on the pizzelle and sipped their tea, the women began to chat. "You were telling me about your daughters," said Loretta. "How did they end up so far away?"

"Work," lamented Francesca. "You know how it is. Everybody thinks you have to go where there's more money so you can have a better life. Nobody ever stops to think that part of having a better life is being close to your family."

"Well, from what you've told me, at least it seems like your children are all happily married," said Loretta.

"Ayyy, not all. My daughters are doing fine. But my son hasn't settled down yet. That one's still trying to sort out his life. Don't get me wrong; he's a good boy. Smart. Hardworking."

"What's the problem?" asked Loretta.

Francesca hesitated for a moment. "Well, I'll tell you," she said at last. "He was all set to get married a few years ago. Then three weeks before the wedding, the whole thing got called off."

"What happened?"

"My son would never say a word about it. But two months later, I read in the paper that his fiancée had married some other guy. Six months after *that*, I see the birth announcement for their first child. So, you do the math."

"Oops," said Loretta with a pained expression.

"Oops is right," Francesca went on. "But, life goes on. He'll find his way. So tell me about you. What's your story?"

"You mean, how did a nice girl like me end up raising two children all by herself?"

Francesca shrugged and nodded.

"Where would I even begin?" Loretta wondered aloud.

"Why don't you tell me about your mother?"

"Ah, my mother," Loretta began. "I guess things started to fall apart after my father died. I was a teenager, and I was really close to him. Mom loved him too. I knew that. But two years later, she got remarried, and I couldn't stand her husband."

"What was wrong with him?"

"Nothing. He just wasn't my father," admitted Loretta. "Anyway, I went through this rebellious phase and made life miserable for everybody at home. I stopped going to church, and that drove my mother nuts, because she's an old-fashioned Catholic—which I guess is why I did it. It was probably a big relief for them all when I went off to college. And that's where I met David."

"Penny and Will's father?"

"That's right," said Loretta. "David was two years ahead of me. He was good-looking, full of philosophy and all these

avant-garde theories about society and rela-
tionships and the uselessness of organized re-
ligion. I thought he was brilliant. Marriage,
of course, was an anachronism to David.
When he graduated, I quit school, thinking I
could always go back someday to finish."

Loretta paused. She looked at Francesca
and rolled her eyes. "Yeah, I was a complete
sucker."

"It happens," said Francesca sympa-
thetically.

"Well, needless to say, my mother was
apoplectic," Loretta continued, "but I didn't
care. So we ended up here in Providence because David found a teaching job. We found a
nice little apartment, and a year later Penny
came along. A little over a year after that, I became pregnant again. I was happy when I
found out, but David wasn't. I didn't want to
admit it to myself, but he had been growing
distant for a long while." Loretta bowed her
head. "He didn't want me to keep the baby,"
she said, her eyes starting to well up. "I was
furious. I told him to go away and do whatever it was he had to do and that I would take
care of my children by myself. It wasn't long
after that he left—to go find himself."

"And did he?" asked Francesca.

"Yeah," said Loretta. "He found himself with another woman."

"So does he at least stay in touch with the children?"

"What for?" Loretta shrugged. "Penny was a baby when he left, and Will wasn't even born."

Francesca nodded as Loretta went on to talk about struggling to raise the children on her own. As she listened, she was struck by the steely determination in the young mother's voice. What impressed her most, though, was her sense of responsibility, her refusal to blame anyone else for her circumstances.

When Loretta finally finished, Francesca could not help beaming a smile of admiration at her. "I didn't know it," she told her, "but you're one tough broad."

Loretta forced a smile. "Oh, I don't know; most days I feel like I'm barely keeping things together. I worry about the kids. Penny needs a father in her life who will be there for her. And poor Will, he needs someone to toss a ball to him now and then. They've both missed out on so much because of me."

"Honey," said Francesca. "Before you go

beating yourself up for no reason, you should know that you've done a great job."

"Then why do I feel so guilty about everything?"

"Why do you think?" laughed Francesca. "It's because deep inside, you're an old Catholic too. If you want to feel better, try going to confession. Works all the time for me."

Loretta groaned. "I haven't been to church in a thousand years. The walls would fall down around me the second I stepped inside. I never even had the kids baptized."

"Well, at least you wouldn't be at a loss for words in the confessional," noted Francesca.

"No, I suppose not," sighed Loretta.

"Well, you'll see; things will work themselves out. They always do, and never the way you expected, almost like magic."

Francesca patted Loretta on the hand and began to collect the teacups and saucers. "That's enough for today. Now you should go back upstairs and get some rest, while I get dinner started. The kids should be home any minute."

Loretta was just pulling herself off the couch when the front door burst open, and Penny and Will came tumbling in.

"It worked, Mrs. C! It worked!" cried Will, beaming with excitement. "I didn't think it would when I went to bed last night, but I tried it anyway!"

"What on earth are you talking about?" said Loretta.

"Show them, dopie," said Penny, giving her brother an elbow in the side.

His eyeglasses sliding at an odd angle down his nose, Will reached in his backpack. "The bus driver said he found it under a seat," he gushed as he rummaged through the sack.

"Found what?" asked his mother, still perplexed.

"Look!" the boy cried triumphantly, holding up his math book.

Francesca looked on and smiled with deep satisfaction. Apparently, Saint Anthony had come through once again.

Chapter Eight

LORETTA awoke on Friday morning reasonably refreshed. With a yawn and a stretch, she got to her feet and went to wake up the kids for school. "Come on, guys, up and at 'em!"

she called, setting the merry-go-round once more in motion.

When she arrived at work that day, Loretta stopped by Mr. Pace's office. The door was ajar, but as expected, the senior partner was not yet in. She left a thank-you note atop his desk, then hurried off to get her workday started.

Later that morning, a golf ball came rolling past Loretta's desk. She peeked out of her cubicle and saw Mr. Pace ambling down the hall in her direction. He smiled at her. "I just stopped by to thank you for your nice note."

"Thank *you* for all the nice food," replied Loretta. "That was really sweet of you. You shouldn't have gone to the trouble."

"Oh, it was no trouble," he said. "Besides, I enjoyed meeting your Mrs. Campanile. She seemed very nice—and she makes an excellent spaghetti sauce, you know."

"Yes, she does," said Loretta, eyeing him with curiosity. "But how did you know that?"

"Oh, while I was there, she let me come into the kitchen and have a little taste test with some Italian bread," he explained.

"Did she really?" said Loretta, nodding thoughtfully. "Now that's very interesting."

"Of course, she seemed quite busy," Pace hastily added, "and I had to get back to the office, so I didn't stay long. But I rather enjoyed talking to her." The senior partner's face flushed. Stooping down, he snatched up the wayward golf ball. Turning to go, he said, "Nice to see you healthy again. Have a good weekend, Loretta."

"You too, Mister Pace," she called after him.

Loretta chuckled to herself as she turned her attention back to her work. "Yes, that was very interesting, indeed."

When Loretta returned home that evening, Francesca and the kids were in the kitchen, sitting around the table. Penny looked at her mother. "What's for supper?"

"Pizza," said Loretta. "How does that sound?"

"Pizza works for me."

"Me too," added Will. "I'm going to play some PS2 while we wait."

"And I'll be upstairs," said Penny, pushing past her brother. And off the two went.

"You know, I would have been happy to cook supper tonight," said Francesca. "You still look tired."

"No, you've already done way too much this week," said Loretta, sitting down at the table. "Anyway, it's Friday night, so who wants to cook?" She paused and could not repress an impish impulse. "I happened to see Mister Pace today."

"Oh, that's nice," said Francesca, betraying no emotion.

"Yes," Loretta continued. "He said he enjoyed meeting you—and getting to taste the sauce you were making that day."

Francesca narrowed her gaze. "So?"

"Oh, nothing," said Loretta innocently. "I just thought it was funny that the first thing you did when you two met was to give him something to eat, that's all."

Francesca's face reddened ever so slightly. "It just goes to show that you have to be careful who you feed," she said. With that, Francesca got to her feet and pushed her chair back. "Well, it's time for me to be going home now."

Ever so pleased with herself for having once gotten the better of her venerable babysitter, Loretta walked Francesca to the door.

"Come say good night to Mrs. Campanile, Will," she said.

"Good night, Mrs. C.," said Will as they passed, his eyes reverting immediately to the television.

"Good night, Will. Be a good boy," Francesca told him.

"Penny!" Loretta called up the stairs. "Say good-bye to Mrs. C." When no answer came, she said, "What is she doing up there?"

"What do you think?" said Will. "She's on the computer."

Loretta shook her head. "I don't know what to do sometimes," she said to Francesca. "I worry all the time about what she's doing on that computer, what she's looking at on the Internet."

"Why don't you just move the computer down here, where you can keep an eye on her?" Francesca said simply.

Loretta scowled with annoyance at the simple, inescapable logic of the suggestion, her smug self-satisfaction of just a few moments earlier gone with the wind.

"Well, good night, everybody," said Francesca, an impish look coming into her own eyes. "See you on Monday." With that, she turned and headed out the door.

Loretta stood there as she watched the old

woman make her way down the steps, until she could contain herself no more.

"Oh, you think you're so smart!" she finally cried out.

From out in the dark, she could hear Francesca break into laughter. Then, in spite of herself, Loretta laughed too. She waved good-bye, closed the door, and went to the window. Will put aside the video game controller and stood beside her.

"You know, Mrs. C is okay," he said, looking out. "But sometimes, she thinks she knows everything, doesn't she?"

"Yes, she does," Loretta agreed. She smiled, though, because Loretta suddenly realized something quite unexpected had happened between her and the old Catholic lady who sometimes made her feel guilty: They were becoming friends.

"WELL, hello, Mrs. Campanile," said a yawning Tony. "It's been a while since the last time I saw you in the store at this hour. Cooking dinner for the family today?" It was Sunday morning.

"Not exactly, Tony," she replied as she put the chicken cutlets and the rest of her groceries up on the counter. "My son decided at the last minute to have some friends over to his apartment today, to watch the big football game, so he called me last night and asked me to make something for them to eat."

"Hey, I don't blame him," said Tony, smiling. "You can't have a Super Bowl party without food."

"Eh, I guess," grunted Francesca, trying to sound annoyed, even though she was inwardly delighted. "It would have been nice if he let me know about it a day or two in advance."

"Ayyy, you know how kids are," laughed Tony. "They're all the same, even after they grow up."

"I'm not sure if all mine are completely grown up yet," Francesca sighed.

"Yeah, but would you want them any other way?" said Tony.

"Probably not," admitted Francesca. Then, leaning closer, she added, "But don't tell them that."

When she returned home, Francesca brought the groceries into the kitchen and put some music on the living room stereo. Francesca loved music. For her, it was as integral a part of Sundays as was dinner

with the family. Later, as it was nearing midday, she listened to Beethoven's Ninth while
sautéing chicken on the stove.

By the time Joey arrived a short while later,
Francesca was in soaring good spirits. Alice
and Rosie had called earlier; both had talked
of a possible trip home to visit in the summer.
And Loretta had surprised her by sending a
nice little floral arrangement to say thank you
for taking care of her all week.

"Hey, there you are," Francesca said mer-
rily as she pushed the chicken from the skillet
into an empty foil pan. "You're just in time.
Listen, they're playing 'Ode to Joey'!"

It was obviously too early in the day for
her son to appreciate the joke, for his only
response was a blank look and a shrug. He
ambled over to get a peek at what his mother
had prepared.

Francesca clicked her tongue at him.
"That's as good a joke as you're going to hear
all day," she said testily.

"Uh-huh," grunted her son.

"Listen to that music," she mused. "Imagine how good it must have felt to write a song
like that. I mean, the first time Beethoven
heard it in his head. What was it like for him?"

"I'm guessing he was joyful," said Joey, deadpan.

"Oh, so the brain is finally up and running after all," she chided him, wiping her hands on her apron.

Francesca bent over and opened the oven door. Reaching in with a pot holder, she pulled out the two foil pans and set them on the counter. "Here," she said, "have a look. I made you some sausage and peppers. The other one is the baked ziti."

"*Madonna mia*," marveled Joey. "You cooked so much. The chicken would have been plenty."

"What, you're gonna be *scumbarì* and not have enough food for everybody?" she scoffed. "Just shut up and take it."

"You're the boss," said Joey. He reached toward the pan to sample the sausage, but his mother swatted his hand away.

"Go sit down if you want to try some." With that, she nudged him toward the table before reaching for the bag of rolls she had bought earlier that morning at the bakery. She opened one of the rolls and layered the inside with some sausage and peppers. She put the sandwich on a dish and set it on the table before her son. "So, anybody special coming to watch the game with you today?"

Joey understood what his mother meant by "special."

"No, Mom," he said. "Just a few friends. So please don't start."

"Who's starting anything?" huffed Francesca defensively. "I was just asking a simple question."

"Yes, but that was just a different version of the same simple question you're always asking me."

"What," pouted Francesca. "I'm not supposed to want to see my son settled down and happy? Go ahead. Shoot me for being concerned."

Joey let out a little laugh. "Well," he said gently, "it hasn't quite come to that yet—not *yet*." Then, looking away to the window, he shook his head, his smile fading. "You know, it's not like I haven't been looking for someone," he admitted. "I'd settle down in a minute if I could find the right one."

Francesca reached out and gave her son a gentle slap across the top of his head. "Maybe you're looking *too* hard," she told him. "Maybe you should try a little less quantity and a little more quality, if you know what I mean."

Joey made no further reply, other than to shrug and take a bite of his sandwich. The subject was once again closed.

"HEY, Frannie," said Peg. "What are you doing here on a Wednesday afternoon? Aren't you supposed to be working?"

It was two weeks later. For the past few days, Francesca had been hanging around the house, restless and bored, so she had come to the library for a change of scenery.

"Winter vacation," she said ruefully as she stepped into the library's computer room to chat with her friends. "The kids are out of school, and the mother took the week off from work."

"Really," added Natalie, turning away from her monitor. "You think you'd be happy getting a week off for yourself."

"Eh, I guess you're right," agreed Francesca with a shrug. "You think I would be, but . . ."

"But now you don't know what to do with yourself, do you?" Peg finished for her.

"*Mannagia,* I'm going crazy!" cried

Francesca. "I don't know what's the matter with me."

"Tell us about the kids," said Natalie. "How's it been going?"

Francesca started talking about her days looking after Penny and Will. She told them of the ups and downs she had experienced getting to know the two children and the wonderful feeling it gave her to see that they were finally starting to warm up to her. Peg reacted unfavorably to the news that Francesca had been baking treats and occasionally cooking dinner for the children—and not charging the mother extra! Just the same, as Francesca rambled on, she caught a faint hint of envy in her friend's eyes. She saw it, in fact, on all their faces.

"So anyway," sighed Francesca, "things have gone pretty well. I just don't understand why I feel so inside out today."

Her three friends looked at one another and exchanged knowing smiles. "Frannie, it's as plain as the nose on your face, what's bothering you," Peg said. "You miss them."

LORETTA managed to keep her kids entertained for the first few days of their vacation.

Come Thursday, though, they had grown restless. She had run short of ideas to keep Penny and Will occupied, so they spent the day hanging around the house, watching television.

"I'm bored," Penny announced late in the afternoon.

"Me too," said Will with a yawn.

"The two of you could try something different, like maybe reading a book," said their mother, who was only too content to stay sitting at the end of the couch while she read the newspaper.

"Please, Mom," sighed her son. "We're on vacation, you know."

"How about skating?" said Penny. "We haven't done that yet."

"It's a little late for that today," replied her mother. "But what do you say we go tomorrow morning?"

"I guess," said her daughter with a sigh.

"What about dinner?" said Will. "What are we having tonight?"

"I haven't made up my mind yet," Loretta told him.

"I wonder what Mrs. C is making for dinner," said Penny.

"That's funny. I was thinking about her too," said Will. "It's been kind of weird not having her here every day, hasn't it?"

"I know," agreed Penny. "I mean, sometimes Mrs. C does get on my nerves, but then other times, I don't know. It's kind of nice to have her here."

Loretta smiled, for she understood how the children felt.

"Hey, I know what to do," enthused Will. "Why don't we call her up and ask her to come over and cook us dinner?"

Loretta chuckled and put the paper aside. "I don't think that would be fair to Mrs. C. After all, it's her vacation week too."

"Yeah, I guess you're right," sulked Will. "It was just an idea."

Loretta looked back toward the kitchen with a thoughtful gaze. A plan suddenly popped into her mind. The more she considered it, the warmer it made her feel inside.

FRANCESCA'S delight knew no bounds when she received Loretta's call Thursday night. Will and Penny wanted to go skating Friday morning, Loretta explained, and they were all wondering—if she didn't already have plans, of course—if she would be interested in spending the day with them. There was no need to ask twice, and they quickly made arrangements for the outing.

Will and Penny were sitting on the front porch with their skates slung over their shoulders when Francesca arrived the next morning at precisely ten thirty, as planned. A few moments later, their mother bustled out the door, carrying her own skates. The four of them piled into Loretta's car, and soon they were on their way.

Loretta and the children took to the ice as a brisk breeze blew across Kennedy Plaza, where the rink was nestled at the foot of Providence's fledgling skyline. Francesca stood by the edge of the rink, smiling and waving to Will and Penny as they called out, "Hi, Mrs. C!" each time they skated by. Loretta, she discovered, much to her surprise, was a marvelous skater. Will, on the other hand, was something of a calamity on skates. Try as he might to stay upright, the young boy spent almost as much time picking himself up off the ice as he did skating on it.

"Did you see us out there?" gushed Will,

his cheeks a bright red, when the family finally came off the ice.

"Yes, I did," Francesca assured him. "Very impressive."

"Did you see me too?" said Penny eagerly.

"Of course," Francesca told the girl. "You looked like a ballerina. I bet one day you'll be a beautiful figure skater. And someday, Will, you're going to be a great hockey player."

Both children beamed with pride.

"So," said Francesca, "where to next?"

The group repaired to the Providence Place Mall, just a few steps away, to grab a bite to eat in the food court. After lunch, the four strolled about the mall, pausing now and then to peek inside the stores. Francesca had promised to buy them each a little gift if they saw something they liked, and so the two eagerly scavenged about to see what they could find. Will made his choice when they came across a man demonstrating windup helicopters that soared up into the air. Penny, however, was not having any luck.

Seeing an empty bench, Loretta and Francesca stopped to take a break. While they sat and chatted, Penny continued her search, with Will in tow. When a few minutes passed without their reappearance, both women started to worry. The two adults were just gathering together their things to go look for the children when Penny emerged from the crowd, with Will close behind. The young girl was bubbling with excitement. "I found something. I know I can't have it today, but I thought I would show it to you anyway."

"What is it?" asked Francesca.

Just then, the young girl did something quite unexpected. She reached out and took Francesca by the hand. It was the simplest of gestures, and an onlooker would have thought nothing of it. Francesca, though, knew better. At the touch of the child's hand, the old woman felt her heart melt.

"Come on," Penny said eagerly. "I'll show you."

Penny led them to the young ladies' section of a women's boutique. There, displayed on a mannequin, was an adorable blue gown with fanciful lace sleeves and a delicate floral pattern stitched into the collar. The young girl gazed at the dress with dreamy, longing eyes. "Isn't it beautiful?" she sighed.

"You'd look just like a princess in that dress," gushed Francesca.

"I know I can't get it now," she started to say, glancing at them with eyes that said she hoped she was wrong.

"Well, not today," gulped her mother after seeing the price tag.

"Oh, well," said Penny. "I didn't think so. Maybe someday."

"Someday," agreed Francesca.

In the end, Francesca and Loretta helped Penny pick out a little knit tam and matching scarf. The distraction of trying them on and looking at herself in the mirror was enough to make the young girl forget about the dress.

In no hurry to go straight home, Loretta took them all on a little driving tour of Providence, letting Francesca act as guide. She drove aimlessly about some of the lovely neighborhoods, until they came to Prospect Park. There, they all got out to take pictures in front of the statue of Roger Williams, Providence's founder.

When at last they returned home, the children seemed to be bubbling with anticipation as they hurried out of the car and up the walk to the front porch. Francesca eyed them with interest, wondering what they were up to.

"Why don't you just sit in the living room and relax for a couple of minutes," suggested Loretta before Francesca had a chance to follow her to the kitchen.

Francesca dutifully settled onto the couch, while Penny and Will did their best to occupy her attention. Looking about, she noticed that the living room appeared to be spic-and-span. She puzzled over just what exactly was going on, until she detected a familiar aroma.

"Okay," called Loretta, just at that moment. "Bring her in!"

Francesca let the two children guide her to the kitchen. She could scarcely believe what she saw. The kitchen was immaculate, not a single dirty dish in the sink nor a stray scrap of paper or homework assignment to be found anywhere. The table was beautifully set with four settings. A pair of candles stood at the center.

"Oh, my," she exclaimed, impressed beyond words. "Well, I see that you three have been very busy."

"Everybody pitched in," said Loretta, who was standing with arms crossed in front of the stove, smiling from ear to ear.

"And what's for dinner, might I ask?" said

Francesca, craning her neck to get a glimpse of what was behind the young woman.

"Ta dah!" announced Loretta, whipping the cover off one of the two pots on the stove to reveal the bubbling tomato sauce within. "I made it this morning. I followed your recipe exactly."

Francesca beamed at all of them with pride. When they sat down to eat, she raved at how wonderful everything looked. Loretta filled their bowls with the spaghetti and passed them out one by one.

"Wow, Mom!" exclaimed Will. "This is delicious!"

"Really, Mom," agreed Penny. "It's excellent!"

Francesca concurred wholeheartedly. "To Chef Loretta!" she said, raising her glass. "Or should I say, *Mamma* Loretta?"

"To Mamma Loretta," laughed the children, and everyone joined in the toast.

When it came time for Francesca to go home, Loretta and the children gathered at the door to say good night. "Thank you so much. I had a wonderful day," Francesca told them.

"And say thank you to Mrs. Campanile for the nice gifts she bought you at the mall," replied Loretta, giving Francesca a nod.

"Thanks, Mrs. C," they both said.

"Oh, you're welcome, children," she told them. "I had a lot of fun. I'll see you again on Monday."

Francesca walked out to her car, opened the door, and climbed inside. She turned the key to start the car.

Nothing happened. She tried again. The engine made a clicking noise and then once again nothing.

No matter how often she turned the key or pumped the gas, Francesca could not make the engine start. She sat there for a few minutes, mulling over her options. Then with a sigh, she came to what she could not have known in that moment would be a fateful decision. She opened the car door and trudged back to the house.

"Is everything all right?" asked Loretta with concern when she opened the front door.

"Yes," Francesca told her, "everything's fine. But would you mind if I used your telephone? I need to call my son."

Chapter Nine

THERE is something sweetly inexplicable that passes between two people who are destined to meet when one day, after wandering often aimlessly through life, the heavens finally fall into alignment, and they happen upon each other unexpectedly. It is not quite, though some might call it so, the proverbial love at first sight that strangers sometimes experience, for in truth, the two find in each other something extraordinarily familiar and comforting. It is more a feeling of profound recognition than anything else, one that brings with it a sense of relief, as if their hearts are simply saying to each other, "Oh, there you are. Where have you been? I've been looking all over for you for the longest time."

Such was the case that night when the doorbell rang and Loretta hurried to the front hall and opened the door, discovering a young man waiting on the front porch. With his hands buried deep in the pockets of his frayed, gray sweatshirt, he was standing there looking about at his surroundings, as if he were not quite sure that he had come to the right place. When he turned his gaze to Loretta and their eyes met for the first time, she felt overcome by a sensation of paralysis, as if suddenly she could not move or speak. The young man seemed to suffer from the same affliction, for he stood there equally immobile and mute.

"Hi, I'm Joey Campanile," he finally said. "I'm looking for my mother—Francesca? Did I come to the right house?"

"Of course," breathed Loretta. "Please come in."

Loretta stepped back and let Joey enter. She saw that he was tall. His features were dark and rugged, and there was no mistaking his striking blue eyes. Not quite able to turn her gaze from them, she self-consciously pushed a stray strand of hair from her face.

"I'm Loretta," she said, extending her hand.

"Nice to meet you, Loretta," replied Joey, gently taking her hand in his own.

"Come on," she beckoned, turning away. "Your mother is waiting for you in the kitchen with my daughter."

"Excuse me for a second," said Joey, touching her shoulder while she was still in reach. "But can I ask you a question?"

Loretta turned back and saw the look of puzzlement on Joey's face. "What is it?" she said.

"Well, I was just wondering. What is my mother doing here?"

"She's my babysitter—well, more like my nanny," Loretta said, and laughed. Then, seeing that he wore the same confused look, she stopped and added, "Didn't you know?"

Aside from a raised eyebrow, Joey made no reply.

"Oh, well, then follow me," said Loretta, leading him on.

As they passed through the living room, Will looked up from his video game at the newcomer.

"This is my son, Will," said Loretta. "Will, this is Joey. Mrs. Campanile is his mother."

"Hey," said Joey. He nodded to the TV screen. "Ace Combat?"

Will's eyes widened. "Ace Combat Zero," he said eagerly.

"Oh, yeah," said Joey. "I heard that's a good one."

"Ayyy, *finalmente!*" exclaimed Francesca, bustling out of the kitchen, her coat and pocketbook in hand. "What took you so long? And look at the outfit he wears to pick up his mother. Didn't I tell you to throw away that old sweatshirt?"

"Sorry I didn't get here sooner," Joey told his mother patiently, "and that I didn't wear a tux, but I was at the gym when you called me on my cell." Joey rolled his eyes for the benefit of Loretta, who put a hand to her mouth to hide her smile.

"Hmm, I see you two have met," said Francesca.

"Yes, and I was just introducing him to Will," explained Loretta. "And this, Joey, is my daughter, Penny."

Penny had just followed Francesca out of the kitchen.

"Hey, Penny," he said.

The young girl stood there staring at him.

Loretta looked down at her daughter and gave her a shake. "Hey, aren't you going to at least say hello?" she chided.

"Oh, hi," Penny said at last, shrinking back behind her mother.

"Well, that's nice. We've all met," said

Francesca brusquely. "Come on now, Joey. Time to take me home. Good night, everybody." With that, she unceremoniously grabbed her son by the arm and oriented him toward the door.

"Whoa, just a minute," said Joey.

"What?" his mother said testily.

Turning to Loretta, Joey said, "Is it all right if we leave the car here overnight? I'll come back tomorrow morning and see if I can't get it started."

"Yes, of course it's all right. We'll be here."

"Great," said Joey with a smile. He hesitated, as if he wanted to say more but didn't dare. "Well, I'll see you tomorrow."

"It was nice to meet you," said Loretta, returning his smile.

"Okay, let's go," said Francesca, giving her son a tug. She swept him out the door and down the front walk to his car.

Loretta closed the door behind them and went to the window to watch them go. She was soon joined by Penny and Will. Penny slipped her hand into Loretta's and rested her head against her mother's arm. "He seemed nice," she said.

"Very nice," her mother agreed.

THEY HAD BEEN driving for some time, and Joey had yet to make a single remark. Francesca had expected him to pepper her with questions the moment they were alone. Instead, lost in thought, he gazed straight ahead, his eyes fixed on the road.

"Okay, let's have it," she blurted out at last.

"Have what?" Joey replied.

"Oh, you're going to tell me that you're not angry or upset now that you know I've been babysitting two children every day without telling you or the others?"

"Oh, that," said Joey with an absentminded shrug. "Wasn't it you who told me not to ask you about your business?"

Francesca sat there for a moment, glaring at him. "Is that how you show concern for your mother?" she finally exclaimed. "What kind of son are you anyway? You'd think you would have been at least a little bit worried when I called you."

"Actually, I was mostly annoyed, because I had to cut my workout short," he jested, giving her a sideways glance.

"Nice," huffed Francesca, folding her arms.

"But how come you called me? Obviously

you've been trying to keep this a secret. Couldn't her husband give you a ride?"

"Did you see a wedding ring on her finger?"

Joey did not answer right away but continued to look straight ahead. After a time, his expression brightened slightly. "No," he said thoughtfully at last. "Now that you say it, I didn't."

"That's because she's not married," Francesca told him. "So, what was I supposed to do? Make that poor girl drag her two kids out and drive all across town just to take me home?"

"Nope," said Joey. "You did the sensible thing." He drove up to a red light and stopped. The light turned green, and he drove on. "So, why did you do it?" he said at last, breaking the silence. "How come you started babysitting? Do you need money?"

"No, of course not," sighed Francesca, the fight having gone out of her. "It's just something I needed to do. It's a long story. I'll tell you all about it some other time, but not tonight. Okay?"

"Yeah, sure." Joey nodded. "Whatever you say. I'll just go back there tomorrow and see what I can do about the car."

"Good," said Francesca. Then she added, "And make sure you wear some decent clothes when you do."

LORETTA was upstairs, watching from her bedroom window when Joey returned to the house the next morning. Despite it being a Saturday, in a vacation week no less, she had sprung out of bed and dressed early so as not to miss him when he arrived.

The crystal blue sky of the previous day had been replaced by a shroud of heavy, slate gray clouds; a thin drizzle hung in the air. Wasting no time, Joey went straight to his mother's car, pausing briefly to cast a glance at the house before climbing inside the car to try the ignition. Having no luck, he climbed back out, opened the hood, and gazed in at the engine.

After a time, Joey walked to his own car, where he opened the trunk and pulled out a toolbox. He returned to his mother's car and, with a wrench in hand, was soon at work on the engine. Just then, the light drizzle suddenly turned into a steady rain and, before long, an outright downpour.

Loretta rushed down to the front hall

and threw open the door. "Hey!" she called. "Come inside before you drown out there!"

At seeing her at the door, Joey's face lit up in a warm smile. He looked up in annoyance at the sky and gave a shrug of resignation before closing the hood of the car and running up onto the porch.

"Come in," Loretta insisted, tugging the sleeve of his sweatshirt, the same tattered gray thing he had been wearing the night before.

"Yeow, it's unreal out there," said Joey, stepping into the hallway, where he shook some of the raindrops from his head. "I don't think I can work on my mother's car anymore today."

Loretta looked up into his eyes, trying her best to project outward calm, even though her heart was galloping. She was desperately trying to think of a way to entice him to stay for a little while.

"Do you think you can fix it?" she asked.

"I don't know. Maybe," he answered. "I mean, I think I should at least be able to get it started."

"It sounds like you're good with cars," she said.

"I know a little bit," said Joey modestly.

"My father had his own shop for a long time, so I learned a lot from him."

Neither of the two knew what to say next, despite the fact that they never took their eyes off each other.

"Listen," Joey said at last, "I was just wondering—"

"Yes?" said Loretta expectantly.

"Um, would you mind if I left the car here one more day?"

"The car?"

"Yes." He nodded. "I'll come back tomorrow and take another whack at it."

"No problem," said Loretta, a bit crestfallen.

"Okay. Well, in that case, I guess I'll get going," said Joey.

There was a hint of reluctance in his voice, but Loretta just watched stupidly as he stepped out onto the porch.

When he drove away, Loretta stood at the door, fuming. Then she slammed it shut and stomped into the living room, where she plopped disconsolately onto the couch. "I am *such* an idiot! What was I thinking? Offer him a cup of coffee, or tea, or a glass of water. *Anything!*"

She sat there for a time before suddenly sitting up straight, for an intriguing idea had occurred to her. As she mulled it over, the makings of a plan began to coalesce in her mind.

It rained the rest of the day and all through the night, washing away the leftover snow. By midday Sunday, the clouds had started to break apart, and the sun once again showed its face just as Joey pulled up to the house. His timing could not have suited Loretta better. She went to the door and waved to him, while he went to work again on Francesca's car. Penny, resting her elbows on the sill of the front window, gazed out at him, while her brother pulled on his coat and hurried outside to watch.

"What's going on out there now?" Loretta called from the kitchen a little while later.

"I don't know," answered Penny. "It looks like he's saying something to Will."

Loretta went to the window and saw Joey leaning over the engine. Now and then, he would turn back to Will and say something to which the young boy paid rapt attention. The pair looked perfectly at ease with each other.

Nearly an hour passed before Joey packed up his tools.

"Here they come!" cried Penny to her mother.

Loretta, wearing a crisp white apron, was just emerging from the kitchen when Will burst through the front door. Not far behind, Joey came to the doorway and leaned his head inside.

"Anybody home?" he called with a good-natured smile.

"Yes, of course," Loretta greeted him. "Please come in."

Joey stepped into the hallway, just as she had hoped he would.

"Did you fix the car?" Penny asked him.

"Nope, it's busted," said Will before Joey could open his mouth.

"Is it really?" said Loretta.

"Technically speaking? Yup, it's busted," said Joey with a laugh. "I'm gonna have to get it towed. It might be the transmission."

"Oh, that's too bad," said Loretta.

Joey was about to say something else when he gave the air a sniff. "Gee, *something* smells good," he noted.

"Oh, that," said Loretta, a picture of nonchalance. "I was just getting ready to put dinner on the table. Nothing special—just some ravioli and pork chops and spare ribs." Then, as if the idea had just come to her, she said, "Are you hungry? Why don't you have a bite to eat before you go?"

"Oh, no," said Joey. "I wouldn't want to impose."

"Nonsense," said Loretta. "There's plenty."

"Are you sure?" said Joey, weakening.

"Yes, I'm sure," said Loretta. "Come on."

Joey relented and came into the kitchen. He washed his hands and sat down with the children. "Well, this is a nice surprise," he said, giving them a wink. "I hope your mom made enough."

"Trust me, there's more than enough," Loretta said. Joey had not noticed that the table had already been set for four.

"WHAT do you mean you couldn't get it started?" said a displeased Francesca later that afternoon. "What did your father and I send you to college for anyway?"

"Chemical engineering," Joey reminded

her. He was once again sitting at a dinner table, this time in his mother's kitchen, looking over the Sunday newspaper.

Francesca let out a grumble and sat down across the table from him. "So now what do I do?" she asked him.

"Don't worry about it," said Joey. "We'll get it fixed."

"That's not what I meant," said Francesca. "How am I supposed to get around without a car?"

"Oh, I get it," said Joey. "You're worried about how you're going to get back and forth to babysit every day."

"Among other things," said Francesca testily. "Are you going to start on me about that now?"

Joey shook his head. "Nope," he replied. "I was just going to say that, if you want, I can take a late lunch for the next few days and drop you off, then come back after work to take you home."

This suggestion was eminently suitable to Francesca. "Are you sure you'll be able to do that?" she said.

"No problem," her son assured her.

"Great," said Francesca, feeling much relieved. "You're a good boy, Giuseppe. I don't care what they say."

"Eh, I try," he said with a shrug.

Pleased to have her transportation arrangements settled for the next few days, Francesca slapped her hand down amiably on the table and got to her feet. "So, what do you want to eat, *figlio mio?*" she asked him. "I've got a couple of steaks in the fridge. Maybe a little risotto and a salad?"

"No thanks, Mom," he told her. "I'm not that hungry."

"Not hungry?" she said worriedly. "It's almost five o'clock on a Sunday afternoon, and you don't want to eat? What's the matter? You feeling sick or something?"

"No, I'm fine," said Joey. "I already had something to eat a little while ago."

"Where did you eat?" said Francesca.

"At Loretta's house," her son admitted.

Francesca stood there, gaping at him. "I see," she said quietly. "I suppose that's why it took you so long to get here."

"Yeah, I guess," murmured Joey. "Plus her son wanted to show me his video game."

"But I don't understand," said Francesca,

her brow furrowed. "What made her cook dinner for you?"

"She didn't cook dinner for *me*," Joey tried to explain. "She just happened to have dinner on the table when I walked in."

"Uh-huh." Francesca nodded thoughtfully. "So, tell me," she asked him, "just what exactly did she cook for you?"

"Oh, nothing special," said Joey. "You know, the usual thing. Some ravioli, and pork chops, and stuff."

"So let me get this right," she said. "The first thing she did when you came to the house was give you something to eat?"

Joey's only response was to turn to the next page of the newspaper.

Francesca's disquiet only grew over the next few days. Each afternoon, Joey insisted on coming to the door when he arrived at the Simmons house to take her home. He invariably lingered on the porch, stopping to exchange a few pleasant words with Loretta, who seemed only too eager to delay their departure. The signs weren't hard to read.

It was not until Wednesday evening, when Joey came to take her home, that Francesca's apprehensions began to abate.

"Good news," Joey announced. "I got a call from the mechanic. He said your car should be ready tomorrow."

"Hey, that is good news," said Francesca. "Now you won't have to be bothered coming here to pick me up."

"Oh, how nice," said Loretta softly, her eyes downcast.

Wasting no time, Francesca gave Joey's arm a tug. "Well, come on now, Joey," she told him. "I want to get to mass. It's Ash Wednesday, you know."

"That's right," said Loretta, all at once perking up. "I'd forgotten that it was Ash Wednesday." Then, turning to Joey, she added, "My boss, Mister Pace—he's a lawyer downtown—he went to mass at *lunch* today and came back with ashes."

The word *lunch* Loretta said with odd emphasis, but for what reason, Francesca could not discern. For his part, Joey only gave a knowing nod before leading Francesca to his car.

THE flowers arrived a little after ten the next morning. Loretta had been at her desk, busy as always, during the early part of the day. She ripped open the accompanying little envelope and tugged out the card inside, which read simply:

How about lunch?
J.

A moment later, her telephone rang.

"There's a call for you from a Mister Campanile on line three," the receptionist informed her. "Do you want to take it?"

"Oh, yes," said Loretta. "I'll definitely take it."

THEY went to a busy restaurant just a few steps down the street and around the corner from her office. Despite the crowd, they were finally alone together for the first time.

"So, Loretta Simmons," said Joey, "at long last, tell me about yourself."

"What would you like to know?" said Loretta.

"Everything," he said with a smile.

"Well, I really like getting flowers," she told him sweetly.

"Ayyy, I bet you get them every other day," said Joey.

"Uh-uh," said Loretta, shaking her head. "Not in a very, very long time."

Joey looked into her eyes. "I find that hard to believe."

"Oh, it's not so hard," said Loretta softly. She gave a shrug. "Such is the life of a single mom."

"That's gotta be tough sometimes," he said gently.

"I'm not complaining," said Loretta. "Things just work out the way they do. I'd like to think that everything happens for a reason, although *that's* hard to believe sometimes. Trust me."

"I know what you mean." Joey smiled. "But if you could do it all over again, where do you think you'd like to be right now?"

"Well, at the moment, I'm kind of happy right where I am," she said, returning his warm gaze. Then, pursing her lips, she added, "I haven't felt that way in a long time."

"I haven't either," said Joey. He let out a long breath and settled back in his chair. "I was almost married once a few years ago," he told her, then shrugged. "I just figured I'd get that skeleton out of my closet right away, while I had the chance."

"What happened?" said Loretta, though she already knew.

"It's a long story. Let's just say that, at the last minute, right before the wedding, things just kind of fell apart."

"I'm sorry," she said. "That must have been painful for you."

"It was," admitted Joey. "It hurt for a long time, and it just wouldn't go away. It was always there, pulling me down on the inside like a lead weight, you know?"

Loretta nodded, because she understood all too well.

"Anyway," he went on, "then a funny thing happened."

"What?" asked Loretta.

"My mother's car broke down," he told her. "Ever since that night, it doesn't bother me anymore. Almost nothing does."

"It's funny about that night," said Loretta, giving him a knowing look as she gently rested her hand on his, "but ever since then, I feel the exact same way."

OVER the weeks that followed, Joey came to the house almost every day—after his mother had gone home—to have dinner with

Loretta and the children and spend some time with them before going home again at night. On the weekends, he helped Loretta around the house and horsed around with Will and Penny. It thrilled Loretta to see how happy he made her children. Will already looked up to Joey like a father, and Penny adored him.

Joey and Loretta decided that, at least for the time being, the best thing to do was to say nothing to Francesca. Both had an inkling that she would be less than pleased by their blossoming affair.

"Let's just keep this to ourselves," Loretta confided in the children, "and we'll all surprise her and tell her one day soon."

Loretta suffered from occasional pangs of guilt, for she had come to care deeply for Francesca and didn't want to do anything to hurt her. Nonetheless, this was one of the most joyous times of Loretta's life. No matter what might have gone wrong in her day, when Joey walked through the door, she felt whole again, as if she had at last found a piece of herself that had been missing for the longest time. And though their private moments together were always stolen and brief, she felt their love for each other deepen with every embrace.

Given enough time, however, all conspiracies of silence, no matter how benevolent, are destined to fail. Francesca was not blind. She was too astute an observer of human nature not to recognize that something was amiss at the Simmons house.

There was an evasiveness about all of them, as if they were reluctant to say too much to her. When she tried to start a conversation with the children, they would hurry off upstairs, using the excuse that they needed to straighten up their bedrooms or do their homework. Had she not known the children as well as she did, she might have accepted these explanations without question.

As for Loretta, the young mother had suddenly found the energy to keep the house in perfect order, and she was trying to expand her culinary repertoire by cooking dinner herself almost every night. It would have given Francesca no end of pleasure to stay now and then, but Loretta always seemed anxious for her to leave. It was all very distressing, and Francesca puzzled over it, until one afternoon when everything became clear.

That afternoon, Francesca had dutifully looked after the children, and Loretta came home at her usual hour, bustling through the front door with a bag of groceries under her arm.

"Cooking dinner again tonight?" asked Francesca.

"Yes, in a little while," said Loretta, hurrying into the kitchen. "Nothing special. Just some hamburgers and stuff."

She put the groceries away, then called for the children.

"The two of you can start setting the table," she told them.

Francesca went to the living room to collect her things. When she returned to the kitchen to bid them all good night, she noticed that Will and Penny had put out four place settings on the table.

"Hey, put that extra plate and silverware away before they get dirty and your mother has to wash them," she said.

"What extra plate?" said Penny.

"Why would you put out four plates when there are only three of you?" asked Francesca quite sensibly.

"Uh, Mrs. C isn't having dinner with us

tonight," said Loretta, quickly coming to the rescue. "Put the extra plate back in the cupboard. You can walk her to the door while I start supper."

It was an odd moment, but Francesca read nothing into it and went on her way, intending to stop at the library before going home. She had driven only a minute or two when she realized that, quite stupidly, she had left her book bag in the kitchen at Loretta's house. She turned the car around, and as she drove back down the street to Loretta's, she was startled to see a familiar car parked out front and an even more familiar person strolling up the front walk. Suddenly, the fourth place setting made sense to her.

It was Joey.

Francesca was thunderstruck. She brought her car to an abrupt halt a few houses away, just close enough to watch what happened next without being seen. As Joey neared the porch, the front door swung open and out dashed Penny and Will to greet him. A smiling Loretta soon appeared at the door. She took Joey's hand and gave him a kiss; then the four of them went inside together.

Francesca sat in stunned silence. A

thousand conflicting emotions beset her. She could not quite put a name to it, but when Loretta and Joey went inside the house and the door closed, she felt an ache deep within her, something akin to what a mother feels on that morning when she leaves her child at school for the first time.

Chapter Ten

"Bless me, Father, for I have sinned."

It was Thursday, two days later, and Francesca had decided to attend the weekly Lenten penitence service at her church. She had been going through the motions the last forty-eight hours, feigning ignorance of what she had discovered and trying to show a happy face to everyone. All the while, though, she felt as low and miserable as she could ever remember.

"It's been a month since I last confessed," she went on.

"Ah, Francesca," said Father Buontempo brightly. "I was wondering how long it would be before I saw you this Lent. So, what's on your mind?"

"I've lied to my children," she confessed

straightaway. "And because of me, my son has become involved with a woman, a single mother with two children."

"I take it you disapprove of this woman?" said the father.

"Disapprove? No, I love her like a daughter."

"Oh, I see," said the priest. "Well, then, I suppose the children are the problem."

"They're angels!" protested Francesca.

"Okay, then I guess what you're saying is that you just don't think your son and this woman are right for each other, yes?"

"Who could think that?" huffed Francesca. "All you have to do is see them all together, how happy they are."

There was a long pause. "Forgive me, Francesca," Father Buontempo finally said, "but I'm having a hard time understanding just what it is that's troubling you."

"So am I," confessed Francesca, heaving a sigh. "I guess what's bothering me, Father, is that I came to know this woman and her children because I needed to be a part of their lives, to do something meaningful again, and I thought they needed me just as much. It all felt so perfect, and I was so happy. But then this all happened, and at first I was so mad and hurt I couldn't think straight. Then I realized something, that after all this time, it wasn't *me* they needed all along. It was my son. And now I feel . . ."

"Left out again?" said the priest. "A little cheated, maybe?"

"Yes, I suppose," said Francesca.

"Francesca," he told her gently, "by now it should have occurred to you that your life has never been just about you alone. It's also about everyone and everything you touch. God has His own plan, and what *you* think you might need to make you happy might not be what God *knows* is the best thing."

"So, what are you saying I should do?" said Francesca.

"What I'm saying," replied Father Buontempo, "is that if your son and this woman are truly in love, then let God do His job. Trust Him, and let whatever is going to happen, happen. In the end, you might even consider lending Him a hand."

"But how am I supposed to do that?"

"Think about it," he said. "Something will come to you."

"You know," griped Francesca, "you and

God could try being a little more specific now and then."

"Well, if you think it would help," said the priest good-naturedly, "say three Our Fathers. And see if you can't stop lying to your children."

FRANCESCA awoke the next morning with her heart not feeling quite so heavy. Outside, the sky was a brilliant blue, and a warm, gentle breeze swayed the trees, whose branches were just starting to show their buds.

Just the same, as the day wore on, Francesca's thoughts dwelled on Joey and Loretta. Later, as she readied herself to drive to Loretta's house, her mind was still unsettled as to what she should do or say. Such being the case, she decided to follow Father Buontempo's advice to stay out of the way and bide her time.

In truth, there wasn't much else for Francesca to do. The moment they came home from school that afternoon, Will and Penny dropped their backpacks and scurried outside to play. Francesca settled onto the couch, but as the hour grew later, she began to eye the clock. It wasn't unusual for Loretta to come home a few minutes late, but it was now nearing an hour past her normal time. Penny and Will came back inside and hungrily prowled the kitchen.

"Where's Mom?" asked Penny testily.

"Yeah, we're starving," said Will.

"Be patient," Francesca told them, regretful that she hadn't baked something for them. "Your mother will be home soon."

No sooner had she spoken those words than the three of them heard a car pull into the driveway. Will and Penny instantly dashed for the front door and out to their mother's car. As Loretta tried to make her way up the walk, the two pestered her with questions.

"Hey, you two, let your mother breathe," Francesca cried to them. She held the door open and let the harried woman in, her still-jabbering children in tow.

"Go back outside for a few minutes," Loretta ordered them. "I'll let you know when it's time for dinner." Will and Penny reluctantly slouched off once more to the back-yard, while Loretta flopped onto the couch. "I'm sorry, Francesca," she said wearily. "I had to work late. I tried to call you from my car, but my cell phone was dead."

"Don't worry about it," Francesca told her. "Just relax for a while. You look frazzled."

Loretta cast a nervous glance at the clock and let out a groan. "I feel frazzled," she admitted.

As Francesca gazed at the young woman, she recognized that beleaguered, frenzied look that parents sometimes wear. A little time to themselves, she knew, was all they usually needed to feel renewed. Just then, an idea unexpectedly came to Francesca, just as her priest had told her one would. She understood exactly what she was supposed to do. "You know, I think you could use a little time to yourself. Just a day, even, to relax and be on your own."

"What, you mean without the kids?" Loretta chuckled. "That's a nice dream. What would I do with them?"

Francesca smiled and came closer.

"Well, actually, I've been meaning to ask you—maybe you'd consider letting me take Will and Penny to my house one day—maybe even let them stay overnight." Francesca paused for effect. "That is, if you think they would want to."

Loretta straightened up, her eyes widening.

"They would love that," she said. "But no, I couldn't possibly impose like that."

"What do you mean, impose?" scoffed Francesca. "I'd be thrilled to do it. So, what do you say? Tomorrow's Saturday. I don't know about you, but I've got nothing on my schedule."

"Neither do we," said Loretta. "Honestly, do you really want to do this?"

"With all my heart," said Francesca earnestly.

Loretta took a deep breath. "Francesca," she said, "there's something *I've* been meaning to tell you. It's about—"

"Another time," said Francesca gently, holding up her hand. "Right now, I need to get home and get ready for tomorrow. I'll call you later tonight, and we'll arrange everything."

Francesca said good-bye, anxious to put into action the second part of her scheme. When she climbed into her car, she sat for a moment, aware that Loretta was watching from the window. She put the key into the ignition and twisted her arm back and forth as if she were turning it to start the engine. This she did several times, before opening the door and climbing back out. Feigning a look of annoyance, she trod back up the walk to the front porch, where Loretta opened the door for her.

"Is there something wrong?" the young woman asked.

"You're not going to believe this," replied Francesca, "but my car won't start, after all the money I spent to have it fixed. Could I use your phone? I need to call my son again."

Francesca was sitting on the porch, waiting with Loretta, when Joey drove up to the house a short time later. He strolled up to the porch and nodded hello to the two women. "Trouble with the car again, Ma?" he said, making an effort to avoid looking at Loretta.

"See for yourself," said Francesca, handing him the keys.

Joey took them and went to the car. Just as Francesca knew he would, he started the engine with no trouble. With a bemused look, he left the engine running and climbed back out of the car.

"Sounds fine to me," he called. "I'll just let it run a minute."

"Well, imagine that," exclaimed Francesca. Just then, Will came bounding around the corner of the house with Penny right behind. "Hey look, it's Joey!" he cried excitedly.

Joey turned to Loretta with startled eyes. The two, in turn, looked in alarm at Penny, who, at the sight of Francesca, had the presence of mind to clap her hand over her brother's mouth.

"Oh, there you two are," said Francesca nonchalantly. She was so pleased with herself. She had them all right where she wanted. "Come over here. I have to tell you something."

"What?" said Penny meekly, looking nervously at her mother.

Francesca looked down at the children warmly before giving a little nod at Loretta. "Your mother said you two can come and stay at my house tomorrow. Would you like that?"

Penny and Will looked at each other and nodded enthusiastically.

"Beautiful," said Francesca. "Now the best part is on Sunday, when all four of us"—she paused and looked Joey in the eye—"or should I say, all *five* of us, will have dinner together. Wouldn't that be nice?"

"Yes!" the two cried.

Joey gave Loretta a sideways glance. "I'm

not sure," he said, sotto voce, "but I think she knows something."

Loretta, her jaw hanging open, could only nod in reply.

Francesca stepped closer to her son and gave him a gentle slap on the cheek. "I'm your mother," she told him. "I know everything." Then she turned to Loretta, who was still too dumbfounded to speak. "So that's that," she said pleasantly. "Now why don't the four of you go inside and have your supper."

Francesca climbed back into her car. As she pulled away, she heard Loretta call after her, "Oh, you think you're so smart!"

Francesca gave a wave in the rearview mirror, and the two women burst out in laughter.

WILL and Penny were waiting on the porch when Francesca came to the house the next morning. The two sprang to their feet and ran to greet her with cries of "Hi, Mrs. C!"

Francesca found Loretta standing in the front hall, staring down with worrisome eyes at Will's and Penny's backpacks, the ones they ordinarily used for school. Emptied of their books and papers, Loretta was using them as suitcases, and the two packs were astonishingly overstuffed. "I just don't want them to forget anything," she fretted.

A word of assurance from Francesca that she was taking the children only to her house and not the far side of the moon put Loretta's mind at rest. By this time, Will and Penny were clamoring to leave, and so there ensued a flurry of hugs and kisses, and before long, the three were off.

"How long will it take to get there?" asked Will as he and his sister buckled themselves into the backseat of Francesca's car.

"And what are we going to do?" Penny chimed in.

"Do?" jested Francesca. "We're going to work. But don't worry. We're going to have fun. Wave good-bye to your mother."

As they drove across the city, Will and Penny stared out the windows at the unfamiliar neighborhoods they passed. Before long, they were driving down the main street toward Francesca's neighborhood; then they turned off the main road and climbed up the hill to her house. "Here we are," Francesca announced when she turned into the driveway. "Okay, you two, grab your bags—that is, if you can lift them—and bring them inside."

When she opened the front door, they were greeted by the pleasant aroma of freshly cooked tomato sauce. "Mmm, it smells like food in your house," noted Will.

"That's what houses are supposed to smell like," replied Francesca. "Come on now. Leave your bags and have a look around while I get your lunch started."

Will and Penny followed her lead into the kitchen, quietly taking in the house's high ceilings and the beautiful old woodwork. It wasn't long before they found their way into the den, where they looked with keen interest at the family photographs. They were most fascinated by those of Joey when he was a boy.

"Hey look, it's us!" a delighted Penny suddenly cried out. She had spied the photograph Loretta had taken of them with Francesca that chilly afternoon in Providence.

"I was hoping you'd see that one," Francesca called to them as she poured some pastina into the now-boiling pan of water. She gave it a stir with a spoon and joined them for a minute in the den.

"Who are these other kids?" asked Will. "Your grandkids?"

"Yes. Those are my granddaughters, Dana and Sara, and that's their brother, Frankie. They all live in Florida. And those two are my other grandsons, Charlie and Will. They live out in Oregon."

"That's right," chuckled Will. "I remember when you first came to our house, you said he and I had the same first name."

"I remember that day too," said Francesca.

"What do your grandchildren call you?" asked Penny. "Grandma?"

"No," replied Francesca. "They call me Nonna."

She gave them both a smile and walked back to the kitchen. The two children followed her. While Francesca went to check the pastina, the siblings stood in the middle of the floor, exchanging questioning glances. "What is it?" Francesca asked over her shoulder as she gave the pan another stir.

"Go on, ask her," Francesca heard Will whisper.

"What's the matter?" asked Francesca.

"Nothing's the matter, really," said Penny. "It's just that . . . we were wondering something." She took a deep breath to find her courage, looking up with the sweetest expression Francesca had ever seen. "We were just wondering if maybe—if it would be all right if we called you Nonna too."

No words could possibly have expressed the old woman's complete and utter jubilation at hearing that request. Her heart bursting with joy, tears flowing from her eyes, Francesca gathered the two children into her arms and squeezed them close.

"Yes, my sweets," she wept, kissing them on their heads, "of course you can call me Nonna, any time you like."

"Nonna?" whimpered Will, who like most boys could tolerate being hugged for only so long. He looked up at Francesca, his eyeglasses all askew. "Could we have lunch now?"

Francesca let out a laugh and released the two from her embrace. "Yes," she said, wiping her eyes dry, "lunch will be ready in just a minute. And after, we get to work!"

"Work" consisted of preparing lasagna for Sunday dinner the next day. When they were done eating lunch, and the lasagna noodles were boiling, Francesca showed Penny and

Will how to make the filling, letting them mix the eggs and the ricotta, the parsley and the other spices. Under Francesca's watchful eye, they took the long, wide noodles and laid them across the bottom of the pan, spooning the ricotta filling on top, before adding each successive layer of noodles, until the pan was filled. Finally, they laid strips of mozzarella all along the top and poured some tomato sauce over the whole thing. Then, Francesca covered it all in foil and stowed it away in the refrigerator.

"What else can we make?" asked Penny eagerly.

"Next, I thought we'd make a nice ricotta pie," answered Francesca. "And the best part is, we get to eat it today."

As the day grew later, and the pies were cooling on the counter, Francesca made them wash their hands and faces. When the two were presentable once more, she directed them to put on their jackets, and the three went out to the car. A few minutes later, they arrived at church, just in time for five-thirty mass.

"Are we going in?" said Penny, looking at Will.

"Yes, I thought we would," answered Francesca.

She had expected them to protest and had been ready to turn around and go back if they did, but in fact, the two seemed intrigued by the prospect, and so she led them in. Before they could step inside, however, Will ran over to the poor box. Reaching into his pocket, he produced a quarter and dropped it in the slot.

"For Saint Anthony," he whispered. Then he hurried back to Francesca's side.

After mass, Francesca led her two charges back to the car, explaining as they went along the significance of the different prayers and rituals. Most mysterious to them was the bread she had received from the priest at Communion.

"That's going to take a little while to explain," Francesca told them as they settled into the car. "Speaking of bread, though, gives me an idea for tomorrow. But we have to hurry."

Francesca drove straight to the market. Tony was at the register, ringing up the day's receipts, when Francesca walked into the store. With Will and Penny at her side, she quickly picked out a packet of yeast and two bags of flour.

"Good evening, Mrs. Campanile," Tony said cordially. "You got here just in time."

"I know," she said. "I decided at the last minute to bake some bread tomorrow morning."

As he rang up her purchases, Tony smiled. "Cooking for the family tomorrow, Mrs. Campanile?"

Francesca looked at the children and beamed.

"You know, Tony," she said. "This time, I think I am."

NIGHT had fallen. Loretta and Joey walked arm in arm along a downtown sidewalk toward his car. The two had just come from dinner at a restaurant and were now pondering where they should go next. It was a pleasant evening, with just the hint of a warm breeze sauntering in from the south.

As they strolled along, Loretta rested her head against Joey's shoulder. She was as happy as she could ever remember. It was a blissful, peaceful feeling, and she wanted to hold on to it for as long as she could.

When they came to the car and climbed inside, the two sat for a moment, neither one speaking. "Any place you'd like to go next?" said Joey at last, taking her hand in his.

"You know, there are lots of places I'd like for us to go sometime," she told him, bringing his hand to her lips. "But tonight, the only place I really want to go is home."

"I think that can be arranged," said Joey, giving her a knowing smile as he started the engine.

Later that night, as she was standing in the darkness by her bedroom window, Loretta looked out at the full moon beaming down through the cloudless night sky. Joey came up behind her, wrapping his arms about her and kissing the back of her neck.

Loretta realized in that moment how much it reminded her of her romantic dreams. True, she was not off in some exotic locale, standing on a balcony overlooking a moonlit bay, but her heart was pounding with anticipation, just as it always had in her most vivid dreams. The reason, she well understood, was because, unlike in her dreams, the man for whom she was burning was real, and his love for her was real, and his touch thrilled her to her soul.

Loretta turned to face Joey, entwining her arms around his neck. She stood there in his embrace, the two of them bathed in the moonlight. Hope had finally triumphed, just as she had always dreamed it would. There was only one thing left now to make it all complete, and at long last she would be his.

Letting him draw her closer, Loretta arched up and brought her lips to his ear. "Tell me you'll stay," she whispered.

EARLY the next morning, Francesca was standing at the stove when the two children came down the stairs in their pajamas, yawning and stretching the whole way to the kitchen, where they unceremoniously plopped themselves down at the table. Their eyes still full of sleep, and their hair an adorable mess, they happily reminded Francesca of her own children on all those many Sunday mornings of so long ago.

"So, what's it gonna be?" she asked, flipping over the bacon sizzling in a pan. "An egg? Some French toast? Or how about blueberry pancakes?"

"How about all three?" yawned a hungry Will.

"Done!" exclaimed Francesca to their surprise.

After breakfast, the children went upstairs to get dressed, while Francesca cleaned up the kitchen. When they returned, they found that she had set out the flour, yeast, sugar, and salt on the table, along with a small bowl of warm water. Before long, Francesca had them mixing it all together and then kneading the big lump of dough to make the bread.

By the time Joey and Loretta arrived just after noon, the house was filled with the aroma of freshly baked bread and the lasagna simmering in the oven. When they came through the front door, the children ran to their mother and hugged her as if they hadn't seen her in days.

"Wait until you see what we made," bragged Will.

"I can't wait," said his mother, giving them a squeeze.

A moment later, Loretta was in the kitchen, raving to Francesca about how beautiful the house was, before shooing Joey away so that she could help his mother get dinner on the table.

When at last the food was ready and the

table set, they all gathered in the dining room. Francesca stood at the head of the table, smiling as she presided over the proceedings, for it was wonderful to once again have her home filled with such happy sounds. She was about to start dispensing the antipasto when Joey suddenly got up and left the room. He returned with a bottle of champagne.

"My, my," said Francesca as she watched her son pop the cork. "What's the occasion?"

"Tell you in a minute," said Joey, filling the adults' glasses before turning to Loretta and asking, "A drop for the kids?"

"Uh-uh," she playfully warned him, rolling her eyes.

"I'll get them some ginger ale," offered Francesca.

When everyone's glasses were filled, Joey stood and raised his own. "Kids, Mamma Mia," he began, "there's something Loretta and I want to tell you. We talked it over last night and—"

"What?" Will and Penny asked impatiently.

Before her son could say another word, Francesca looked at Loretta and noticed that the smiling young woman was now wearing a diamond ring on her finger.

"Oh, my God!" cried Francesca joyously. She jumped up and kissed and hugged Loretta, then Joey, and then Loretta again, and then both the children.

"What is it, what is it?" cried Penny above the hubbub.

"*Dio mio!*" Francesca sighed happily. "What it means, young lady, is that one day very soon, we're going to go back to that store and buy you that nice blue dress!"

THE first thing Francesca did that beautiful afternoon in August, after Loretta and Joey had exchanged vows at the church before Father Buontempo and he pronounced them husband and wife, was to open her purse and pull out her rosary beads. Rolling one of the dark, smooth beads between her thumb and forefinger, she whispered a quick prayer for the two newlyweds. Beside her sat Loretta's mother, Jane. The two had only just met the previous evening at the rehearsal party, but they had hit it off at once. She seemed a feisty, high-spirited sort, though at the moment, she was dabbing her tear-filled eyes with a handkerchief while gushing to her husband about how beautiful her daughter looked. With Penny as the flower girl in her beautiful new dress, and Will the ring bearer, Loretta's stepfather had gladly acquiesced to Loretta's request that he walk her up the aisle.

Everyone had flown home for the wedding, and later at the reception, Francesca was in all her glory when the photographer gathered them all together to take a picture. After dinner, when the plates had been cleared away and everyone got up to dance, Francesca sat for a time alone at the table, taking in the beautiful scene. It wasn't long, though, before she spied Mr. Pace moving in her direction.

"Is this seat taken, madam?" he asked.

"Only if you sit down in it," replied Francesca with a nod.

"In that case, I'll do so," said a smiling Pace.

"So, how was your dinner?" she asked.

"Not bad," he replied. "How about yours?"

"Eh, it was okay." Francesca shrugged. "But the sauce on the macaroni gave me *agita*."

"That happens to me sometimes too." Pace nodded.

Francesca gaped at him for a moment. "Now how would a Yankee like you know what *agita* is?" she asked.

"Like I said once before," he told her with a smile, "I'm not as much of a Yankee as people think."

"And how is that?"

"I'll let you in on a little family secret," said Pace. "When my grandfather, whom I was named for, first came to this country, he realized it would be a lot easier to get along if he introduced himself to people as William D. Pace, instead of his real name."

"Which was . . . ?" Francesca asked.

"Guglielmo Di Pace, of course!" The old man chuckled. "He came from a little town in Abruzzo, just like my grandmother. The two of them wanted their children to do well in America, but they also didn't want them to forget where they came from, so when they began to go by the name of Pace, they made sure to give all their children the letter *D* for a middle initial."

Just then, the sound of cheers drew their

attention to the dance floor, where Loretta and Joey and Will and Penny were holding hands, dancing together. Francesca blew them a kiss.

As she watched them happily whirling about hand in hand, Francesca marveled at Loretta and Joey, and how they had finally become a family. "Well," she said with a wistful sigh, "I guess they won't be needing me anymore."

"Oh, I don't think that's the case at all," Pace assured her. "I think all of them need you now more than ever." The old gentleman got to his feet and offered his hand to her. "What do you say to joining them on the dance floor?"

"Oh, I haven't danced in years," said Francesca. "I don't think I even remember how."

"Maybe now would be a good time to learn again," he noted.

Francesca looked up into his earnest face and warm eyes. She wanted to go with him but hesitated. Something she couldn't quite put her finger on was holding her back. It reminded her of that moment of fear in the airplane, just before it was about to take off. Part of her wanted to stay there, safely alone in her seat, but another part was equally afraid to sit idly by and just let life fly away without her.

"Yes, Guglielmo Di Pace, you might be right," she finally told him, giving him her hand. "Maybe now *would* be a good time for me to dance again."

And off she went, leaving her fears behind. After all, sometimes in life, it was good to take a little chance.

A WHOLE
NEW LIFE

BETSY
THORNTON

A HUSBAND is jailed for the murder of his wife, while an offbeat cast of characters does whatever it takes to prove his innocence.

Prologue

THE monsoons come to southern Arizona in July and August, dumping a good percentage of the rainfall for the year, often in quick, violent thunderstorms that briefly turn the Cochise County high desert into a green oasis. The monsoons come from the south, flooding the washes and sweeping away cars whose drivers are foolish enough to cross the barriers put up to warn them.

One monsoon evening in late August, in the foothills of the Mule Mountains halfway between the newish, big, and booming town of Sierra Vista and the old, small, and arty town of Dudley, a woman walked out of a house. It was a nice house, not too big, built of cedar boards that had grayed enough to blend in with the surrounding landscape of mesquite, ocotillo, and desert willow.

Down the road a ways was the Norton place, and beyond was the house being built by the man from Phoenix. The man from Phoenix rarely showed up, but he had a crew working there every day. They'd been there that morning, hammering, sawing, the cement mixer going full blast, until the drenching rains arrived.

Now a light drizzle was falling. The woman carried her purse and a bottle of spring water and wore loose black drawstring pants, a white T-shirt, and a wedding ring. She was in her forties, pretty, with long dark hair held back with a pink terry-cloth headband. It was early in the evening, but the dark clouds made it seem later.

The woman walked quickly to a blue Toyota Tercel and got in. She fastened her seat belt, then remembered: She hadn't taken her pill yet, her probiotics, special ones from some kind of soil organism, popular now among the eternally fit. She took them twice a day, big white gelatin caps. She would tell anyone that she felt a million times better since she'd begun taking these probiotics.

She rummaged in her purse for the bottle, shook out a capsule, and swallowed it. Then she started the car. The clock on the dashboard lit up—almost seven. She was running late. So you're late, she told herself. Calm down. You'll get there. Yoga breaths.

She pulled out of the driveway, turned

right, and headed down the small road past the skeleton of the new house. Her throat felt dry, so she stopped and gulped down some water. The highway started rising into the mountains, and the rain came down harder.

Her mouth was still dry. She finished off the water. She forced herself to slow down, the visibility badly obscured by the rain. Already the clock said seven twenty. Hours. This was going to take hours. A car came up from behind, its headlights hitting the rearview mirror. She accelerated just a little, but the car stayed right on her tail. It was so irritating; her skin felt hot, tingly. Calm down.

She slowed to let the car behind go by. Her face felt funny, kind of numb—her throat, too. The car passed. She accelerated again.

Her throat was so tight she could hardly swallow. Maybe getting a cold. She never got them, she was so healthy—she ought to be; she did everything right. A panic attack? Relax. Probably some kind of allergy; the pollen count would be high with all this rain.

The wipers hurried across the windshield, but her heart was going even faster. She tried to focus on the road as it steepened toward the tunnel that led into town, but now she couldn't even breathe.

Something was really, definitely, terribly wrong. She had to get help, the mountains so dark, the road slick, slick, slick: *swish clunk, swish clunk.* Hurry. Suddenly she was six years old again, swinging on a wooden swing, her big brother on the one next to her, both of them going higher, higher—she reached for his hand . . .

Breathless, terrified at what was happening to her, she floored the accelerator. The car swerved, almost fishtailed; then she saw the taillight of the car that had passed her going slow now on the final hill. She jammed on the brakes.

The blue Toyota Tercel hydroplaned, sailing off the road, over the mountainside. In a brief but seemingly eternal moment, she reached for her brother's hand, missed; she fell off the swing, then lost consciousness as the car hit the rocks below.

IT WAS around nine when the man driving the gray Volvo turned off the rain-slick dark highway onto the smaller road that led to his house. He was in his late forties, with sandy hair thinning at the forehead, and he wore wire-rimmed glasses. He taught English at the local college and had spent the past few hours in his office getting organized for the fall semester.

He passed the house being built by the man from Phoenix, shadowy in the dark. He always read a poem to his first class, and earlier that day, he'd driven all the way to Tucson, a three-hour round-trip, just to get a copy of a certain Louise Bogan poem.

So, with stiff walls about us, we
Chose this more fragile boundary:
Hills, where the light poplar, the firm oak,
Loosen into a little smoke.

Magical. He'd marked those lines in pencil. Would they get it, the class? It was a junior college; they were working-class kids, which was fine with him, but they didn't have the background of kids from middle-class homes. It was up to him to bridge that gap.

As he pulled into the driveway, he noticed with relief that his wife's blue Toyota wasn't there. He got out, breathing in the smell of the rain, unlocked the door, and went inside.

Only one light on, a dim bulb in the lamp by the terra-cotta-colored wing chair. The rest of the house was dark. He sat down and took off his wire-rimmed glasses. He listened to the rain drip-dripping from the eaves, feeling the house settle around him, soft in its emptiness without his wife there.

The phone rang, like some noisy intruder. Damn.

"Hello?" He made a face. "Oh. Hi, Anita. No, she's not here." His voice was polite. He didn't like Anita, and she didn't like him.

He said, "She's still at her yoga class."

Anita's voice shrilled. He held the phone away from his ear.

"No," he said. "Why should I be? They probably just went somewhere afterward for coffee or something. . . . Sure, I'll do that. Soon as she gets home." He hung up. Damn that pushy Anita. His peaceful mood was shot. He went into the kitchen, turning on lights. Turquoise canisters stood in a neat line, containing nothing readily available to eat. He pulled open the door of the refrigerator, stared inside at vegetables that would have to be cooked, closed it.

Down the hallway to the front door was

something strange. Lights, red and blue, flashing through the window by the front door.

What the hell? A police car was in his driveway. A sheriff's deputy was coming down the walk. Then he heard knocking.

Annoyed, then all at once nervous, he stepped back, took a deep breath, turned the knob, and opened the door to a whole new life.

One

JACKSON Williams knew how his wife died. It was her tires. She never had them rotated. She never even looked at them. Just a week before her death, he'd said to her, "Jenny, you need to do something about your front tires. The treads are worn." But she hadn't. She'd driven over the Mule Mountain Pass on bare tires in the rain, lost traction, swerved, gone over the edge, and crashed and died.

Now they were going to do an autopsy. Because he hadn't been able to get an answer about when her body would be released, Ruth Norton, Jackson's neighbor and friend, had suggested a memorial service in Dudley, followed by a reception at Ruth's house.

There could be a quiet burial later when Jenny's body was released.

He'd gotten through the memorial service, but after half an hour at the reception, he'd felt he couldn't go on. So he'd slipped away, gone out back and up the rise where the mountain began at the end of Ruth's yard to a big rock. There he sat now, polishing his wire-rimmed glasses and thinking about that autopsy.

Couldn't they tell how Jenny had died without cutting her up? It seemed especially hard that it was her body they were cutting up; she had tended it so carefully, worked so hard at keeping it fit.

He put the glasses back on, and Ruth's backyard below came into focus. The guests were milling around down there—some of his colleagues from the college, including Sid Hamblin, that envious ass, braying as usual; Jenny's friends from various exercise classes; her best friend, Anita, who had pointedly ignored him. There was Ruth, talking to Grace Dixon, Jenny's mom, under the apricot tree. Amazingly, he hadn't seen Grace in three years. Jenny had driven over to Green Valley, a retirement community near Tucson, to see her a couple of times a month, but she never took him along.

Ruth had looked nice at the memorial, elegant even, in some long, dark gauzy dress that set off her reddish-brown curly hair with the streak of white that went back from her forehead. She never got dressed up except to substitute teach, and afterward she always changed into sweats and some old T-shirt the minute she got home.

His mind drifted. The first time he saw Jenny, six years ago, he was skiing with a friend. He didn't ski well, and he'd been floundering at the bottom of a slope when this amazing butterfly-like creature floated down a hill and alighted right in front of him. She was so graceful. A *mystery*. It had seemed like destiny, inevitable. He should have left her there on the slope, a beautiful image. But instead he'd pursued the puzzle he saw as Jenny; God help him, he married her, and the more the puzzle of Jenny had unraveled, the less of Jenny there seemed to be.

All those arguments he'd had with her— arguments about what she called his lack of ambition, arguments about the time he spent away from home, as well as the times he was home but not doing what she wanted. Now he wished he'd kissed her—just once, even—during those arguments instead of always trying to have the last word.

He heard a rustling behind him and turned his head, and there was Tyler, Ruth's eleven-year-old.

Tyler was okay. Tyler wasn't like the people in Ruth's backyard; Tyler was real. "Hey, sport," Jackson said.

"Hey." Tyler hunkered down beside him, stiff in dress khaki pants that were too big. He was a skinny kid still, though if he was anything like his two older brothers, he would fill out in a couple of years. "What are you doing up here?"

"Well . . . actually, it's hard for me to talk to people right now."

"Yeah," Tyler said in a hushed voice. "And they're *laughing*."

"People laugh for all kinds of reasons," said Jackson. "Like when they're nervous or tired, or sometimes to keep from crying."

"I guess so," Tyler said.

Tyler adored his two older brothers, Dan and Scott. Jackson tried to remember how long Dan had been gone. Three years, he thought, but Scott had left only six weeks ago to see his father before he went to college at UCLA. Tyler must be lonely.

"When all this is over," said Jackson, "we'll play basketball again. I'm getting out of shape."

"Cool," said Tyler.

THIS reception will never be over, thought Ruth Norton, coming out of her house with a glass of water for Jenny's mom, Grace Dixon. Never. Sid Hamblin, one of Jackson's colleagues from the college, was sitting on the outside stoop, blocking her way.

"Excuse me," she said.

"Sorry!" Sid jumped up, a big man in his forties with a black beard, wearing a Hawaiian shirt—his idea, apparently, of what one wore to a memorial service. He bowed and made a sweeping arc with his arm. "Madame," he said.

She inched past him, trying not to make physical contact—he radiated a kind of jocularly aggressive sexuality that both annoyed her and made her nervous—and went across the yard to Jenny's mom, handed her the water, then sat down beside her.

I am in purgatory, thought Ruth, sitting with Mrs. Dixon. Someone had to look after her because Jackson was hopeless at that kind of thing and, in fact, had disappeared. Mrs. Dixon, an elderly widow, had been driven here from Green Valley by a friend.

Ruth patted Mrs. Dixon's hand. "Are you doing okay?"

Mrs. Dixon looked at her without recognition. A white-haired old woman with some of Jenny's prettiness but faded, she was dressed in a black pantsuit with a silver-and-turquoise necklace.

"It seems to me," said Mrs. Dixon, "they could have had better flowers for Jenny at the memorial than those weeds."

"Wildflowers," said Ruth gently. "Asters. Jenny loved to run. She would have seen them by the side of the road. They were to kind of evoke her memory."

Mrs. Dixon sniffed and reached for her purse. With a shock of guilt, Ruth saw she had tears in her eyes. For heaven's sake, how could she sit there feeling trapped—she, Ruth, of all people, with three boys who were all alive, all healthy? Mrs. Dixon had lost a child. No, *two*. She remembered that now—Jenny's brother was dead as well. All Grace Dixon's complaints were just to cover her pain. How could there be anything worse than to lose a child?

Where was Tyler? Ruth realized she hadn't seen him in a while. As Mrs. Dixon blew her nose, Ruth glanced around the yard, and then she saw him, crouched by a big rock, talking to Jackson. Tyler was safe. Thank goodness. Tyler and Jackson, both safe.

IT WAS two days after the memorial service. Tyler trudged down the road from the highway where the school bus had dropped him off, past the house being built by the man from Phoenix. The cement mixer was grinding away. He hated where he lived, out in the middle of nowhere. Not one single kid lived there but him.

At least there was Jackson. Tyler looked up, hoping Jackson would be home and might play basketball. His Volvo was there in front of the house, along with a sheriff's deputy's car.

A sheriff's deputy car. Wow.

His mom's car wasn't in the driveway. She was substitute teaching, wouldn't be home till four thirty or so. Tyler went inside to the kitchen and drank some milk from the jug in the refrigerator. He usually played video games after school unless Jackson was around and wanted to play basketball. But today Tyler pulled up a chair to the window that had the best view of the front of Jackson's house.

A deputy in uniform came out of the house carrying a big box, followed by another uniform carrying Jackson's computer. They put everything into the deputy's car. Then Jackson came out with a tall man carrying a clipboard in his hand.

The man gave the clipboard to Jackson, and Jackson looked at it, then wrote on it. They were taking his computer, and Jackson used his computer all the time. Why wasn't he stopping them?

THE next evening Ruth, in sweatpants and a faded red T-shirt, walked over to Jackson's house carrying a bowl with what was left of the Million Dollar Chicken she'd made for dinner. Jackson's gray Volvo was in the driveway. The front door was open.

"Jackson?" she called through the screen.

No answer.

Ruth opened the screen door. "Jackson? It's me."

"Out back!"

Ruth walked through the living room to the kitchen. The outside door was open, and Jackson was sitting on the back stoop.

"What are you doing out there?" she asked him.

He didn't turn his head. "Listening to the doves."

Ruth smiled. "I brought you some Million Dollar Chicken."

"Thanks."

She placed the bowl inside the refrigerator, then came out and sat down beside him. He was wearing jeans and his old plaid shirt with a rip in it that Jenny had always wanted him to get rid of. He looked so vulnerable. She touched him lightly on the shoulder.

"Ruth," he said, "when I went to identify her, they told me she had been swerving all over the road, like she was drunk."

"Drunk." Ruth laughed. *"Jenny?"*

"Her tires were so bad. I should have just taken her car myself and gotten new ones. I feel so guilty."

"Don't. It's not your fault. Jenny was a grown-up, responsible for her own tires."

They sat in companionable silence. The

cottonwoods rustled in a little breeze, and the doves cooed.

Then Ruth said softly, "Tyler told me about the police coming. He said they took your computer and some other stuff."

Jackson rested his forehead in his hands. "They had a search warrant. I asked the detective why, but he said it was just routine."

"What else did they take?"

"A whole bunch of stuff. They had me read through this list, but nothing on it *meant* anything. Then I signed it." He paused. "They took away half the stuff in the medicine cabinet. Old prescriptions, all Jenny's vitamins."

"Jenny and her vitamins." Ruth sighed. "Maybe she was drunk on vitamins. Hadn't she been taking some weird pills lately?"

"Probiotics."

"What's that?"

"Don't ask me. She got them at the Co-op."

"Here's a thought," said Ruth. "What if she was swerving because she was having a bad reaction to those probiotics?"

"I never thought . . ." said Jackson. "That would explain why they took everything in the medicine cabinet and why it's taking so long to release her body."

"Makes sense to me," said Ruth.

"Wow." Jackson whooshed out a sigh of relief. "That's what I love about you, Ruth. You always make me feel better."

"So stop worrying." Ruth took his hand and gave it a squeeze. "Everything will be okay. You'll see."

CREATIVE writing was Jackson's favorite class. It took place Tuesday and Thursday nights. At the first meeting, he'd assigned a topic. No more than two paragraphs: What I Didn't Do on My Summer Vacation, but if I Could Have, I Would Have.

He'd been looking forward to this next class, but now, as some of the students read their papers out loud, Jackson found himself distracted, thinking about the police. The search warrant. He'd felt sick, weak when they left, but he'd gone over to Ruth's and played some basketball with Tyler, and that had helped. Then Ruth had come over, and he'd felt a lot better, but maybe, if he didn't hear from the police soon, he should call them, tell them about the probiotics.

Jackson wrenched his thoughts away from that to focus on the students.

"I would have gone to the Tucson Mall," read a beautiful girl with long purple fingernails, "to the Gap. I would have tried on everything in the whole store that was pink. Then I would have—"

Jackson glanced at the clock. "Oops." He raised his hand. "I'm sorry. We've run out of time. We'll finish up at the next class."

As the class began to file out, he added, "Carlos? Could I speak to you a minute?"

A gangly Hispanic kid with a shaved head and a wide humorous mouth stopped dead in his tracks. "Hey, man, what'd I do?"

"Do?" said Jackson. He held up Carlos's paper. He'd read it once before class, then twice, with rising exhilaration. "You wrote this."

What I didn't do on my summer vacation, but if I could have, I would have gone to the North Pole to see my dead nana. She lives there in an igloo under the Northern Lights with a sled pulled by tired penguins. When she was alive, she made tamales wrapped in bitter words that froze my poor mother's heart. She was the Queen of Snow and Ice, but if I could see her now, I would melt her in my arms and I would say, "Nana, sing and dance for me like you used to when I was a little boy, before you were old."

"This is *really* good," said Jackson. "*Alive.*"

Carlos smirked, ducking his head. "You think so, man? Thanks, Mr. Williams. Thanks a lot."

Jackson paused. "Did you do much writing in high school?"

"Naw." Carlos looked bemused. "The smart kids did that. My mom didn't finish high school. I'm just a dumb Mexican."

"What does that mean? A dumb Mexican?"

"Aw, man, you know. What'd they ever write, Mexicans?"

"Are you kidding me? There are some fine Mexican writers. I'll lend you a couple of books."

"Hey, that'd be cool. Thanks." Carlos cocked his head. "You got kids, Mr. Williams?"

Stunned for a moment, Jackson didn't answer. "Yes," he said finally. "A daughter. She's back east, with her mother."

"Bet she misses you," said Carlos. "Bet you're a good dad."

Uncomfortable, Jackson involuntarily looked at his watch.

"Well, later, man," said Carlos.

"Later," said Jackson.

He sat at his desk for a few minutes after Carlos left. A good dad. His daughter was twenty-one, and he hadn't seen her since she was three. *Tired penguins.* Maybe he could get Carlos published somewhere, some little magazine. Jackson had a friend, Casey, in Chicago, a professor with connections to the literary scene. They e-mailed each other all the time. My computer, he thought. When will I get it back?

Suddenly anxious, he stood, gathered up his things, and left the classroom. As he walked outside, he saw the campus cop standing in the parking lot talking to another man, whose face he couldn't see. There was something familiar about him. Then Jackson realized he was the detective who'd come to his door with the search warrant.

A prick of fire stung Jackson's chest. What was he doing here at the college? Come to update him on the investigation? The detective came closer. He had a piece of paper in his hand.

The detective looked at Jackson apologetically. He cleared his throat. "Jackson Williams, I'm here to serve you with a warrant for your arrest for the murder of your wife, Jenny Williams."

No. No. How could that be? Surely he had made a mistake.

"You have the right to remain silent," the detective went on. "Anything you say can and will be used against you in a court of law. You have the right to an attorney. . . ."

Two

THIN, high clouds streaked the morning sky. After Jackson's call from the jail last night asking her to hire a lawyer for him—he'd been adamant about which one, Stuart Ross, over in Dudley—Ruth hadn't fallen asleep till after four a.m. And even though she'd showered an extra-long time, she was still a little groggy.

What to wear to see the lawyer? She'd recognized his name as soon as Jackson said it. Stuart Ross. He'd won a big murder case over in Tucson several years ago, defending a homeless man accused of killing a city councilman. It had been on the news for days. Why on earth, she wondered, had Stuart Ross moved to Dudley?

In the mirror—oh, no—she saw that her hair had dried with a cowlick on top. She pulled on a pair of black pants—black went with everything—and a white blouse. She took a red jacket from the back of the closet, found an old tortoiseshell headband to take care of the cowlick, dabbed on lipstick. Shoes, what shoes?

Her face felt flushed; beads of sweat were forming on her forehead. The sooner she saw the lawyer and got him to straighten out this terrible mistake, the sooner Jackson would be out of jail. Out by this afternoon, she hoped. What if Stuart Ross was really busy, a famous lawyer like that. What if he refused to take the case? She would have to be persuasive. There was a time when she'd been good at dealing with people, *grown-ups,* but it seemed so long ago.

OVER in Dudley, Stuart Ross, attorney at law, was thinking about how he probably wouldn't ever bother with marriage again. He'd been married twice—first to an okay person, really, but she was far away, remarried long ago. His second marriage had been to an alcoholic, which made sense, considering that at the time, he'd been supporting himself by picking up legal work in bars. It was amazing how many times he'd shown up in court half drunk and no one had noticed. Until everybody did.

A month of rehab, then years of AA. That was behind him now.

Stuart sipped coffee from the Dudley Coffee Company and leaned back in the chair in his office on Main Street, just a short walk from the courthouse. He had a good view of the tourists ambling past the Western Art Gallery, across the street.

Stuart hadn't had a drink for six years. When he first moved here from Tucson, he'd taken a job as a deputy public defender with the county, but he'd struck out on his own after a while and was now fully self-employed. Some private clients, but mostly contract work from the county for indigent defendants. All that was left now of his former renegade status was his empathy for the down-and-outs he usually represented and, of course, his ponytail.

He wasn't rich, but he wasn't poor, either;

in fact, he was doing A-OK. And outdoors it was a nice fall day, sun-filled and breezy. Stewart relaxed, savoring the feeling of well-being. A woman strode determinedly down the sidewalk toward his office, stepping out into the street to get by a clot of tourists. The woman looked employed, nice red jacket, black pants. Somewhere in her forties. Like me, thought Stewart sadly, and belched. Too much caffeine.

He opened the top drawer of the desk and popped three Tums Ultra, losing sight of the woman. Then almost immediately the bell in the outer office tinkled. Ellie, his office manager/secretary, chosen for her good looks and air of impenetrable rectitude, was out on another extended coffee-cum-shopping break.

"Hello?" someone, a woman, called out.

Stuart swallowed hurriedly and went out to the reception area. It was the woman in the red jacket. Bad lipstick—too pink or something; lines that softened rather than hardened her face; thick reddish-brown curly hair with a streak of white going back from the hairline, held in place with some sort of plastic headband. An odd smell filled the air—musty, medicinal, somehow familiar.

"Well, hi there," he said in his Ben Matlock voice. Taller than she was by half a foot, he looked down at her.

Up close, he could see that the jacket was from another era, shoulder pads like a football player's. Thrift store, maybe. Suddenly he realized what that smell was—mothballs.

"Are you Stuart Ross?" she asked.

"I sure am." Still Matlock.

"My name's Ruth Norton." She took a breath. "I'm here to see about hiring you on behalf of my neighbor. He—"

"Hold on. It's better if we talk it over in my office."

Stuart smiled magnanimously as he escorted her into his office. She sat in the straight-backed, unforgiving client chair. Stuart closed the door, which made the smell of mothballs almost overpowering. Stuart's nose twitched.

"I'm sorry," she said. "I need to get rid of this jacket. It-It—" She sneezed, stood, and slid it off her shoulders. Without it, she was instantly better-looking. "It smells."

Stuart stood up gallantly. "Here." He took the jacket from her. "I'll put it on the coat-hanging thingie outside."

After he did so, he sat in his chair and got down to business.

"Here's how it works," he said. "First thing we discuss is a retainer, which varies depending on the nature of the case—"

"What happened is—" Ruth cut in.

He held up his hand. "Wait. You haven't hired me yet, so there's no confidentiality. They could haul me into court as a witness."

"But how can you know if you'll take the case or not if I don't tell you anything?" she said.

"We'll get to that. A retainer covers my expenses, and if it's not used up, you get a portion back." Stuart's lawyer voice swelled; he'd made this speech a million times, but he still enjoyed it.

"Can't we cut to the chase?" Ruth exploded suddenly, startling Stuart into silence. "When they arrested Jackson—"

"Jackson?"

"Jackson Williams, my neighbor. They told him he'd been indicted. What does that mean, exactly?"

"He's been formally charged."

Ruth shuddered. "I'm authorized up to ten thousand, okay? This damn headband. It's giving me a headache." She ripped it off her head and snapped it in two, right in front of him, then dropped the pieces onto the carpet. "There."

Menopausal, thought Stuart, but he kept his cool.

"Jackson teaches English at Cochise College in Sierra Vista," Ruth went on. "He's a good man. He's charged with first-degree murder for killing his wife, Jenny." Her voice rose. "Mr. Ross, it's completely untrue, and I'm begging, *begging* you to take this case."

First-degree murder. Momentarily stunned, Stuart cleared his throat. "Well then, we'll go with the full ten thousand." He paused. "For starters."

"So you'll take the case?"

"Yes. I'll go see him at the jail today, make it official."

A teacher, he thought. That was an edge right there. Depending on circumstances, maybe not a plea; a trial, way way down the road, of course. Easy there, Stuart, he told himself, but years had gone by since he'd had a murder case. He could almost taste it, him in his three-piece suit, arguing to a full jury at the pinnacle of the criminal justice system—the awesomeness of it, the majesty.

"He needs to get out of jail right away," said Ruth urgently. "Can you do it by this afternoon?"

"Depends on his conditions of release."

"What does that *mean?*"

Stuart held up a finger, picked up the phone, and punched in numbers. "Stuart Ross here. What's the bond on Jackson Williams?" He waited, staring at a shard of headband on the floor. "No kidding." He hung up and said to Ruth, "Five hundred thousand dollars."

Ruth blinked; then her eyes widened in shock.

"But," Stuart went on, "he'd only have to come up with ten percent. That's fifty thousand. He got it?"

"I—I don't see how."

"Then he won't be getting out this afternoon," Stuart said briskly. He glanced at Ruth's crestfallen face. "I'll work on getting it lowered. Best thing for you to do now is go home."

MARA Harvey's mom had told her once that the first minute after a plane took off was the most likely time for it to crash. A month past her twenty-first birthday, Mara closed her eyes and gripped the armrest, feeling the plane bump along fast, faster, then leave the ground and go sailing into the sky.

Mara wore tiny black sunglasses, three silver hoops in each ear, and a rose tattoo. Her mother was dead. How could she be dead? Mara thought for the millionth time. How *could* she? Don't cry. The creepy man sitting next to her would see.

Her father wouldn't be creepy. He was an English professor. And a poet—her mom had told her a long time ago he was a poet. All Mara remembered was being swung into the air by a man with long sandy hair who was laughing and saying, *Got you now!* Her mom had liked him. She'd said, "I loved him, but I liked him, too. He was fun. He noticed things no one else did and got excited about them."

"But, mom, why—"

"You can't live on poetry," she'd said abruptly, and wouldn't talk about it any more. Her mother had died two years ago, when Mara was nineteen. Mara didn't think about it as much as she used to, but when she did, it was still like it just happened.

On Mara's twenty-first birthday, the man

she knew as Dad had handed her an envelope with her name on it in her mother's handwriting. Mara had carefully slid a paper knife under the flap. When it was open, she touched her tongue to the flap where her mother had to have licked to seal it. Stupid.

Inside was a piece of paper with her real father's name and his address, in Dudley, Arizona. "Ooh," said her best friend when Mara told her about it, "are you going to write him?"

Write him? All she'd done was write, answering all those sympathy cards, till her hand had felt paralyzed. Her whole being had felt paralyzed since her mother's death. She needed a jump start to get back into a life. Seeing her real father might do that, but she couldn't afford to take the chance he would say no to a meeting. So she'd gone online and bought plane tickets with money she'd saved.

Mara walked though the arrival gate in the Tucson airport and ducked into a restroom before she reached security. She bent down and brushed forward her short streaked blond hair to give it body, then flipped her head over and combed her hair into place with her fingers.

Mara was only four when her mom married Roy Harvey. Her real father had moved out west when she was three, and before he left, her mom had made him sign a paper giving up all parental rights so Roy could legally adopt her. Her real father—had he been upset giving her up? Laughing, sandy-haired. Got you now! Did he ever think about her, wonder what she was like?

A poet. Even though he hadn't been told she was coming, she had this fantasy of someone superintuitive, who, like destiny, would be waiting in the airport to meet her.

She put her sunglasses on and left the restroom. Groups of people waited for arriving passengers. Relatives, friends, *moms*. There was no actual reason why he would be there, and he didn't know what she looked like. Maybe he'd be holding a sign with her name on it. Men of all ages glanced at Mara. None of them held a sign.

She lingered till the crowd dispersed. Then she bit her lip, wanting to cry. Mara, you are a stupid idiot, she told herself. Shape up. Why would he be here? He doesn't even know you're coming.

SIERRA VISTA IS THE biggest town in Cochise County, but the courthouse is in Dudley, left over from the days when Dudley was the county seat and not just a tourist town. Ruth lived between the two, but she spent more time in Sierra Vista, where there were bigger grocery stores and a Wal-Mart. Dudley was quainter, more charming, and now that Scottie and Dan were both gone, Ruth tried to come to Dudley more, as part of some vague plan for a new life.

Not this kind of new life, though. More or less dismissed by the lawyer, Ruth strode down Main Street carrying her smelly jacket, dodging tourists. *Fifty thousand dollars for Jackson to get out of jail.* Jackson didn't have that kind of money. Ten thousand dollars for the lawyer's retainer had been a stretch.

Ruth would have been happy to help, but all she had was two thousand three hundred and forty-two dollars, down from almost four thousand due to the lack of substitute-teaching jobs over the summer. If she didn't get called in soon, it would be even less.

That lawyer—she couldn't believe she'd broken her headband right in front of him. It was just that he was so pompous, she'd had to do something to get his attention. A ponytail. Who did he think he was kidding? She felt sad about the jacket; it had always worked for her back when she and her ex-husband, Owen, had run a business in California. "Aha. Your power jacket," Owen used to say. Now she would probably never wear it again.

Ahead of her was the Convention Center—a pale green art deco structure—and to her left, the Mining Museum and what everyone called the Grassy Park, where they set up booths from time to time and held crafts festivals. She'd dragged Tyler to one this summer.

At the corner by the post office was the guy with the long gray beard, dressed in an orange satin robe and a pointed cap, who was—though Ruth had no way of knowing this—an occasional client of Stuart Ross. He was almost always there, tinkling a bell. The Magician, they called him. He lived in a cave in the hills above Dudley. Half the residents wanted to get rid of him, but the other half, led by an aging activist called Ken Dooley, wanted to keep him. Ken Dooley wrote letters about various causes to the local paper every week, and in a recent one, he had defended the Magician.

The Magician tinkled his bell at her now, muttering to himself. Poor man, she thought as she passed him. Mentally ill.

She reached her old Honda Civic, opened the trunk, and threw in the red jacket. As she started the car, it hit her full force: *Jackson was in jail*. Dear God, please get him out as soon as possible.

From Dudley, Ruth drove all the way to Sierra Vista for groceries. When she finally got home, work was going full blast at the construction site down the street. Muscular men swarmed around the half-finished structure, a cement mixer grinding away.

Inside her house, Ruth kicked off her shoes and put away the groceries. The house had been a shack when she and Owen bought it twelve years ago as an investment, liking its isolated mountain setting. Then they'd flown in from L.A. with Dan and Scott on long weekends to work on the remodel, gutting the kitchen and adding rooms. When they were done, the kitchen, with its black tiles and stainless steel fixtures, looked like it came from a magazine.

They'd only just finished and had gotten back to L.A. late at night when Owen had blurted out his confession. "I'm in love," he'd said, "with Tony." Tony? "Who the hell is she?" Ruth had said blankly, in shock, not really taking it in. "He's not a she," Owen had said.

The next morning, Ruth, eyes swollen from crying and pregnant with Tyler, had hustled Scott and Dan into the old van piled with as much stuff as would fit and driven all the way here without stopping. A place that was nowhere. The people, nobodies: *normal.*

Looking back, she was ashamed at her thinking. By now she'd long forgiven Owen. How could he help who he was?

All these years later the black ceramic tiles looked smudged, the stainless steel embossed with water marks. Tyler had left his bowl on the table, dried-up Cheerios stuck to the bottom.

Ruth felt a pang. Her two big boys, Dan and Scott, gone out in the world. And now Jackson in jail. *Fifty thousand dollars to get him out.* But his lawyer had said he would get the bond lowered.

She put Tyler's bowl in the sink and stared out the window.

It was hot. Her face flushed, and sweat gathered under her hair. Her body felt weak. She sat down heavily in a kitchen chair. It wasn't any hotter than usual. What was wrong with her?

She remembered she'd woken up a few nights ago, in a drenching sweat, suffocating under the covers. Oh, *no*. Ruth stood up with a start. A *hot* flash. Wasn't she too young? She hurried to the bathroom and looked in the mirror. She looked the same. She pulled the bathroom curtain aside for better light and froze.

A white Toyota was parked at Jackson's house, and a woman stood beside it. She was young, blond, and pretty. As Ruth watched, the woman opened the gate to Jackson's house. Who was she? Ruth pulled on her old Reeboks and went out the door.

"Hello?" she called as she reached the driveway. The woman, younger than she'd thought and wearing tiny sunglasses, was knocking on the door. "No one's home. Who are you looking for?"

"Jackson Williams. He lives here, doesn't he?"

"Yes." Curious, Ruth opened the gate and

came into the yard. "I'm Ruth Norton. I live next door. Are you one of his students?"

"No." The woman smiled tentatively. "Do you know him well?"

"Friends for years," said Ruth.

The young woman took off her sunglasses, and Ruth could see now she was really young—barely into her twenties, if that. "I'm Mara." Her voice lilted up at the end of the word, hopefully.

Mara? Ruth knew the name from Jackson, but surely this wasn't . . . How old would she be now? "*Mara? Jackson's daughter?"

"He talked about me?"

"Yes," said Ruth. "He always hoped he'd see you again."

Mara's face lit up.

Ruth's heart broke for Jackson, his daughter finally coming to see him and he was sitting in jail accused of murdering his wife. What was she going to tell the poor girl?

"Look," Ruth said, "he won't be home today." She hesitated. The key to Jackson's house was under a rock by the door, but she didn't feel right about just letting Mara in. "Where did you come from?"

"New York."

"Ah. Well . . . it's hot out here. Why don't you come back to my house. There's iced tea, and we can talk." She paused. "All the way from New York. You must be hungry."

Three

STUART sat at a wooden table in the windowless law library at the Cochise County jail. He had to get the contract signed to make it official so he could call over to the county attorney's office and ask the prosecutor assigned to the case for the disclosure file.

The door opened. A man came in wearing the regulation orange-and-white-striped jumpsuit.

Stuart got up quickly. "Jackson Williams? Stuart Ross." His hand shot out, and Jackson took it.

Jackson's hand was cold as ice. "Thanks for coming."

Stuart sat down again, and Jackson sat across from him. Behind the wire rims, his eyes were green; straight nose, high forehead, sandy hair thinning at the hairline. An English professor.

Jackson began, "Listen—"

"Wait." Stuart held up his hand. "I'm going with the full ten thousand as a retainer. That covers hiring an investigator, among other things. You need to sign this contract." Stuart reached down, pulled it out of his briefcase. "That way I'm officially retained, so whatever you tell me is protected by client confidentiality."

Jackson signed and pushed the contract back over to Stuart. "I have no idea what this is all about. I mean, it's . . . it's crazy, *Kafkaesque*. I thought of you because of that big murder case you won in Tucson. The homeless man?"

"Robert Buehler," said Stuart casually, as if it were just another case and not the apex of his career. "Sure."

"Mr. Ross," Jackson said imploringly, "I need you to get me out of here. There's a big misunderstanding. I didn't kill my wife."

"And you'll plead not guilty at the arraignment," Stuart said. He took a pad out of his briefcase. "I don't have the disclosure yet, so I can't fill you in on any details. You understand about disclosure?"

Jackson gave a little smile. "Like in *My Cousin Vinny*. All the information that goes to the prosecutor gets disclosed to the defense."

"Right," said Stuart. "I thought we might chat a bit and you could give me an idea of what went down. We'll get to specifics after I've read through the disclosure."

"All right." Jackson blinked as if to clear his vision. "Jenny was driving over the Mule Mountain Pass in the rain, and her car went over the edge. She was dead before anyone got to her. The police told me the man in the car in front said she was swerving all over the road, like she was drunk. I know she wasn't drunk; she never drank. At first I thought it must have been a blowout or she hydroplaned—her treads were pretty thin."

That was it? There was nothing there. Stuart leaned back in his chair and waited for him to say more. Finally he said, "I'm your *lawyer*. You can be straight with me. Why do you think they arrested you?"

"I don't know. But I have a theory. She took pills—probiotics."

"What the hell is that?"

"Some sort of herb and mineral mixture they sell at the Co-op that's supposed to cure everything. She'd been taking them about a month. She might have been having an allergic reaction, or maybe the stuff builds up over time and affects the nervous system."

"That's a thought," Stuart said. "I haven't seen the autopsy report yet. Everything's speculation till then." He leaned across the table. "I'll have more questions for you after I've read the disclosure. But I have one more for now. You and Jenny? Good marriage?"

"No," said Jackson.

Stuart stared at Jackson, taken aback. "How so?"

Jackson's face flushed. "It was my fault."

"Really." Stuart regarded his client with something approaching wonder. Could it be he was dealing with an honest man? "Any domestic violence convictions? That kind of thing?"

"No. We argued quietly, always very polite." Jackson sighed. "Jenny tried so hard to make everything nice, like she was running a marathon of perfection or something, and the more she tried, the more . . . *tired* I got." His eyes met Stuart's. "I was exhausted."

For a second, Stuart drifted back to the last plodding days of his first marriage. He looked across at Jackson with fellow feeling. "Marriage is a hard road," he said.

The guard was at the window in the door.

Stuart rose. "Unfortunately, our time's up. I'll go over the disclosure and get back to you soon."

"*Wait.* What about getting me released?"

"There's a five-hundred-thousand-dollar bond. You'll need ten percent. You got fifty thousand?"

"No." His eyes were urgent. "Surely you can get it lowered."

"Probably. I'll file a motion to modify the conditions of your release. What's the most you can lay your hands on?"

Jackson shrugged. "Ten thousand?"

"That's ten percent of a hundred thousand. I should be able to get it down to that."

The guard came in. Stuart shook Jackson's hand and put a paternal hand on his shoulder. "Hang in there," he said.

TYLER lunged and grabbed the ball from Mara. He bounced it down the cement drive and aimed. The ball whooshed through the net. "Three-pointer!" Tyler pranced, holding his arms aloft, his eleven-year-old elbows like little knobs. "The crowd goes wild!"

Mara flopped down on the grass by the

driveway. "Good shot," she said, kicking off her shoes. Ruth had told her this most incredibly awful thing—her father had been arrested for killing his wife. Ruth said it was all a big mix-up, but before she could tell her more, Tyler had come home from school, and now here she was playing basketball. Ruth had said right off that her father was a really nice person and they were sure to find out soon it was all a mistake.

Tyler flopped down beside her, using his ratty white T-shirt to wipe his face. "How come you've never seen your dad?"

"He's not my dad," said Mara. "I've got a dad in New York."

"Where's your mom?"

"My mom died of cancer."

"I have a dad," said Tyler. "He doesn't live with us. He's gay."

He looked over at Mara to see her reaction. He hardly ever told anyone his dad was gay. He guessed he told Mara because she had all those earrings and a tattoo and was from New York.

"No kidding." Mara looked up at the clouds. "Cool."

Tyler brightened. "Yeah. He lives in L.A.

with his partner, Tony. Me and Scott and Dan go see him every summer." His voice faltered. "I mean, we did."

"Scott and Dan?"

"They're my brothers. I'm the youngest, Scott's next—he goes to UCLA—and Dan's the oldest. He's twenty-two. He lives in Seattle with his girlfriend." He stole another glance at Mara. "You're going to stay with us, right?"

"Um-hmm. For now, anyway."

"Take Dan's room. Scott's is still full of junk." He paused. "Mom didn't marry Dad when he was gay. He got gay later."

RUTH sat in her car at the mailbox out by the highway and unfolded the *Sierra Vista Review* to the front page.

LOCAL ACTIVIST ACCUSES BORDER PATROL OF HARASSMENT

In a letter to a Dudley weekly, Ken Dooley, fifty-three, stated that the border patrol had come on his land several times without permission to look for illegals and twice had threatened him. Dooley went on to say that as a proud citizen of the United States of America, he owned a gun and was not afraid to use it against intruders. . . .

Ken Dooley, the local activist, who'd written the letter to the *Dudley Weekly* defending the Magician. Thanks to him, Jackson wasn't the lead story. Then Ruth saw it: COCHISE COLLEGE PROFESSOR CHARGED IN WIFE'S MURDER. Her stomach lurched.

Jackson Williams, popular professor, was arrested last night and charged with the murder of his wife, Jenny, after an autopsy revealed traces of a lethal poison in her system.

A lethal poison. Ruth felt a little nauseous. They didn't say what it was, didn't mention the probiotics. But surely, even unregulated items didn't contain any lethal poison. She read on. Just a recounting of the night Jenny died, nothing new, nothing to tell her why they had arrested Jackson.

She shoved the paper under the seat and drove down the road. She parked at Jackson's, got out, and found the key under the rock. Mara might want to see her father's house, and Ruth wanted to check it out first, maybe tidy up a little.

She opened the door. The living room looked just as it always had when Jenny, an anxious housekeeper, was alive. In the kitchen, Ruth sat down on a wooden chair at the farmer's table Jenny had refinished three years ago in a frenzy of activity after her miscarriage.

It was so strange sitting here. She could see Jenny clearly, five three, perfectly proportioned, wearing sweats because she always seemed to have just come back from working out. They'd never really been close. Ruth always felt clunky with Jenny and her pert little nose, her brown inquisitive eyes. Inquisitive? More like relentless. Ruth had learned to field her questions ever since that day . . . Why think of that now? That was over two years ago. But she couldn't stop.

"I've been meaning to ask you this for so long," Jenny had said, the two of them drinking coffee. "You know how the boys go see their father and his partner every summer?"

"Yes."

"You don't mind?"

"Mind?" Ruth laughed. She loved Owen as

much as she ever had once she'd gotten over the initial shock. "Why would I mind? They have a great time. Owen's an excellent father."

Jenny nodded. "But don't you worry?"

"Worry?"

Jenny folded her hands at the table. "*You* know. A gay man and his partner." She lowered her voice. "M-O-L-E-S-T-A-T-I-O-N."

Ruth felt as if someone had thrust a sharp knife into her. "Of *course not.*" Ruth's voice was thick with hurt. "What? If Owen were straight and I had daughters, does that mean he'd . . ." Tears came to her eyes. "If you knew him, you'd never—" She stopped.

"Ruth." Jenny stretched her hand tentatively toward her, then withdrew it. "I didn't mean . . ." She fell silent.

They sat, the two of them, paralyzed by good manners.

"Look," said Jenny finally. "My brother—I never tell people this, so please, please, don't say anything ever to Jackson, but . . . well, he was molested by a homosexual. When he was ten."

"Where's your brother now?" Ruth asked.

Jenny blinked, as if startled, then bowed her head. "Dead."

"I think," Ruth said, her voice like ice, "that *pedophiles* molest children, not *homosexuals*."

"You never know." Jenny's voice rose. "Children don't tell. They think it's all their fault. You should be careful to protect them."

"How dare you," said Ruth. She stood up, wanting to strangle her. "How dare you accuse me of not taking good care of my boys."

Jenny had never even apolo— Forget it.

Ruth came to in the present. It amazed her how this incident still had the power to upset her. She'd never told anyone about it, just carried it around inside her.

Outside, something rumbled. Thunder. Maybe it would rain tonight. They needed it. The desert always needed it.

A SPRINKLE of rain fell on the tin roof of Stuart's little wooden house in Dudley and on the two chinaberry trees growing in the front yard. Inside, Stuart lay stretched on his secondhand beige couch reading through the disclosure file on Jackson Williams.

Photocopy of Jenny Williams's driver's license. Pretty, dark-haired. Five foot three, one hundred and four pounds. Not an organ donor. A request for blood work on blood drawn from the defendant. That was odd. No reason for it that Stuart could see at this point.

What exactly had killed Jenny Williams? He skimmed the autopsy report. Respiratory failure and cardiac arrest, brought on by a lethal dose of aconite. Aconite. *What the hell was that?* Aha. Jackson had mentioned something about probiotic buildup—maybe aconite was one of the ingredients. If it was, then case closed.

Stuart skimmed the evidence sheet. One of the items seized by the police was an amber plastic bottle of prescription medicine, dated two years ago, labeled JACKSON WILLIAMS, AMPICILLIN CAPSULES, but containing not ampicillin capsules but traces of aconite, the same deadly substance found in Jenny Williams's body.

So much for the probiotic buildup.

Was Jackson that stupid to poison his wife, then leave the evidence right in his own house? They'd photographed the amber plastic bottle from two angles before they'd collected it from under a bed. Under a bed? The defendant had meant to dispose of it, the prosecution could argue, but when he went to get it, it was gone.

Nonsense, the defense would say; anyone could have planted it to frame my client. What *was* aconite? Where did it come from?

Nothing else on the evidence sheet seemed damning. A book, *Herbal Remedies,* probably something to do with that probiotic stuff. Right now Stuart was still skimming, getting the gist of things. He turned pages of depositions. Man in the car in front who witnessed the accident; colleague of Jackson's from the college, Sid Hamblin, saying it was common knowledge the only reason Jenny and Jackson didn't divorce was because the house was in her name and Jackson never had a dime. *Common knowledge.* Stuart snorted. The most egregious form of hearsay.

But *was* the house in Jenny's name?

And here, Anita Selby, who worked for a real estate agent, thought you should know, just had to blah, blah, best friend of Jenny Williams, blah, blah, remembered a conversation, *more hearsay,* Jenny was pretty upset. Jenny said to Anita two days before she died, *I'm thinking about leaving my husband. Anita, he'll kill me.*

It was raining harder outside now, the tin

roof amplifying the sound. Stuart sat back, suddenly tired, letting the deposition fall to the floor. Enemies. He needed some good solid enemies of Jenny Williams. Lots of investigating to do. George Maynard. He reached for the phone and punched in George's number. George was the best, as long as he stayed off the sauce.

MOST of the people who'd been at the AA meeting were gone when George Maynard stacked the last chair in the room at the church where it had taken place. "See ya," he said to the quartet cleaning up the coffee fixings. He opened the door and stepped outside into the dark. It was raining and had been for a while.

The air smelled fresh, filling him with energy, making him want to be doing something significant, important, not like that piddley feuding-neighbor civil case he'd just finished up for the attorney in Sierra Vista. He'd almost reached his car, a yellow fifty-six Cadillac Coupe de Ville, when his cell phone chimed.

He punched on the cell. "George Maynard here."

"Stuart Ross. Got a big case for you. Are you free?"

"Yep. What kind of case?"

"Stop by my office tomorrow, say ten thirty, and we'll talk."

"Not even a hint?"

"First-degree murder," said Stuart.

George smiled.

THE Magician walked slowly down Main Street. It had rained all night on the town of Dudley and on the mountains surrounding it and on the mountain pass where Jenny Williams had lost her life.

Now it was morning, seven o'clock and cloudy, but the rain had stopped, though it still dripped from the eaves of the houses and turned the brick buildings on Main Street a rich, deep red.

In his ancient black sneakers, the Magician hobbled down Main Street. His long beard was sodden, and the damp intensified the stale smell of his orange robe. The tip of his cap pointed downward, and his shoulder ached from the weight of his leather bag.

He was carrying a rock, quite a beautiful one he'd found by his cave, streaked with quartz, turquoise, and malachite. Malachite, malachite, malachite. Three times. Nothing got through when you thought three times. My rock, my rock, my rock.

How his bones ached. All the shops were still closed, but he stopped outside a restaurant, the Cornucopia, and looked at the pictures on the menu posted in the window. An orange, a banana, a pineapple, something green. His mouth watered. Kiwi, kiwi, kiwi.

Then, out of the corner of his eye, the Magician saw a police car cruising slowly, headed his way. He backed away from the restaurant, stepping off the sidewalk. My rock, my rock, my rock.

The police car was coming closer. The Magician raised his arm; the rock flew out of his hand and hit the window of the Cornucopia restaurant. Glass tinkled like wind chimes. The police car skidded to a stop and an officer jumped out.

"What the hell is going on here?"

The Magician raised his arms high over his head, as if invoking spirits from the four corners of the heavens. "It flew, Officer," he said. "It flew, it flew. My rock flew like a bird."

A bird, a bird, a bird.

AT NINE A.M., Stuart walked into his office, the Jackson Williams disclosure file under his arm. "See if you can run down Victor Robles," he said to Ellie. "He's the prosecutor on this case."

"He already called. He said, 'Welcome aboard.'" Ellie looked up from her desk, dark bangs flirting with her eyelashes.

"I'll call him back right now."

"No. You don't have time. You've got an initial appearance at nine thirty over in Justice Court. Your pro bono. The Magician threw a rock through the window of the Cornucopia restaurant." She paused and added pointedly, "Ken Dooley's already called."

"Aw, damn," said Stuart disgustedly. "Don't tell me I have to deal with Ken, too." The guy was a pain. What was with him, anyway? He'd appeared out of nowhere four months ago, and his rabble-rousing letters had become a fixture in the *Dudley Weekly*.

Stuart went into his office and put the file down on his desk. He was all fired up to work on the case this morning, but what could you do. He came back out and took a tie from the pocket of the jacket he kept ready on the coat-hanging thingie. Then he shrugged on his jacket and picked up his briefcase.

"It's the rain," he said to Ellie. "That cave must get damp."

Ellie giggled. "And Ruth Norton called you twice," she said.

Stuart frowned. The headband snapper. He was working for Jackson, not her. He needed to have George Maynard talk to her at some point since she might have useful information as a neighbor, but she was down the list from, say, Anita Selby, the dear friend.

"She says it's important," said Ellie.

"If she calls again, tell her I'm in court. Get her number and tell her I'll try to get back to her. George Maynard's supposed to be here at ten thirty. If I'm not back by then, get him to wait."

Stuart pulled into the last remaining parking spot in front of the Justice Court and got out, carrying his briefcase. Led by Ken Dooley, a line of picketers walked slowly up and down in front of the building. Ken wore sunglasses, a Hawaiian shirt, jeans, and sandals, his graying hair a boyish tangle of curls. The rest of the picketers were mostly women. They carried signs held aloft: ONE PERSON'S

HOMELESS IS ANOTHER'S HOLY MAN! FREE THE MAGICIAN!

Watchdogs for civil liberties. Stuart was glad to have them around, but they needed to understand that all the Magician, otherwise known as Ikan Danz, wanted right now was a nice dry jail cell.

"That's his lawyer," someone said.

"Hey, Stuart, you with us or against us?"

"I'm for the Magician," Stuart said, heading for the steps.

"Counselor Ross!" Ken Dooley loped over.

The air filled with a whiff of patchouli oil. Stuart stepped back. "Got to get to court," he said hurriedly.

"Just hold on a sec," Ken said. "I have someone here who wants to talk to you." He turned and beckoned. "Come on, Frieda."

A woman with dangly silver earrings walked over, wearing a dress embroidered by Guatemalan peasants. She was thin as a stork, her black hair streaked with gray and pulled back into a long braid.

"Mr. Ross?" she said. "I kind of look after the Magician." Her face was earnest, a do-gooder. "He's a free spirit. He doesn't belong behind bars." She held up an envelope. "I've raised the money to pay for the window he broke. Two hundred dollars."

"Wonderful. I'll tell that to the judge."

"Don't you want to take it?" she said.

"Give it to the owner of the Cornucopia for restitution. Got to go." Stuart turned, dodged Ken, and ran up the steps.

Inside, it was calm. The cloudy light shone off the beige linoleum. The big clock on the wall said nine twenty-five.

"Counselor Ross?" The bailiff was at the door to the courtroom. He gestured with his head. "Got your client inside."

Stuart strode into the court. Greatly diminished without his robe and pointed cap, the Magician, a.k.a. Ikan Danz, sat at the defense table dressed in an orange jumpsuit. Of indeterminate age, with his matted graying beard and pouchy eyes, he looked like one of those winos who hang out on city streets muttering to themselves.

Stuart sat down at the table next to him, standard reassuring hand going out. Touch, touch, touch; part of the job. Of course the guy was nuts, but was there a diagnosis? Couldn't find one in the file. "It's okay," he said.

"What, what, what?"

"A week," Stuart said. "I think I can get you a week."

The Magician's rheumy eyes cleared. He smiled, revealing surprisingly white teeth. "That'd be good," he said.

RUTH stood by the sink wearing silver beads, black pants, and one of those long tunic tops in burgundy that everyone wore a few years ago. She had pretty hair, dark reddish brown, so thick and curly, with that cool streak of white. Was it natural? Looking at Ruth, Mara thought it probably was.

"You look nice," Mara said.

"Thank you." Ruth smiled self-consciously. "Tyler's gone to school. Have some breakfast."

Mara spotted a box of Cheerios. "I'll have these," she said. She got a bowl, opened the refrigerator, and took out the milk.

Ruth sighed. "I was hoping Jackson would call last night to tell me what happened with the lawyer, but he didn't. When they did the autopsy, they found some kind of poison in Jenny's system. It was in the paper."

"Poison?" Mara picked up her spoon. "So

they think my father poisoned her," she said matter-of-factly. "Do you think he did?"

"Of course not," said Ruth. "I think it was these homeopathic pills she was taking. Probiotics. They'll have to analyze them to confirm it." She paused. "Jackson couldn't do something like that. Trust me. He's—helpful, *kind*—just a very nice person."

"What about Jenny? Was *she* nice?"

"I've known—knew—Jenny for years from being neighbors. Talking-over-the-fence kind of thing, except"—Ruth gave a forced little laugh—"there's no fence."

"Oh," said Mara.

"Anyway," said Ruth, rallying, "I've been trying to reach Stuart Ross—that's his lawyer—to find out what's going on."

"Is he a good lawyer?" Mara asked anxiously.

"He came here from Tucson. He won a big murder case there. He's kind of arrogant, but I guess that's how they all are. I've called him three times and he hasn't called back. I've got some shopping to do; then I'm thinking I'll go park myself in his office. You'll be okay here on your own?"

"Sure." Mara yawned to hide her disappointment that Ruth hadn't asked her to come along. "Is it okay if I take a shower?"

"Of course." Ruth picked up her car keys. "I'll get going, then."

"Do you think my father will be released soon?"

"I hope so."

Mara heard the front door close. Ruth hadn't answered her question when she asked if Jenny was nice. *Ruth hadn't liked Jenny.* That was interesting. Why not?

Mara left the kitchen and went down the hall and into Tyler's room. Through the window she could see the back of her father's house: a wooden stoop leading to a door. What if her father wasn't released right away? Could she go see him in jail? Were visitors allowed? Yes, they were; she'd seen it in a thousand movies.

"MAN, this feels good," George Maynard said happily as he closed the file, tilted back in the client chair, and swung his feet in their dusty tan cowboy boots up on Stuart's desk. "A first-degree murder case." He raised his bushy gray eyebrows. "That friend of Jenny's—Anita Selby? One who quoted her as saying—what was it?—'He'll kill me'? They can use that? It's not hearsay?"

"I'm not sure," Stuart said. "Might be excited utterance."

"I'll start with her, see if she's maybe holding a grudge against the husband. It'll give me an idea of Jenny's life, too."

"Good a place as any." Stuart tried not to look at the scuffed bottoms of George's boots digging into the finish of his wood desk. George was a former cop out of Sierra Vista, in his late forties, big-nosed, with a full head of gray hair, combining hard-edged energy and a laid-back attitude that had deceived more than one suspect.

"Not drinking now, are you, George?" Stuart asked casually.

"Nope. Been sober six months and three days. Got me a sponsor and all that good stuff." George's brown eyes twinkled.

"Good." Stuart paused. "Heard about you and Sandy. I'm sorry."

"Yeah. But what can you do? I put her through hell for years with my drinking."

George shrugged nonchalantly, but his eyes veered away. "Another thing." He rubbed his hands together. "Got any idea how come they wanted blood work?"

"Nope. Wondered that myself," Stuart said.

"Well, I guess that's it for now. Stay in touch, okay?" George swung his legs down from the desk and stood up. "Have Ellie make me a copy of everything. I'll stop by and pick it up later."

He walked out of Stuart's office to the reception area, leaving behind a residue of free-floating energy and a whiff of tobacco.

"You be good now, Ellie," Stuart heard him say.

Ellie giggled like a little girl. "You, too, Mr. Maynard."

Ellie never giggled like that around him. Stuart didn't know if George had ever actually cheated on Sandy, but there'd always been plenty of women who would have liked him to. How did he do it, Stuart wondered as he opened a paper bag and took out a sandwich from the Dudley Coffee Company. Early lunch.

His phone rang. "Stuart Ross here."

"Stuart, hey—Victor Robles."

The prosecutor in the Jackson Williams case, a good man; Stuart could work with him. "Well, what do you know," he said, imagining Victor sitting in his office. "Victor. My favorite prosecutor."

"So you got the Williams case." Victor laughed. "It'll be good to see you keeping busy for a change. You picked up the disclosure?"

"Yep. Very interesting." Stuart chuckled; he and Victor, just two good guys having a good time. "I see you've gotten a statement from the infamous Anita Selby."

"Infamous?"

"She *will* be. George Maynard's on it." He paused. "What's up?"

"I got some more disclosure, results on some blood work."

"Ah," Stuart said. "Noticed the request for blood work in the file. Couldn't figure out why."

"Guess you'll know soon enough, huh?"

"I'll send Ellie over to pick it up."

Stuart hung up. *Blood work.* Why? He opened the disclosure file on Jackson to reread the part about the blood work.

The front-door bell tinkled. *Damn.* Ellie

had gone to lunch. He went out, and there was that woman. The headband snapper.

RUTH had found a parking space in the alley behind the post office and pulled down the rearview mirror to check her hair and, though she normally didn't use it, spritzed on a little hairspray.

Why had she bothered? The lawyer with the ponytail was glaring at her, wearing the ugliest tie she'd ever seen.

"Look," he said, "this is a bad time. It's always a good idea to make an appointment."

Ruth bridled. "And how do I do that? Your secretary, who seems completely bored, if not brain dead, says she has to check with you, and you're never here. I need to know when Jackson's getting out."

"I'm about to start on the release motion right now."

"About to?" Ruth was aghast. "You haven't even started? You have ten thousand dollars and that's the best you can do?"

"The judge isn't going to consider a release motion till after the arraignment," the lawyer said. "That's not for a couple of days."

"A couple of *days?*"

"They'll set a date for the release hearing at the arraignment. It's the best anyone could do. Maybe you should go home and study up on our criminal justice system."

Ruth's eyes flashed. "What kind of case could they possibly have? I *assume* you're looking into it. Did Jackson tell you about the probiotics Jenny was taking?"

"Sorry." He held his arms wide, palms up. So theatrical. "I'm not at liberty to discuss what I talk about with a client."

"This release hearing," said Ruth. "Can I go to it?"

The lawyer looked at her thoughtfully. "It's an open hearing, but I think it would be better for Jackson if you didn't."

Ruth whooshed out a breath. "They'll have the hearing, and then he'll be out. You promise?"

"It's out of my control. But yes, I don't see why not. He's a solid citizen, employed, no record, unlikely to flee."

Ruth backed away toward the door. "You have to let me know as soon as it happens. I'll need to pick him up."

"Right. Sure. Fine."

Ruth left the lawyer's office, dodging

tourists, passing the Cornucopia restaurant, whose plate-glass window had been replaced with brown cardboard. Only yesterday she'd walked this same way, coming back from that same office in humiliation. Today the Magician and his bell were gone from the corner by the post office. Her face flushed. *No, not another hot flash. Ignore it.* At least it hadn't happened in the lawyer's office. It had gone well in the lawyer's office. She hadn't let him intimidate her at all.

It had been a while since she'd felt so good. She'd been a mom for so long she'd forgotten how it was to be anything else. Since Dan and then Scott had left home, she'd been in a kind of mourning for her boys, but years before that, with Owen's confession, a part of herself had been lost. Now, with that lawyer, it felt as though she'd rediscovered the person she used to be, who wasn't afraid to say anything.

Four

JACKSON sat on a gray metal bench at one of the two gray metal tables, bolted to the floor like everything in the pod, staving off dread and pretending to read *One Hundred Years of*

Solitude. In reality, he was studying his surroundings, the inside of a jail.

The fluorescent lights were intense, glaring
off the beige linoleum, the shiny pale green
cinder-block walls, the glass window where
the guards could look down and see what
everyone was doing. At the end of Jackson's
table, three inmates stared at the TV, limited
to two undisturbing channels, twitching and
batting at each other's arms as the animal
channel explained how jellyfish mated.

"Go, jelly man, give it to her!"

"Hey, Jackson!"

Jackson looked up and saw Leroy from
across the room playing cards with three other
inmates. Leroy grinned at him. His head was
shaved, and he was missing several teeth.

"How come you're always reading, man?"
Leroy said.

Jackson looked at him with interest. How
had he lost his teeth? A fight? Bad dentistry?
Why was he in jail? There was a fascinating
story there, he was sure. " 'Cause I'm not
playing cards," he said.

"College professor," Leroy guffawed to
the other three guys.

For a moment, all three looked at Jackson

with awe. "Cheez," one of them said. Then they went back to their cards.

In a way, thought Jackson, it was like a class. You walk in that first day and you don't know who anyone is, but you make assumptions. Then they begin to sort themselves out, and you find out that half the time your assumptions were wrong. Look at Carlos with that wonderful paragraph: *Tamales wrapped in bitter words* . . . He needed to get out, if only to see what Carlos wrote next. He would get released, he was sure. His lawyer was coming tomorrow with the disclosure, and then he would know what was going on.

The new guy, the old man with a gray beard they called the Magician, sat on the floor in lotus position. The Magician's eyes were closed, and his head rolled around as he muttered to himself.

What if I don't get out? Jackson thought suddenly, and the dread he had been staving off rose to confront him. Suddenly he was tired. His back ached for his reading chair at home; his stomach gurgled around a leaden mass of half-cooked macaroni.

The Magician stood up and began to walk, stately and careful, like a drunk on the way to the next bar. He muttered to himself, "Kiwi, kiwi, kiwi."

Totally nuts, poor guy. Jackson stood up, keeping his place in the book with one finger; he thought he would go lie down in his cell.

The Magician kept coming closer until Jackson could see the little pits on his red nose. He looked straight at Jackson.

"Kiwi, kiwi, kiwi."

Embarrassed for the guy, Jackson wanted to look away, but he couldn't. The Magician raised one skinny arm and plopped it down on Jackson's shoulder. As if restored by the touch, suddenly the Magician's eyes, like blue marbles in their pouches of flesh, turned remarkably clear. Then he spoke, so softly only Jackson could hear.

"Jenny," he said. "Jenny, Jenny."

RUTH and Mara had gone to Sierra Vista that afternoon to return Mara's rental car. Since Jackson wouldn't be getting out right away, Ruth decided Mara could just as well drive the old gray Volvo. Then they'd cooked dinner, and now Mara, Ruth, and Tyler sat in the living room on two couches draped with colorful Mexican blankets, a Scrabble board on the low table between them.

Ruth put her last tiles on the board to spell ELATE. "Why, I do believe I win," she said, smiling smugly. "And now I think I'll go to bed and read. You guys can put the Scrabble stuff away."

"Ruth?" Mara said, a little anxiously. "I want to talk to you about something."

Smile gone, Ruth sat down next to her on the couch. "What?"

"I was thinking, when Jackson gets released, the lawyer's going to call you to pick him up?"

"That's right."

Mara took a deep breath. "Let me do it."

Ruth's brow furrowed. "He won't know who you are."

"I'll introduce myself. *Please.* I really want to."

"He'll have just gotten out of jail."

"All the better," cried Mara. "Don't you see? It's my way of saying, Even if you were in jail, I know you didn't do anything."

"Oh, why not," said Ruth, giving up. "Then if they call me to sub, I can go." She stood up and left the room. "Night-night."

Mara folded the board and dropped the

tiles into the pouch and put everything into the Scrabble box. Tyler watched her.

"I want to go with you when you pick up Jackson," he said.

"You can't. You have school."

"What if I'm out when the lawyer calls?"

"I won't be at the house." She lowered her voice. "I'm going to the release hearing. I'll sit in the back. Jackson won't know who I am, but that way, I'll recognize him when I pick him up."

"Cool," said Tyler.

"That's me," said Mara. "The very coolest of the cool."

Tyler giggled. Mara glanced down the hall that led to Ruth's bedroom. "Come on, let's go in the kitchen," she said.

At the kitchen table in the semidark, Mara leaned toward Tyler conspiratorially. "Tell me about Jenny. Did you like her?"

"My brother Dan liked her. They used to run together."

"What about you?" Mara studied Tyler's face. His pupils were big as an owl's. "You didn't like her, did you?" She smiled at him reassuringly. "It's okay. You can tell me. I'm cool, remember?"

Tyler giggled again. "Well . . . she was kind of a drama queen. Like everything she did was really important, even if it wasn't. She lied, too. After you talked to her for a while, you just felt tired."

"What about Jackson?" Mara bit her lip. "Did *he* like Jenny?"

Tyler rolled his eyes. "He was stuck with her." He scooted his chair close to Mara. "I know something," he whispered. "There's this guy. He used to come to their house when Jackson wasn't there."

"You mean, to see Jenny?"

Tyler nodded.

"So. Maybe he was a friend."

"Jenny had girlfriends, not *guys*. Besides, he was kind of sneaky, like he didn't want anyone to see him. He went in the back door—the only place you can see it is from my bedroom window. And," said Tyler, "the last time I saw him go in was the day Jenny died."

Mara looked at him in astonishment. "The day Jenny *died?*"

"I know who he is," he whispered. "Randy."

"Randy who?"

"Dunno. But you can't tell Mom. Not yet."

"When can I?"

"When Jackson gets out. The guy might figure out I told and come after me. Mom can't protect me like Jackson would. He works right down the road at that house they're building. That's how I know his name. I heard one of the other guys talking to him."

STUART stretched out on his couch. Aaah. He leaned over and took the lid off the coffee he'd bought on his way home. The red disclosure file, along with the additional disclosure in plain manila, lay on top of the stack of newspapers.

He picked up the new file and opened it. Results of some blood work. He scanned through the jargon, looking for the point, and found it on the last page: Physical examination of the blood given by the defendant rules him out as the donor of the sperm found in Jenny Williams. Holy crap. Jenny had had sex the day she died, and not with her husband.

Well, well. While Jackson sat home nursing his *ennui*, Jenny had found a way out of *her* boredom. A lover. Was this good? On one hand, it brought in another suspect. On the other, it gave Jackson a motive. Nothing like infidelity to rouse murderous passions.

IT WAS AIR-CONDITIONING cool in the law library at the jail, but tiny beads of sweat collected on Jackson's forehead as he read the results of the autopsy. He looked up at his lawyer.

Stuart sat across from him wearing a navy jacket with metal buttons, staring at the green cinder-block wall, not exactly twiddling his thumbs, but looking as though he could be.

"Aconite?" Jackson said. "A lethal poison? Homeopathic remedies often have very small amounts of poison in them. I hope—"

"Herbal remedies," Stuart cut in. "They seized a book with that name."

"It was Jenny's," said Jackson. "I was about to say, I hope they analyzed the probiotics."

"Uh, you might want to keep reading," Stuart said.

Jackson went back to the red disclosure file. He read everything once except the part about the amber bottle under the bed containing traces of aconite. That he read twice. Then he looked at Stuart. "This is a mistake," he said. "There *were* ampicillin capsules in that bottle, just like the label says. I took them a couple of years ago when I got an ear infection. You can call my doctor and confirm it."

Stuart threw up his hands. "You're missing the point. Who cares what the label says?"

"But how can it be aconite? I don't even know what aconite is!"

"I'll tell you what it is," said Stuart. "It's what killed Jenny. My guess is someone spiked those probiotics."

"If I didn't know the truth," Jackson said, "and I read this, I would actually think I'd done it." He stopped as the realization rushed over him. Jenny had been *murdered*. It was completely out of the realm of his experience. "I didn't do it, I swear." His throat felt dry. "And if I did, why would I leave the stuff under the bed?"

"Exactly the point I would make," said Stuart.

"Somebody's trying to frame me." Jackson shuddered. Hanging there in the empty air, the words sounded absurd, the kind of thing some cartoon criminal might say. Except they were true.

"I hear you," Stuart said. "I'll be checking out who might have access to aconite, and also who had access to your house."

Denial, Jackson thought. Being so sure

about the probiotic stuff—that was just a form of denial. He should have known they wouldn't have arrested him if the probiotics had been what killed Jenny. But this—this was worse than he could ever have imagined. Who?

". . . doors?"

"What?" Jackson blinked. "Sorry. I can't think. I need to digest everything. What's the worst that can happen? I mean, what if I was convicted?" He swallowed. "Are we talking death penalty?"

"No, no," said Stuart. "It's not the kind of thing that gets charged as a capital crime. The most you could get is natural life."

Jackson took a deep breath.

"We were talking about who had access to your house," Stuart went on. "The way I see it, I could make a case for someone spiking Jenny's pills with the aconite, then planting the rest in that bottle and putting it under your bed. You lock your doors?"

"Yes, but we hide a spare key under a rock by the door."

"Is that common knowledge?"

"I suppose so. Anyway, it's an obvious place to look." He clenched his fists. "Who would hate Jenny that much? And that bottle under the bed—who could hate *me* that much?"

"Well," Stuart said, "we got a couple of people don't exactly like you, right here in the disclosure file. Anita Selby? Sid Hamblin?"

"Anita hates me, for sure."

"Why is that?"

"We used to get along okay; then she kind of turned on me." Jackson paused. "You know what? Anita called that night, just before they came to tell me about Jenny."

"Yeah?"

"*She* knew about the key. Maybe . . . No. She was Jenny's best friend. As for Sid, he's the biggest gossip at the college. He'd say anything if he thought it would get people's attention."

"Is it true what he said?" Stuart asked. "The house is in Jenny's name?"

"No. It's in both our names. See?" Jackson added disgustedly. "Sid didn't know what he was talking about."

"Okay, Sid's irrelevant. Jenny's death makes the house yours?"

"Yes."

"But if you had divorced, you could have lost the house in a settlement. The prosecution could argue that killing Jenny was a way to make sure you got the house."

Jackson's face reddened. "That's ridiculous."

"Just covering all the bases. Enough of that; let's move along."

"Wait," said Jackson. "There's something I wanted to tell you. Last night in the pod something really weird happened. There's this crazy man; they call him the Magician."

"I know him." Stuart looked annoyed. "He's in your pod?"

"Yes." Jackson leaned across the table. "He acts like he's completely nuts, but he came up to me, put his hand on my shoulder, and said, 'Jenny, Jenny, Jenny,' clear as a bell."

Stuart shrugged. "Probably heard the other inmates talking about your case. He's what they call chronically mentally ill. He'll babble along, and then out of the blue he has these moments of lucidity, but they don't mean anything. Look, we're running out of time and I want to get to this." He handed another file to Jackson. "A little more disclosure. Results of some blood work." He paused. "What it says is, Jenny had sex with someone the day she died."

"*What?* But we didn't—" Then he caught on. "No. Are they sure? Who with?"

"You tell me."

"I don't know. Jenny had a lover?" he said wonderingly. "I had no idea. Who—" He gazed past Stuart's shoulder at the wall.

"The investigator's working on it," Stuart said.

"Then that's it. It had to be the *boyfriend.* Maybe she wanted to break it off. Or maybe he's married and she threatened to tell." He tried to imagine this new Jenny. "I could find out if I weren't stuck in this damn jail. *You will get me out of here, won't you?*"

Stuart nodded. "Seventy-thirty your favor I can get you out on your own recognizance. And if not, at least I should be able to get the bond reduced to a hundred thousand."

GEORGE Maynard was parking his yellow Cadillac Coupe de Ville in front of the Sierra Realty Company, a tidy stucco building in a newish upscale complex outside Sierra Vista, when his cell phone chimed.

"George? Stuart here. You talked to Anita Selby yet?"

"Just about to. What's up?"

"Got some new disclosure." Stuart paused. "Jenny Williams had sexual relations the day she died. And not with her husband."

"Hot dog." George perked up considerably. "Then who?"

"I have no idea. Jackson doesn't, either, but maybe Anita does."

George punched off his cell, shrugged on his tan corduroy jacket, and slipped on a bolo tie with a turquoise clasp. Sam Elliot, he thought, favorite movie star of cowboy rednecks everywhere. I'll play it Sam Elliot. He smoothed the front of the jacket, patted the pocket with the little voice-activated tape recorder, and got out.

Behind the plate-glass window of the realty company were listings of houses and acreage for sale, along with a photograph of a woman with a tiny nose—Anita Selby, Realtor of the Month.

Sam Elliot opened the door and sauntered into the office. Six desks stretched to the back, but only two were occupied: one by a blond man; the other by the Realtor of the Month, in her forties, big gold earrings, white hair either premature or the color stripped out.

"Miz Selby?" he said, advancing closer.

She got up right away, a little hustler, smiling a big warm smile for the man she thought was a buyer. She wore a bright red pantsuit and was way too thin. "You must be the man who called about the Hereford property," she said brightly. "Mr. Jenkins?"

"No, ma'am. Name's George. George Maynard." He lowered his voice. "I'm an investigator for the attorney Stuart Ross."

She frowned. "Stuart Ross . . . that lawyer in Dudley? Why—?"

"He's the attorney for Jackson Williams."

She looked shocked. "I don't have to—" She stopped. "Do I?"

George smiled apologetically. "You kind of do. Sooner or later. There's a little place nearby we could have some lunch, talk."

Ten minutes later at the Lone Star Café, George and Anita sat on red vinyl seats in a booth at the back and ordered from menus with little cowboy boots designating the restaurant's specialties.

Anita glanced at George, then touched her perfect hair. "I'm feeling nervous," she said. "You're not taping this, are you?"

"Taping this?" George raised his eyebrows.

"Sure, I'm taping this, got a little microphone right here in my carnation."

"What carnation?"

George looked down at his lapel. "Oops, no carnation."

Anita laughed. "So we're just going to talk and that's it?"

"You might be asked to give a deposition to the defense later, but there's a good chance we'll just talk and I'll be on my way. Look at it like this: Everyone's entitled to a defense, right?"

Anita looked doubtful. "I guess so."

They paused as the waitress set down a burger and fries for George and a salad, dressing on the side, for Anita. George picked up his burger. "You and Jenny were pretty tight, huh?"

"She was my best friend." Anita poured two drops of dressing onto her salad, then disconsolately speared a tomato. "I miss her."

She sighed and gave him a look, up from under her eyelashes, flirtatious in its helplessness. Coming on to him a little bit. Divorced, George would bet on it.

"We were on the phone almost every day,"

she went on, "and Fridays I'd meet her after work at the Outback Bar and Grill."

"Sure," said George. "That place over in the foothills."

"It's nice there," said Anita. "Everyone's friendly. We'd have a couple of drinks—you know, yak it up."

"I bet." George chuckled. "Couple of attractive women out on the town, leave hubby at home and have a blast, huh?"

For a second, Anita looked uncertain. She touched her hair again. "I mean, you couldn't expect her to spend every second with her husband," she said. "She had to have her own life, too."

George held out his hands, palms up. "Course she did."

"Let me backtrack a little," said Anita. "Jenny liked the atmosphere at the Outback, but she didn't really drink. I mean, she quit three years ago when she got pregnant."

George paused, surprised. "Pregnant?"

"She miscarried. It was so sad. The doctor said she should forget about having children. But Jackson would never talk about it. *Never.* Jenny said it was like he was just *gone.* And after that, when her brother Kevin died, Jackson wouldn't talk about that, either."

"Her brother? Must have been young. What'd he die from?"

"I'm not sure. I never met him, but"— Anita lowered her voice—"I think it was drugs."

George tsked-tsked and changed the subject. "You didn't like Jackson much, did you?"

"I hated him." Her face reddened. "I mean," she said, "because of the way he treated Jenny."

"You ever see him hit her, be violent?" George asked.

"No, not *that,* but it's almost as bad to be ignored. Jenny was always anxious around him, like whatever she did wasn't going to be good enough. Finally she gave up; she just wanted out. She told me that. It's all in my statement. Didn't you read it?"

"Sure, but why don't you run through it again for me."

Anita rolled her eyes. "The day before she died, Jenny called and said she needed to talk. We went out to lunch, and afterward we went and sat in the park—over by the old high school?"

George nodded understandingly. "Yes."

"That was when she told me. She said, 'I'm going to leave Jackson. I'm going to tell him tonight.' And then she started crying. 'Anita,' she said, 'I'm *so* scared. He'll kill me.' "

Word for word, thought George, the way she had told it in her statement. Word for word, nothing added the way it might be if you were really remembering. "Whew." He raised his eyebrows. "So did she tell him she was going to leave him?"

"Of course she did." Anita stared at George as if he were crazy. "She had to have. That's what this is all about."

"Called you and told you after she broke the news, huh?"

"She didn't have to. It's obvious. I knew she'd told Jackson, and he'd killed her just like she said he would."

"I used to be a drinker," said George. "Out in the bars till late, and when I left, I'd say to people—this was back when I was married— 'Gotta go, my wife's gonna kill me.' "

"*No*," said Anita emphatically. "It wasn't casual like that. Anyway, when you look at the whole picture, it doesn't even matter if she actually said it or not."

"Wait." George scratched his head. "She didn't say it right out?"

"Weren't you listening? It was basically the gist of the whole conversation."

"The gist? So she didn't actually say he'd kill her?"

Anita looked exasperated. "She *did* say that."

"She'd put up with him for a long time. Why'd she suddenly decide to leave, I wonder."

"It wasn't sudden. It all accumulated till she'd finally had it."

"Or maybe *he'd* had it. Gave her an ultimatum."

"Who? Jackson?"

"No. What's-his-name. The boyfriend."

"*What* boyfriend?"

"That miscarriage," George persisted, a shot in the dark. "Maybe the baby wasn't Jackson's and that's why he wouldn't talk about it."

Anita's gray eyes hardened. "You bastard." She stood up, reaching into her purse. "You think I was born yesterday? You butter me up, then move in for the kill! You're trying to smear her reputation! Isn't that what defense lawyers do? Blame the victim?" Anita's voice was like steel. "I've *cooperated*, but this is as far as I go." She flung a twenty on the table and stalked out.

George sat alone in the booth. There were other ways of finding out who Jenny's boyfriend was. What he did get made it clear Anita hated Jackson, which should make a dent in her credibility. He was sure she was lying, the way she told the story so precisely the same, lying to get even with Jackson. Any reason for that other than Jackson's treatment of Jenny?

WHEN Tyler got home from school, Jackson's Volvo was parked in front of the house, but his mom's car was gone and the house was empty. His mom and Mara must have gone somewhere together. Having Mara around was almost as good as having his brothers back, but he wished he hadn't told her about seeing the man go into Jackson's house, because now he had a stomachache.

Mara got along well with his mom; they talked and talked. What if she blurted it out accidentally before Jackson got home? Then his mom would get upset and throw all these questions at him.

Tyler roamed the house from room to room, ending up in his bedroom. He looked out the window at Jackson's backyard. He could see the stoop where Jackson liked to sit in the evening. Sometimes he would look out his bedroom window and see Jackson sitting there and Jackson would wave at him. He wished Jackson were home right now so he could talk to him. At least he hadn't told Mara *everything*.

"HELLO?"

When he heard her voice, so sweet, so familiar, Jackson's knees almost buckled. He turned his back to the guard down the hall and cupped his hand over the receiver. "Ruth," he said, "it's Jackson."

"Oh," she said. "Oh, my goodness. How are you?"

"Okay, but listen, I can't talk long. I talked to my lawyer. It wasn't the probiotics. It was something called aconite. They found traces of it in a bottle under the bed."

"*What?*"

"Someone must have planted it."

"Who?"

"I don't know. But I just found out Jenny

was having an affair with someone. I don't know who. Ruth, can you try to remember everyone who went to the house when I wasn't there?"

"I don't . . . I can't . . . I'm still taking it in."

The guard was coming toward him down the hall. "I have to go," said Jackson. "If you think of anything, tell my lawyer."

Stunned, Ruth sat on the beat-up couch in the living room. In a matter of minutes, everything she had assumed about Jenny's death had shifted from faulty probiotics to deliberately planted poison and a mysterious lover. How awful that Jenny had been having an affair. Why couldn't she just ask for a divorce? From Tyler's room, Ruth could hear Mara and Tyler giggling, playing some game. Keep them out of this, she thought. Children, innocent.

She could hardly remember the days before Jenny died, much less remember who had gone to Jackson's house. She'd been innocent, too. Like she'd been with her ex-husband while he was falling in love with another man. An innocent, faithful dupe.

She focused back to the present. The only person she could think of offhand that she'd seen going to Jackson's was Jenny's friend

Anita Selby, and she had nothing to do with anything.

Five

"C-R-TWO-zero-zero-zero-five-zero-six-seven-one. State versus Jackson Williams!"

Mara gave a little gasp. Sitting near the back of the crowded courtroom, she craned her neck to see better. Ruth had been called to sub that morning, so Mara jumped into Jackson's Volvo and drove over to Dudley. She'd thought she might recognize her father right away, but in the jumpsuits, the prisoners all looked alike.

One of them rose; it must be Jackson, since they'd called his name. He had wire-rimmed glasses, sandy hair. He was shuffling toward the podium where a lawyer waited, shuffling because he had chains on his ankles. His hands, too. Mara sat rigid with embarrassment for him. How cruel. The lawyer at the podium must be Mr. Ross—a ponytail?—waiting for her father.

"Motion to modify conditions of release. You may proceed, Mr. Ross," said the black-robed judge.

"Your Honor." Mr. Ross rested a fatherly hand on Jackson's orange shoulder. "As you can see in the motion, my client is a highly respected member of the community. No priors whatsoever. He owns his home and has no reason to flee. I'm asking that he be released on his own recognizance."

"Thank you, Mr. Ross." The judge's voice was weary. "Prosecution? Are there victims present?"

A woman rose from a table up front. "No, Your Honor," she said, "but I do have a letter from Mrs. Grace Dixon, the victim's mother, and one from Mrs. Dixon's doctor." She waved sheets of paper. "I made copies for the defense"—she walked over and handed them to Stuart—"and Your Honor, if I may approach, copies for the court."

Mara watched as the judge read the letters. Then the judge set them down. "Let it be noted that the court has read the letters from the victim's mother and her mother's doctor. You may proceed."

"Your Honor, the state opposes this motion," said the woman. "The defendant is facing life imprisonment, so he has every reason to flee. The victim's mother lives in Tucson and is elderly, or she would be here today. As you can see from her letter, Mr. Williams has put her in a state of terror for her life. It's already affected her health. The defendant's release could damage it further."

"Your *Honor*," said Mr. Ross, "this is slander. No one has threatened Mrs. Dixon in any way, and my client is presumed—"

The judge cut in. "That's enough, Counselor. I'm ruling on the motion." He banged his gavel. "Motion to modify conditions of release is granted."

Mara's heart fluttered.

"Bond is reduced to two hundred and fifty thousand dollars."

Two hundred and fifty thousand? Was that good? Mara had never been in a courtroom before. There was no one to ask. But the lawyer's shoulders slumped. Her father put his head in his hands.

It wasn't good. What was going on? The lawyer could tell her. She'd just wait outside the courtroom till he came out. Mara stood up. A good-looking Hispanic kid in a black T-shirt with a shaved head, a few seats down from her, stood up, too.

Stuart walked at full speed out of the

courtroom, just ahead of the Hispanic kid.
He had to be in Justice Court in fifteen minutes, needed to pick up a file at his office on
the way. He dodged a pretty blond teenager
coming toward him just outside the door.

"Mr. Ross—"

"Sorry. Not now," he said without stopping.

"Wait!" she called. "Is Jackson Williams going to be released?"

Who was she? One of Jackson's students?
"No," he said.

"Why *not?*"

"Call my office. I'm running late."

What was the point of calling his office? He
wasn't even there. Mara stood disconsolate in
the big marble lobby of the courthouse.

"Hey, you here for Mr. Williams, too?"

She looked up. There was the Hispanic kid.

"I saw you trying to talk to his lawyer.
Those lawyers. No time for anyone." He gave
her a smile so cockeyed that she smiled back.

"How do you know Jackson?" she asked.

"He's my teacher. He's supposed to be
really good, but I only had him a couple
classes and then they arrested him."

"Oh!" said Mara. "I'm Mara. I'm his
daughter."

He looked at her with interest. "He mentioned he had a daughter back east. Cool. I'm Carlos."

"He was supposed to be released."

"Guess his lawyer screwed up." Carlos shook his head sadly. "You'll have to go see him in jail. Tell him I said hello."

STUART left the courthouse, drove to his office, parked illegally, and ran in to get the file he needed for Justice Court.

Ellie handed it to him. "I called over to the jail," she said. "They transferred the Magician into the nut pod."

"Good. Call Ruth Norton, okay?" Stuart said. "And tell her Jackson's not getting released."

"Okay," Ellie said. "And Ken Dooley was here, asking about—"

"Tell him I died," said Stuart.

"And, Mr. Ross?" She looked upset. "I need to talk to you."

"Not *now*, Ellie."

"Soon!" she called as he went out the door.

On the way to Justice Court, Stuart thought about Jackson's case. George Maynard had told him about the interview with

Anita. Story too pat, and she hated Jackson. Not credible, according to George. But would a jury see her that way? See if George could dig up some dirt, maybe a little slippery real estate deal, a dissatisfied buyer. Nothing from Anita about the boyfriend.

Stuart was liking the boyfriend better every day. Sure, the prosecution would say that gave Jackson a reason to murder his wife, but the burden of proof lay with them. The more players, the more it confused the jury. Got to find that boyfriend.

He parked at the Justice Court, ran up the steps, and pushed open the door. The bailiff was standing just inside. "Sorry, Counselor, everything's been continued."

"What?"

"Judge went home with the flu."

What next? Stuart turned on his heel and trudged back out the door. He got into his truck and drove back to the office, circling the parking areas several times before he found a place far, far away.

Ellie was at her desk, reading. What was she doing reading on his time? She looked up. "Mr. Ross? I have to quit."

Stuart stared at her blankly. "You what?"

Ellie looked like she might cry. "I have to quit working for you."

"When?" Stuart asked flatly.

Ellie bit her lip. "Tomorrow."

"Tomorrow." Stuart sat down in disbelief. "Ellie," he said. "You can't quit tomorrow. Whatever happened to two weeks' notice?"

"My mom needs me." Her voice was plaintive. "My grandmother had a stroke up in Phoenix. She's in the hospital, and we have to go there and help her."

"Help her?" Stuart threw up his arms. "She's in the *hospital,* Ellie. That's what they do in hospitals; they help people. You can't wait, maybe a week? What does she need *you* for?"

"To hold her hand. It's lonely in hospitals."

"Your mom can still go. You can join her later."

"My mom's scared to go to Phoenix by herself. There's all that traffic." Ellie began to cry. "Oh, Mr. Ross, why do you always have to argue so much?"

MARA had just finished cleaning Ruth's kitchen when she heard the sound of the school bus on the highway and went out to meet Tyler. "Listen," she told him, "Jackson didn't get released."

"Oh, man!" Tyler threw down his backpack on the driveway. "How come? I miss him. And I wanted to tell him about Randy."

"Speaking of Randy, when you walked past the construction site," said Mara, "did you see him?"

"No. He hasn't been around for a while."

"We're going to fix this Randy thing right now," said Mara decisively. "I'm going to go talk to those guys, see what I can find out."

"No," said Tyler. "What if they tell?"

"I won't say who I am." She paused. "I'll go out the back and around to the road so they can't see where I'm coming from."

Tyler followed her to the back door. "Be careful," he called.

Mara went around Jackson's house and out to the road to the half-finished house belonging to the man from Phoenix. Two sunburned men in red bandannas, muscular arms gleaming, were loading bits of wood into a battered brown pickup.

"Hello?" she said.

One of them kept loading the truck, but the

other one grinned at her. He looked like a pirate. Maybe this wasn't the greatest idea.

"I'm looking for Randy," said Mara. "Randy, Randy, um . . . I can't remember his last name."

"You must mean Randy Gates," said the pirate man. "He quit a couple, three weeks ago."

The other man got in the truck, but the pirate man came closer. Mara could smell his sweat. She backed away, heart beating fast.

"What do you want with old Randy, anyway?" he asked.

"Nothing," she blurted out.

"I bet." He grinned again, slow and sure, as if he knew exactly why she was there. "There's nothing Randy can do for you that I can't."

"*Earl.* Let's go," said the man from inside the truck.

"Think about it," the pirate said to Mara as he got into the truck. He leaned out the window. "You know where to find me."

His partner gunned the engine loudly, and the truck careened down the road to the highway. What did he mean, Mara thought, *There's nothing Randy can do for you that I can't?* Then it struck her. Mara took off, loping down the road. Tyler was waiting by the front door.

"Did it work?" he asked.

"Yes," said Mara. "His name's Randy Gates. Listen to me." She hustled Tyler inside the house. "He quit a couple, three weeks ago. Around the time Jenny was killed. We *have* to tell your mom."

RUTH pulled into the driveway as it was getting dark. She hated subbing. Considering what they paid, was it even worth it? Her middle was rigidly compressed by her tummy-control panty hose, and her feet, in red flats fashionable ten years ago, ached.

Tyler came running out. "Mom!"

"You're home," said Mara at the door. "How was your day?"

"Where's Jackson?" Ruth asked.

"Come into the living room," said Mara, "and sit down. Would you like some tea, coffee, fruit juice, water?" asked Mara brightly.

"Water." Ruth sank to the couch. "Where's Jackson?" she said again.

"Jackson didn't get released," Mara said.

"No!" cried Ruth. "Why not?"

"I think it was because Jenny's mom had her doctor write a letter saying she might die if he got out."

"What?" said Ruth. "That mean old bi—
How could she?"

"Tyler and I need to tell you something,"
Mara said.

Ruth stared suspiciously at Mara. "What?"
The phone rang. "Get it in the kitchen, Tyler,
would you?" she said absently. "Tell them to
call back." She paused. "What?" she said to
Mara again.

"Wait till Tyler gets here," said Mara.

"Mom!"

Ruth felt her face flush suddenly, sweat
prickling the back of her neck. Oh, God, not
another hot flash. "*What*, Tyler?"

He came into the living room, carrying the
phone. "It's Jackson."

Ruth grabbed the phone. "I'm going to tell
him about you now," she said to Mara.

LIGHTS out, but Jackson tossed and
turned. *Hi, this is Mara. Hi, this is Mara. Hi,
this is Mara.* Her voice rang in his head.

"Mara," he'd said, shamed that he would
be talking to her for the first time in eighteen
years from the county jail. "How is Maggie?"

"My mother died," Mara had said. "Two

years ago. Of cancer." Then the guard had said time was up. "I'll come visit," she'd said.

Maggie dead? Maggie, who had taught him to dance, *you klutz, funny*. So light on her feet even when she was pregnant.

So many times he'd imagined what Mara might be like. Little Mara. The name had been his choice. He would have gone with naming her after Maggie, but she hadn't wanted that.

Maggie hadn't wanted a lot of things she used to want before the baby came. Things like freedom and spontaneity. He knew now that those things were meaningless, really. Maggie said he didn't care about the baby, but he did, more ferociously than he ever could have imagined. He just couldn't see why the baby couldn't join in with them in the life they already had. He'd been so immature.

Well, how much better had he been with Jenny? Things had been all right once—until the miscarriage. It might have brought them closer together, but instead he'd withdrawn and Jenny had thrown herself into self-improvement. Maybe they should have talked about it more, but he'd been unable to.

Six

THE door to the office of the English Department out at Cochise College was half open. Inside was a big dark-haired bearded man in a denim shirt and buckskin vest. He was tilted back in his chair, feet on the desk, reading through a sheaf of papers. George tap-tapped on the doorjamb, and the man looked up.

"Sid Hamblin?" said George.

The man took his feet down. "That's me. Come on in."

"I'm George Maynard, investigator for Stuart Ross—an attorney over in Dudley?" George took out a card and passed it over.

"Sure," Sid said heartily. "Office right there on Main Street. I live in Dudley—One fourteen C Moon Canyon—moved there when I got divorced a couple of years ago. I know why you're here. Sit down."

George sat on an old oak chair. The office was small and cluttered. Behind Sid was a poster of the Grateful Dead and next to that a window. Outside, George could see his yellow fifty-six Cadillac, two male students hovering around it like wasps around fruit.

"Hell of a thing, divorce," George said.

"But it sure beats murder, huh?"

"Let's talk about that," said George. "Jenny's murder."

Sid stroked his beard. "Speaking of Jenny," he opened a drawer and took out a colored plastic bottle. "Probiotics. Jenny turned me on to them. They really give you a boost. Jenny was a wonderful woman, by the way. Used to see her at those departmental get-togethers— a bright light in an otherwise dreary scene."

"Where else did you see her?"

"Sad to say, that's about it." Sid reached down and brought up a bottle of water. He opened the pill bottle, shook one out, and swallowed it with the water.

"Let's talk about Jackson," said George. "You seemed pretty anxious to let the police know the lousy state of his marriage. Some kind of rivalry going on there?"

"No rivalry, not at all. I'm not into these ego trips—more of a live-and-let-live kind of guy. Except when it comes to people murdering their spouses. That kind of gets to me." He looked at his watch. "Uh-oh, time's up. Got a class." He rose from his desk. "Young minds are waiting."

George stood, too. From somewhere, a bell rang.

At the door, Sid said, "Wish I could have helped you out more."

THE phone rang in the office of Stuart Ross, attorney at law. Stuart clenched his head, tugging at his hair with both hands. Not again. It could just ring.

Ellie and her damn grandmother. Wow, he thought, I'm turning into a heartless monster.

The phone rang again. Stuart jerked involuntarily, knocking over his cup of coffee. He stood up hurriedly to escape the stream of liquid seeping over the edge of his desk. Wasn't he supposed to be in court in twenty minutes? No, it was okay. That was yesterday.

Stuart went out of his office through what had once been Ellie's domain, where little piles of documents seemed to have swelled into mountains overnight. In the bathroom, there were no paper towels. He grabbed a fistful of toilet paper and started back through the reception room, knocking a stack of papers off Ellie's desk. He knelt to pick them up.

The bell tinkled.

Stuart looked up, and there at the door was that headband-snapper woman. *Damn.*

The phone rang.

It rang some more as Stuart, crouched and vulnerable on the floor, armed only with toilet paper, stared up at Ruth. She looked a little spiffier than he remembered, not so thrift store.

"Aren't you going to answer your phone?" she said.

"What?"

Ruth came over to the desk and picked up. "Mr. Ross's office." She paused, glancing at Stuart.

Stuart shook his head back and forth.

"I'm so sorry," said Ruth, her voice melodious. "Mr. Ross is in a meeting. All right. Fine." She hung up. "No message," she said.

"In a meeting," said Stuart gratefully. "How'd you know to say that? And it sounded so true."

"My ex-husband and I ran a very successful business in L.A. I know all about office management." Ruth looked around. "This place is a pigsty. No wonder Jackson didn't get released."

"I resent that," said Stuart hotly. "He

didn't get released because Jenny's mother opposed it. And my secretary quit." His voice turned whiney. "Now I don't know where I have to be or when."

Ruth walked to the desk and sat in Ellie's chair. "Why don't you look at your calendar? It's right here." She held it up. "You have a one o'clock this afternoon in Division Five and a four o'clock in Division Two. And"— Ruth shot him a meaningful look—"it looks like Jackson at two thirty." Her expression changed. "Oh, dear."

"I didn't forget that," said Stuart defensively.

"I told him about Mara last night."

"Who's Mara?"

"Jackson's daughter," said Ruth.

"Ah. Didn't know he had one."

"Well, he does." Ruth straightened some papers on the desk and picked up a stack of catalogs. "Junk," she said, dropping them into the wastebasket. "Sit down. You're making me nervous."

"You're"—Stuart's voice was hopeful— "you're not a legal secretary, are you?"

"No, I'm not."

Not a legal secretary. Stuart sat down.

"There's something I have to tell you," Ruth said.

"What?" Stuart's voice was weary.

"My son Tyler told me this last night. He was home alone the day Jenny was killed. They're building a house near us, and Tyler knows some of the construction workers because he stops and watches them work sometimes." She paused. "He saw one of them go into Jenny's house by the back door when Jackson wasn't home—it was around noon, the day she was killed. He saw him go in other times, too, when Jackson was gone."

"You're kidding me." Jenny was banging this construction worker? "Maybe she hired him to do some work on the side," Stuart said neutrally. "I don't suppose you got his name?"

"Yes, we did get his name. Randy Gates."

Randy Gates. He'd never been a client, but Stuart had seen the guy in court plenty of times, seen him graduate from marijuana to methamphetamine. Randy Gates, habitual criminal.

"Interesting," he said.

"Interesting?" said Ruth. "More than that. He might have been Jenny's lover. He might have planted that poison. And"—Ruth's voice was triumphant—"he quit right after Jenny was killed."

MARA turned the key and pulled open the door to Jackson's house. It smelled dusty inside. She took a deep breath and tiptoed into the living room. The room was oppressively neat. Mara kept her hands to her sides, as if to touch anything would be a violation—of what, she didn't know.

She went down to the end of the hall, opened a door, and there was her father. His presence, anyway, in the rows of books in the built-in bookcase, a desk with a computer monitor and keyboard but no hard drive, stacks of papers, photographs on the wall.

She went closer for a look. A man in wire-rimmed glasses, with a mustache and an earring, grinned at her rakishly from a place of mountains and a stream—Jackson; but in that place of freedom, he looked nothing like the chained man in the courtroom. Next to that was a photograph from the same place, but a woman. Jenny.

Mara made herself look. Jenny, little nose, dark hair, shining eyes, in a tank top that showed off buff and burnished arms, legs strong in hiking shorts.

Mara opened drawers at random— here were his pencils, pens, old photographs. She riffled through photographs not suitable for framing, blurred or damaged. Mara looked down at a photograph of herself: tanned and laughing, taken at a beach when she was two.

Her mother had had one just like it, except this one had been torn into four pieces, then taped together.

Why was it torn? Had Jackson done it, then had a change of heart and taped it together? No, probably it was Jenny. The Jenny that Ruth didn't like; Tyler, either. But why would Jenny hate her so much she'd torn up her picture when she'd never even met her?

"Hello? Anybody home?"

Mara jumped guiltily. A man's voice, coming from the front of the house. She picked up the taped photograph and hurried down the hall. The door she'd left ajar was now wide open, and a man stood in the opening.

He walked into the hall, smiling. "Saw you go in earlier," he said. "Never introduced myself the other day. Name's Earl Kershaw.

Thought I'd stop by, seeing as how you know Randy and all."

The man from the construction site. The flirty pretend-friendly one who looked like a pirate. What was he doing here?

He stepped closer. "Randy and I go way back. Told ya, there's nothing you can get from Randy that you can't get from me."

Turn. Run. Run to the back door. But Mara felt paralyzed. "Like what?" she said coldly, trying to keep her voice from shaking.

"Like maybe"—he reached behind to his back pocket, pulled out a baggie, and dangled it in front of her—"a little weed?"

"Marijuana?" said Mara.

"Sure. Randy told me he sold to the woman who lived here. The one who was . . . uh . . . Who're you? Her kid?"

"Not exactly," said Mara. "Jenny smoked marijuana?"

"Regular customer, according to Randy," said Earl.

RUTH left Stuart's office before he got back from his afternoon court date. She pulled the door behind her so it locked. Presumably he would have a key, though you couldn't assume much with someone so disorganized. Well, it was better now. Ruth had tidied up. Stuart had kind of explained how things worked, and they'd gone over the billing before he'd gone to court. She'd even typed up a motion on the computer and laid it neatly on his desk.

Now she drove home into a sun that was blinding, thinking she'd told Mara she would be home no later than two and it was nearly five. She felt uneasy, nerves jangling. Why?

She turned off onto her road and passed the construction site; no men working there now, all gone home. As she pulled into her driveway, Tyler came barreling out the door.

"Mom, listen to this!" said Tyler excitedly as she reached the house. He and Mara followed her into the living room. "This friend of Randy's came to Jackson's when Mara was there!"

Ruth blinked. "A friend of Randy's came to Jackson's?"

"Earl," said Mara. "Earl something."

Ruth sank onto the couch and put a book she'd brought home with her on the coffee table. "What did he want?"

"He tried to sell her some dope!"

"Dope?"

"I told her she should call the cops, but she won't."

"I'm not calling the cops," said Mara, her voice worldly. "It was only marijuana. Earl told me Jenny smoked marijuana all the time."

"Oh, she did *not*," said Ruth, aghast. "If you'd known Jenny, you'd have known he was lying. He saw her smoking it?"

"No, but he said she was a regular customer of Randy's."

Ruth shook her head. "I don't think so."

Mara sat down next to Ruth and picked up the book from the coffee table. "What's this?" she asked, changing the subject.

Ruth brightened. "Arizona Rules of the Court. I'm going to study it. I have a job—working for Jackson's lawyer."

Seven

GEORGE pushed open the door of the Outback Bar and Grill, and the first thing that hit him was the sweet smell of alcohol. Ahhh . . . years of nights full of warm and instant camaraderie; hilarious jokes, long-winded stories, teams that won, teams that lost. And here now, tonight, Johnny Cash on the juke-box. Wow, if that didn't take him back a long, long way.

George stepped back outside and used his cell phone to call Stan, his sponsor.

"Hiya. George here," he said when Stan answered. "I need help."

"Where are you, George?"

"In front of a bar."

"Go home, George."

"Can't. It's part of an investigation. I started in and had a moment of weakness, is all. Johnny Cash was on the jukebox, and all of a sudden it was déjà vu all over again."

"How's this for déjà vu, George? Remember that time you woke up in your car at the Circle K parking lot at eight in the morning and those kids were staring at you through the car window? Shouting, 'A wino! A wino!' Remember how Sandy cried when you got home, worried you'd been killed in a car wreck? Then, when she saw your condition, sort of sorry you hadn't been?"

There was a long silence. "Yeah," George said finally.

"You okay?" asked Stan.

"Yeah, I am. I can handle it now. Thanks."

George ended the call and went back into the bar.

The jukebox was silent now, the place dim. A weeknight, it was nearly empty. George sat down at the near end of the bar.

The female bartender was late thirties, blond with a snub nose. She saw George and came over. "Hi, there." Big warm smile.

"Ginger ale," said George.

"Ginger ale it is," she said. "That'll be two dollars."

He gave her three. "Name's George Maynard." He reached into his coat pocket, pulled out a card, and gave it to her. "You're—?"

She looked at the card, then wiped her hands on the towel tucked in her belt and shook his hand. "Mickey Dings."

"Maybe you wouldn't mind if I ask you a few questions about a customer—Friday-night regular. Jenny Williams? You knew her?"

"Yes." She flinched. "Little Jenny. It makes me sick. Imagine her husband doing that."

"What have we got here?" George smiled to take out any sting. "The judge and jury?"

"Looks pretty cut-and-dried to me, from what I read in the paper." She raised her eyebrows. "What? You're saying it's not?"

"We'll see. Tell me about Jenny."

"She came in most Fridays with Anita Selby. You know, come with a friend; if you don't score, you can still have a good time."

"Jenny was looking to score?"

Mickey shook her head. "Not Jenny. Anita. Jenny was a good choice to come with 'cause usually she'd stay out of Anita's way."

"What do you mean, stay out of her way?"

Mickey smiled. "Anita could get B-I-T-C-H-Y if you moved into her territory. I saw it happen once with Jenny. This was three or four months ago. Anita shows up with some guy Jenny knew, and Jenny starts talking to him, kind of flirtatious. Pretty soon he's not paying attention to Anita anymore. She got all pissed off and stormed out. They kind of laughed about it, like, What's with her? But I think something was going on there 'cause they left together."

"Oh?"

"Jenny and Anita didn't show up together the next week, but after that they did—dear friends, same as usual."

"Some guy," said George. "You got a name?"

Mickey shook her head. "A big guy, late

forties maybe, beard. Talked a lot. I think, yeah"—she snapped her fingers—"he worked at the college, like Jenny's husband. That's how she knew him."

Big guy, beard . . . Sid Hamblin, thought George. Sid, who said he only saw Jenny at departmental get-togethers. Liar.

Two pounds heavier from a steady diet of bread, bologna, and pasta, the Magician, in his ancient black sneakers, stepped out into the sunlight, his leather bag over his shoulder. The bag tinkled when he moved; they'd given him back his bell. Due to the vigilant efforts of his fans in Old Dudley and the crowded conditions at the jail, he'd gotten early release. He blinked, screwing up his eyes.

"Free at last," chirped the woman who'd met him in the lobby. "I'm from SEABHS." See bus. She wore a purple pantsuit and was overweight and looked very clean. "Isn't it a beautiful day!"

The Magician wiped his watery eyes on the sleeve of his orange robe. The bell tinkled. "See bus, see bus, see bus," he said.

"SEABHS," said the woman in the same chirpy voice. "Southeastern Arizona

Behavioral Health Services. Ken Dooley called me about giving you a ride back to town." She took his arm gingerly, steered him over to a red car, and stood aside for him to get in.

"Robot, robot, robot," said the Magician, standing his ground.

She smiled. "Go on," she said encouragingly. "Get in. We'll have you in town in no time."

He got in the car. His pointy cap hit the roof, so he took it off. The woman came around to the driver's side and got in, too. She sniffed, then pushed a button and the window slid open.

She glanced over at him. "Let me ask you something, sir. I don't know your history, but you must have meds. Are you taking them?"

"His story, his story, his story," he said.

"Yes," said the woman. "Well. It's shocking they didn't see to your meds in jail. Always trying to save money."

They had reached the far end of Main Street. "It's odd," said the woman. "I can't get a handle on what your diagnosis would be. You're not like any . . . I should have looked at your file. I could run you over to the doctor. He could update you a bit on the meds."

"Stop. Stop. Stop." The Magician put his hand on the door.

The woman braked and pulled to the curb. "Sir," she began, but the Magician stepped out of the car.

One foot, two foot, onto the sidewalk. Tinkle, tinkle, tinkle, he put on his pointy cap. One foot, two foot, free again. He left the SEABHS woman behind, walked past the houses, and climbed slowly up the dirt path to his cave. He smelled creosote and prickly dust and jasmine. Jasmine, jasmine, jasmine.

The path turned around a stand of mesquite, and then he saw the balloons. Red balloons, their strings moored under rocks on each side of the cave entrance. Frieda had been here. Frieda, Frieda, Frieda. He reached the balloons. They were a little deflated, slack, as if their air had slowly leaked out while they waited for him.

He stooped and went into the cave. There were three gallon jugs of water, his sleeping bag, and on top of it a paper sack. He looked inside. Dried apricots, currants, walnuts, pecans. Frieda, Frieda, Frieda. He opened his leather bag and took out three bologna sandwiches and put them in the paper sack.

Then he lay down on the sleeping bag and went to sleep.

GEORGE yawned as he turned down Moon Canyon and headed for Sid Hamblin's house. He was driving the clunker, an ugly gray '85 Oldsmobile; it was what he drove anytime he went to talk to a suspect who would be looking for the Caddy.

He drove up the steep hill at the end of Moon Canyon. The road had turned to dirt a little way back. Halfway up, George parked and got out. It was hot, but he wore his tan corduroy jacket to conceal the Colt Commander pistol in his shoulder holster.

Above him was Sid's house, an A-frame of gray aged wood with a big deck. A black Ford Explorer was parked a little way down the driveway. Um-hmm. Sid had looked like the kind of guy who would drive a big bully vehicle like that to look down on people from.

Over the blur of cicadas, his cell phone chimed. *Damn.*

"George Maynard here."

"George? Stuart. Listen, the kid that lives next door to Jackson's saw someone going in to see Jenny the day she was killed. Saw him some other times, too, but never when Jackson was home."

"As in, maybe that's the guy that was making it with Jenny?" said George. He glanced up at Sid's house.

"Maybe. Guess who."

"Sid Hamblin."

"Sid Hamblin? What does he have to do with anything? No, it was Randy Gates. You remember Randy."

"The *druggie?*" George said in surprise.

"Yep. He was working construction down the street from Jackson's, but he quit when—" Stuart's voice faded out.

"I'm losing you," said George.

"Check it out, okay?" Stuart shouted. "See if you can locate—"

But Stuart was gone. Damn cells. Especially in Dudley. The hills blocked them. Randy Gates, that little turd. Jenny seemed too classy for him. He didn't fit in. Maybe important. George knew from experience that things that didn't fit in were important.

George trudged up to steps that led to a porch on the side of Sid's house. He knocked on the door, listened, knocked again. A terra-cotta sun hung by the door, and next to that was a window, slatted blind down. He peered in, trying to see through the slats.

"No one's home," someone said. "Just called him on my cell."

George turned. A man with curly gray hair and sunglasses stood a few yards below. He was wearing a long cream-colored collarless shirt that George wouldn't be caught dead in and sandals with tire bottoms, and he carried what looked like a *purse*.

"Yeah?" said George. "I just used my cell, and they don't work too good around here."

"You have to get to know the blind spots," said the man.

George gestured toward the Ford Explorer. "That his?"

"It is." The man shrugged. "He probably walked downtown."

"So even though he's not home, you came up here anyway?"

"I wanted to drop this off." He brandished a newspaper. "Here." He tossed it up, and George caught it: the Dudley local weekly.

"Thought he'd get a kick out of my latest," said the man.

"Your latest?"

"Letter. I'm Ken Dooley," the man explained.

Ken Dooley was that guy who'd threatened the border patrol. *He and Sid were friends?* "Hey," said George, "did you know Jenny Williams?"

"Jenny Williams," said Ken. "I met her a couple of times."

"Here at Sid's?"

"Can't remember where," said Ken glibly. "If I see Sid, I'll tell him you stopped by. Who'd you say you were?"

"Harry," said George, reaching. "Harry Potter."

Ken laughed. "Bet you get razzed about that, big time."

George looked at his watch and suppressed a yawn. "Got to run," he said. "Sales rep meeting in twenty minutes."

"WHAT'D you find out about Randy Gates?" Ruth eyeballed Stuart significantly from behind her desk in his office. "It has to be important. I mean, Jenny would never smoke marijuana. She was one of those my-body-is-a-temple kind of people."

"My investigator's working on it," Stuart

said, and finished off a cheese Danish. "What's on for the day?"

"Court appearance at ten in Division One," said Ruth, "then another at eleven thirty over in Justice Court. Files are on your desk."

Stuart groaned. "Busy day." He went into his office for the files.

"You could eat healthier," said Ruth. "All that sweet stuff raises your blood sugar; then it plummets. What are you doing Saturday?"

"Nothing."

"Then come to dinner at my house. I'll have Million Dollar Chicken, and you can meet Mara and Tyler."

"Sure," said Stuart, coming out with the files. "Why not."

"Your tie's crooked," Ruth called as he went out the door.

Alone in the office, Ruth went to work. Billing. That was the key; not the legal stuff. Billing could make or break you. She worked for an hour, then sat back in her chair and looked out the window.

All she'd done since she'd moved to Arizona basically was substitute teach, working with other people's kids so she could be home with her own when they got out of school. Now here she was in a grown-up's place. Ruth felt as though without even knowing it, she'd been living in a dark closet, and now a door had opened and she could see the vibrant world outside and be part of it again.

The bell tinkled, the door opened, and a man walked in. He had curly graying hair and tinted wire rims and wore jeans and a loose white Indian kurta. "Hello there," he said. "I was just walking by, and I saw you sitting at Ellie's desk."

"It's mine now," said Ruth with a touch of pride. "I'm Ruth Norton, Mr. Ross's new office manager. Ellie quit."

"Ken Dooley." He smiled modestly. "Maybe you've read some of my letters in the paper."

Ruth brightened. "Yes, I have. My goodness. Is the border patrol still giving you trouble?"

"Sure, but I'm fighting the good fight," said Ken. "Trouble is my business. Guess my friend Stuart doesn't mind a little trouble, either. Heard he got the Jackson Williams case. I was thinking about it just the other day. Who's the investigator Stuart's got on it? Guy with the bushy eyebrows, fiftyish—forgot his name."

"I haven't met him," she said. "You were thinking about the case?"

"Yes. Wondering if it was something I might want to look in to."

"Oh." Ruth flushed with excitement. "That would be so wonderful if you could help. Jackson is definitely innocent."

"Really?" His eyes met hers. "Why don't you tell me about it."

"I can't," said Ruth. "But I can make an appointment for you to talk to Mr. Ross."

"Not now." He shrugged. "Maybe later. I'll call."

GEORGE drove back home and called Stuart from his apartment.

"Stuart Ross, attorney at law."

"Ellie?"

"No. Ellie quit. This is Ruth. I just started working here."

"Ellie quit? Damn. Well, hello, Ruth. This is Stuart's investigator, George Maynard."

"George Maynard. Oh, good. Someone asked me your name and I didn't know it. Now I do."

"Stuart around?"

"No. He's really busy today. I can have him call you."

"That's okay. I'll call him at home this evening."

George hung up. Stuart had asked him to locate Randy Gates. He picked up the phone again and spent the next half hour calling around to friends in law enforcement to get a lead on Randy's whereabouts. Couple of possibilities, which he wrote down.

Then something occurred to him, and he called a cop he knew in Sierra Vista. "Anita Selby," he said. "Got anything on her?"

"The real estate lady?" his cop friend laughed. "You're kidding me. Woman of the Year here in Sierra Vista two years ago. She got a plaque from the mayor."

So the only thing Anita had ever done to get the attention of law enforcement was get an award. Well, he planned to talk to her again, spring Randy's name on her. Randy was a lowlife, and Stuart couldn't see a connection to Jenny Williams, but that was all the more reason to check it out. For all he knew, Jenny had been a big-time dealer, hiding behind respectability. Just thinking this made him tired.

He stretched out on the couch and fell asleep.

George woke suddenly. What? Where? He rubbed his arm, still asleep from being wedged under the sofa cushion. The light coming through the window was dim—dusk. He'd slept for hours. Damn. Sid Hamblin. His AA meeting. Forget that; Sid had priority.

He groaned, got up and strapped on his shoulder holster, put in the Colt Commander, jacket over everything, then staggered outside to the Olds. He picked up a Whopper on the way out of town and ate while he drove, window down, cool air blowing in. By the time he got to Dudley, it was dark, half moon low in the sky. He drove slowly up Moon Canyon and parked a ways down, where he couldn't be seen from Sid's A-frame, then got out and walked.

George saw the Ford Explorer and, even better, a light coming from a back window of the A-frame. He reached the steps and hiked up to the door. The newspaper Ken Dooley had tossed to him was by the door. Guess old Ken wasn't that important.

George knocked, then knocked again. He went around to the deck. Double French doors, uncurtained. He could make out a living room, a big leather couch. He went closer. The French doors were not only unlocked, they were slightly ajar.

"Hey, Sid," he called. "George Maynard here."

Silence.

He'd spent years as a cop knocking on doors, and something here didn't feel right. George unholstered his gun and stepped inside without touching the doors. A light came from a hallway.

He skirted the big leather couch. At the end of the hall was an open door, and through the door, George could see a computer.

Suddenly he felt a presence: eerie but familiar, not human. Something cracked underfoot. Green disks the size of big buttons were scattered on the floor. He saw the empty bottle. Tums Ultra.

"Sid?" he called again, but he knew what that presence was. He took a deep breath and went through the open door into the room.

Sid Hamblin was lying on the floor, facedown. He was wearing only a pair of boxer shorts, gray with red hearts.

George got to Sid fast, thinking heart attack. He checked the pulse, then saw the purple bruising on the outstretched arm, and the legs where they touched the floor. *Lividity*. The guy was dead and had been for a while. Probably already dead when George had knocked on his door that morning and chatted with Ken Dooley.

He took a deep breath, thinking of the Tums Ultra scattered in the hall. Heart attacks sometimes masqueraded as indigestion. But what came to mind was poison, just like Jenny Williams. And Jackson in jail, so maybe he was off the hook. Something nudged at the corner of his mind—something related to Jenny Williams that Sid had said—but he couldn't get hold of it.

STUART was lying on his couch virtuously watching the Discovery Channel when his phone rang. "Stuart Ross," he said.

"George here. Sid Hamblin's dead."

Stuart sat up on the couch *"What?"*

"Yeah. I found him, couple hours ago. Couldn't rouse anyone at his place this morning, so I went back there tonight, walked right in; doors weren't locked. He was lying on the floor, dead. I called Dudley P.D., then hung around to make sure they did the scene the way they should. They're calling it an apparent heart attack."

"Heart attack." Stuart felt a twinge of anxiety. "How old was he, anyway?"

" 'Bout your age. Reason I went to see him was he lied to me the first time I talked to him out at the college. He might have been having a thing with Jenny Williams."

"What? And you didn't tell me?"

"You were big on Randy Gates. Besides, the cell was fading."

"I'm still big on Randy Gates. He was at Jackson's the day Jenny died. He could have planted the aconite under the bed then."

"If he did, I'm betting he was someone else's pawn," George said. "The more I think about Randy, the more unlikely it seems, him and Jenny, a health nut. She— *Bingo, I got it.*"

"Got what?"

"What I was trying to remember. Sid was taking the same stuff she was. Those probiotics. In fact, he took some right in front of me in his office. Said she turned him on to them."

"Damn," said Stuart. "Someone spiked his pills, too? Hot dog. That would get Jackson off the hook." He paused. "Uh, maybe."

"Yeah, maybe. If Sid bought the pills after

Jackson got arrested. Wait for the autopsy. Could have been a heart attack. For all we know, he choked on a Tums; they were all over the floor."

"I'll try to get a rush on it." Stuart gave a hollow chuckle. "Throw out those magic words, *serial killer.*"

THE Magician woke in the night. The sound that woke him was mingled with whatever he'd been dreaming. But he knew his sounds. Bug sounds, bird sounds, animal sounds. This sound had not been bug or bird or animal. Then he heard it again. Not close yet, but coming. *Human.* Robot, robot, robot.

Dressed except for his old black sneakers, he rolled off the sleeping bag and pulled them on fast, no time to tie, grabbed his leather bag, stooped his way out from the cave.

Human coming. *And he knew who it was.* Someone who'd figured things out—that they didn't add up. Robot, robot, robot. He hurried as quietly as he could up the rise behind the cave. Human getting closer. He began to run, tripped on a rock, grazed his ankle, rubbed it, smelling the copper penny of his own blood. Bleeding, bleeding, bleeding. The shoelaces on one shoe had caught on a mesquite bush branch, and he tugged his foot free, leaving the shoe behind.

He smelled human. Closer, closer. Robot, robot, robot. Jail had weakened him. The bag was heavy, full of treasures weighing him down. He tossed it away and ran.

Eight

TO JACKSON'S left was a Mexican man, and beyond the plate-glass window were three members of the man's family: a boy, a girl, and, with the phone to her ear, a wife. To Jackson's right, a straggly-haired Anglo talked to a sobbing woman on the other side of the plate glass.

He was suspended in a time eighteen years ago, when he had lived in a scruffy apartment in New York City, waking to a child jumping on the bed, Maggie beside him. Now Jackson waited for Maggie's daughter, *his* daughter, to come into the visiting room. She was late; he'd thought maybe she wasn't coming—too ashamed or scared.

Then the guard had showed up. "Williams, you got a visitor."

A breathless young woman appeared beyond the glass in front of him. She wore a lilac-colored T-shirt and tiny sunglasses. She was tall and blond and beautiful. His daughter. Pride swelled inside him, unearned pride, but he couldn't help it.

She removed her sunglasses and picked up the phone. "Can you hear me?"

"Yes." He paused. "You look like your mother. Beautiful."

"Thank you," said Mara. "Everyone always says that. I mean"—she flushed—"that I look like her."

"It's true."

"She died. She had cancer." Beyond the glass, Mara's eyes filled with tears, and she blinked them away. "Sorry."

"For what?" said Jackson. Maggie, beautiful Maggie, was dead. He already knew, of course, but Mara telling him again now brought it closer to home. "You have every right."

Mara took out a Kleenex from somewhere and blew her nose. "Anyway," she said matter-of-factly, "Ruth and Tyler say hello."

Jackson felt relieved. Even though he'd spoken to Ruth on the phone, somehow he'd imagined that she and Tyler would soon forget him. With Mara there, maybe they would remember him a little longer. "Give them both a hug for me," he said.

He looked at her, trying to think what to say. If only he were out, they could go somewhere and talk.

"Carlos says hi, too," Mara said.

"Carlos?" said Jackson, astounded. "You met him? Where?"

"At the release hearing. He says you're a really good teacher. Listen, I know you like poetry." She looked at him obliquely. "I thought since I don't know you yet, I would read you a poem."

She opened a book and began to read. *"Come, let us tell the weeds in ditches—"*

The Louise Bogan poem, the one he'd read his class that first session, lifetimes ago. Jackson closed his eyes. It was magical in a way, but in another way, the worst thing she could have done, because it made him see things clearly. He was living in a sterilized world, everything neutral-colored and fluorescent, and he would be here forever, hardly ever get to see his daughter. Even now the guards were hustling the visitors to go. He began to cry.

"Oh, my goodness," said Mara. "I didn't mean to upset you."

He lowered his head until he got himself under control. Then he raised his head. "Thank you for the poem. Please come again."

"Oh, I will." Mara hung up the phone and stood up. Then she leaned down and picked up the phone again. "Don't worry," she said. "We'll get you out of here. I promise."

THAT evening, Stuart came to dinner at Ruth's, and afterward they all sat in the living room and played Scrabble: Mara, Tyler, Stuart, and Ruth. "Sid Hamblin certainly looked like the kind of person who would have a heart attack," said Ruth. "Overblown." She sighed. "I didn't like him much, and now I feel bad about it."

"Save your guilt," said Stuart, "for something that matters." No reason, he thought, to freak her out by telling her about his suspicions concerning Sid's death unless they were confirmed.

"Sid Hamblin? That fat guy at Jenny's memorial?" Tyler asked.

"Stocky," said Ruth.

Stuart lined up his Scrabble tiles on the little wooden holder. He scowled. He was in third place, behind Mara and Ruth. It was only a game, but he couldn't help wanting to win. It was in his blood.

Mara placed some of her tiles to make JIV-ING, hitting the double word space with the G. "That's thirty-four," she said.

"Very good," said Ruth. She wrote it down.

"I have an idea," Mara said to Stuart. "About what you could do to get Jackson released."

"Yeah?" Stuart looked at Mara warily. They hadn't talked much about Jackson over dinner. It had been a good dinner, too—something called Million Dollar Chicken, made with salsa and honey. Everything had been fun. Now here was the price tag. "What?"

"You could talk to Jenny's mother, make her understand he couldn't have done it. Then maybe she'd write a new letter saying it was okay for him to be released."

"No way," said Stuart. "As Jackson's attorney, I'm not allowed."

"Her name is Grace Dixon," Ruth said to no one in particular.

"Grace Dixon," said Mara. "You *know* her?"

"I sat with her after the funeral." Ruth sighed. "What an ordeal."

"*I* could talk to her," Mara said to Stuart. "Where does she live?"

"Some retirement community outside of Tucson. But you can't." He stared down at his tiles; he had something there, but he couldn't figure out just what. "It would be the same as me talking to her." Stuart moved his tiles around. He looked at the board. Aha!

"There must be something I can do," Mara persisted.

"Sorry," said Stuart distractedly. He glanced at Ruth as he put down his tiles: ABETTING on the triple word space. "Used up all my letters," he said triumphantly. "Eighty-three points."

TAPED to the open door of the office of Victor Robles, the deputy county attorney prosecuting the Jackson Williams case, were several cartoons about lawyers. They had been there all the years Stuart had known Victor. Stuart tapped on the doorjamb, and Victor looked up from his desk.

"Stuart. Hey." He stood up, extended his

hand, and shook Stuart's. "Good to see you. Come in and close the door."

Stuart settled back in the chair. "Jackson Williams. Some case, huh? A real can of worms."

"A can of worms?" said Victor neutrally.

"You heard about Sid Hamblin?"

"Yeah, about an hour ago. I was out of town this weekend." Victor steepled his fingers. "A heart attack. How old was he, anyway?"

"Our age."

There was a little silence. Victor studied the ceiling.

"My investigator found him," Stuart said.

Victor leaned forward. "George Maynard?"

"Yep," said Stuart. "Best there is."

"When he's sober."

"He's sober," said Stuart firmly. "Been going to AA six months now." He paused. "They sure saved my life once upon a time."

There was another little pause.

"Anyway," said Victor, "George was probably wasting his time, talking to Sid. His statement wasn't admissible, so his death is neither here nor there, as far as Jackson Williams goes."

"You think not?" Stuart said. Might as well

put his cards on the table. "What if the cause of death turns out to be the same as Jenny Williams? Sid was taking that probiotics stuff, too."

Victor shrugged. "So what? Aconite is not an ingredient of probiotics. For all I know, half the college is taking it. It's not relevant. That book they seized, *Herbal Remedies?*"

"It was listed in the evidence inventory, but I haven't seen it yet."

"Oops, sorry," said Victor. "Guess my secretary forgot to include a copy in the disclosure file. It was sitting there right in Jackson's house, and it's got a couple of pages devoted to aconite. *Aconitum napellus,* monkshood. Talks about fatal dosages and everything."

Crap, but outwardly Stuart's expression didn't change.

"Is that damning or what?" said Victor smugly. "Not only that, but you can buy *Aconitum napellus* right off the Internet. Haven't got the report back from the computer guys yet."

Stuart shrugged dismissively. "I think Sid was poisoned, too, and my guy's been sitting in jail. I asked Dudley P.D. to put a rush on the autopsy. If the cause of death turns out to be the same as Jenny Williams, then case dismissed; Jackson goes free."

"Unless Sid bought those pills before Jackson got arrested. They work in the same place. Plenty of opportunity."

Stuart already knew this, but a good offense was the best defense and all that. "In my opinion," he said, "the case sucks. There's more. I have a witness who saw someone going in the back door of Jenny's house the day she died. Guess who? Randy Gates."

"No. Randy Gates?" Victor looked appalled. "You're kidding me. She's way out of his league."

"I didn't say they were engaged."

Victor laughed. "You think it was Randy who had sex with her and that looks good for your client?" He leaned across the desk confidingly. "Between you and me, if my wife was screwing around with Randy Gates, I'd consider poisoning her myself."

"Randy's a good suspect whether they had sex or not," said Stuart, treading water. "Sleazy guy with a history of violence. He was at the house, could have planted the aconite."

"Not Randy." Victor shook his head. "Too dumb to do anything that complicated."

"So he's working for somebody else. What-ever. Someone had sex with Jenny, and if it wasn't Randy, all the better. It brings in even more suspects. Reasonable doubt."

"It's a toss-up," said Victor.

"That's your headache, isn't it?" Stuart tried to look smug. "Toss-ups are fine by me. Toss-ups are what reasonable doubt is all about." He looked at his watch. "Got to run." He stood up. "Good talking to you, Victor."

Stuart walked out of the office. He hadn't paid much attention to the fact that they'd seized that *Herbal Remedies* book. A book about aconite right there in Jackson's house. If Sid had been poisoned like Jenny, unless they could prove Sid had bought the pills after Jackson was arrested, then Jackson was screwed—all that Randy Gates stuff was just a smoke screen for a jury.

And Victor didn't even know if Sid had been having a thing with Jenny. Hadn't had time yet to think about that perfect motive and put two and two together and try for a match with the sperm found in Jenny. Two homicides. *Aw, man.* Next thing he knew, he could be begging Victor for a plea to save Jackson from the death penalty.

What the hell. Wait for the autopsy report. Proceed normally until then and hope for the best.

GEORGE parked the Olds in the strip mall across from Sierra Realty. He'd rather have driven the Caddy, but Anita had already seen it. It was a workday morning, early, and the parking lot was full of cars, including Anita Selby's, a red Honda. He knew the Honda was Anita's because fifteen minutes ago he'd watched her pull in.

He kept thinking about Anita. A cold person under that phony smile. Poison—a woman's crime, people said. Had Jenny been carrying on with Sid and lied to Anita about it, then Anita found out?

George took the lid off his coffee cup and sipped. He didn't think asking Anita to lunch would fly after that last time, and he didn't want to walk into an office full of staring people while Anita threatened to call her lawyer. He needed an unguarded moment.

Ten minutes later Anita sashayed out of the office and got into the Honda. George started up the Olds and followed, three or four cars behind, as she drove south, going toward the foothills. When the cars thinned out, he drove slower so he would still be pretty far behind, just a harmless old codger in his crummy Oldsmobile.

Coming up on Jack Rabbit Road, her blinker flashed. George slowed even more. There wasn't much up Jack Rabbit Road except three or four high-end houses, so he wasn't afraid of losing her. The road curved, sides thick with live oak and bird of paradise. No sign of her car. Then there it was, in front of a house—another car, too.

He pulled over to the side, opened his window, and heard voices.

". . . love it," Anita was saying. "Big fireplace in the family room, oak floors throughout."

"It didn't say there wasn't a pool," whined a woman's voice. "We're really set on having . . ." The voice faded away.

George kept the engine running for the air-conditioning but left the window down. He heard voices again. Car doors slammed. Engines started up. George realized, too late, he should have turned his car around before he parked. A Jeep Cherokee drove by, tires spitting dust, the Honda Accord just behind. Oh, well, just let her go by; she wouldn't recognize him in the Olds. The Honda passed him, too, then braked, pulled over, stopped.

Anita Selby got out, slamming the door behind her. She marched over. "What do you think you're doing!" she shouted. "Stalking me?"

"Easy, easy" said George soothingly. "A few more questions, is all."

"More?" She stamped her foot. "This is ridiculous. Wasting your time digging up dirt on Jenny, stalking me, when there are people you *should* be talking to, people a lot more involved than I was."

"Like Randy Gates?"

"Who?"

"Why don't you get inside," said George. "Air-conditioning's on. Take a load off."

Reluctantly, she got into the car. "I've never heard of Randy Gates. Who is he?" she asked lightly, her voice a little too casual.

"Drug dealer."

"A drug dealer. Great. More slander." She slouched into the seat. "Jenny *never* did drugs. She didn't even drink alcohol."

"He was seen at her house the day she

died," George said. "Other times, too. If you got an explanation, I'd like to hear it."

Anita sighed wearily and put one hand on the dashboard as if to check out her manicure. A good one—pale polish, French tips. "Probably," she said, "she was buying drugs for Jackson."

"Jackson," repeated George. "Good one. Throw the slander right back in my face." He paused. "How about this? How about she was buying dope for Sid Hamblin."

Anita froze, the hand on the dashboard stiffening to a claw. "Sid's dead," she said. "I read it in the paper. A heart attack."

"High blood pressure, probably," George said. "They haven't done the autopsy yet. Gee, I hope the stuff Jenny was getting for him from Randy was marijuana and not methamphetamine. You rev up a bad heart with meth and there's no telling . . ."

"Oh, God." Anita fanned the air.

"You can go all night, I hear, on meth," said George. "I figure Jenny was buying it just to keep things interesting in the sack. She was sleeping with Sid, wasn't she?" He paused. "Must have pissed you off when you found out."

"I don't believe this," said Anita through her teeth. "As if I cared. Okay. Here's something that you're not going to want to hear."

"And why not?"

"Because it's about Jackson. Jackson and Ruth Norton."

"Who the hell is Ruth Norton?"

"His neighbor. Jenny used to complain how she could never get him to fix anything, but if something needed fixing next door, he'd be over there in a shot. He spent all his time next door."

"And?"

Anita looked at him in disgust. "How obtuse can you get? They were having an *affair*. Jenny told me, crying, that Ruth Norton and Jackson were having this blatant affair right under her nose."

STOPPING by for a quick update before heading over for a hearing in Division Two, Stuart squared his shoulders and looked at Jackson across the table in the law library at the jail. "Sid Hamblin?"

"What about him?"

"He's dead."

"Dead?" Jackson looked genuinely shocked. "How?"

"Apparent heart attack."

"Apparent?"

"They always say that until it's confirmed by an autopsy." Stuart paused. "He have a history of heart problems?"

"Not that I know of." Jackson leaned back in his chair and blew out a long breath. "Whew. I'm still taking it in."

"On a lighter note," said Stuart, "I've hired Ruth as my office manager."

"You have?" Jackson's face lit up the way it always did when Stuart mentioned Ruth. "That's really great. You can discuss my case with her anytime. You have my permission."

"Listen to me," Stuart hurried on. "They seized your hard drive in the search. Is there anything incriminating on it? Searches on the Internet for various poisons? Late-night diatribes in a chat room or e-mails about how much you hate your wife?"

"I've never gone into a chat room," said Jackson. "As for e-mails, I delete them."

"They can retrieve deleted e-mails."

Something flickered in Jackson's eyes. He

looked down at the table and back up. "Casey," he said reluctantly.

Stuart pounced. "What? Who's Casey?"

"He's a professor at the University of Chicago," said Jackson. "A friend from the old days."

"And?"

Jackson shrugged. "It's hard to explain. Let me think about it."

The guard came into the room. "Time's up, Counselor."

Stuart rose. "Think hard," he said. "I don't want any surprises."

IT WAS late afternoon when George cruised slowly by the Santa Rita Apartments, a low-rent complex. In the parking lot, an ancient Toyota Corolla was jacked up, and a young woman stood beside it looking down at a pair of legs that extended from underneath.

George pulled over to the curb. The young woman had short black hair and was painfully thin. The sleeves of her red sweat-shirt were pulled down, and she was walking in place, shivering, though it wasn't especially cold. George wound down the window.

"Hey, Rosie!"

She looked over, and her mouth formed an O. "Hi, Detective Maynard," she said flatly. "Long time no see, thank God." She pushed up a sleeve and scratched at her arm.

"Nathan around?" he asked.

Her eyes veered down to the legs under the car. "No way. I have no idea where he is." Her voice rose. "I haven't seen Nathan in years, Detective Maynard. Not in years and years and years."

"You can come out now, Nathan," George said loudly to the legs. "I'm not a cop anymore."

After a moment, the legs scooted forward, then the rest of Nathan, a muscular young man with black hair. He stood up and brushed at his faded jeans. "I haven't done anything."

"Neither has Randy Gates," said George, "but I'd like to talk to him."

Nathan looked past George's car, eyes as far away as the mountains outside of town, then back at George.

"Sorry. Can't help you. He moved away."

"If you run into him, give me a call. Here's my card." He handed it to Rosie. He could see little red spots all over her face as she took it. He remembered how pretty she was the first time she got into trouble. "Aw, Rosie," he said sadly. "You ought to know better than methamphetamine. Speed kills."

"Speed kills." She stared at him, muscles in her face twitching. Then she laughed. "That is so, so sixties." In her eyes, though, he saw a scared little girl.

He reached his hand out to that little girl, caught her wrist. "It's okay," he said soothingly. "Calm down. It's *okay.*"

For a second, she did calm down. "At Sunset View," she whispered. "That trailer park across from the café in Huachuca City. Lot Twelve." Then she was gone.

George thought he should drive immediately to Huachuca City in case Rosie was telling the truth, but he was too tired.

The neighbor, thought George. Anita said Jackson was having an affair with the neighbor. Ruth somebody. Norton. Maybe look into this Ruth Norton.

Ruth. Wasn't that Stuart's new secretary's name? Aw, so what. Anyway, Stuart would have to be pretty desperate to hire someone who was connected to a homicide he was working on.

George turned onto 92 away from town,

headed for his apartment. It was getting toward sunset, and because he was tired, he decided to skip the AA meeting. Maybe he'd call the pizza parlor near his place and order a meat lover's pizza. He punched on his cell, but—damn—the cell had run down.

The mountains were purple now in the late afternoon light. The mountains, the mist in the trees, the trees themselves tore at his heart. In the purple light, it seemed to George that the trees were actually bleeding, bleeding into the ground. Everything was dying.

Up ahead, on his right, the red-and-blue neon glowing in the twilight, was the Qwik Stop liquor store. A beer would be nice, he thought. Or maybe a six-pack. He slowed as he approached and pulled in, just like that, hardly even noticing.

Nine

THE morning sky was overcast, the sun diffused, leaving no shadows. Without the interplay of light and dark, everything seemed uglier, Frieda thought as she climbed the rocky path that led to the cave. Her long skirt of woven fabric kept catching on the creosote bushes, and the string bag she'd bought last year to replace paper bags and save the trees was heavy and dug into her bony shoulder.

You couldn't do everything, she thought, but if everyone did something, it could make a difference. Ken was always saying that. Lots of people didn't like Ken, and she could understand why—he irritated them on purpose, just to get them to react—but often he said profound things, and the most profound was, "Choose something to care about. Just one thing can be all it takes to change a life."

She'd chosen the Magician, and in her string bag was more food. He really wasn't as out of it as people thought. They'd actually had conversations, and sometimes he said things that were really smart.

Just one more turn of the path and there was the cave. The red balloons she'd left were still there, strings tangled on some bushes.

She went to the mouth of the cave and looked in, but there was no sign of the Magician. Probably already downtown. She wrinkled her nose against the musty smell, and the first thing she saw on top of his sleeping bag was his pointy cap. He never went downtown without wearing it, so he must be around.

She took everything out of the string bag, then went back outside. "Hello!" she called. "Mr. Magician, are you there?"

She climbed the little rise by the cave but saw nothing except rocks and bushes and weeds. She went a little ways farther up and saw something brown caught on a mesquite bush.

Frieda gathered her skirt and ran up the slope. It was his leather bag, upside down, hanging from a branch. What? Frieda felt numb. Then she noticed three pennies and a ten-dollar bill on the ground.

"Mr. Magician!" she called anxiously. "Hello?"

She walked farther up the slope and found a red-and-green braided yarn bracelet, a white card that said STUART ROSS, ATTORNEY AT LAW, a paperback book, *Stranger in a Strange Land*—she'd given him that—and then his gold metal bell. There she stopped.

"Hello?" she called again. "Mr. Magician!" Her voice caught in her throat. "Please answer!"

MARA had waited till the next day to search Jackson's house so she could do it while Tyler was at school. She had the key to the house, which had been Jenny's house, too, so Jenny's mother's address was bound to be there somewhere.

There were a lot of men working at the house down the street. From the living-room window, she could see the pirate man, Earl, having a smoke with another guy. He probably wouldn't come back, but just in case, she locked the front door.

Then she looked around. Jackson had an office with a desk. Did Jenny have a desk somewhere? Mara entered the bedroom, a large room with a king-sized bed and a desk with a black leather chair.

She opened the top desk drawer, all paper clips and pens. Where was Grace Dixon? She pulled open the side drawer and found files, neatly labeled. In the middle was a file labeled MOM—full of letters.

She glanced at some envelopes, and they all had the same address: Grace Dixon, 212 E. La Cholla Way, Green Valley, AZ. Green Valley, where was that? She could check it out—go to Mapquest on Tyler's computer. Then she sat and stared at one envelope with a letter inside, postmarked two years ago.

Dear Jenny,

I see no reason why I should pay for your training to be an aerobics instructor. I don't know why you quit your real estate job. Surely that was more lucrative than teaching people to bounce around like idiots. The next time you need financial assistance, don't come to me. I realize Jackson is ineffectual, with no earning power, but it was your choice to marry him, so you must live with the consequences.

Bitch! Mara stopped reading.

ORGANIZED by Ken Dooley, a raggle-taggle band of people and three dogs wandered the hills above the Magician's cave. Frieda stood watching from the top of one of the higher hills, her long skirt blowing in the wind. They'd been here for an hour already and found nothing but more odds and ends from the Magician's bag.

Ken, in a leather jacket and a bright Peruvian knit cap, strode up a hill. One of the dogs barked. Another answered. Someone shouted from across the way. Frieda saw Josh, one of the men, waving his arms, beckoning to her. She came toward him.

"What?" she asked when she got there.

Josh pointed to the ground at an old dirty black sneaker.

"His shoe," she said. "He only has one pair."

"Don't touch it!" Ken came up behind her.

Frieda straightened up. "His shoe," she said again, numb. "It's got paint all over it."

"Frieda," said Ken gently. "I don't think it's paint."

"Blood," she whispered. "It's blood, isn't it?"

"Heavy-duty voodoo," said Ken.

Frieda's mouth trembled, "Should we go to the police?"

"The police." Ken's mouth turned down in disgust. "What are they going to do? They don't care. We need representation, and he has a lawyer. Here's what I think you should do, Frieda."

RUTH had almost finished the billing when the bell tinkled. She looked up and saw a thin middle-aged woman in a long skirt. The woman looked familiar, but Ruth wasn't sure why. Her face was plain, her hair loose and wild, as if she'd been walking in the wind.

Ruth smiled at the woman. "Hi. How can I help you?"

"I need to see Mr. Ross right away. It's urgent," she added.

"Mr. Ross won't be back for a while," said Ruth apologetically. "Maybe I can help."

"My name's Frieda. I—"

"Frieda," Ruth cut in. "Now I know why you look familiar. You had a booth at the crafts fair in Grassy Park this summer. I went with my son. You sell herbal oils and stuff like that."

But Frieda went on as if Ruth hadn't spoken. "Mr. Ross and I met over at Justice Court last week. I was one of the people protesting the Magician being arrested—"

"The Magician," Ruth cut in, surprised. "You mean, with the hat and the bell? That man?"

"Yes. Hasn't Mr. Ross ever talked about him? He's his client."

Ruth stared at Frieda in disbelief. "He is?"

"Yes." Frieda looked as though she might cry. Then she did.

Ruth grabbed a box of Kleenex— something she had brought from home—

pulled a tissue out of the box, and offered it to Frieda.

Frieda took the tissue and blew her nose. There was a little silence.

"Are you okay?" said Ruth.

"Yes." She closed her eyes. "No."

"Look," said Ruth kindly, "why don't you tell me all about it. Maybe I can do something."

WHERE the hell was George? Stuart's head throbbed and his throat was raw as he drove back from Justice Court over in Sierra Vista after a tough case. All the way back he'd been calling George and getting nothing but a recording.

Now he stood in his office with a sore throat, a headache, and two women: Ruth and Frieda, that woman he'd spoken to outside of Justice Court in Dudley the day the Magician was arrested. She was sobbing, saying something about the Magician being missing, his leather bag, blood. *Blood?* Damn. A harmless old guy.

"So what are you going to do?" wailed Frieda.

Stuart felt dizzy. He went over to Ruth's

desk to prop himself up. "I'm just a lawyer," he said. "Have you reported this to the police?"

Frieda shook her head. "Ken said they wouldn't do anything."

"Ken can go to hell." Stuart picked up the phone, punched in numbers. "Hi. Stuart Ross here. Tell Sergeant Nelson I'm sending someone over. A woman named Frieda." He hung up. "It's all set," he said to Frieda. "Sergeant Nelson—Jack Nelson—that's who you need. If you really want to help the Magician, get over there now."

"That was excellent," Ruth said to Stuart after Frieda left.

"Thank you." He was exhausted; the phone call had taken the last of his reserves. He clutched the edge of the desk.

"That poor man," said Ruth. "I passed him by the post office just the other—" She stopped. "What's wrong? You look awful."

"I don't feel good." Stuart sat down heavily. "And I'm worried."

"What about? The Magician?"

"Sure. Among other things. George Maynard, my investigator. I can't locate him; I've been trying all day."

"Oh," said Ruth. "Well, I'm sure he'll turn up."

"My *head*." Stuart groaned.

Ruth put a practiced hand on his forehead. "It feels like you've got a fever," she said. "You should go home and go to bed."

"It's only two thirty," Stuart whined.

"So what. I can hold down the fort. Besides," she added sternly, "what good are you if you're sick? It's not fair to your clients."

"Okay. Okay." Stuart rose.

"Stay in bed," Ruth called after him as he lurched out the door, "and drink plenty of fluids!"

"HEY, Jackson!"

Jackson looked up from his book. "Yeah?"

Leroy, one of the inmates, walked over and sat down.

"Whassup?" Jackson asked. If I spend much more time here, he thought, my friends won't be able to tell me from the other inmates.

Leroy whooshed out a breath. "Remember that old guy that was in here one night? The looney tunes with the beard?"

Jackson stared at Leroy. "The Magician?"

"Yeah. The Magician. Didn't you and him know each other?"

Jenny, Jenny, Jenny. "Not exactly. What about him?"

"Somebody offed him, man."

Jackson's stomach lurched. "What do you mean?"

Leroy shrugged. "He's gone, man. Blood all over the place."

"What?" said Jackson. "Who told you that?"

Leroy shrugged, suddenly losing interest. He stood up.

The Magician was dead? *Jenny, Jenny, Jenny.* Jackson had bought Stuart's explanation about the Magician picking up on things. The guy hadn't seemed that crazy. Maybe he'd known something about Jenny's death.

His mind whirled. Who on earth had Jenny been screwing around with? He should call Stuart.

But there was that e-mail to Casey. Jackson had written it in a low period, hadn't meant it, not really. If they retrieved that, how was he going to explain it to Stuart? And how was Stuart going to explain it to a jury? Call Ruth. Ruth was working for Stuart now.

JUST WHEN YOU figured you were through the hardest part, thought George, you weren't safe at all. He saw now that it had been there the whole time, that *need,* waiting for him. Six-pack on the seat beside him, he'd gone way over the speed limit getting to his sponsor's house. He and Stan had stood and popped the tops, poured all the beer out onto the driveway.

He'd spent the night on Stan's couch; then the next day he'd gone to five different AA meetings, thinking about the case and not thinking about it as he drove. Tomorrow talk to Ruth Norton. Stupid to wait. Give her priority over Randy Gates. He drove to Willcox, the Junction, Douglas, Elfrida—must have gone to every AA meeting in the whole damn county.

CARRYING two bags of groceries, Ruth walked down a cement path to Stuart's house. A television was on inside, loud. She went up the porch steps and knocked on the door. Did someone say to come in? She wasn't sure with the noise from the TV. She tried the door, and it wasn't locked. She opened it partway.

"Stuart? Hello?" she called over the television. "It's Ruth!"

"Come in!"

Stuart lay on a beige couch, bleary-eyed, covered up to his chin with a sleeping bag. Ruth looked around. The furniture was old, and newspapers were everywhere. What a mess. He was a lawyer. Somehow she'd expected something a little more . . . middle class.

"Could you turn that off?" shouted Ruth.

Stuart picked up the remote, and then there was silence.

Ruth shifted the bags. "I brought you apples, bananas, orange juice, tea, honey, and four cans of chicken soup."

"Thank you," croaked Stuart.

She moved a stack of newspapers and set the bags down, then came closer and put her hand on Stuart's forehead. "You don't feel so feverish anymore. It's probably a twenty-four-hour virus. Want me to heat up some chicken soup before I go back to the office?"

"I just had a doughnut."

Ruth opened her mouth to say something about that, then remembered she wasn't his mother. Thank God. "Listen, Jackson called me last night. He was really upset. One of the inmates told him the Magician was murdered."

"We don't even know if he's dead," Stuart protested.

"Jackson thinks the Magician knew something about Jenny's death," Ruth went on as if he hadn't spoken. "He told me the Magician came up to him and said Jenny's name. *Three times.*"

"He says everything three times," said Stuart. "It doesn't mean anything."

"But what if it does? The Magician. Does he have a name?"

"Ikan Danz."

"What?"

"I can dance. Get it? Look"—Stuart struggled to rise—"he got arrested a couple of months ago because some store owners thought he was scaring away the tourists. I represented him, pro bono. So they just called me the second time. SEABHS did some kind of psychological workup, and he's a D.S.M. something-or-other."

"A D.S.M. something-or-other what?"

"I can't remember. Actually, I didn't read it. But there must have been a diagnosis.

What does it matter? Those psychology people, they just take a bunch of characteristics and squeeze them into a label. They gave him some meds, but he quit taking them."

Ruth sighed. "There's something I need to tell you. It's about Jackson and me. We—"

The phone rang. Ruth jumped.

"Damn," said Stuart. He picked up. "Hello? Stuart Ross here. . . . George—where the hell have you been? . . . No kidding?"

Waiting, Ruth gazed past the couch, through a dining room, into a kitchen. Dishes were piled high in the sink. I will not offer to do his dishes, she thought. I absolutely will not.

"Norton," said Stuart.

Ruth looked over at him.

"Sure . . . Yeah . . . When? Look, she's here right now. I'll ask her." He put his hand over the phone. "It's my investigator. He wants to set up an interview with you at your house. Today, if possible. Why don't I tell him one o'clock."

"Fine," said Ruth.

"One. Yeah." He hung up. "You were saying?" he asked Ruth, but the phone rang again. He picked up again.

"Aha." It was Victor. "Caught you at home."

"Had a little virus or something," said Stuart. "I'm fine now."

Ruth stood up. "Got to go," she mouthed to Stuart, and went out the door.

"Got the autopsy report on Sid Hamblin," said Victor. "Cause of death same as Jenny Williams."

Stuart sat down. "And?"

"Well," said Victor, "they seized those pills, the probiotics? Three months' supply. About two-thirds gone."

Jackson had been in jail less than a month. It was pretty simple math, but Stuart did it twice. "So what? Where's the connection?"

"Couple of other things. Sperm in Jenny's vagina? Looks like we got a match. Sid Hamblin again. How's that for a connection?"

"What else?" said Stuart hollowly.

"This is nothing, really." Victor chuckled. "I mean, compared to the rest. Just a little e-mail your guy wrote to a friend. Dot E-D-U, must be some kind of professor. Looks like in Chicago."

Stuart closed his eyes. He didn't want to hear this. "You don't have to fill me in on that. I'll pick up the disclosure first thing in the morning," he said, and hung up.

ALL MORNING, TWO uniformed officers had been searching around the Magician's cave. Frieda, wearing a sweater knit by Peruvian children, had watched as Sergeant Jack Nelson, a middle-aged man with a big mustache and sad eyes, lifted a sample of soil from the ground where the shoe had been and put it into an evidence bag.

Now he came up to her where she sat. The cave and the area around it were strung with yellow crime-scene tape. In plain clothes—windbreaker, red plaid shirt, and jeans—Sergeant Nelson hunkered down on the ground. "I don't know how to say it any better way." His voice was kind. "There's mine shafts all over these hills. Someone goes down one, well . . . they might never be found."

Frieda bit her lip. She pulled the sweater close around her.

"Are you going to be okay?"

She nodded.

He paused. "I'm going to have one of my men stand guard over the cave. I got a fingerprint guy coming up here later. You better go down to the station and get fingerprinted yourself."

Frieda looked at him in horror. "Me? Why? I'm not a criminal."

"Course you're not. But you've been in the cave, probably left some prints. It's for purposes of elimination, is all."

She looked stricken. "Other people went in there, too, when we had the search party."

"Not smart," Sergeant Nelson said. "Who went in? Everybody?"

"No." She paused. "I think actually just Ken."

"Tell Ken to stop by, then."

Frieda lowered her face into her hands and said in a muffled voice, "I can't believe this is happening. That poor, poor man."

"Now, now." Instinctively, Sergeant Nelson reached out to pat her shoulder. "Listen," he said. "His leather bag and his hat? Hopefully there'll be something on them for a DNA match so we can make sure the blood is Mr. Danz's. All that's down the line, of course; we got to send it to a lab in Phoenix. It's not like you see it on *CSI.*"

"*CSI?* What's that?"

"*Crime Scene Investigation.* On TV," Sergeant Nelson said.

"I don't watch TV," said Frieda. "I don't even own one. I don't read the newspapers, either."

"Then how the hell do you know what's going on?"

Frieda held out her arms and made a circle that seemed to encompass Sergeant Nelson, the cave, the mountains, the sky. "This is what's going on," she said.

A BASKETBALL hoop hung from the garage door at Ruth Norton's. Kids, she has kids, thought George. He smoothed his hair back with his hands and walked up to the front door. He was a little nervous; the last couple of days had thrown him off balance. You are a professional, Sam Elliot, he told himself.

A woman opened the door. She had a pleasant face, natural, not hidden behind a lot of makeup, and thick reddish-brown curly hair with a streak of white going back from her forehead. She wore a pale blue long-sleeved shirt and black pants.

Suddenly he felt awkward. "I'm George Maynard," he said. He fumbled in his pocket for his card and handed it to her.

"Well, I thought as much." She smiled. He noticed her teeth were an average off-white color. "And I'm Ruth. Come on in."

He stepped inside. "Pleased to meet you, Ruth. How do you like working for our boy Stuart?" *Our boy? Where did that come from?*

"Pretty intense."

He laughed, and she laughed, too. "I made coffee," she said. "We can talk in the kitchen."

George followed her to a cluttered room with black ceramic tiles and stainless steel fixtures dimmed with use. On the refrigerator were snapshots and children's drawings. He sat a little farther back in his chair, comfortable. "This is nice," he said. "Homey."

This was Anita's evil temptress—the woman who supposedly was having a blatant affair with Jackson? George wanted to keep an open mind here, but what struck him about Ruth was that she was normal. When was the last time he had met a woman who was normal? He couldn't remember.

"Let's get started," she said expectantly. "Tyler was the one who saw Randy Gates going into Jenny's house."

"Yeah?" said George. "Guess I should talk to Tyler, too."

"He'd love that. But now, shoot. Give me the third degree."

"Aw," said George.

"The day Jenny was murdered," offered Ruth, "I was at orientation for substitute teachers, so I can't tell you much about what happened." She paused. "And now Sid Hamblin's dead, too." She shivered. "It's kind of scary. I mean, you don't think—?"

"Don't know. Have to wait for the autopsy. You knew Sid?"

She nodded. "Slightly. He was here in my house, at the memorial for Jenny. To be honest, I didn't like him. He gave me the creeps."

"Heard a rumor that something was going on between him and Jenny. You know anything about that?"

"That's who Jenny was having the affair with? *Sid?*" She looked flabbergasted. "Oh, yuck, how could she?"

George bit his lip to keep from smiling. "It's just a rumor right now. How about Anita Selby? Did you know her?"

"Jenny's friend. I met her once in passing, is all."

"Let's get back to you. You're pretty close to Jackson, huh? Been neighbors for years."

"Years," said Ruth. "My boys love him."

"And you? You love him too?"

Ruth was silent for a moment, then said slowly, "What I feel has to do with brotherly love. A warm feeling of camaraderie. That's what I feel for Jackson."

"What about Jenny? You felt camaraderie-like about her?"

"No. To be honest, I thought she was kind of a blight on Jackson's life, that he would have been happier without her."

George raised his eyebrows.

"Let me explain," said Ruth. "I loved my ex-husband very much." She closed her eyes. "He was understanding and sensitive and good. He was the best father. My two oldest boys are strong, confident men now because of him. Tyler, he's eleven; he didn't get all that as much because of the divorce."

"Poor little guy," said George. "I'm divorced myself. Seems like nowadays a lot of people don't even try to stay married."

"In our case, it wasn't not trying. Owen is gay. I didn't know it when we got married, and I don't think he did, either." She blinked. "What were we talking about?"

"Uh . . ."

"Jenny," said Ruth. "Of course. I was trying to explain about Jenny." She paused. "I never told anyone about this, because it hurt too much." She put her hand over her heart. "It still hurts. I liked her at first, then later not as much, but I kept trying to like her— you know, for Jackson's sake. Then one day we were talking and she said wasn't I worried about sending the kids to see Owen because he was gay and he might molest them." Ruth's eyes filled with tears. She grabbed a napkin and wiped her eyes. "Sorry," she said.

"No," said George. "I can see how it would upset you."

"She did things like that," said Ruth. She smiled. "You seem like a nice person. How long have you been divorced?"

"About a year," said George.

"A year." Ruth leaned toward him, eyes full of concern. "I guess it must still be pretty painful."

He nodded. She had a nice voice, he thought suddenly, *kind.* Bet she was one hell of a good mom. "Twenty years I was married to Sandy. I had a drinking problem, but . . . aw . . ." He shrugged. "I got no excuses. No one to blame but myself, that's the real truth.

But I've been sober now more than six months."

"Good for you," said Ruth.

"She calls me sometimes," George confided, "and asks me to do things for her. I kept hoping it meant she still cared."

"Maybe she does and she's afraid."

He shook his head. "She doesn't." He shrugged, looking pained.

"Hell is other people," said Ruth.

George looked at her with surprise and admiration. He ran his fingers through his hair. "That's deep."

There was a silence.

"You must be a very good investigator," said Ruth. "Just look at the stuff I've told you that I never told anyone before."

"I was a little talkative myself," said George. "Damn!"

"What?" said Ruth, startled.

"I got this voice-activated tape recorder." He patted his jacket pocket. "Right here." He took it out. "I've gone and taped this whole conversation."

"Ooh. . . . If I'd realized that, I wouldn't have . . ." She giggled nervously. "You're not going to play it for Stuart, are you?"

George suddenly had the sense of a whole interview gone awry. "Are you kidding?" he said.

He opened the recorder and took out the little cassette. You lost your grip, Sam Elliot, he thought. He unwound the tape and crumpled the shiny ribbon. "I'm not going to play it for anyone," he said.

Ten

RUTH woke up that morning with old songs in her heart. *"You go to my head,"* she sang in her kitchen. *"Da da dum, da da da dum."*

"You're in a good mood," said Mara. "What's that song?"

"Some old standard," she said. "It just popped into my head."

How Owen had loved those old songs. They used to dance around the living room to Cole Porter, Owen swooping her around. She hadn't danced now in years. *Oh, wouldn't it be loverly.*

"I'm thinking about going to Tucson today," said Mara.

"Tucson?" said Ruth. "What's in Tucson?"

"Malls," said Mara. "Lots of them."

"Tyler!" said Ruth. "Don't forget you're sleeping over at Buzzie's tonight. You got your pj's and a toothbrush?"

"A sleepover?" said Mara. "On a school night?"

"They're doing a history project together," Ruth explained. Then she turned to Mara, "There's a Tucson map in the right-hand kitchen drawer on the top. Why don't you take it."

"I— Sure. Thank you."

Tyler shrugged into his backpack. "You'll be here when I get home tomorrow?" he asked Mara on his way out to catch the bus.

"Probably."

"I'm running late," said Ruth when Tyler was gone. She ran her fingers through her damp hair. "The hair dryer conked out."

"Use mine," said Mara. "It's in the boys' bathroom."

In the boys' bathroom, Ruth looked at herself in the mirror. It seemed to her she looked better than usual. Younger, more animated. She hadn't had a hot flash in a while.

She turned on the dryer. *You go to my head* . . . What were the other lines? There was a mint julep in there somewhere, and champagne bubbles. A whole lot of alcohol. George had said he used to be an alcoholic. Maybe that was what put the song in her head. She giggled, and her heart sang, thinking about what George had said as he left yesterday. *I'll have to stop by the office more often.*

A short time later, after Ruth left, Mara finished the dishes and got dressed in jeans and a sedate navy knit polo. Then she checked her purse to make sure the map she'd printed out from Mapquest was still there. Green Valley, where Mrs. Dixon lived, was outside of Tucson—one hour and forty-seven minutes' driving time.

HEY there, Casey. I was thinking. Here we are, two professors, and all we do is bitch about our wives. Jenny's mad at me, and I don't care. We haven't spoken for two days, and you know what? I'm enjoying it, in a sadistic kind of way. I used to be a nice guy, but you know what they say. Hell is other people. Sometimes I even think about her being dead and all I feel is relief.

Inadmissible, thought Stuart automatically. Written eight months ago. He groaned. A plea. The only way out of this mess was to get Victor to offer a stipulated plea. Twenty years. But would he—

The bell tinkled, and then Ruth appeared at his door, smiling, almost radiant. What did she have to be happy about?

"You're late," said Stuart grimly.

"Sorry," said Ruth without remorse. "My hair dryer broke. Why are you so upset?"

"Upset? Why would I be upset? Because I have a whole bunch of new disclosure on your friend Jackson? Really damning stuff."

Ruth sank into the client's chair. "Jackson told me he gave you permission to discuss his case with me. Tell me about it."

And he did. The prescription bottle with the poison under the bed, the sperm matchup, the probiotics and the cause of Sid's death—everything.

Ruth sat there looking stunned. "Sid was murdered?" She glanced at Stuart worriedly. "Have you told Jackson all this yet?"

"Not about Sid. Tomorrow." Stuart's eyes shifted away. "I'm swamped today, and I'll need time to lay it all on him."

"You're forgetting something," Ruth said. "The Magician. He knew about Jenny. You said yourself he had moments of lucidity. He spoke to Jackson, and now something's happened to him, too, and Jackson couldn't have done that. Besides, isn't it true that the more things you throw at a jury, the less likely they are to convict?"

"Jeez," said Stuart, "you're a lawyer now?" He rubbed his face. "I'll run over to Dudley P.D., get a copy of the file on the Magician. You make copies of the new disclosure for George to pick up."

Ruth's face brightened again, and Stuart scowled. What did she have to be so happy about?

GEORGE drove into the Sunset View Trailer Park where Rosie had said Randy Gates was staying. Stuart had called him last night about the autopsy report and the results linking Sid to the sperm found in Jenny. It fit nicely into a theory George already had: Jenny had been screwing Sid; Anita Selby found out and offed both of them. That whole Ruth–Jackson affair, a smoke screen created by Selby, was doubly worse when you considered what a fine, decent person Ruth was. George's hands tightened on the steering wheel.

From her reaction when he'd asked, he was pretty sure Anita knew Randy Gates; probably she'd scored grass from him. And Anita had plenty of access to Jenny's house. She could have gone over to Sid's later—to commiserate about Jenny or whatever—and spiked his pills then.

And that guy Ken Dooley—he was a friend of Sid's, and he'd admitted to meeting Jenny. He might know something. That took the investigation to Old Dudley, where Ruth worked. He could pop in and say hello.

He drove on down to lot 12. The trailer was nondescript, with a dirt yard, a wire fence, and no vehicles parked in its vicinity. George stopped, got out, then reached into his jacket pocket and turned off his cell. Nothing like a cell going off at the wrong time.

He went up a couple of splintery wooden steps and knocked on the door. No one answered. He went back to the Olds, got in, and drove out to the street where he had a view of lot 12.

While he waited, he sipped at watery coffee he'd bought at the café up the street, so unlike the coffee he'd had yesterday at Ruth's.

IN THE distance, Mara could see a golf course smack dab in the middle of the desert, bright green, dotted with white sand traps. She turned down a street lined with pink stucco town houses and parked Jackson's Volvo three doors down from the Dixon address because Jenny's mother might recognize the car and freak out.

Mara marched down the street, opened a low wrought-iron gate, and went into the yard. Before she could push the bell, the door opened. A woman stood in the opening. "Oh!" she said. "I'm just on my way out."

"I'm sorry," said Mara. "I thought Mrs. Dixon lived here."

"Of course she does," the woman said heartily. "I'm Betty from home health, looking in on her. I'm new. That's why you don't recognize me. I bet you're a granddaughter."

"I'm Mara."

"Well, you're a sweetie to come see your grannie. I'll take you to her in the living room; then I'll be on my way."

Mara followed Betty down a hall, the walls painted peach.

"Grace!" Betty called. "You'll never guess who's here. Mara!"

"Who? Mara who?" said a woman's voice gruffly.

"Why, I don't know," said Betty. "She didn't say. I thought—"

Mara took a deep breath and turned the corner into a light-flooded room that was all white and peach, white carpet, white couch and chairs, and peach pillows everywhere. A white-haired old woman, wearing beige and masses of silver-and-turquoise Indian jewelry, was sitting in the center of the couch, resting both hands on a cane. Her eyes, behind tinted glasses, met Mara's.

"Harvey," Mara said awkwardly. "Mara Harvey."

"Never heard of you," said Mrs. Dixon abruptly.

"I thought . . ." said Betty. "I'm sorry, Grace. Shall I stay?"

Mrs. Dixon looked Mara up and down. "Well, she doesn't look like she's on drugs. Go, Betty, shoo, shoo. And you," she said to Mara, "sit down. There, where I can see you."

Mara heard the door close as Betty left. Mrs. Dixon leaned toward Mara. "Not from a religious group, are you?"

"No." Mara looked at Mrs. Dixon. "Jackson's my father."

There was a silence so deep Mara could hear the cars out on the street and, as the silence lengthened, the whack of a golf ball.

Then Mrs. Dixon said, "I didn't know Jackson had a daughter."

"I haven't seen him since I was three," said Mara. "I mean, until I came out here." She bit her lip. "I was hoping you could write a letter saying it's okay if they let my father out of jail, lower the bail to something he can pay," she said in a rush. "I know Jenny was your daughter, but Jackson didn't kill her. I know he didn't."

"You're wrong," said Mrs. Dixon. "He *did* kill her. Even if he didn't actually poison her, he still killed her. He ignored her and neglected her. He killed her spirit every day. I know that from what Jenny told me. That memorial—I could hardly stand to be there in the same room with him. Mourning when he didn't love her."

"He loved my mother," cried Mara. "I'm sure he did."

"Your mother was probably just a fantasy to him," said Mrs. Dixon relentlessly, "because she left him. Some men, all they can love is fantasies. She gave you a better life than he would have."

"That is so . . . so not true." Mara's eyes watered.

Mrs. Dixon's eyes were a blur of blue. "My little Jenny," she said sadly. "I lost my little girl. I can't write that letter."

"It's okay," said Mara, giving up. "I understand. I do. And I upset you. I'm so sorry."

"I'm fine. I think you should go, though."

Mara stood up. "You'll be all right?"

"I'll be fine. I have a gentleman friend coming over soon—Henry." She paused. "I have friends. And once in a blue moon there's Kevin."

"Kevin?"

"You wouldn't have heard of him. Jenny never spoke of him to people. She more or less disowned him a while ago, acted like he never existed. He's my son, Jenny's brother."

"Oh," said Mara.

"I don't know why she had to be like that. I know Kevin upset people sometimes, but he was her brother. And he's highly intelligent. He's traveled the world."

"Where is he now?" asked Mara.

"Alaska." Mrs. Dixon looked at the floor. "He's been in Alaska for months." She looked up. "Time to shoo, little Mara," she said.

As STUART approached the Dudley police station, Ken Dooley was just coming out. Ken was back in sunny Mexico today in huaraches and a guayabera shirt.

"Hey there," said Stuart. "Shot any border patrol guards lately?"

"Not yet." Ken smiled genially. "But I'm loaded and ready. You gonna defend me?"

"You got the money," said Stuart, "then I got the time."

"What?" Ken said. "No pro bono for human rights?"

"I'm pro bono now," said Stuart. "I'm here about the Magician."

"Great. But who cares about a homeless guy anyway, huh?"

Stuart thought there was possibly some

truth in this, but he said, "I imagine they're doing their best with limited resources."

"Well, I'm doing whatever I can," said Ken glibly. He held up his palms. His fingers were gray with ink. "Just got fingerprinted."

Stuart raised his eyebrows.

"For purposes of elimination," said Ken. "I went inside the Magician's cave when we were out there looking for him."

"Okay," said Stuart. "Excuse me. Got to run." He turned and went into the police station.

"Mr. Ross," said the young woman behind the glass. "Sergeant Nelson's waiting. You can go on back." She buzzed him in.

Jack Nelson sat behind a desk piled with folders. "Come in," he said to Stuart. "I hear you're busy. First-degree murder case, huh?"

"Yeah. Jackson Williams." Stuart sat on a rickety folding chair. "You involved in the Sid Hamblin investigation at all?"

"Nope. You said on the phone this was about the Magician. Got something for me?" Sergeant Nelson asked hopefully.

"Not really. What have you got?"

"We talked to a bunch of people, names that Frieda gave us, but nobody knows anything, nobody saw him. What's your interest?"

"He's my client," said Stuart.

Nelson looked skeptical. "So maybe he said something to you about someone being after him, having a grudge?"

"Are you kidding? He was barely coherent," Stuart said. "Why don't you give me copies of the reports and maybe something will ring a bell."

"Anything," said Nelson dolefully, "before that Dooley ass starts writing letters."

JACKSON'S Volvo was parked in front of the house when Ruth got home. Mara was safely back from Tucson. Ruth crossed that off her list of little worries. Her big worry was all the new stuff about Jackson that Stuart had told her. How much should she tell Mara?

Inside the house, it was very quiet, too quiet. Where was Tyler? Then she remembered: He was sleeping over at Buzzie's to work on his history project.

"Mara?" she called.

"In the kitchen." Mara was sitting at the table where yesterday Ruth had sat with George Maynard. The thought warmed her.

"How were the malls?" Ruth asked brightly.

"I didn't go to any," said Mara.

"I guess you saved yourself some money, then." Ruth sat down.

Mara's mouth quivered. "I went to see Mrs. Dixon, Jenny's mom. I went to ask if she'd write a letter to get Jackson released."

"What?"

"I had to do something, and then when I talked to her, I realized that Jenny was a person, you know? And except for Mrs. Dixon, nobody even cared that she was dead, including my father."

For a moment, Ruth was shamed into silence, and the worst of it was that it was true. "Oh, Mara," she said finally. "I'm sorry."

"Mrs. Dixon isn't going to write the letter. I don't blame her."

"Your father and Jenny weren't suited to each other," said Ruth gently. "I think he tried to love her, but he wasn't any good at it."

"And there's something else Mrs. Dixon said," Mara went on. "I didn't realize Jenny had a brother."

"I only heard her mention him once." Ruth shrugged. "I guess it was too painful."

"Mrs. Dixon told me Jenny disowned him," said Mara.

"Did she tell you how he died?" Ruth asked curiously.

"Died? He's not dead."

"Of course he is. Jenny told me," said Ruth.

"No, he's not. His name's Kevin, and he lives in Alaska."

Jenny's brother was alive? *Dead*, Jenny had said. How many times was she doomed to re-play that scene in the kitchen with Jenny? Every time she did, it seemed to get worse. Jenny had lied—she'd lied about her brother so Ruth would feel sorry for her and let her off the hook for saying such terrible things about Owen.

And Mara was a grown-up. Jackson was her father. She should be told what was going on in the case—Sid Hamblin, his affair with Jenny, the Magician, everything. She'd hear about it anyway, and who was there but Ruth to tell her kindly, gently.

GEORGE had been parked here for hours. No one had gone in or out of the trailer at lot 12, no sign at all of Randy Gates. One foot had gone to sleep, pins and needles. I'm too old, he thought.

George got out and stamped his foot. He

walked around a little bit, then headed across the street to Nell's Café. What the hell. He could take a seat by the window, keep an eye out.

He pushed open the door and sensed the warmth inside, the smell of—what? Meat loaf. He loved meat loaf.

The waitress was delivering an order at the back booth. George started for a seat at the counter, then saw the customer in the last booth, a youngish handsome man with curly black hair.

Randy Gates.

George slid into the booth. "I hear the meat loaf's pretty good."

"Detective Maynard," said Randy Gates, a cheeseburger halfway to his mouth. For a moment, he glared at George. "I could walk out of here." He half rose. "Who's going to stop me?"

"Not me." George raised his hands. "Don't have the authority. I'm not a cop anymore; I'm a private investigator, working for Stuart Ross, the attorney who's representing Jackson Williams. I just want to talk to you, is all. Where's the harm in that?"

The waitress came back and set a glass of

water in front of George. "I'll have the meat loaf," George said. "And coffee." He looked at Randy. "You can put his cheeseburger on my bill."

Randy sank back into his seat. "I don't know what the hell there is to talk about anyway."

"Sure you do," said George. "Jenny Williams."

"Who's that?"

"Right," said George. "Except we got an eyewitness saw you go into her house the very day she died. Other times, too."

Randy sighed. "Okay. So I'd stop in and see her sometimes. She used to run past the construction site every day, and we struck up some conversations."

"Some conversations," said George. "And here you are, hiding out like you did something wrong. Course, you were selling her dope on a regular basis, but big deal. I don't care about that."

"One meat loaf," said the waitress. She plunked it down.

George grabbed his fork and stabbed a chunk of meat loaf with some mashed potato. "You quit your job right after Jenny got killed.

You've been running and hiding ever since. How come?"

"She got murdered, is how come," said Randy through clenched teeth, "and I got a record. A bunch of phony trumped-up convictions. Once you got those convictions, everything you do is wrong."

"I'll tell you what I think," George said. "You didn't kill Jenny. But I don't think her husband did, either. All we know is someone did. She ever ask to sample the goods, smoke a number with you?"

"Never," Randy said. "She was a clean liver, that lady."

"Then who was she buying it for?"

"You got me. Her husband, maybe?"

"Sid Hamblin. She ever mention that name?"

Randy shook his head.

"How about"—George leaned across the table—"Anita Selby?"

"Anita," said Randy. "She's your so-called eyewitness saw me going into Jenny's house? That lying bitch," he went on. "You tell Anita she wants to rat out me, I can rat her out big time."

"How's that?" George pounced.

"How'd that go over with her boss? A doper, out there selling fancy real estate."

"That all?"

"It ain't enough?"

"I heard," said George, "even though she and Jenny were supposed to be best friends, Anita didn't like Jenny all that much."

"Who cares if she didn't?"

"Help me out here," said George in exasperation. "We're talking Jenny was murdered. Think. She say anything to you strange or paranoid about Anita? Or anyone else, for that matter?"

"Only strange thing she ever said to me was about a letter."

"A letter?"

"She said she was going to have someone write a letter." Randy scratched his head. "It was strange, you know, 'cause she looked like a lady who knew how to write."

"Who?" said George. "Who was going to write the letter?"

"Some guy." Randy's forehead wrinkled. "What was the name?" He snapped his fingers. "Ken. That's it, Ken. Ken Dooley."

STUART WALKED down Main Street carrying a mocha java from the Dudley Coffee Company. It was eight at night. It wasn't till he'd gone home that he realized he'd left the reports on the Magician from the Dudley P.D. in his office. Might as well go over them before he talked to Jackson tomorrow.

The Cornucopia restaurant had been closed for hours. A few die-hard tourists still wandered down the street looking into the shopwindows, and one of them was standing in front of Stuart's office, a middle-aged man in a baseball cap, a green-and-yellow-striped polo, and khaki pants, camera around his neck.

He smiled genially as Stuart approached. "Evening," he said. "Nice night."

"Yep." Stuart walked past him to the office and pulled out his keys.

"Say, do you know anything about the architecture of this building?" asked the man.

"Sorry," said Stuart. "Not a thing."

He turned away to forestall any more conversation and unlocked the door. The bell tinkled as he stepped inside, closing the door firmly against the tourist. He went into his office—there was the file right where he'd left it. He sat at his desk, put his feet up, and opened the file for Ikan Danz a.k.a the Magician.

Stuart flipped through the reports; nothing new to add to what he'd been told by Frieda and then Jack Nelson. He paused at the inventory of evidence seized and read that more thoroughly.

Sleeping bag, three water jugs, paper sack, apricots, walnuts, three empty baggies. One red hat. Six tea bags, a bottle of echinacea. One large Mexican tin box. Contents of box: one dried mesquite pod; four blue stones; one button saying FRODO LIVES. One paperback book, *Stranger in a Strange Land*, inscribed "from Frieda." One braided yarn bracelet. One bell. One white handkerchief. One twenty-dollar bill, two tens, three fives, nine ones, and change. One card, STUART ROSS, ATTORNEY AT LAW. One card, KEN DOOLEY, AT LARGE IN THE UNIVERSE.

The guy had had absolutely nothing of value except the cash. Unless you counted the two cards. His own and Ken Dooley's. Stuart smiled. His manager and his publicist. What the hell else did you need in this world? He yawned, closing the file.

Eleven

MARA drove Jackson's Volvo slowly around the mining pit, an enormous hole in the ground, with crumbling terraces that led to the bottom, where toxic-looking water pooled. At the point where the pit reached its maximum depth was a sign saying SCENIC VIEW. Who did they think they were kidding?

Last night Ruth had told her everything about Jackson's case. Everything. Mara swallowed hard, remembering.

"But what can we do?" she'd cried.

"The Magician," Ruth had said. "Jackson thinks he might have known something about Jenny's murder." She hesitated. "We could talk to Frieda; she's his friend."

"I'll talk to her," said Mara. "Where—"

"I don't know. You could try the Co-op. They might know."

Just past the pit was another sign that said DUDLEY FOOD CO-OP with a big arrow pointing to the right. Mara turned and went by a stand of old brick buildings to a big building on the corner. She parked in front and got out.

Inside she saw rows of herbs, bins of beans,

nuts, and grains, and shelves of canned goods, but no people except a blond guy with a goatee and a pierced eyebrow at the cash register reading a book.

He looked up and smiled. "Hey there," he said. "What's up?"

"The sky," said Mara from behind her sunglasses.

"You live in Dudley?" he asked. "Haven't seen you before."

"I'm just visiting."

"I'm Josh."

"Mara," she said.

She drifted through the store looking for something small to buy and stopped in front of a bulletin board. In the middle was a sign, hand-lettered: HELP US FIND THE MAGICIAN!

Under that was a fuzzy picture of a bearded man wearing a pointy cap and what looked like a bathrobe. "Our dear friend has vanished," it said below. "If you have any information concerning his whereabouts, leave a message here for Ken Dooley or Frieda."

"Oh!" said Mara. She turned to the cashier, who was back to his book. She pointed to the poster, about to ask where she could find Frieda, but he spoke first.

"Pretty sad, huh?" Josh leaned across the counter. "He was a great old guy, lived in a cave. I was part of the original search party," Josh added eagerly. "With Ken Dooley."

"Yeah, I see his name on the poster," said Mara. "Who is he?"

"He's, uh—kind of this activist." Josh lowered his voice. "Anyway, we're pretty sure the Magician was murdered."

"That's awful," said Mara. "Um, Frieda. How can I find her?"

"You can't right now. She's the one that found him missing." He lowered his voice. "She's so traumatized, she went on a retreat."

"Oh," said Mara, disappointed.

GEORGE knocked on the screen door of the house next to Sid Hamblin's. Through the rusty squares he could see a young man on a couch, hunched over a guitar. *"Oh, baby, baby, ba—"*

"Hello?" called George loudly.

The singer looked over, then got up and padded barefoot to the door. His blond hair was braided into dreadlocks. "Yeah?"

"Sorry to bother you while you're practicing," said George. He held up his card, and the man squinted at it through the screen.

"Wow," he said. "An investigator. This about Sid?"

George nodded. "Since you're his closest neighbor, I thought maybe you could help me out, answer a few questions."

"I didn't even know the guy." He gestured up the hill to Sid's. "I'd say hi if I saw him on the street and that's about it."

"Maybe you noticed his visitors," said George. He opened a manila envelope, slid out a photograph of a brightly smiling Anita Selby. "You ever see her go up there?"

"Jeez." He snorted. "Middle-class chick like that? Don't think so." He paused. "There *was* one middle-class lady went there a few times, but it wasn't her."

"You're sure?"

"Yeah. The one I saw had long hair, dark. Looked athletic."

Jenny. "So who did go up there?" George asked.

"Ken Dooley went there a lot." He tilted his head, considering. "Saw Frieda with him a couple of times."

"Who's Frieda?"

"Older lady, hangs out with Ken sometimes.

You could show her the picture. She lives over on Wood Canyon—two-oh-three C." He paused. "One of the times I saw her going to Sid's, she had the Magician with her, not that he'd be much— Damn."

"What?"

"Somebody offed the Magician, too, right?"

"*Offed* him?" George stared at the young man, suddenly alert. *Someone else was murdered?* "Who's this Magician?"

"Old looney-tunes guy, hangs at the post office. Pointed cap. Dressed in orange. You never saw him there?"

"No," said George. "I work out of Sierra Vista, mostly."

"Ask Frieda. She'll tell you all about him. Man." He hit his head with the heel of his hand. "What is this? Dudley's the murder capital of Cochise County now? I should move back to New York City, where it's safe."

George left the neighbor and drove out toward Wood Canyon, just off Tombstone Canyon. The road wound around in a meandering way. Big cottonwoods dropped their yellow leaves onto pitted asphalt. Half the little wood and adobe houses didn't even have numbers, at least none that were visible. George found an adobe that said 200 at the curb. He parked in the dirt and got out.

A Mexican man in overalls stood by a wire fence, holding a rake. "You got any idea where two-oh-three C is?" George asked.

"That's Frieda's house," said the man. "You go down two houses, go up the steps to the third house on the right."

"Thanks," said George, turning away.

"Hey, man, she's not a doper," the man called after him.

I'm that obvious? thought George as he climbed the steps to 203-C, a wood house painted silvery green with a brick front yard and a pot of red geraniums by the front door. He opened a wooden gate.

"She's not home!" said a woman's voice behind him.

He turned. Couldn't see anyone but sensed invisible people watching him everywhere here on Wood Canyon. He walked over to a spot where he could look into the yard across where the voice had come from.

A thin red-haired woman wearing a long purple batik skirt stood near a wooden porch painted a fading white. She was feeding a bright-patterned cloth into an ancient wringer washing machine.

"Son of a gun," said George. "I remember my grandmother used one of them machines out on the ranch forty years ago."

"I'm a batik artist," said the woman. "This saves energy."

"I'll bet." George half smiled. "But maybe not time."

"What's time for?"

What's time for. For some reason the phrase struck George with some special significance. What *was* time for? To practice a guitar, to make bright patterns on cloth? No. He drew himself up. To catch a murderer. "Got any idea when Frieda will be back?"

The woman stopped feeding the cloth into the wringer. "Why?"

"Just want to talk to her."

"Are you a Realtor by any chance?" she asked suspiciously.

"No," said George, surprised.

"I hate Realtors." She looked disgusted. "They have no shame. They come around trying to get you to sell your house for nothing so they can turn around and sell it again for double."

"I'm not a Realtor. I wanted to ask her about the Magician."

"Oh." Her face brightened. "You can ask Frieda about the Magician anytime and she'll go on and on. But right now she's away on a retreat. She should be back tomorrow, though."

"You look like a local," said George. "One hundred percent. Maybe you can tell me where I might find Ken Dooley?"

"Everywhere." She gave the wringer a turn. "Ken is everywhere. At the Co-op. Or the Coffee Company. Or the post office."

"He got a house?"

She smiled. "A school bus. Lives in an old bus out on Highway Ninety-two. I can give you directions, but he's only there at night."

A SHORT time later the sun winked off the silver of the bolo on George's tie, set with a chunk of genuine malachite, as he ambled down Main Street, headed for Stuart's office and Ruth. As he walked, a feeling came over him that felt like certainty and made up for everything—all the frustrations and wrong turns and backslidings. Everything would be okay. He was invincible.

Up ahead, the sun shone on the front window of Stuart's office. He could just make out Ruth sitting at Ellie's desk. He pushed open the door. The bell tinkled. In the second before Ruth looked up, he noted how ladylike she looked with that silver streak in her hair.

Then her face lit up. "George," she said.

"Ruth," he began. "I—"

"You—" said Ruth simultaneously.

They both stopped. Ruth giggled.

"Uh," he said, "is the boss man in?" The boss man. Why had he said that? He'd been planning to ask her to lunch.

"No," she said, "but he should be back in a little while"—her voice lilted up hopefully—"if you want to wait."

"Sure," said George. "What's time for." He sat on a chair, tilted it back. "Maybe you can help me with something. Stuart's never mentioned it, but it might be relevant to the case. Tell me what you know about this guy, the Magician."

"Oh!" Ruth stared at him in admiration, her face luminous.

Beautiful, he thought. You might not notice it unless you knew her, but she was beautiful.

"The Magician," she said. "Yes."

"The hell with Ross," said George. "Let's go have lunch."

Twelve

To the Editor:

A man sits in the Cochise County jail awaiting trial for the murder of his wife. Did he do it?

Meanwhile, our dear friend the Magician is still missing. Is there any hope we'll ever see him again? He is likely dead, maybe even murdered. For what? Knowing too much? What could he know, a simple soul like our friend? The Dudley P.D. say they are looking into it. But are they? They look pretty busy. They've fingerprinted some of us, questioned some of us, too. We have to ask, Why us? We are his friends.

But what, you might ask, is that troublemaker, yours truly, Ken Dooley, getting at? Well, folks, the Magician and the accused murderer were once in the same pod in the jail. Not only that, they were seen conversing together. About what, no one knows—except the accused, of course.

Gas prices are rising everywhere, so maybe Dudley P.D., with their limited resources, can't afford the gas it would take to drive out to the jail to question the alleged murderer about his conversation with the Magician. Limited resources is the only reason I can think of. How about you?

Ken Dooley

IT WAS late afternoon when Stuart strode into his office, a copy of the *Dudley Weekly* under his arm. The office was full. Ruth was there with George and Mara, all of them drinking coffee.

"This just came out," he said, holding up the newspaper. "Our friend Ken Dooley is at it again."

"What?" said Ruth.

Stuart flung the paper on Ruth's desk. "Page three, upper right."

George and Mara read it over Ruth's shoulder.

"How can he write that?" said Mara, looking sick. "It isn't fair. What a terrible man. What does he have against my father?"

"Conversed?" Ruth looked up at Stuart. "Jackson didn't say they conversed."

"Of course they didn't converse," said Stuart in exasperation. "Nobody conversed with the Magician. He'd pick up a word and say it over and over."

"Then what the hell is this all about?" said George.

"It's about nothing. It's about saying things to get yourself noticed. The guy's a narcissist." Stuart sat down. "He should stick to shooting at the border patrol."

"I'm going out to talk to Dooley tonight," said George.

"Why?" Stuart looked at George in amazement. "Because of this letter?"

"Because of a lot of things," said George, "but not this letter. Did you know he was friends with Sid Hamblin?"

"It's libel," said Ruth. "You can sue Ken Dooley for libel."

Stuart shook his head. "It's not libel. He says alleged, he covers himself. The guy isn't stupid. He just enjoys upsetting people."

"How could anyone enjoy that?" said Ruth in disgust.

"That's funny," said Mara suddenly.

"What?" Ruth asked.

"Just something somebody said. I wonder—" Mara stood up. "I'm going over to the Co-op."

Ruth looked over at her. "Why?"

Mara opened the door. "We need some kind of vegetable for dinner. I'll get something there."

Ruth tried not to look worried.

George put his hand on her shoulder. "Let her go," he said soothingly. "She's all grown up."

THE letter haunted Mara, so nasty, insinuating. *The guy isn't stupid. He just enjoys upsetting people,* Stuart had said. She mulled over the organic vegetables in the back of the Co-op and decided on green beans. She filled a bag and took it up to the register.

Josh was ringing up an interminable purchase of mostly grains and vegetables for a young mother with a baby strapped to her front. His face reddened slightly when he saw Mara.

Mara plunked her beans onto the counter when the mother left.

"I guess this person Ken Dooley cares a lot about the Magician," she said, handing him a five. "I mean, his name's on the poster. You said he was, like, this activist, but who is he exactly?"

Josh put the change in her hand and shrugged apologetically. "I don't really know who he is," he said. "He hasn't been in town that long, but I heard he lived in Mexico before he came here. But then somebody else said Thailand, so who knows. He's doesn't talk about his past." He lowered his voice. "I did hear this rumor . . ."

Mara waited. "What?" she said finally.

"I heard Ken Dooley isn't his real name— that he changed it. Got in trouble with the feds. He was an activist. I guess he was big time, offended a lot of people. Been running ever since."

"Alaska," said Mara urgently. "Did he ever mention Alaska?"

"I—" Josh put his finger to his lips. "Here he comes now."

Mara stepped away from the register as a man strode in, a sheaf of paper in his hand.

His curly hair was tousled, and he wore sunglasses, a Mexican guayabera shirt, jeans, and huaraches.

"Hey there, Josh," he said, but his sunglasses were aimed at Mara. "Got a bunch of flyers to post. Thought I'd leave you some."

"Sure thing," said Josh. "I read your latest letter, man."

"What'd you think?" His sunglasses were still aimed at Mara.

Even though she couldn't see his eyes, she could feel his interest—he was the same age as her dad, as Jackson, maybe even older, but his attention didn't feel fatherly.

"Cool," said Josh.

Mara moved around him, headed for the door, and opened it.

"Who was that?" she heard Ken Dooley saying as the door closed behind her.

Mara walked to her car, swinging the bag of beans. Parked next to Jackson's Volvo was a big old van, its blue paint faded to gray. As she reached the Volvo, someone called out to her.

"Hey, Mara!"

She turned.

Ken Dooley had come up so fast he was right behind her.

"What?" she said.

He smiled. "Josh says you're visiting. Just like to say hi to pretty ladies who are new here and make them feel at home."

Mara put her hand on the handle and pulled, but she couldn't open the door far enough to get in because he was standing in her way. "Excuse me," she said. "I have to go."

"What's your hurry?" His voice was relaxed. He rested his hand on the car. "You could at least tell me your name."

"You know my name."

"Your last name. Who you're visiting." He smiled again. "Might even be someone I know."

"Well, it isn't." Mara pulled on the door with all her strength, and Ken stumbled backward. She got inside fast and locked the door.

"I can find out, you silly girl," shouted Ken Dooley, his face red and venomous looking. "I know everybody in this town!"

GEORGE shoved his Colt Commander pistol into its holster and shrugged on his tan corduroy jacket. If he was going out of town to some school bus in the desert to see a guy who liked to shoot at the border patrol, it didn't hurt to be careful.

Ruth had asked him to dinner and he'd had to say no, because of needing to check out Ken Dooley, but he'd given her a definite yes for tomorrow night. Wouldn't want to get himself killed before he had a chance to have dinner at Ruth's.

He drove down Highway 92 till he came to the bridge over the wash that Frieda's neighbor had told him to watch for, then slowed, looking for a dirt road. It was close to seven, the purple sky deepening to indigo as the sun slipped behind the mountains.

It was so empty out here that that Dooley guy could shoot a border patrolman and bury him without anyone noticing. George was driving the Olds for its inconspicuousness, but he realized now the Caddy would have been better—if he went missing, someone might remember the big yellow car.

George spotted the dirt road and saw the school bus a quarter of a mile down, its windows all lit up. Must be on a generator, and Dooley must be home. George killed his lights, made the turn, and stopped to debate his next move.

Maybe he should reconsider the whole thing. Then George remembered Ruth's face when he'd told her he was going out to Ken Dooley's place to talk to him. Bright and soft at the same time, and so full of confidence in him. Well, what the hell.

He turned on the headlights, started the Olds, and headed down the road. You didn't want to sneak up on anyone out here in the desert. Soon he heard music, loud. Some chanting New Age stuff.

A shabby blue Dodge van was parked to the right of the bus. George pulled in behind it. The music was so loud the guy probably didn't even know anyone was out here.

George got out of his car, and the first gunshot blasted a few yards away from him, cutting through the air like fast-flying insects. The second round raised a cloud of dust close to his foot. He ducked down beside the Olds, but that didn't necessarily mean anything because of ricochet. *Watch out for ricochet.*

Abruptly the music stopped.

George felt something pierce his left arm as another round ripped through a mesquite tree near him. His arm began to burn. A pellet from the shotgun blast—that son of a bitch had shot him.

RUTH wiped her hands on a kitchen towel and turned off the rice. "What was it you wanted to tell me?" she asked Mara.

"It's about Ken Dooley."

Tyler came into the kitchen. "I'm starving. What's for dinner?"

"A roast chicken from Safeway," said Ruth. She looked at Mara. "What about Ken Dooley?"

"He came into the Co-op when I was there," Mara said, "and he followed me out. When I tried to leave, he threatened me."

"What?" said Ruth. "How dare he!"

"But that's not important," Mara said. "Remember what Stuart said about him, that he was smart but he liked to upset people?"

"Yes," said Ruth.

"That's exactly what Mrs. Dixon said about Kevin."

Ruth frowned. "Kevin?"

"Kevin Dixon, Jenny's brother. They didn't get along. And Mrs. Dixon looked like she had money. So if Jenny died, Kevin would probably get all their mother's money, not just half. And he could have planted that poison at Jackson's so Jackson would be arrested and no one would come looking for him."

"But I don't see—" Ruth began, but Mara cut her off.

"Mrs. Dixon said Kevin was highly intelligent but he upset people, just like Ken Dooley. And she said he'd traveled the world." Mara's voice rose excitedly. "I asked about Ken Dooley at the Co-op, and he's traveled the world, too. He hasn't been in town that long. And he never talks about his past."

"Ken Dooley! Kevin Dixon!" shouted Tyler. "Who cares?"

Mara almost dropped the bowl. "Ken Dooley and Kevin Dixon. They have the same initials."

"That does it," said Ruth. "I'm calling George right now."

DIMLY, George was aware of chimes. What—? His cell phone was ringing in his car. He'd forgotten to turn it off. The phone chimed. The shotgun clicked. Out of ammo, thought George. Wasted it shooting wildly, an amateur. He stepped out from behind his car before the guy had a chance to reload.

Ken Dooley, naked except for jeans, stood in a circle of light by the door of the school bus holding a short-barreled shotgun.

The profound calm of total focus descended on George, and in some visceral way, he remembered that this kind of thing was what he had liked about police work: All your worries and anxieties gone away, it was just you and the situation at that moment.

"Hi, Ken," said George, making sure the Colt Commander was in plain sight. His left arm felt strangely numb. "Could we get a little civilized here? Drop the gun, please."

Ken let the shotgun go, and it fell to the ground. "Hey, don't I know you?" he asked suddenly.

"We met at Sid Hamblin's."

"Stuart's investigator. That's just great." Ken's voice turned snide. "Now he's hired you to terrorize innocent citizens?"

"It's not like I had a choice. What do you expect? I drive down the road, an ordinary citizen, and you come out shooting."

"I thought you were the border patrol. What are you doing here?"

"I just got a couple of questions for you."

Something trickled down George's arm—sweat, probably. He ignored it.

"Then ask away," said Ken. "I've got nothing to hide."

"About Jenny Williams," said George.

Ken put his hands on his hips, cocky. "What about her?"

"I heard she came to see you," said George, "right before she died. Something about a letter she wanted you to write."

Ken looked at him blankly. "Man, you are totally off the map here. I saw her at Sid's a couple of times, but she never came to see me about any letter."

George had no idea whether Ken was lying or not. His left arm tingled; the adrenaline calm had worn off and he was very tired.

"Now I got it!" said Ken triumphantly. "Payback time. This is really about the letter in the paper today, isn't it?"

"What kind of crap was that, anyway?" said George in disgust. "There's no connection between what happened to the Magician and Jackson Williams. Williams was in jail and you know it."

"The guy's a jerk," said Ken. "For all I

know, he killed Sid, too. Thought I'd sling a little mud—for Sid and Jenny's sake."

"What? They were saints? Jenny screwing Sid behind her husband's back?"

"She was just trying to survive the best way she knew how. To make up for Jackson and his little affair."

"What affair?"

Ken looked self-righteous. "He never mentioned that, huh? Him and the woman next door."

"That's bull!" The blood rushed to George's head. His arm throbbed. "Anita Selby told you that, didn't she?" The sleeve of his corduroy jacket was dark with blood. Seeing the blood made him feel light-headed. He felt himself sway a little. "Anita," he said doggedly. "What do you know about her?"

"Hey, man, I don't know beans about Anita," said Ken. "You better go to the emergency room, have someone look at that arm."

George thought maybe he was right and it was time to go. "You should have aimed," he said, needing the last word with Ken. "Then you wouldn't have hit me."

"JUST GIVE IT TO me straight, Doc," said George in the emergency room of the Sierra Vista Hospital. "Am I going to live?"

"I think so, now that I've given you the tetanus shot." The nice lady doctor smiled, then turned serious. "That barbed wire can be nasty stuff." She glanced at him. "Odd wound for barbed wire."

George's eyes veered away. "Yeah." No way he was going to tell her it was a gunshot wound—she'd have to call the cops.

"It's just a flesh wound, but you need to take all of those antibiotics. Change the dressing once a day and don't get it wet."

"Sure thing," said George. He moved toward the door.

"Wait," said the doctor. "Let me give you some samples of Vicodin for pain, save you getting that prescription filled."

George took care of business at the front desk. His arm ached dully, so he stopped at a drinking fountain and took two of the Vicodin, then went out to the parking lot. He drove home, unlocked the door to his apartment, and flicked on the light. His knees felt like they might buckle under him. Oops. Pills were kicking in.

He went to the living room, sat on the couch, and took a few deep breaths to re-orient himself. Then he reached for the new disclosure on Jackson Williams he'd brought home with him.

He opened the file and began to read an e-mail, but the phone rang. "George Maynard here."

"Oh, good. It's Ruth." Her voice lilted up. "I know it's late, but I was worried. I've been calling your cell all evening."

"Yeah? Too busy dodging buckshot to answer it. Ken Dooley thought I was a border patrolman and got me in the arm with a shotgun. Just got back from the emergency room, had it taped up. Just a scratch. Nothing to worry about."

"But—but—" Ruth sputtered. "Ken Dooley—is he in jail?"

"Uh-uh. Make-my-day law. You go on someone's private property in Arizona, they got a right to shoot you." George rallied briefly. "Not that he isn't an ass. Only thing that really pissed me off is, I got nowhere with him."

"Maybe you didn't ask him the right questions."

George paused. He was really tired. "What does that mean?"

"Mara and I . . . well, there's something we need to tell you. Did you know Jenny had a brother? Kevin Dixon?"

Anita had said something about a brother. What was it? He couldn't focus. Then he remembered. "Yeah. He died."

"No, he didn't. It was one of Jenny's lies. I think you should go see Jenny's mother. Let me give you her address in Green Valley."

George scrawled the address on the front of the file, letters veering upward. "What am I seeing her about?"

"Ask her for a photograph of Kevin."

"Why?"

"Because Mara found out a few things. I'll tell you about it later, but we think Ken Dooley might be Kevin Dixon."

"No kidding. Interesting," said George. It *was* interesting, but it didn't make sense. Maybe it would make sense tomorrow. He wanted to get off the phone while he still made sense. "I'll get on it first thing in the morning," he said. "Got to go now, okay?"

George hung up. He took a deep breath;

then he picked up the disclosure file and started to read the e-mail again.

Hey there, Casey. I was thinking. Here we are, two professors, and all we do is bitch about our wives. Jenny's mad at me, and I don't care. We haven't spoken for two days, and you know what? I'm enjoying it, in a sadistic kind of way. I used to be a nice guy, but you know what they say. Hell is other people. Sometimes I even think about her being dead and all I feel is relief.

George registered in a vague sort of way that this probably wasn't so good for the case, but that wasn't what bothered him. He went back to the line *Hell is other people*. Ruth had said those same words to him in her kitchen. So Jackson said it to her and she said it to you, he thought.

So what?

He threw the file across the room. Ken Dooley had told him tonight that Ruth had been having an affair with Jackson—that made two people. Two people, and he hadn't checked it out at all.

NINE O'CLOCK IN the morning and the golf course was bright green, thousands of gallons of water wasted every year so people could go out and hit a ball with a stick. Where was the sport in that? George turned down the street to Grace Dixon's house feeling not exactly chipper but at least clearheaded.

He'd virtually passed out on his couch the night before and slept heavily. That morning the first thing he did was flush the rest of the Vicodin down the toilet. Too powerful, too much like booze. It had screwed up his thinking.

He didn't know why Ruth thought Ken Dooley might be Kevin Dixon, but he liked the idea, especially now that he saw where Grace Dixon lived. Definitely some money there, best motive there was. He checked the numbers on the pink stucco town houses till he found the one he was looking for.

He parked and got out. He wore jeans and a blue polo shirt, the only polo he owned. His ex had given it to him to upgrade his image, but he'd only worn it once. It was hot—must be near a hundred degrees. He took a deep breath. Time to get lucky, he thought.

Beyond the wrought-iron gate at Mrs.

Dixon's, a big spiky yucca grew in the center of the gravel yard. He went up to a red door and knocked. He was about to knock again when the door opened. A skinny old man in pink walking shorts, a pink-and-blue-striped polo, and spotless white running shoes looked at him inquisitively.

No one had mentioned a husband. "Mr. Dixon?" asked George.

"Mr. Dixon died some time ago," said the man.

"I'm sorry," said George. "Actually, I'm looking for Mrs. Dixon."

"Grace is in the hospital under observation," said the man. "Her heart's not too good, and she was having chest pains yesterday." He peered out at George. "Who might you be?"

"George Maynard. I'm an investigator looking into the death of Mrs. Dixon's daughter." He produced his card. "I was hoping Mrs. Dixon could answer a few questions."

"My, my." The man took the card. "It'd be good to put a few more nails in that Jackson Williams's coffin, hey?" His hand shot out. "I'm Henry Bradshaw. Old friend of the Dixon family."

George gripped his hand. The flesh felt like parchment paper. *Nails in that Jackson Williams's coffin*—guy wasn't biased or anything.

Henry went on. "I thought I'd better make sure everything was okay here. Come on in. Maybe I can answer some questions."

George followed him into the living room. Henry sat on a white couch, and George sat on the edge of a white armchair.

"Hurt your arm, did you?" asked Henry.

George nodded. "I got shot."

"You don't say." Henry looked at him with admiration. "All you policemen, you deserve a medal, every one of you. I'm a big supporter of law enforcement. Watch *Law and Order* faithfully. What did you want to know?"

"Jenny's brother, Kevin?" George said. "Maybe they kept in touch, family members and all. She might have said something to him that could add a few more nails to that coffin you were talking about. How can I reach him?"

"Oh, my." Henry rubbed his jaw. "That's a hard one. Grace told me she spoke with him not too long ago, but I don't think she has an address for him. He's somewhere in Alaska."

"Alaska," said George blankly.

Henry laughed. "Makes sense if you know him. He's an oddball—never could stay put, hold down a job."

"Maybe you could find a number where he could be reached."

"I don't think Grace ever calls him. He calls her." He scratched his head. "And I doubt if Kevin talked to his sister, 'cause they were estranged."

"Oh?"

"Had the most on-again off-again relationship you've ever seen. Even when they were growing up, crazy about each other one week, hated each other the next. But I'll tell you one thing, Kevin loved his little sister to—well, he loved her. Even if she didn't always love him back, especially when he got . . . older."

George leaned toward Henry. "We'd really like to find him. Maybe Grace has photographs lying around?"

"Photographs." He brightened. "Sure, she's got photographs."

"Maybe I could borrow a couple of the most recent."

"Grace wouldn't mind, I guess, if it will

help pound in those nails!" He smiled, stood up, and started out of the room.

George looked around as he waited for Henry. More pillows on the couch than anyone could ever use, and so clean.

Henry came back holding a manila envelope. "There's two pictures. I put 'em in here," he said, handing the envelope to George. "They're not real current—maybe six or seven years old."

George took the envelope and slid out the photographs. One was of a man with a neatly trimmed beard near a mountain, holding a pair of skis; the other a clean-shaven man on a couch in a living room. Not this couch or this living room and not Ken Dooley. George had never seen this man in his life.

MARA woke up late to an empty house. Tyler was long gone off to school, and Ruth's car wasn't in the driveway, so she must be at work. She showered and dressed and went into the kitchen. She didn't feel like cereal, so she ate leftover chicken from last night.

She nibbled at the wing, staring out the window at the bird feeder in the backyard. At that moment, she had a flash of insight: When this is all over, she thought, I'm going to go to law school.

Right now, however, she was going to do what she'd planned to do last night. She went into Tyler's room, turned on his computer, went online to Google, and typed in "Ken Dooley." Only eight hundred and twenty-one entries.

WHAT the hell is going on? George thought, driving back on I-10. Ruth sending him all the way to Green Valley for this—he glanced at the envelope containing the photos of a stranger. And he'd had other things to do, like check up on Frieda and the Magician. Maybe Ruth wasn't as straight-on wonderful as he'd thought. Aw. Maybe she was, but he needed to watch himself. Two people had told him she'd been having an affair with Jackson Williams. And Ruth herself had said, hadn't she, there in her kitchen, that Jenny was a blight on Jackson's life.

"YOU shot my investigator," said Stuart, steely-voiced.

"It was out-and-out intimidation!" Ken Dooley shouted. "I had a right to. He was on my property. There are statutes protecting a man on his own property in this state, and you know it!"

"Let's take a look at some of those statutes," Stuart sneered. "How about that?"

"Fine with me. You go right ahead."

There was a silence, maybe Stuart looking things up.

Ruth closed her eyes. It was late morning, close to twelve. Ken Dooley had been in Stuart's office for the last twenty minutes arguing. She hoped he wasn't carrying a gun in that leather bag.

The bell tinkled. She opened her eyes.

George walked in carrying a manila envelope. Ruth was so relieved, the blood rushed to her cheeks. She saw George's blue polo shirt first, because she'd never seen him wear anything like that, then the dressing on his arm, before she looked at his face.

"George—" she began tentatively, then stopped. His eyes were opaque. He was mad at her.

"I went to Grace Dixon's house," he said, looming over her desk. He tossed her the manila envelope. "Have a look."

She undid the clasp. Inside were two

photographs. She slid them out and looked at a man with skis, a man on a couch. She looked up at George. "Who is he?"

"Kevin Dixon," said George.

"Oh, shoot." Her face fell. "Then he's not Ken Dooley after all."

"Kevin lives in *Alaska*. You sent me on a wild-goose chase."

"What if I'd been right? I was only trying to help." Her voice wavered. "Why are you mad at me? You hung up on me last night."

He blinked. Then the blankness went out of his eyes. "I did?"

"Yes."

"Look, Ruth. I wasn't in my right mind. I took some Vicodin for the pain, and my thought processes were just all fouled up."

There was a little silence. Ruth bit her lip.

"Aw, Ruth. I'm sorry." He ducked his head as if he were ashamed. "I'm just a jerk."

"You are not. And look at your poor arm," said Ruth. "Does it hurt? You know you need to change that dressing once a day."

"I'm fine."

"This Ken Dooley stuff, Mara and I really really thought . . . We didn't mean . . ." She lowered her voice and glanced at the closed door to Stuart's office. "He's in there now. Ken Dooley."

George looked disgusted. "Then I'm outta here."

"George? Are you still coming to dinner tonight?"

"I'll be there."

GEORGE drove to Wood Canyon, where the big cottonwoods were shedding their yellow leaves. He walked down the pitted asphalt street that dissolved into dirt on the edges and trudged up the steps to Frieda's house.

The front door was wide open. He tapped on the wood frame.

"Anybody home?"

"Who is it?" a woman called.

"Uh, George Maynard, looking for Frieda."

"Oh." A woman in her fifties came to the door. A loose embroidered dress hung from her bony shoulders; her graying hair was pulled back tight, displaying long silver earrings.

"I'm an investigator," said George. "I thought you might—"

She interrupted. "I know. You're asking about the Magician. My neighbor told me. Please come into the kitchen. I just made a pot of tea. There's something I'd like to show you."

The kitchen was large, with an ancient gas stove and a white porcelain sink. Jars and bottles lined the walls. But the first thing George noticed was the flowers. The place was full of dead flowers, twisted into wreaths on the walls, hanging from rafters, sticking up from mason jars on the counters.

George sneezed. His arm hadn't been bothering him, but now it started up again. He sneezed a second time.

"Oh, dear. It sounds like you've got allergies."

George looked at the flowers. "Good way to find out, I guess."

"Are you with the Dudley police?"

"No. I'm a private investigator for Stuart Ross's office."

"Oh, *him*." Frieda made a face. "I like his secretary, though. She's nice. She came to my booth with her son when we had a festival in Grassy Park this summer. Ruth. You must know Ruth."

"Great woman," said George heartily. "Great." He paused. "You were going to show me something."

"Yes, it's fabulous." She pulled open a kitchen drawer and handed him an envelope. "It was with my mail. Go ahead, read it."

George took the letter out of the envelope and began to read.

Dear Freeda, me and a friend of yers are here at the halfway house and he asked me to write this for him. Yer friend had to leave fast becaws the soshul servish were comin to make him take his meds. He ran away and a pikup gave him a ride to Tuson. He's had a ruff time, but now he's got different meds and feels better. He still has the peecock feather you gave him and he's waving it right now to say hello and to thank you for all that you dun for him. I guess you know by now who I mean. It's yer old friend the Magishun.

George looked up. "Son of a gun," he said.

"I'm so happy," said Frieda. "I was about to go downtown to tell Sergeant Nelson when you showed up."

George blew his nose. He looked at the envelope. It was postmarked from Tucson a few days ago, with no return address.

"Let me give you something for that allergy," said Frieda. She scanned the wall with the jars and bottles. "Let's see."

George sneezed again and felt the ache in his arm. Then the jars and bottles came into focus, rows and rows of them, and near one end were several labeled clearly with skull and crossbones. He went closer for a better look. "What are these?"

"They're poison," said Frieda. "I label them as a precaution."

Curious, George took down a bottle. "Why even have them?"

"Some of them are only poison if the dosage is too high, and others are for teaching, like when I have my booth."

"What's the worst you got?" asked George. "Poison-wise."

"The worst, well, monkshood, but I don't have it anymore."

"Monkshood? What's that, exactly?"

"A plant. Its scientific name is *Aconitum napellus.*"

Aconitum napellus. George felt like he'd

been hit with a brick. Aconite. Aconite was what had killed Jenny, and Sid as well. "You said you don't have it anymore? Why not?"

"One day I was going through my supplies and I noticed it was gone. It was so annoying."

"When?" asked George. "When did you notice it was gone?"

She stepped back. "I don't know."

"Think," he thundered.

Frieda flinched. "For heaven's sake, why are you being so rude?" She snatched the letter off the table. "The police need to see this. I have to go downtown right away."

George followed her out through the living room. She stood at the door, waiting for him to leave. "I need you to go now. I'm very busy."

"You said it was poison. Don't you feel any responsibility?" He raised his voice again. "Who had access to it?"

Frieda's face was pale. "Please, won't you leave," she said.

He walked to the door. "Tell me one thing," he said. "This summer at your booth, when Ruth stopped by, was it gone then?"

"I don't think so." Her voice was defensive. "I can't say for sure. It's not like I keep track every single day. One day I looked and it wasn't there, that's all."

George turned and walked down the stairs. Ruth had been at Frieda's booth. Ruth, wonderful Ruth. She didn't like Jenny, *a blight on Jackson's life*. Ruth, always worrying, always trying to help, always trying to fix things. And Sid Hamblin—she didn't like him, either. He was at the memorial service at her house. He could have had the probiotics with him there.

They'd found the bottle with the aconite under the bed. Why would Ruth leave it there to incriminate Jackson, her friend? Because all that rigmarole she'd given him about brotherly love was bull and she *had* been having an affair. Had it turned sour? Maybe she wanted to get even. That nice woman—in her kitchen, they'd shared secrets. Were all her confidences just a ploy to get him to overlook anything incriminating against her?

No. It couldn't be—it was just a paranoid fantasy. How did he know? Hell is other people.

Thirteen

MARA drove fast over the Mule Mountain Pass in Jackson's Volvo. She went through the tunnel, down Tombstone Canyon, past the courthouse, and onto Main Street. She finally found a parking space two blocks from Stuart's office.

She grabbed a clutch of papers from the passenger seat and walked over. Through the window, she could see Ruth at her desk and Stuart standing.

Stuart was talking when she walked in.

"Guys?" Mara said.

Ruth looked at her. "Goodness," she said. "What's with you?"

"He was never any kind of activist," said Mara, all in a rush. "I went online and I found him. I found Ken Dooley."

"You want a medal?" Stuart said. "We find him all the time."

"Hush," Ruth said to him.

"Online," said Mara. "I got a picture from the newspaper and everything. I made two copies. Here." She put half the papers on Ruth's desk, gave the other half to Stuart. "I don't see how he could be who we thought he was, but this is almost as good."

"A certified public accountant," Stuart said after a moment, "for a firm in Pittsburgh."

"That's Ken in the picture, all right," said Ruth. "In a suit. Receiving a certificate for thirty-five years of service."

"A certified public accountant," Stuart said again, with glee. "His reputation will be ruined."

"That doesn't mean he isn't dangerous," said Ruth. "Maybe he's wanted for fraud and Jenny found out. . . ." Her voice trailed off, and she looked at Mara. "I already knew he wasn't Jenny's brother. I sent George all the way to Green Valley to check it out."

"What are you talking about?" said Stuart.

"Mara and I had this idea Ken might be Jenny's brother—"

"I didn't know Jenny had a brother," said Stuart.

"It's too hard to explain," said Ruth. "I told George, and he went to Grace Dixon's and got pictures of her son, Jenny's brother. They're right here." She held up a manila envelope.

"George went all the way to Tucson 'cause

you guys were playing amateur detective?" Stuart looked annoyed. "And for what? Damn it. You're wasting his precious time."

Ruth waved the envelope at him. "Don't you want to see?"

"Why would I want to see? It's not even relevant." Stuart grabbed the envelope and tossed it into the wastebasket.

GEORGE drove from Frieda's house back to the highway and into town. He turned up Main Street and found a place to park. Then he sat in his car, trying to think. Maybe he was overreacting. It just fit so well into what George knew in his heart was his basically pessimistic view of the world that he had from being a cop.

Okay. I am a professional. What would a professional do?

He had no idea. Just play it by ear. He got out of his car and walked to Stuart's office.

Mara was sitting with her feet up on Ruth's desk when he came in. Ruth was probably there, too—well, of course, she had to be—but George didn't look. The door to Stuart's office was closed.

When she saw George, Mara took her feet down. "Guess what!" she said in an excited voice. "Ken Dooley was a certified public accountant for thirty-five years! In Pittsburgh!"

"Don't you think that's amazing?" Ruth chimed in eagerly. "Mara went online and found this picture of him in a suit."

Ruth wasn't speaking loudly, but her voice hurt his ears.

"No kidding," he said without affect. "Stuart around?"

"He's in his office sulking," Mara said. "Because you went—"

"Mara," said Ruth warningly. "What's going on, anyway?" she asked George.

"I need to see Stuart," George said, not meeting her eyes. "I don't want to talk right now."

"Ooh!" Mara said. "Maybe you can tell us at dinner tonight? Ruth is making pork roast with prunes!"

"Dinner." George banged the side of his head in a way that must have looked completely phony. He looked right at Ruth, but he didn't see her. "Can't make it," he said. "Something came up."

"That's all right," Ruth said quickly. Suddenly the air was so charged with tension it felt as though it might ignite.

"Excuse me," said George. He edged past Mara to Stuart's office.

"I feel terrible," Ruth said to Mara. "Like I'm getting a migraine."

"You get migraines?" Mara said in surprise.

Ruth rose. "I think I'll take the rest of the day off."

"CLOSE the door," said Stuart as George sat in the client chair. "You don't look so good." He looked at George's arm. "That where Ken Dooley shot you?"

"Yep."

Stuart's mouth twitched. "They tell you?"

"What?"

"Ken Dooley was a certified public accountant in Pittsburgh."

"Yeah," said George. He paused. "Yeah, they did."

Stuart looked at him with concern. "You sure you're all right?"

"So," said George, not bothering to answer. "You know the poison that killed Jenny Williams?"

"Sure. Aconite."

"I found the probable source."

"You're kidding. Hot *damn*." Stuart looked at George. "You don't look exactly joyous about it." He frowned. "So what's the source?"

"Her name's Frieda. She—"

"Frieda?" Stuart interrupted. "Frieda!"

"And," George went on heavily, "that Magician guy? She got a letter from him. He's in some halfway house in Tucson."

"I wouldn't bet on that," said Stuart. "Listen—"

"Let me finish," George interrupted. "Frieda sets up a booth in Grassy Park when they have these festivals." He sighed. "They had one this summer, and"—he paused— "Ruth was there."

"Ruth," said Stuart guiltily. "I guess I was a little hard on her. But I was mad. Sending you off on these errands, wasting your time." He held up a manila envelope. "She gave me this, and I threw it in the trash; then I fished it out again. Recognize it?"

"The photographs of Kevin Dixon I got from Jenny's mom's."

"Do they mean anything to you at all? Look carefully."

George took the envelope and slipped the

photographs out again—the bearded man with skis, the man on the couch; the photographs that had taken five hours of his time, at Ruth's urging, to get. "Nothing," he said. "They don't mean anything."

"Maybe you never saw him. I forget you've never spent much time in Dudley." Stuart paused. "I didn't realize it till today, but he came back. He was here one night, in front of my office."

"Who? Kevin Dixon?"

"Yes. Dressed like a tourist, camera and everything. He asked me about architecture. I recognized his voice, you know, subliminally, but he looked so different I didn't make the connection."

"You already knew Kevin?" said George in surprise.

"Yes, but I didn't know I knew him. It wasn't till later I had a sense of something screwy."

THE sun shone on the golfers in their bright clothing. The man in the tangerine-colored polo shirt parked the red Volkswagen, a birthday present two years ago, on the street of pink stucco town houses and got out, smiling.

It was good he'd decided to stop taking the meds again. He was so clear today, remembering old friends; they'd brought flowers and gifts to his cave. He had mingled with the tourists and taken pictures of the lawyer's office and the post office and Frieda's house. Frieda. His best friend. In his polos and khakis, he'd passed her once going to the post office and she'd never blinked an eye.

He wished he could tell his mother the whole story, but he knew she wouldn't understand, and besides, she'd just come home from the hospital. He would tend to her like a good son.

A police car drove down the street patrolling the neighborhood, and he waved at the officer inside. The officer waved. And why not? He was wearing his polo shirt and khakis. People believed you or not because of clothes. That's all it took was clothes.

Down the way, a few houses past his mother's, a man got out of a big old yellow Cadillac. He wore a striped shirt, a bolo tie, jeans, and cowboy boots. He didn't quite fit in. Probably going to see his mother. The man in the cowboy boots walked toward him.

Another police car drove slowly by. Or

maybe the same one as before. He couldn't remember.

"Kevin Dixon?" said the man wearing the bolo tie.

He blinked. "Yes."

"Name's George Maynard. I'm an investigator for an attorney in Dudley, Stuart Ross. I think he was your lawyer once."

"Not mine," said Kevin Dixon.

"I just have a couple of questions." The man took his arm. "Let's take a walk down to my car. Don't want to get your mom upset."

"Not mine," Kevin said again. "Mr. Ross is not my lawyer. He's the Magician's lawyer. I'm Kevin Dixon."

"Your lawyer says you're the Magician," said George. "He recognized you from some photos. Jenny Williams is your sister."

"I walked over the mountains to her house," said Kevin. "She never let me come around except at night when her husband wasn't home because she was ashamed of me. But deep down she loved me from when we were kids, playing games."

"And you loved her?"

"I loved her," Kevin Dixon said, "every way you can love a person. I was thirteen and she was seven, but I loved her like grown-ups love each other."

"Ah," said George.

"She said it was wrong, that she'd tell Ken Dooley about me if I didn't take my meds and he'd put it in the newspaper how much I loved her when we were kids." Kevin looked at George confidingly. "I have my own kind of meds—if I concentrate on thinking things three times, it blocks the bad stuff. But she said that was stupid. She wanted me to go with her to a counselor to talk about everything."

"Ah," said George again.

"Counselors won't talk to you unless you're taking meds, but when I take them, everything's so sad. I wanted to just be me, my real self. But I started taking them for her." He glanced at George. "But I still acted like my real self around my friends so they would keep on liking me. *Frieda.*"

"And then what happened?"

"The meds made me understand what Jenny *really* wanted."

"What was that?"

"She wanted to die, of course. Jenny wanted to die so much."

George stared at Kevin Dixon. He hadn't

thought it would be so easy. "Jenny wanted to die," he said cautiously. "Why is that?"

"He made her so unhappy, her life wasn't any good anymore."

"Sure," said George. "I can see your point. But most folks, if they feel that way, they just get a divorce."

"No. She didn't have the strength to do it on her own."

"Do what?"

"Die. She couldn't die. She cried all the time, but she couldn't die. I took the poison stuff from Frieda's." He stopped. "Just in case. And then—she told Sid about us when we were kids." His eyes jittered. "She said he wouldn't tell, but he threw me out of his house. And I think he told SEABHS about me. I heard someone walking on the path to my cave, and it had to be that SEABHS lady coming with my meds."

"So Sid had to go, too, huh?" said George.

"It was the meds." His voice rose. "They weren't good. They made me cold. Cold and—and thoughtful. And I really didn't need them. I had to put on an act instead of being myself. I dumped out Sid and Jenny's capsules and put some of that powder in. I put the rest of it in a bottle I found with her husband's name on it and put it under the bed so they would blame it on him. It was the right thing to do because he's the one who really killed her."

"Not exactly," said George. "Those meds, you taking them now?"

"Coming off," said Kevin. "She shouldn't have told Sid, and she was going to tell Ken Dooley, too, but Jackson was the one who killed her. I was just the agent." His voice rose wildly. "You ask my mother. She'll tell you the same thing. Jackson killed Jenny." He backed away. "I have to go now. My mother needs me. I'm wearing my best polo shirt just for her."

"Uh," said George, "I thought we could go for a little ride first, over to the police station."

"The police station?"

"Sure. It's comfortable there. You can tell your story again. It's a good story. Everybody will be interested."

"My best polo," said Kevin. "Polo, polo, polo."

"JENNY said her brother was molested as a kid," said Ruth sadly, "when it was herself she was talking about. I think maybe she wasn't really so concerned about Owen and my boys—she just wanted to bring up the topic. But I was so mad I just turned off on her. She might have told me everything if I'd let her talk."

"And if we had some apple pie, we could have pie à la mode, if we had some ice cream," said Stuart. "What's the point in beating yourself up about it?"

"At least Kevin confessed." She sighed. "Now it's simple."

"Simple!" said Stuart. "Ha! A confession means nothing. The guy was a babbling idiot by the time George got him to the police station."

"Maybe," said Ruth. "You never read the workup SEABHS did, did you?"

"Scanned it."

"Well, I read it. I've got it here. One of the things the psychologist said was"—she read out loud—" 'This guy is all over the map. I can't get a reading on him, and I suspect possible malingering.' "

"Possible malingering," said Stuart. "His mom has money—for every shrink that finds possible malingering, there's another that will say there isn't."

"So what's going to happen?"

"His mom will get him some hotshot Tucson lawyer, and the first thing that lawyer's going to do is file a Rule Eleven."

"What's that?" asked Ruth.

"Motion to determine competency to stand trial," said Stuart. "If he's found not competent, they'll send him to a hospital, pump him full of pharmaceuticals. If and when he's restored to competency, the case goes forward."

Stuart shrugged out of his jacket and hung it on a hook. "I'm taking the afternoon off," he said. "You can close up if you want."

"Then I will," said Ruth. "I have a lot to do. Don't forget tonight," she called as he left. "Jackson's welcome-home party."

"JACKSON'S still sleeping," said Ruth, "and I'm making a list for the party. Mara and Tyler are going to the store."

"Steaks would be good," said George. "I can grill a steak like nobody's business. Salt, pepper, a little Worcestershire."

"I could do baked potatoes in the oven," said Ruth. "But maybe takeout potato salad would be better. I don't know. Do you think people would mind takeout stuff?"

"Naw. It's your party. People eat what you give them. Ruth?"

"What?"

"Your ex." George cleared his throat. "All those years you were married, you didn't know?"

Ruth sighed. "I think, every now and then, deep down I did. I guess I was selfish, just wanted to hang on to what I had."

"Selfish." George took her hand. "I don't think so."

"I had a boyfriend in high school," said Ruth, "and then Owen. There was someone a few years ago, but it wasn't much. I don't . . . I'm kind of . . . nervous."

"It's nice, holding hands," said George. "I can handle a lot of hand-holding, at least for a couple of years."

Ruth giggled. "You were so *mad* at me," she said in a rush. "Like you didn't trust me. Like I'd done something wrong."

George sighed, looking out at Ruth's back-yard. "It was more me," he said. "I didn't trust my own luck, that anything good could happen to me anymore."

A little breeze scattered the leaves around the apricot tree.

"What if the wind picks up?" Ruth said. "Won't it be hard to grill if it's windy?"

"You worry too much. Worry, worry, worry." He looked down at her fondly. "You could take a break sometime, Ruth. Let me do your worrying for you."

An alcoholic, thought Ruth. He'd said he was an alcoholic. What if he started drinking again? What if . . .

THERE had been a flurry of welcome when Stuart had brought Jackson home in the late afternoon yesterday. A banner had hung from his door: WE LOVE YOU, JACKSON. He hadn't touched another human being for a long time, and there were Ruth, Tyler, and Mara waiting by the gate, all talking at once, all hugging him. Mara, his daughter. He'd felt shy. He didn't know her. What to do or say.

"There's Million Dollar Chicken in your refrigerator," said Ruth. "We're saving the official welcome-home party for tomorrow. And I thought we could get hold of a cot, put it in the exercise room so Mara can move in with you after the party."

Tyler tugged on his arm. "C'mon. You have to play basketball."

Mara played basketball, too, the three of them in the driveway as the sun started to go down, until finally Jackson started to stumble, missing all his shots, and Ruth came out of the house. "Go home," she said to him. "Get some sleep. We'll all be here in the morning."

He felt as though he hadn't slept in a hundred years. Exhausted, he'd gone home, walking blindly to the bedroom, where he fell into bed. But the king-sized bed seemed too large and he'd spent a restless night. Near morning he'd finally slept, far into the day.

Now he stood in his living room, staring blankly at the beige couch, the terra-cotta-colored wing chair. There was the carved wooden screen that Jenny had bought at Cost Plus World Market. On the coffee table were the round brass tray and the brass jar from India that Jenny had bought at Cost Plus, too.

I'll give it all away, he thought—no, yard sale, then take the money and get different stuff. I'm pretty broke. Get rid of the brass but maybe keep the coffee table. We can put the board on it when Ruth and Tyler come over to play Scrabble.

He looked out the window. He could see Ruth's place. Her car was parked in the

driveway behind the yellow Cadillac that be-
longed to a man he'd never seen before. Ruth
was with him now, coming around the side of
the house. They were holding hands.

So much had changed; different people
lived next door now. They were all getting
ready for his welcome-home party. In a couple
of hours he would shower, put on clean
clothes, and walk over to Ruth's. Mara would
be there—his daughter, the daughter he didn't
know yet. I guess, he thought, we'll talk. And
talk and talk and talk.

UGLY cinder-block walls, painted pale
green. Bright fluorescent lights. A babble of
voices. Men in orange jumpsuits sat in the row
of chairs in front of the glass in the visiting
room. The Magician shuffled to an empty
chair and sat down.

She sat behind the plate-glass window
holding a phone, wearing a blouse covered
with flowers. Her hair was braided into two
circles around her ears where silver earrings
dangled, but her lined face was plain and
pure.

He picked up the phone. "Hello, Frieda."
She smiled. "Hello."

"Thank you for coming," he said. "It's good to have a visitor."

"You're so different now," said Frieda.

"I have to take my meds all the time. They watch to make sure." He paused. "Does that mean you don't like me?"

"I didn't mean it that way. I'll always like you," she said. "You're still you. I'll come see you every week. I promise."

"They're going to take me to a hospital in Tucson," he said.

"Tucson. I can easily come see you in Tucson."

He nodded. "That would be nice." He looked down at the floor, then looked up again. "I guess they probably told you. I'm not a good person. The things I did."

She smiled again. Frieda, Frieda, Frieda. There was nothing in her smile that was hidden, held back.

"We're all God's children," she said.

PETER PEZZELLI

Peter Pezzelli was born and raised in Rhode Island, although he traces his Italian roots back to Abruzzo and Avellino. A graduate of Wesleyan University, he first worked as an administrator in his family's nursing home business. After he entered a writing contest on a whim, his girlfriend (and future wife) encouraged his literary ambitions by buying him a typewriter for his birthday. In his spare time, Pezzelli enrolled in writing workshops and eventually began submitting articles to local publications. An award for one of his short stories inspired him to pursue a career writing fiction. His other two novels are *Home to Italy* (2004) and *Every Sunday* (2005).

© Corinne Pezzelli

BETSY THORNTON

Betsy Thornton was born in Wilmington, North Carolina. After college, she married and lived in New York City, where her son Alex was born. She and her second husband, an artist, lived in Rome for a while, then moved to a small Greek island, Skopelos, where Thornton began to write seriously for the first time. Eventually they moved to Bisbee, Arizona, where she got a job as a victim advocate with the Cochise County attorney's office. "Being a victim advocate was probably the most meaningful job I have ever had. It brought me in touch with a wide range of people in crisis and taught me as much about life as any journey to a foreign land ever could."

Cathy Murphy; hat by Optimo Hats

Helping to enrich the lives of thousands of visually impaired individuals every day
www.rdpfs.org

Reader's Digest Partners for Sight is a non-profit foundation established in 1955 by DeWitt Wallace, co-founder of Reader's Digest. Originally created with the purpose of publishing high-quality reading material for the visually impaired, the Foundation has helped to enrich the lives of thousands of visually impaired individuals.

Now, through its program of carefully directed charitable grants to qualifying organizations, the Foundation is also a vital source of support on local, regional, and national levels for the blind and visually impaired community. **Partners for Sight** supports the grant program as it continues to provide new technology, new opportunity, and new hope for the visually impaired.

If you would like to contact the Foundation, write to: **Reader's Digest Partners for Sight Foundation, Inc.,** Pleasantville, NY 10570.